"Thomas joins the ranks of first-rate masters of misdirection who delight in artfully distracting us readers from the terrible truths planted right before our eyes."

—Maureen Corrigan, *The Washington Post*

"A compelling, ingenious novel about grief, love, the healing process, and what it means to mother . . . Perfect for fans of psychological fiction, in particular Alex Michaelides' *The Silent Patient*."

—*Booklist*

"*A Good Enough Mother* is both a heartbreaking story of love and loss and a hopeful meditation on the winding path to healing."

—*BookPage*

"[An] exceptional debut . . . Thomas melds astute psychological insight with powerful storytelling in this moving thriller."

—*Publishers Weekly* (starred review)

"Riveting . . . A gripping debut . . . Thomas knows how to fashion a story."

—*The Sunday Times* (London)

"An intelligent novel on the dilemmas of the therapist-client relationship and good parenting."

—*The Guardian* (London)

"*A Good Enough Mother* is not just everything a great thriller should be—haunting, emotional, charged with depth and power—it is also a gorgeous and devastating examination of motherhood that cuts right to the heart."

—Aimee Molloy, *New York Times* bestselling author of *The Perfect Mother*

"Thomas combines all the tension of a thriller with the emotional resonance of a powerful family drama."

—Paula Hawkins, #1 *New York Times* bestselling author of *The Girl on the Train*

"This powerful story of love, loss—and ultimately, healing—will resonate with anyone who has ever loved a child."

—Kim Edwards, #1 *New York Times* bestselling author of *The Memory Keeper's Daughter*

"The suspense is raw and enthralling, with a strong emotional ache at its center." —Hilma Wolitzer, author of *Silver*

"Both a riveting account of what goes on behind the scenes at your therapist's office and a dark meditation on motherhood, marriage, and grief. I couldn't put it down."

—Lisa Gabriele, author of *The Winters*

"Packs an emotional punch and is a gripping, original read. It is a novel full of loss and longing and the complexities of human relationships." —Kate Hamer, author of *Crushed*

"A beautiful, compelling book about the hopes and terrors of motherhood. You'll stay up reading way too late, desperate to find out what happens next . . . and even when you manage to put the book down, Ruth's story will haunt you."

—Gin Phillips, author of *Fierce Kingdom*

PENGUIN BOOKS

A GOOD ENOUGH MOTHER

Bev Thomas was a clinical psychologist in the NHS for many years. She currently works as an organizational consultant in mental health and other services. She lives in London with her family.

Look for the Penguin Readers Guide in the back of this book. To access Penguin Readers Guides online, visit penguinrandomhouse.com.

A GOOD ENOUGH MOTHER

Bev Thomas

PENGUIN BOOKS

PENGUIN BOOKS
An imprint of Penguin Random House LLC
penguinrandomhouse.com

First published in the United States of America by Pamela Dorman Books/Viking,
an imprint of Penguin Random House LLC, 2019
Published in Penguin Books 2020

Excerpt from a letter by Everett Ruess to Waldo Ruess, November 11, 1934,
from *Everett Ruess: A Vagabond for Beauty*, edited by W. L. Rusho.
Reprinted with permission of Gibbs Smith Publisher.

A Pamela Dorman/Penguin Book

ISBN 9780525561606 (paperback)

THE LIBRARY OF CONGRESS HAS CATALOGED THE
HARDCOVER EDITION AS FOLLOWS:
Thomas, Bev, author.
Title: A good enough mother : a novel / Bev Thomas.
Description: New York, New York : Pamela Dorman Books, 2019.
Identifiers: LCCN 2018039700 (print) | LCCN 2018043177 (ebook) |
ISBN 9780525561262 (ebook) | ISBN 9780525561255 (hardcover) |
ISBN 9781984877741 (international edition)
Subjects: | BISAC: Fiction / Contemporary Women. |
Fiction / Family Life. | Fiction / Thrillers.
Classification: LCC PR6120.H639 (ebook) | LCC PR6120.H639
G66 2019 (print) | DDC 823/.92—dc23
LC record available at https://lccn.loc.gov/2018039700

Printed in the United States of America
1 3 5 7 9 10 8 6 4 2

Set in Adobe Jenson Pro
BOOK DESIGN BY LUCIA BERNARD

For Colin

ACKNOWLEDGMENTS

Throughout my career in the NHS, I've had the privilege of working with exceptionally talented clinicians and colleagues. Particular thanks go to Mary Burd, Jane Gibbons, and Yvonne Millar who have been inspirational in shaping my thinking and approach to my work. I'm also very grateful to William Halton for his ongoing care, wisdom, and insight. I'd like to thank all my colleagues at Tavistock Consulting, and Brian Rock and Laure Thomas at the Trust for their support.

I wrote a lot of words before this book, and I've had the pleasure of being part of many different writing groups along the way. From Tufnell Park to Taos, I'd like to thank all my fellow writers for encouragement, a sense of belonging, and the shared love of words and stories.

Writing can feel like an act of blind faith, but it's one that's been helped by the support of my truly extraordinary friends. I am indebted to all those who have encouraged or read my writing over the years; particular thanks to Vicky Browning, Fliff Carr, Isanna Curwen, Maggie Greene, Sara Holloway, Anna Jones, Rebecca Lacey, Emma Lilly, Shirley McNicholas, Megan Meredith, Chris Murray, Sally

Norton, Carey Powell, Liz Stubbs, and Kay Trainor. Extra special thanks to Sam Cook for endlessly reading my writerly offerings, and for keeping the faith when I came close to losing it.

I'm also grateful to Christopher Wakling, whose unequivocal words on a Shropshire Arvon helped me to the finishing line. A big thank you to Sean Larkin QC for help with all my legal queries—all errors or liberties taken are entirely my own. I'd also like to thank Jon Krakauer for *Into the Wild*, which unexpectedly found its way into the pages of this story.

I'm beyond grateful to my fantastic agent Karolina Sutton; for her energy, joy, curiosity, and excellent matchmaking skills—but also for seeing something in my early chapters that kept me going to complete the rest.

A very big thank you to my brilliant editors. To Louisa Joyner in the U.K. and Pamela Dorman in the U.S.—to their assistants Libby Marshall and Jeramie Orton and the whole teams at Faber & Faber and Penguin Random House respectively for looking after me so well—and thank you, too, to Anne Collins and Amanda Betts in Canada. Their collective enthusiasm from the outset was amazing— as was the editorial care, insight, and thoughtfulness over the months. It has been a real delight to work with them all and I feel so incredibly fortunate to have found a home with these publishing houses. I'd also like to thank my copyeditors, Tamsin Shelton and Jane Cavolina, for forensic work on timelines and the rest.

Finally, this is a book about family, and it would not exist without my own. Love and gratitude to my parents for instilling a passion for books, a spirit of persistence, and for the stories we are given that make up who we are. Huge love and thanks to Paul, for many things, but especially for coming to the Hackney writing group, which sparked our best creative endeavours. Most of all, my love to Joe and Nate, such wonderful traveling companions on this unexpected journey. *Have faith, work hard, dream big.*

A GOOD ENOUGH MOTHER

ONE

On paper, Dan Griffin was nothing out of the ordinary. He was anxious, he was urgent, he was like any other patient we see at the Trauma Unit. "Unremarkable" was how I described him to the police. When they looked for answers in those early therapy sessions, they read about the bruise on his face, the terror in his voice, and the flashbacks that were so visceral they took his breath away, but there was nothing to hint at his capacity for violence. Nothing at all to suggest what he was capable of. It took a while to understand that the question to ask wasn't *Why didn't I see it coming?* but *Why didn't I move out of the way?*

It's a Friday afternoon in April when I see Dan for his first appointment, at the end of a difficult week—an onslaught of new referrals, an email about the budget cuts, and then, that morning, the unexpected phone call about the death of a patient, Alfie Burgess. The hospice nurse is kind as she tells me what happened. "Peaceful," she says, "and surrounded by family," then some other things I don't hear. "You'll let the team know?" is how she ends the call. Of course, it should be me as head of department to tell them all, and in the past I'd happily rise to such leadership requests. It was something I was good at—competent, capable, and in control, spreading my arms wide to contain the distress of the department. But that day, in the run-up to Tom's birthday, my hand is shaking as I replace the receiver.

It's a feeling that's been getting worse. The once fluttery sensation in the pit of my stomach has become a band of tension across my chest. It could be the death of anyone, a next-door neighbor's friend, or even a story in the news; but when it's someone I know well, like Alfie, it tightens, until it becomes hard to move. There's never a picture or image that forms in my head, just a creeping sense of dread about Tom. I try to focus on Alfie, on how I will tell the team, but my body is rigid, like it's gone into hiding.

Tom's birthday has become an obsession. I knew it would. It did last year. But lately, almost any event can serve as a marker of time— the first autumn leaves, the first dusting of frost, or the first smudge of purple and yellow crocuses. All small signs that the world is turning without him. But the day of his birth? His *birthday?* What mother doesn't want to transport herself back to the glorious cocoon of that moment, whatever the age of her child? There's a nervous kind of anticipation that I know will come to nothing. The date will come and go without him, the balloon of hope will deflate, and sometimes, the sheer effort required to pump myself back into shape simply feels too much. I've had days like this before, and I know it will pass. For the moment, however, I am too full of it. If it were anyone else, any other member of my team, I'd tell them they shouldn't be at work. "Go home," I'd say, "be kind to yourself." But for obvious reasons, home is the last place I want to be.

That day, I am like an overfull bath. Drip. Drip. Drip. I feel heavy with the weight of it all, as if one more small request will send me sloshing and spilling out all over the floor. And yet, still I hold up my hand for more. Another referral? An extra supervision group? A paper to present at a conference? *Yes, I'll do it,* I hear myself say. And I do it in the hope it'll fill the void. I'm not making excuses. There are no excuses. But my state of mind on the day I first meet Dan Griffin cannot be denied.

After the phone call, I sit at my desk for a while. I think about imparting the news about Alfie, and I know exactly how it will go. There will be grave faces. Sadness, tears, hushed tones, and hugs. We will make tea and remember him, his cheery "What's up?" when he arrived at reception. Our thoughts will be with his parents, their quiet-spoken dignity; together we will rage against the injustice of it all. We will remind ourselves that he was ill, that porphyria was a degenerative condition. That he defied all expectations, "he did so well," we'll conclude, "considering." Beneath all the camaraderie and commiseration, there will be an undercurrent of competition—who knew him best, who's entitled to grieve the most. We will think about how long he'd been coming to the department for his needle phobia, on and off for more than eight years, maybe more. I remember telling Tom about him once. No names, of course, but in the face of his own nightmares, it was an attempt to normalize his fears. I remember how he sat wide-eyed as I told him about Alfie's panic and what we did to help him. "You see," I said, stroking his hair, "everyone has worries."

We will recall how well Alfie seemed the last time he came in.

There will be a card to sign, a collection for the flowers; I feel dizzy just thinking about it all. Tasks that I have both welcomed and risen to effortlessly over the years today feel insurmountable.

I don't want more grief. More death. I already feel stalked by it. I want to put the phone down and pretend it hasn't happened. But I can't do that. It falls on me. Ruth Hartland. Director of the Trauma Unit. I am in charge. It says so on my door.

In the event, I am lucky. After telling my colleagues in neighboring offices, I bump into Paula in the corridor, and given she delights in the status of her new position as office manager, I know she'll tell the rest of the team and have a collection organized by lunchtime.

I manage to steer clear of everyone for the rest of the morning, but in the afternoon it's my responsibility to log all new patient referrals in the main office. I can feel the quiet sadness. There's also an air of stoic resilience. Look at us, it seems to say, we're clinicians, we're trained to manage and contain difficult feelings—including our own. Tom used to joke about it. "Mum," he'd say, "you're at home. You can stop being the therapist now." Still, I can feel the heightened sensitivity, people treading carefully around each other, as though bruised and tender after an accident. After ten minutes, I can't breathe for the kindness and the solicitous glances.

Things soon shift. Death makes us selfish—and eventually it pushes everyone inward, to reflect on their own lives and families. For once, I am grateful for Paula, who always speaks with flourish on behalf of the team. She glances up from her paperwork. "Makes you think about what we take for granted," she says, looking around at everyone. "I just want to get home and give my kids a hug." She wraps her arms around her waist and gives herself a squeeze. "I'm sure we all do."

I don't say anything. I don't call her to one side, remind her about Eve, who has no children and wishes she had. I just smile and nod. I don't speak about myself. I can't. No one knows about my situation. It's better that way.

Dan Griffin is my last patient that afternoon. My consulting room is around the corner from the waiting area and the walk to collect a patient takes about a minute—a journey I have made hundreds of times over the last twenty-five years. Tom and Carolyn used to visit me here sometimes when they were small. I remember how Tom liked the "swingy" chair in the main office, where he'd sit gazing out of the window over the tops of the trees. They'd both be surprised to see how little it's all changed; the carpet and the furniture are exactly as they were. Over the years, there have been a few additions to the walls in the corridor, the framed Beacon Award, the Trust commendation for clinical excellence. Otherwise, it's the same—the seascape by the lift, the row of abstract pictures with scattered geometrical shapes, and the one Tom liked best, the shaggy dog jumping in the rain. It's what we offer here, a sense of stability, something constant and reliable for people who've known terror in their lives. These days, David would shrug in the face of any psychological theorizing. *What difference does any of it make?* he'd say. But maybe that's because of what's happened to our own family.

Usually, as I walk to collect a new referral, I spend a few moments clearing my head, orienting myself to the new patient and the process about to begin. Today, I don't. I'd like to say I was thinking about Alfie and his parents, but that would be a lie.

I walk slowly and deliberately, my eyes on those swimming-pool-blue carpet tiles. It's just as I pass the stairwell that I look up and see him in the waiting room at the end of the corridor. I stop and stare. Everything else falls away.

He's hunched in the chair by the door, head in hands, hair hanging down over his fingers. I hear myself make a noise, a muffled sort of cry, and then suddenly a wave rolls gently through me. I feel suddenly light. Elevated. He's grown his hair long again. David would hate it, but I'm pleased. One of the last times I saw him, he'd hacked it off completely, leaving long golden curls in the bathroom sink that made me want to weep. Now it's grown back down to his shoulders. It suits him long, I think, as I reach a hand to the wall to steady myself.

As I move closer, I can see his donkey jacket. The one we bought him for Christmas. The one with the tartan lining. My heart is thumping now. There's a new shirt, one I don't recognize, and a red rucksack on his lap. On his feet, Doc Martens boots. Always those black boots. The sight of them makes me smile. *Tom, here you are*, is what I think, or perhaps I say out loud. My chest rises and falls and I break into a clumsy run, startling the patients in the waiting room. Some look up. One of them is Tom. As he lifts his head, I feel a dull pain in my solar plexus, swift, like a punch. It is not him.

I come to a jarring halt. I pull back, a strange lurching movement. The young man who looks up—just a boy, really—glances at me briefly, his expression blank, then he looks back down into his hands. I take in the black eye, the bruise on his cheek, and his bandaged hand. It is not Tom. I feel light-headed, sick. I reach for the door frame and hold on tight.

I am used to seeing my son in odd places. I've come to understand that it's normal, something we all do. I have "seen" him many times over the last year and a half. Only last week, I spotted him walking up the hill to his old primary school. It was just before his growth spurt in Year Six. He was walking with Finn, kicking his bag and laughing and joking as they jostled into each other.

Sometimes I see him when he's older. It's the smallest thing that pulls me in—the curl of hair on his neck as he's getting out of the Tube, or his floaty, airborne walk as he strides across a beach. Sometimes, and these are the times that upset me most, he looks exactly as he did when I last saw him. Seventeen, with a haunted face and a brutal haircut. These glimpses are always fleeting, images that shimmer then disappear when I look more closely. Usually, I know exactly what I am doing, that I am willfully conjuring him up, turning unsuspecting strangers into the face I want to see. As I stand in the doorway that day, the likeness does not fade or shift, it is clear and hard and unsettling.

"Dan Griffin?" I say, eyes scanning the waiting room, knowing exactly who will get up and rise to his feet. At the sound of his name, he jerks up awkwardly and nods in response. After that, I don't remember much. Perhaps he is sweating, perhaps his hands are shaking when he picks up his rucksack; I don't recall any of these details. I am thinking very little about him. As I walk back to my office, all my efforts are concentrated on keeping my body in an upright position and my steps even and balanced along those blue carpet tiles.

The referral letter said he was twenty-two, but he looks much younger. He'd been fast-tracked by Dr. Jane Davies, a substitute GP in Hackney I'd never met.

Dear Ruth Hartland,

I would be grateful if you could urgently assess this young man, who has just moved to the area. Dan Griffin has recently experienced a highly traumatic event and is displaying the classic PTSD symptoms. He was unable to disclose the event, but I believe it was a vicious attack in a park. Given the severity of his anxiety, however, I did not press him for details. I have requested notes from his previous GP. . . .

Yours etc.

Dr. Davies

Dan is looking down at the floor, his rucksack hugged to his chest. His body is tense, his eyes uncertain. I introduce myself, ask how I can help him today. There's a long pause. He looks up, swallows several times, then stares at me with such intensity I want to look away.

Perhaps it's because he's so preoccupied with his own distress that he doesn't notice my own. My flushed face, my heart still thumping wildly, it's impossible to believe he can't see it under my blue fitted jacket. Is it shock? Disappointment? Or rage or shame at my own stupidity? *What was I thinking?* What would David have thought? I imagine eye rolling, but really, I wonder too if he might have seen what I am seeing.

Dan talks a lot at the beginning of the session. His voice is clipped and breathless as he tells me he's "desperate, not coping," and reveals the extent of his flashbacks. I am grateful for this detail. I use the opportunity to ease my way back into my body, but even as he speaks I feel a surge of resistance, wild and hopeful thoughts that want to reject the reality of who's in front of me. I sit still. I breathe.

Soon, I am aware of my legs on my chair, my hands on my lap, and I listen as he moves away from his symptoms to talk about his sense of disappointment about coming to the clinic. How small it was. How shabby. How difficult to find.

"I was surprised," he says, "for a place with such a reputation." He mentions the scuffed carpet. The lift that wasn't working. The walls that need a "lick of paint" and the inadequate and ambiguous signs. "I mean, *hello?*" he says. "Was it some kind of test? An orienteering challenge?" And then a vague hint of paranoia. "As if you want us to fuck up all over again." And on he goes, filling the session with complaint and dissatisfaction. "The unit came highly recommended. *Experts* in your field. *Once a week*, the letter said. *Six sessions?* How will that be enough?" His tone is not angry, more resigned. The clinic. Our approach. *Me.* He expected more. We've already let him down. And somehow, this comes as no surprise to him. I realize, quite quickly, this is what he's used to. What he's come to expect. That he views the world through a lens of disappointment. He shrugs. "I guess I thought the whole thing would be a bit more"—he pauses, trying to find the right word—"*special.*"

When I ask about what he hopes to gain from coming to the unit, he says he "wants things to go back to how they were before." And at this point, he leans forward, assuming a position of intimacy like we're acquaintances, or friends reuniting. It's a struggle to stay still. To resist the urge to move closer to him. He draws an invisible line on the leg of his jeans with his finger.

"Before—and after. And I want to be back here," he says, jabbing the "before" section on his thigh. He looks up at me expectantly.

That's the thing I remember most about that first session with Dan Griffin, his preoccupation, obsession almost, with getting back to "how he was before." It's a common wish for many of our patients and it's a relief for me to be back on familiar territory, in a world I feel in control of.

"When terrible things happen," I say, "it's understandable to want to go back to a time before." I tell him that whatever has happened, the purpose of therapy is not to try to erase an event, but quite the opposite. "Here at the unit, we work on how to incorporate the traumatic event or events back into your life," I say.

He sits rigid in his chair, beads of sweat in a line on his forehead.

I am speaking, saying the right things, nodding and asking all the appropriate questions, all the while I am drinking him in, my eyes poring over him, like a blind man's fingers on a face. Teasing out all the Tom-like bits of him. The way his hair falls forward. The curve of his chin. The look of vulnerability that sometimes shoots across his face. "We are simply unable to make terrible things *un*happen to us," I say. And of course, I can say this with real conviction. "Any event in your past now makes up who you are."

"I've done it before," he cuts in. "Things have happened to me before—years ago. I just blocked them out." He stares at me intently. "It worked then."

I open my mouth to speak, but he continues. "I simply didn't allow it to affect me. It meant nothing." His voice rises, then he shakes his head and flicks a hand through the air as if waving away a fly. "I just need to make it work for me now."

His gaze is defiant, as though daring me to disagree. There's a flash of anger. And I'm pleased. In my experience, this can be a good thing. Anger at what has happened. Anger can be a sign of the healthy part of the psyche. The part that wants to fight. The desire to get better. It can be a sign of energy, of hope. But not always.

"This thing that happened, it was so stupid," he snaps. "Some arseholes. Some stupid wankers in the park—and now look." He lifts his hands up to show me the trembling in his fingers. "What the fuck?" And then he weaves his hands around his rucksack. "Some days I can't even get out of bed. I'm missing college. I used to walk everywhere. Felt invincible. Like the Terminator." He laughs. "Now"—he shakes his head—"even coming here today—" and he falters. "Turns out," he says, "one of the guys was on parole. I mean, Jesus Christ. *Parole?* What's the matter with these people? Why can't people do their jobs properly?" He slumps back in his chair, small and defeated. Perhaps it's his despair, the darkening shadow on his face, but I feel a flutter of anxiety in my chest.

I'm aware of a strong urge to help. To not let him down. It's my job to notice this feeling. Pick up on what's going on in the room between us. *Why can't people do their jobs properly?* This is the time to comment on his disappointment in "the system," the unit, and to wonder whether he's worried that I, too, might prove a disappointment. But in that moment, the counter-transference feels muddied and unclear. So I don't say anything.

We sit together in the silence. I can hear the quickness of his breath, and as he looks down at his now still hands, I peer again at the yellowing bruise on the side of his face, the stitches on his lip, and the grubby bandage on his left hand. When he next speaks, his voice is a whisper. I need to lean in to hear him. As I get closer, I see Tom's mouth, the way his lips make a shape around his words. The way he chews on his bottom lip when he's nervous. I watch his mouth tell me how the world has changed for him. The panic attacks, the flashbacks, and the sleepless nights. However, he skirts around what actually happened. *The thing in the park* is what he keeps saying. I don't press him for details. I know I must wait; being asked too soon can feel like another violation.

I ask other questions, perhaps more than I would do ordinarily. I ask about his family. "Parents? Siblings?"

"No family," he says, and his tone is dismissive. "Father's dead. No brothers or sisters. And I lost my mother."

"I'm sorry—"

He shakes his head. "It's not what you think. She's still alive—as far as I know." He shrugs. "I lost her to someone else."

"To someone else?" I say, both intrigued and confused by his choice of words. He shuts me down.

"I don't want to talk about my family." His tone is brisk. Then, in a softer, almost apologetic tone, he adds, "I just want to get better. Put it behind me and move on. Learn some techniques, some tools, perhaps?"

"We don't offer tools," I say. I tell him we offer a place to talk. "Talking therapy. And given you have come, perhaps there are some things you'd like to talk about."

I ask him for the questionnaire. "The one we sent in the post?" He looks blank. "I didn't get a questionnaire."

I fish another one from my drawer and ask him if he can fill it in and hand it back at reception. He takes it, folds it in half, and puts it straight in his bag. Clearly, he has no intention of completing it. After a moment, I lean forward. "Many people who come here want a quick fix," I say. "I'm afraid it doesn't work like that. The questionnaire will help me understand the meaning of this traumatic event for you. That's why there is no set of tools. It's all about getting to know who *you* are."

He looks stricken for a moment.

I tell him that the people we see have come here because they are unable to get on with their lives. "They have been invaded by something that is often shocking, violent, or brutal, often in the form of flashbacks and invasive thoughts."

He doesn't move.

"It's as if the event has torn something," I say. "Like a protective layer. The trauma has become a kind of wound, one that won't heal on its own."

"A wound," he repeats, "yes, it feels like that."

"Sometimes this wound gets opened because it triggers something else—an association or an event in the past, and it is this," I explain, "that needs facing, in order to move on."

I have his full attention, his eyes not moving from my face.

I explain that it's common for trauma to leave people with a sense that the world has become a dangerous place, random, disordered, and unsafe.

For the first time, he's nodding as I speak.

"I feel like someone has taken my world," and he mimes placing a ball on the tip of his finger, "and spun it upside down." His voice speeds up as he talks about feeling powerless, "out of control."

"Have you ever felt like this before," I ask, "in the past?"

"Have I ever felt like this before?" he replies, nodding again. "Yes, I have. And it feels awful," and he goes on to give me more details about the dizziness, the light-headed feeling. "Things go all fuzzy," he says, "like I'm going to faint."

It's the first time I'm aware of it. This habit he has of answering a question about his past by repeating the question, but then failing to answer. It gives the impression of being both focused and vague, and at the end of the session, I feel a hollow intimacy—like I know everything and nothing about him. There are other things, too—the desire for the quick fix, the reluctance to talk about the past. It feels like there's a chasm between his need and my capacity. Like he's hungry, ravenous, and I'm left with a feeling that I won't be able to nourish him. At the time, I put this down to his difficulty with trust, common in patients who have been traumatized and let down. None of these things are unusual. They are simply things to note, some indication of the landscape that is to come. And yet, of course, our session is not a normal first session. That day, after he leaves, there's no blank canvas to sketch out the beginning of our work. The tabula rasa? It was a scribbled mess before we began.

It's only later, when I'm writing up my case notes, that I notice something else. It happens when he's talking about the world, how it has tipped on its axis. "The world is not safe" is what I write down, but as I look at what I've written, I realize this is not what he said at all. His actual words could mean the same thing—or something very different.

I don't feel safe is the phrase he used. I know this as I stare at the words on the page. But for a reason I can't explain to myself, and much later to my solicitor, I don't make the alteration in my notes.

TWO

It's said that the way babies come into the world is like a small blueprint of how they go on to live their lives. My daughter, Carolyn, was first—and she proved every bit as punctual and determined as she grew up. After a red-faced and indignant entrance into the arms of Beatrice, the midwife, she swiftly composed herself in a way I've gone on to see replicated many times over the years.

After the slippery rush of my daughter's arrival, a quiet lull descended on the labor room. Beatrice moved around the bedside, the sounds of rubber soles on lino, the gentle bleep of the monitor, and the small popping breaths of the newborn in my arms. There were no worries or concerns about her expected twin brother, no medical explanation for his late arrival, and so his reticence was put down to choice.

"He's happy in there," said Beatrice, laughing and patting my arm. She had a strong Jamaican accent and long eyelashes. "He wants you all to himself for a few minutes . . . wants to stretch those little legs. And who can blame him?" she said, smiling at me and my husband.

As the minutes ticked by, David grew worried, and any fanciful thoughts shaping a narrative about this second baby did nothing to assuage my husband's anxiety. "What's happening?" he fretted, desperation in his voice. Every so often I'd catch a flash of the blue of his shirt as he paced up and down the room. He was solid and handsome. It was the first thing that attracted me to him. His height, his physical presence. The very shape he made when he came into a room. But when tense or anxious, he seemed to cave in, becoming small and loose-limbed. Gently, Beatrice suggested he get a coffee, or a walk outside to get some air. As for me, I knew what was to come and I shut down, closing my eyes, like an animal going into hibernation.

Perhaps it was this self-preservation, or simply the presence of Beatrice, who hummed as she moved wordlessly around the bedside, but whatever it was, I felt calm. It was David, shrinking fast, who called for the doctor. Beatrice smiled as she leaned in with chips of ice for me to suck. "Your boy will be along when he's good and ready. Just you wait," she said, squeezing my hand. "He's a chap that likes to do things his way. He's not a people pleaser, this one."

When Tom did finally emerge, he did so with an angry, scrunched-up face, into bright white lights and a bustle of green and blue gowns. "All those people. All that noise," Beatrice clucked as she gathered him up, and sometimes I wonder if it was a shock he was to spend the rest of his life recovering from.

Afterward, I would learn that it was twenty-eight minutes between the birth of my babies. That the average length of time between twin births was seventeen minutes. Years later, when I thought about those twenty-eight minutes, I imagined Tom quiet and alone for the first time in nine months. And although there is much written about twins and their kinship, there's very little attention given to the fact that they are rarely alone. From conception to birth and through the early years, they are always together, rubbing along, side by side with a sibling.

My mother swept in that afternoon, glassy-eyed and desperate to see the babies. As always, she was in midsentence as she appeared in the doorway, and when she leaned in toward me, I caught the whiff of lunchtime gin and the telltale twitch of anger on her forehead. But I was shiny with drugs and hormones and her words slid off me.

Perhaps she finished, perhaps she took a breath; either way, I launched right in.

"Carolyn was out," I garbled, "just like a bullet. But Tom," I said breathlessly, "he wanted to hang on. He wanted his space. To take his time—"

In my postbirth euphoria, my guard was down. As I continued to fashion the modes of their births into aspects of their personalities, I forgot the rules of our relationship.

"It was almost as if he wanted to stay with me," I rambled on, "before the onslaught of the big wide world." My mother tried to listen. Her head cocked to one side. After a while, I realized her face was frozen.

"Don't be silly," she scoffed, like I was a toddler misbehaving at the dinner table. "It's the amniotic sac. It's not about free will." Then, in a final act of restoring order, she reached across to smooth out the ridges on the hospital blanket. She sat back in her chair, her face serene, satisfied that all thoughts of a fanciful nature had been chased from the room.

It wasn't just the drugs and hormones that made me immune that day. It was me. I was different, holding my two babies, one in each arm. As she continued to scratch out the details of her journey—the incompetent taxi driver, the difficulties of coming into London at rush hour, the canceled charity lunch—I felt so full and plentiful that her roar of desperation failed to touch me. I was battered and bruised, but I barely heard it. I watched her mouth move. Letters that formed words that curved into twisted sentences. *Heavy traffic on the motorway. All so last minute. No time to prepare. Wished I'd known earlier.* These words. These small, angry pellets simply bounced off me. As she swelled with fury, I swelled with love. And as she sat at the side of the bed, with fingers that itched to press and prize into the flesh of my newborns, I felt a surge of power. I smiled and hugged my babies close like a shield. I grew in stature, in the knowledge that for the very first time, I had something that didn't belong to her. Something she couldn't have.

After she left, David climbed onto the bed next to me. The color had returned to his face. He held the babies shyly, one after the other, grinning like a fool. When he went to the café to get drinks and snacks, I laid them carefully in the cot and sank back into my pillow. The April sunshine caught the trees outside as it shone through the window. I watched as the pattern of leaves danced and fluttered on the blanket of my bed. There were still some visitors on the ward and I felt lulled by the sound of the surrounding chatter. One conversation caught my attention. It was the two women opposite. I'd watched them earlier, the woman in the bed gently handing her new baby over to what I guessed was her own mother. The new grandmother. As the woman reached for the baby, her face lit up with such pride and joy. I listened as they spoke about someone called Alex. About a fence that would need fixing. "Will you have a christening," the older woman asked, "or have you not decided?" "Not sure," her daughter replied. The older woman nodded and the conversation flitted back and forth. *The tiny fingers. The long eyelashes. His peachy skin.* It was so simple, easy, and uncomplicated. I was in awe. Envious of that ease. That normality.

"Why?" my mother said, her face a twist of displeasure when I mentioned my plans to breast-feed.

"I never did," she said decisively, as if this would somehow be the end of it.

"I know."

"Both of them?" she asked incredulously.

And in those early weeks, my mother became obsessed with feeding. Even the smallest cry or murmur from either of the babies was confirmation that they were grossly undernourished. "Hungry," she nodded, peering over at whichever one was clamped to my swollen breasts. "Ravenous," she'd conclude, her fingers poised to rip open the box of baby formula that she clung to like a handbag. It was David, in the end, who engaged more directly with her own insatiable hunger. "Come along," he said, hooking his arm through hers. "Let's go and buy some cake."

My daughter took to breast-feeding in the manner she would take to pretty much everything in life, applying herself studiously and vigorously until she was a model of efficiency. But almost as quickly as she'd mastered the task, she got bored, and refueling soon became a duty, something to complete, while her gaze wandered around the room to other more exciting things. "Penelope Pitstop," we called her in those first months.

Tom was the opposite. He struggled to make sense of it all, but when he did "latch on," as they say, he was utterly focused. In contrast to his sister, he'd look up at me, small gray-blue marble eyes fixed on mine, his tiny fingers clutching on to the edge of my cardigan.

What I remember most about those early years was the sheer physicality of it all. Small fingers on my cheek. A belly on my hip. Legs climbing onto my lap. A hand slipping silently into my own. And all this amid the haze of sleeplessness. It was Tom who slept badly, but they both had their moments. And for what seemed like months, mornings would shock us awake, finding the three of us, and very often the four of us, sprawled across the sheets, like battered objects washed up on the shore. Yet there was such joy in that physicality. Bodies entwined. Pressed up against each other. Safe.

As they grew from babies into toddlers, I'd watch their different approaches to life. Carolyn was quick and bright, and she only had to watch me do something once and she'd soon be trying it out for herself. She had an innate understanding about the world, a knowingness, together with a fierce independence that often made me feel redundant. It wasn't so much that Tom couldn't do things, but his default position was always one step behind. Just as he was turning his attention to something, she was away and on to something else.

I remember those family occasions when your child stands up, takes a step, or draws a line on a page for the first time and the whole gathering is in rapturous uproar. Carolyn would look up, dip her head, and beam, then repeat the act as her whole body lit up with the electricity of approval. Tom, on the other hand, seemed immune to the external applause. He was often startled by the attention, and he'd turn away with a furrowed brow, embarrassed by the fuss.

Some parents of twins go out of their way to reinforce their separateness and their individuality. We were not those parents. For us, they were always "the twins," from the second they were born, and even long beforehand. I used to love those moments when a stranger on the high street would peer into the pram. "Ah—twins," the look seemed to say, and was a mixture of surprise, admiration, and wonder all rolled into one.

In those early years, they looked alike. We have so many photos of them, with the same wild, curly hair, almost indistinguishable. Tom was always happiest outside. He loved wide-open spaces— beaches, mountains, and fields—and he'd run about with joy, climbing trees and collecting sticks. Even when at home in London, I'd often find him at the back of our garden, digging in the dirt or making a den in the bushes. Carolyn, in contrast, could sit for hours at a table, working on small intricate drawings with colored felt-tip pens. She drew clothes mainly; patterned dresses and skirts and funky shoes that she'd carefully cut out and arrange into beautiful outfits. I look back fondly on that time, before the structure and rigidity of school. They were our golden years, the years when they were small. When we knew exactly where they were and what they were doing. Our worries then were about identifiable hazards—traffic on the road, the jagged edge of a slide, or a deep garden pond. As they got older, their "twinship" suited me more. I continued to reinforce their sameness and probably encouraged joint playdates and outings for longer than I should have. I'd say it was because they liked it, but now I know it was for me, that it served to mask the differences between them that I didn't want to see.

ONE OF THE LAST HAPPY MEMORIES of my son was a year and a half ago, several days before the accident. We were in the garden. It was a warm afternoon on the last day of July, a clear blue sky and small wisps of cloud, and after the heavy rain of the previous week, the lawn shone a bright, jeweled green. The foxgloves were in flower, perky and upstanding with their flutes of purple and white. Tom had completed the first two terms of his carpentry course and we'd grown accustomed to the smell of wood shavings, and the fine dusting on his clothes and hair and eyelashes when he got back home. He'd been working weekends at the canoe club since the spring.

It was a while before then, when he'd first mentioned Julie. "She's one of the full-time members of staff," he said. "She organizes the volunteers. She's really nice," he grinned. "She's got pink hair. She gives me the funny kids to work with," he laughed. "And she always makes me cups of green tea when I get back." He pulled a face. "Says it's better for me than all the black coffee I drink. It's actually growing on me—though I can't tell her that." It was the first time I'd ever heard him mention a girl. There were so many questions I wanted to ask. What's she like? How old is she? Perhaps you could invite her round? *Pink hair?* I opened my mouth. Then closed it again. As time went on, he talked about her more. "Just friends," he said when I asked. But his cheeks colored whenever he mentioned her name. I

met her once, at the center when I came to pick him up. They were
huddled together at the front desk, laughing. I fought the urge to
look too interested. What mattered most was how happy he looked.
It was obvious the outdoor life suited him. He seemed different,
older somehow. His shoulders had broadened and his body had
lengthened and grown into itself. His hair was long and bleached by
the sun. He tanned easily, and his skin was a deep, burnished brown.
The horror of the past year seemed long gone, erased by the sun, the
job, and his newfound confidence. I remember feeling smug. A little
self-congratulatory. I allowed myself to relax. Perhaps that was my
mistake.

I stood at the back door, a hand shielding my eyes from the sun,
gazing out over the small grassy slope that the twins used to roll
down as children. Tom was at the back of the garden, up a ladder,
holding the birdhouse against the silver birch. We'd already missed
the nesting season, as David had promised, and failed, to put it up
for the spring. Tom said he'd do it now. "You never know," he
laughed, "you might get a few latecomers."

"Here?" he called out. "Then you'll be able to see it from the
kitchen."

"Yep," I called back, "that's great."

He placed the birdhouse on the branch and reached for a nail
from his pocket, then gripped it between his teeth as he picked up
the hammer.

The birdhouse had been his Christmas gift to me.

Tom's gift giving was often random, depending on his fluctuat-
ing feelings about the evils of consumerism. That year, in spite of
the fact that Tom was so influenced by that book about Christopher

McCandless, he surprised us all when he handed out wrapped presents.

My gift was in paper patterned with small silver angels.

"Thank you so much! Fantastic," I said, staring down at the parcel in my lap.

On the other side of the room, Carolyn bristled at my exuberance.

"It's not just any old birdhouse," he said when I opened it up and thanked him.

"It's fitted with a camera"—he leaned in to show me—"so when a bird lays eggs, you can connect it up and watch the live feed on the telly."

"Tom," I said, "that's lovely. So thoughtful."

He sat forward in his chair, overexcited. "It'll be like the Big Brother house," he said, "for birds."

We all laughed. Even Carolyn.

A YEAR AND A HALF ON, the garden has been neglected. The box is now hidden under thick, dense foliage. You'd have to be a ferret to fight your way into that hole.

There had been a bird the spring after Tom disappeared. A blackbird. I switched on the camera every day and spent each evening watching the mother carefully fashion a nest out of twigs and fluff and leaves. There were four speckled eggs, each a pale turquoise blue. As the time came near, I would rush home from work and spend hours on the sofa sitting by those jet-black feathers in a state of nervous expectancy. While I knew she couldn't see me, it felt like the two of us were watching over each other. As I sat still on the sofa, I felt safe under the small orange bead of her eye. Naively, I felt her arrival might somehow trigger Tom's return.

When the babies hatched, the nest was a writhing frenzy of movement. I saw them only briefly before I had to leave for work. They were gray and helpless and blindly clamoring for food, as the mother patiently fed their open mouths one by one.

I remember the day was unseasonably hot for March and the therapy rooms were stuffy and airless, even with windows pushed wide open. I felt a pressing eagerness all day, and when a patient canceled her afternoon appointment, I left work early.

I switched on the television; the screen was blank. There was nothing to see. I checked the connection, fiddled with the remote. Nothing. Just the dark brown of the inside of the box. The blackbird had gone, and as I zoomed in closer, I saw the lifeless bodies of her babies strewn around the nest like scraps of leftover meat.

THREE

On Monday morning we have the departmental case discussion, and it's my turn to present. It's obvious who I should bring for discussion. Only three days earlier, I'd been explaining the format to Stephanie, our new trainee. "Patients we find challenging," I said. "A space to explore the unconscious, and how it might affect the work."

She nodded enthusiastically, the cut of her bob slicing neatly back and forth.

I mentioned "projection of emotion," and made a point of talking about transference and counter-transference. I deliberately used terminology that I knew would be unfamiliar to her. But in the space in which I was expecting questions, requests for clarification, or at the very least confusion, there was nothing.

"Every fortnight?" she wanted to know, as she tapped the date into the calendar of her phone.

Stephanie had made herself known to the department well before her start date. In the two weeks before, she was either emailing or phoning on a daily basis. For the most part, she had petty administrative inquiries—a parking permit, library membership, and requests for forms she didn't need. The ones that came my way included a query about attending a conference on trauma and attachment theory, and a request for "relevant literature" to read before she started. "Seems very keen!" Paula observed in her forwarding email.

When I read her student report, I saw a high achiever—a first from Oxford and (just like me, many years ago) the offer of a place on a clinical psychology training course after only a year of work experience. But I also saw someone whose previous three placements had been in cognitive behavior therapy. She had no experience of our therapeutic approach; and reading her personal statement, it was hard for me to fathom her reason for choosing her specialist placement here with us. As I took in the neat symmetrical bob, the manicured nails, I realized Paula had been wrong. It was anxiety, not eagerness, that was her motivator.

Toward the end of our first meeting, I'd tried to find a way in by asking about the papers.

"They were good," she said.

"What did you make of Melanie Klein?" I persevered, knowing how most students struggle with the density of her papers.

"Really interesting," she nodded blandly. "Thanks very much for sending them."

And that's when I understood my irritation. It wasn't the fact that she had gaps in her understanding and theory. Nor was it her avoidance, or capacity for denial. It was the fact that she thought her performance was credible. That somehow she believed she had fooled me.

As I'm walking to the group room, I run through the possible case options in my head. I know I can't talk about Dan. Bringing

Dan would mean talking about Tom—and without Tom, there wasn't much to say about Dan. So instead, I pick another patient who is challenging in a very different way.

Most of the staff are here, except for Stan and Maggie, who are representing the team at Alfie's funeral. The room is full, and besides Stephanie, we have a medical student for the week. He's busy on his phone, and wearing a disconcertingly bright red tie. It's easy to spot the budding male surgeons—the jazzy accessories, the manufactured busyness, all preludes to viewing psychological thinking in much the same way they might a workshop on crystal healing.

"Hayley Rappley," I say, and as I mention her name, there's an air of anticipation. Excitement even. People draw breath, lean forward.

I took Hayley on as a new referral a month ago. I was already overloaded, I didn't need another patient. Especially one like that. But when I heard the details of the case at the allocation meeting, I didn't hesitate. Maggie was chairing that day and handed her straight over. There was relief in the room. After my work with Matt Johnson, all the complex young ones come my way. I can't resist them. That pull to dive in. To help. To make things better.

"Most people are familiar with the tragic circumstances surrounding this case," I continue as I open my file. "I have seen her three times," I say, and look up, "and as you know, she agreed she'd come for the standard six sessions." The group nods, recalling the unusual setup between her and her father.

"No sign of flashbacks . . . intrusive thoughts . . ." I flick through my notes. "And I'm still of the mind that she needs something—but not necessarily our service."

"I don't understand," Stephanie says. "Why wouldn't she?"

"Because having a traumatic experience doesn't necessarily mean a person has a *traumatized response*. They might be struggling, finding it extremely difficult to cope—but they may not have PTSD symptoms. And I'm not sure Hayley has," I explain.

I tell them she's been turning up, "but she's been ticking off the sessions like items on a shopping list. On week two, she spent much of the session in silence, staring out the window. I am very aware of the arrangement—and how it's affecting the work. Her promising her father she'll come. His expectations of me. I feel pressured, and also aware," I say, "that this is fueling my efforts to engage her."

At the end of the second session, I'd asked her to bring in something that reminded her of her mother. "It's not something I would normally do," I explain, "though as I've outlined, this was a slightly odd situation."

I tell the group that when I collected her from the waiting room for her last session, she was wearing a tight red dress, high heels, and a layer of heavy makeup.

"She teetered into the room—then said *ta-da!*, waving her hands down her body, then looked at me, face all angry and tight. '*The thing that reminds me of my mother?*' she said. '*You asked me to bring something. Well, here it is. I'm wearing it!*'"

"As it transpires," I say, looking around at the group, "the red dress was what triggered the argument that Hayley and her mother were having at the time of the accident. I don't know the details. She still hasn't talked about it. In fact, she hasn't talked about anything much at all."

I'm about to continue, when Jamie cuts in. In that gentle, lilting Scottish accent, "Ruth," he says, leaning forward. "Earlier, you said you felt under pressure to engage her." He pauses. "I'm wondering what it would be like if you didn't?" he asks. He strokes a finger over the bridge of his nose as he speaks. Naturally shy, it's a habit he's developed when he speaks in a public forum.

All eyes turn from Jamie to me, as they wait for my response.

Jamie is good. He should be. I was his supervisor. He's doing exactly what I'd do if the roles were reversed. He knows I'm playing it safe, focusing on the details of the case, keeping the spotlight away from me. He's fishing, while I'm doing my best to wriggle off the hook.

The room waits expectantly. Stephanie is sitting next to me, poised with her pen. I feel a prickle of heat at the back of my neck. I want them to stop looking at me.

"If I don't engage her," I repeat slowly, "then I fear she will be lost. Lost and angry. Lots of fifteen-year-old girls feel lost and angry." I hesitate. "Not many have witnessed the death of their mother," I say quietly.

"In the absence of her real mother," Jamie observes, "you have to help her internalize the 'good mother' that she knew. Even though she is no longer here."

For the benefit of Stephanie and the student, he explains a little about Klein and the "good mother," and how her ideas were later developed by Winnicott. Stephanie scribbles furiously in her notebook. The medical student is glancing down at his watch.

Jamie looks back at me.

I nod. "At the moment," I say, "her mother and I are very much the 'bad objects'—her real mother because she has abandoned her. Me, simply because I am not her mother and because I'm getting her to talk about her loss. It will be difficult for her to see me in any other way."

"Of course," he nods.

"Anger is safer," I say, "easier. Much less painful."

"And what about you?" asks Jamie, switching on the spotlight once again. "You chose to bring her today. There must be a strong maternal pull. Where are you in all this?"

I pause for a moment.

"What do I feel?" I close my eyes briefly. "I feel—I feel a tremendous weight of responsibility," I say, and I'm shocked to feel my eyes well up. Quickly, I look down, to reach for my file. "I feel I need to get this right," I say. "To find a way to help her."

"So perhaps that gives us some insight into what Hayley might be feeling," Jamie offers gently. "The tremendous weight of responsibility."

At the end of the case discussion, there's a slot to review the new referrals. I run through the list and when I mention Helen Cassidy, Eve holds her hand up. "She's been allocated to me. Please can I hand her over to someone else?" She hesitates. "I hadn't realized she was pregnant."

People shift in their seats.

I flush. I can't believe I've referred a pregnant client to a member of staff who's just had a miscarriage.

"I'm so sorry."

"It's OK," she says quickly, "not your fault. The GP had left it out of the letter. Admin error. It's fine. Any takers?"

After we allocate the case, I look at the GP letter.

"Hasn't this happened before?" I ask. "Same GP?" There are

nods around the room. I shake my head. "We rely on accurate information from our GPs. Often our *only* source of information. To say nothing of the fact that this particular patient will need linking in with perinatal services." I take the file. "I'll follow it up."

After we move on, this is the moment for me to offer up Dan Griffin. A patient who's vulnerable and estranged from his mother. A patient who's undoubtedly got attachment issues.

A patient who looks like my son.

"Any other business?" I say, looking round.

Several shakes of the head. Then Anna speaks up. "A quick feedback," she says. "Andrew Doornan," she smiles, "he's gone back to work."

There are nods. Murmurs of appreciation.

"Well done," I say. "Great work. Anything else?" I scan the room.

Eve mentions Matt Johnson's latest blog. "Might be useful for our students to read a patient's perspective," and she nods around the room.

It is a good learning opportunity, but I wonder if it's an attempt to appease me, after exposing my inadvertently clumsy referral.

"Good idea. It's certainly worth reading. Matt's an A and E doctor," I say, making a point of looking over at the medical student.

Stephanie makes a note in her book.

"That's everything?" I glance around the room. "OK. Let's finish there for today."

IN THE WEEK between Dan's first and second appointment, I think of him often. Alongside this preoccupation grows the knowledge

that I must call Robert. Supervision is something I've been giving
and receiving for the last twenty-five years. I know what it's for. Robert has been my supervisor for most of my career, and while I have
picked up the receiver several times during the week, something has
stopped me making the call. I imagine it's because I know exactly
what he will tell me to do. He will tell me I must stop seeing Dan,
that the issues with my own son will get in the way of our work together. And I know this is precisely the reason that I don't pick up
the phone.

Instead, I tell myself a different version of the story. I tell myself
it's all in my head. That the likeness to my son is something I have
conjured up, and that the whole episode has taken on a dreamlike
quality, one that I will wake from when I see Dan again. But when
he arrives on that Friday afternoon, a week to the day of his first appointment, I'm not sure whether to be disappointed or relieved that
he looks just as I remembered.

He comes in wearing a black hoodie pulled up over his head.
He drops the hood when he sits down, revealing hair that is greasy
and lank.

"Sorry," he says, trying to make a joke of it, "I know I look terrible." He slumps back into the chair. There are dark circles under his
eyes. His skin is gray, sallow.

"Dead ringer for Gollum," he says.

I note the jokey banter. A lightness to direct me away from his
distress. To keep me at a distance.

"I saw the GP. She gave me tablets. To help me sleep."

"And are they?"

He shakes his head.

The mention of the GP reminds me I haven't yet received his records from the Hackney practice. I make a mark on my notes and circle it twice as a reminder.

The bruise on his cheek is now a faded yellow, his hand still covered by the grubby, frayed bandage. I have the urge to move closer, to reach out and encase his hand in my own. To inspect the wound, and find a crisp white bandage to wind gently around his fingers.

"I want to tell you what happened in the park," he says.

Before I have the chance to answer, he launches into the story.

"It was early evening, still light," he says. "I was chatting to my mate on the phone, when three of them appeared out of nowhere, wearing skullcaps. They dragged me into the trees."

He is talking quietly and matter-of-factly, staring down at the patch of carpet between us as he speaks.

"At first, I thought they wanted my phone. So, I'm all ready . . . to hand it over."

He scratches at the side of his face.

"They just laughed. One of them took it and turned it over in his fingers, then stamped on it. *We don't want your phone*, he said. So now I'm getting worried. One guy, who I never actually saw at all, was holding me from behind, around my neck. All I could see was the tattoo of a snake on his forearm, curling around his fingers. He was sort of pulling me farther into the wooded area, behind the tennis courts."

I nod for him to continue.

"The one with his arm round my neck was still laughing. *Jim, he thought we wanted his phone. Shall we tell him?* Then he pressed his mouth close up against my ear. *We don't want your phone,* he said very quietly, *we want you. We want a piece of you.* And then he punched me in the stomach."

Still his tone is flat. There's an absence of anger. When I go to speak, Dan isn't even looking up. I can see he wants nothing from me.

"They dragged me into the woods. Pinned me facedown," he says. "I couldn't move. I had one on each shoulder. They were heavy. Big blokes. I mean, I tried to wrestle free, but it was hopeless. I could hardly breathe," he says, "let alone move."

He stops for a moment, and picks at his fingers.

"The guy with the tattoo flicked a lighter, right by the side of my face. I thought—" He falters, and looks down at his hands.

"He held it close to my skin, then he just lit a cigarette. That smell—" He shudders. "The lighter. The flame. Burning. I felt like I couldn't breathe."

He's silent for a moment. I wait for him to continue.

"That's the flashback I keep seeing," he says quietly.

I nod. "Is it lots of images," I ask, "like a camera shutter?"

He thinks about this. "It was at first. Now—just one. That moment. The feeling of being trapped. Held down. Now, I don't always *see* it. It's just a feeling."

I probe gently. "A feeling of . . . ?"

He looks up. "Being small and useless. Unable to do anything."

His voice wavers an instant as he picks up the story again.

"After that one had finished, it looked like the other guy was going to have a go too. Then there's this rustling in the bushes. The sound of someone calling a dog. *Trixie,*" he scoffs. "Can you fucking believe it? And then there it was, this small black dog, standing in the clearing, tongue hanging out, and panting at my bare white arse."

He stops for a moment, then looks up at me. "I hate fucking dogs," he says, "always have. But I've never been so happy to see a dog in my life. Then just like that," he snaps his fingers, "they went. One of them stamped on my back and shoulders as he ran away. I got up and left. Never even saw the dog's owner."

He asks for water and I fill a glass from the jug on the table. He drains it quickly.

When I speak, my voice is careful, gentle.

"I'm very sorry," I say, "that this happened to you."

He waves a silencing hand through the air and tells me he went to the Rape Crisis Center. He had tests. Reviews. "A full inspection." He pauses. "It was an awful place," he says. "They were kind, but it was so clinical. I spent hours in a hospital gown, while they prodded and poked and did all sorts of tests." His voice drops down low. "It was humiliating. The whole thing was"—he searches for the right word—"degrading. I felt ashamed. Like I'd done something wrong. Not them. Not the blokes that did it. But me—I was all wrong."

He presses fingertips at each side of his temple. "Two weeks later I was offered an appointment with a counselor," he mocks. "I didn't go. It was shit. But hey—I was OK. Not great, but I was coping."

At this moment, he falls into silence and absentmindedly twists a lock of hair around his finger. I feel a pull in my gut. That was Tom's default gesture, the thing he'd do when he was worried, or deep in thought. I am suddenly back in my kitchen. Hours of late-night conversations with my son, watching him do the exact same thing. It was a habit that started in primary school, when he was learning how to write. He'd sit with one hand gripped around the pencil, the other twisting around a strand of hair, his brow creased in concentration. As he got older, it became a comfort, helped him think, he said. It pained me when he shaved his hair just before he left. It felt like a punishment.

Dan is staring at me, and I realize I have drifted.

"So, when exactly did this happen?"

"About five months ago."

"In London?"

He shakes his head. "Bristol. I moved to London just a few weeks ago. For my film studies course."

"So things were OK," I ask, "immediately after the park?"

He nods. "I was OK. Eating . . . sleeping. I'd started my new course. Things were good. Then just a few weeks ago, all this stuff started to happen. My breathing. Dizzy spells. Feeling faint and spacey."

I'm confused by the time lapse.

"Was there any kind of trigger?"

He nods. "It was just after the police got in touch. They asked me to come in and identify one of the guys. The guy with the tattoo. That's when I found out he was on parole. That he'd attacked another bloke the week before. The parole officers had fucked up. Big time." His voice gets louder. "I blame the solicitors too. All this offender rehabilitation shit. What about the victims?" He bunches his hand into a fist. "It's me who's suffering now. Dropping behind at college when I'm too panicky to leave the house. These so-called *professionals* should be held to account. My own solicitor said I should make a formal complaint. Thinks I've got a case."

Why don't people do their jobs properly?

"So, after the police got in touch, you went to your GP and she told you it was panic attacks?"

He nods. "I had all the tests. Nothing physical. Gave me a leaflet on *how to manage your anxiety*," he snorts. "And then the flashbacks started."

"From the park?"

He hesitates. "First from the park, but then"—he looks away—"other stuff."

I wait for him to continue.

"I can't describe it. It's a panic about feeling small. Being alone. When I went back to the doctor, she told me about this unit. I read up about it. Asked to be referred."

It's then that I hear the rhythm of his breathing starting to change—quick, labored, like he's supping at the air.

"The thing is," he says, "last time I came, you talked about the randomness. How it can make things feel unsafe."

And then all of a sudden he stands up and starts moving from side to side.

"The thing is, I don't think it was."

"Don't think it was what?"

"I mean—I'd love it to have been a random thing. But I think there was more to it," and he picks at the edge of the chair.

"What do you mean?"

"Do you believe in karma?" he asks, looking at me wide-eyed and pale.

"Karma?"

"Maybe it happened for a reason. Because I'm bad. Deserved it. . . ."

"Why would you think you deserved it?" I ask gently.

He's now taking great gulps of air in between his words. He's down in his chair. Then up on his feet again.

"Karma. Perhaps they were sent. A punishment. Sent for me," he says quickly. He drags his hands through his hair.

I can see exactly what's about to happen.

"Dan," I say quietly.

He doesn't hear me.

"Dan," I say again loudly, "I need you to sit down."

I repeat my request, but still he doesn't respond.

His eyes are glazed and distracted. He's sweating profusely. His forehead and neck are drenched.

"It's very important that you concentrate on your breathing," I say, my voice clear and firm. "I need you to come and sit down."

I get up and guide him back into the chair.

"And your hoodie," I say. "You need to take it off."

He doesn't move. I repeat the instruction, then he lifts his arms in the air like a child, and I pull it over his head.

No sooner has he sat down than he's sprung up, unable to sit still. He is pulling at his face. His breathing is now erratic and labored.

"Dan," I say, a little louder, "look at me. You need to look—at—me."

His eyes are wild, darting about the room, and for a while he resists, unable to focus. Eventually, he seems to see me.

"We are going to breathe together. You need to slow your breathing right down. Right now. Breathe in—two—three. Breathe out—two—three."

I repeat this over and over, clearly and calmly, until eventually his breathing slows and then falls in line with mine.

It's been a while since a patient has had a full-blown panic attack in a session; still, I know the drill. Slow the breathing. Stop the influx of carbon dioxide. Prevent hyperventilation. I have dealt with many anxious patients during my career, but his reaction that afternoon is one of the more extreme manifestations of fear I have seen.

When he's calm, I pass him the hoodie, and he slips it over his head. He knows I have seen the marks on his arm. The deep laddering of cuts from his wrist up to his forearm. A crisscross of old white scars, and several fresh ones that have recently scabbed over, leaving small spots of dried blood on his shirtsleeves.

Just as I'm about to mention them, he waves a hand about dramatically. "Woah. Sorry about that," he says, sitting back, "that was all a bit Billy Bibbit, wasn't it?"

Seeing the confusion on my face, he adds, "The film? *One Flew Over the Cuckoo's Nest?*" Before I have the chance to speak, he's asking if that's happened with any of my other patients.

"What about that girl," he asks, "the one who comes before me? Why does she come? Does she get panicky?"

When I tell him I'm not at liberty to discuss other patients, he looks around distractedly, as if wanting to find something else, something new to focus on.

"Your plants are dead," he says, nodding toward the windowsill. "What would Freud say about a therapist who can't keep her plants alive?" He shakes his head. His tone is light, jokey. "Hope you do better with your patients."

He turns back toward me. "Perhaps I should make a complaint?" he asks.

I feel muddled, wrong-footed.

"The parole officers?" he says. "What do you think?"

I know he wants me to collude with his view of the world as an unjust place. A place that let him down. The police. The legal system. The justice system. They've all conspired against him. By agreeing with him, I am being called to set myself apart from these other professionals and to ally myself with him.

I want to say something about my confusion. About how his anger is with "people not doing their jobs properly," rather than the men who attacked him. I want to comment on the fact that his making a complaint feels like some kind of warning. That perhaps I won't do my job properly. Somehow, in my uncertainty about what belongs to me and what belongs to him, I can't find the words for any of this. He's speaking very quickly. And I feel left behind somewhere—running to catch up.

I look up. He's still talking. "—And then I reread the letter about the six sessions," he says. "This is my second. Six simply won't be enough. I mean, how can it?" he asks, "after what has happened to me?"

His tone has changed. The panic has gone. He sits tall in his chair. He looks full of confidence and charged with a glorious sense of entitlement—something, in my experience, that often goes hand in hand with a sense of deprivation. I think about the sort of unimaginable experiences people have had when they come to see us. I think about Mr. Begum, Matt Johnson, and other patients whose images and events still haunt me to this day, although I know this is irrelevant. What's relevant is that everyone, no matter what they've experienced, is offered the same six sessions. It doesn't mean they then can't be offered more, but the principle is that everyone is offered the same at the outset. Boundaries. Containment. It's what we always do.

I blink back at him. The clock behind his head tells me it's time. That we must finish. And when I do reply, it's as if the words come out of my mouth without any thought at all.

"You can have as many as you need," I say.

Satisfied, he nods, then gets up and leaves before I have the chance to draw the session to a close.

FOUR

W hy not?" she says. "It's my neighbor's stuff. It's practically
brand-new." Before I have time to speak, Stephanie is reeling
off a list. "A kid's bed, loads of clothes, toys, a high chair. I mean,
Samira *really* needs them."

We're in my office, the Monday after my session with Dan, and
Stephanie's telling me a little about Samira: her refugee status, how
she left Somalia, and the fact that her husband and older child were
murdered in the village by militants. She's talking very fast and her
face flushes with anger as she speaks.

"She's got nothing. Her daughter comes in wearing this dirty undershirt and skirt. When I volunteered at the camps in Calais," she
continues, "the donations made a massive difference. We could
transform people's lives."

For a moment, I feel bewildered. I could simply tell her the Trust
has a policy about giving gifts to patients, but I know that wouldn't
teach her anything.

"The thing is," I begin, then I stop, because I don't know where
to start.

She's sitting neat and upright, pen in hand, like an interviewer. She looks back at me expectantly.

"Do you remember how we talked about our approach here at the unit?"

Again, there's enthusiastic nodding, but her face is blank. There is no lightbulb moment.

"Yes, but I'm not sure what—"

"Our work has a focus on boundaries; the fifty-minute appointments, the lack of self-revelation, and the offer of six sessions," I say. "Six sessions," I repeat. And as I speak, I can hear the firmness in my voice—as if I am somehow reprimanding myself in the wake of my own deviation with Dan. I tell her that when people come to us in chaos it's these very boundaries, *rules*, if you like, that enable you to do the work. "The frame," I say, "around a very messy picture."

She makes a note in her book, but she looks unconvinced. She has no idea what any of this has to do with baby clothes.

It reminds me of my own initiation into the psychodynamic approach. A placement in North London, where I was astonished by how long the staff spent on their own feelings in staff meetings, rolling my eyes at what I thought was self-indulgence. At first, along with a fellow trainee, we railed against the model. Together, we mocked the strict boundaries. "Detached. Pedantic. What difference does it make?" Two weeks later, I was accompanying my supervisor on a home visit. We were seeing a teenage girl with an eating disorder. "What should *I* do in the session?" I wanted to know as she was parking the car. My supervisor was a small, slight woman with a fierce work ethic. "Just observe," she said briskly, "and focus on yourself." *Myself?*

"Use your emotions as data," she said as we walked up the driveway of a neat semidetached house.

The girl had a pale, gaunt face and wore a baggy pink tracksuit. As my supervisor sat and talked with her on the sofa, I felt consumed by a powerful sense of exclusion. Of being on the outside. And the more I felt it, the more anxious I became. The more I tried to find a way back in, the more detached I felt. I tried to listen—*A family that had moved three times in four years . . . A father in the military . . . Difficulties settling into school . . . No friends*—but my sense of alienation only grew. My head ached. I couldn't concentrate. I felt useless and superfluous. *Emotions as data.* Then something opened in my chest.

All of a sudden, I saw beyond the meticulous weighing of food, and the punishing exercise regime, and I knew I was feeling something of what it was like to be this young girl—anxious, out of control, and trying to make herself smaller, to fit into a life that didn't feel like her own. While I didn't know the theory, it was strangely familiar, like threading my arms into a much-loved coat. I'd spent my childhood creating small boundaries, little frames around the chaos. Mundane and pointless tasks that became a way to manage my anxiety—counting a particular alphabet letter on the back of a cereal packet, studying the weave on the arm of a sofa, keeping a neat and tidy room. After that home visit, something shifted. I read the books, then signed up for two specialist psychodynamic placements. A frame around the mess? I felt like I was coming home.

Now, I look at Stephanie in her neat, buttoned-up cardigan. I take in the color-coded binder perched on her lap. I imagine her on previous placements. Her joy in being able to help patients. Her comfort in the clear treatment objectives, and the use of patient rating scales to map out progress and measure her own efficacy. It's seductive, all that structure and certainty. I often feel jealous of it myself.

Gently, I remind Stephanie of the importance of the blank canvas. "An empty space to be filled with whatever picture they bring. The less they know about us, the more possible that is."

I pause for a moment.

"This approach might feel difficult," I venture, "after the orientation of your other placements." It's like a hand outstretched. An opportunity for her to talk. But when I look back at her, there's nothing. No snag of uncertainty, no hint that she might be finding the concepts tricky. Her face is impenetrable. A mask of competence. In that moment, I am reminded of my daughter. How her own competence is a defense against vulnerability, and how sometimes I see a look of uncertainty flit across her face, but whenever I try to catch it, it slips away, butterflylike, from underneath my fingers.

"What impact do you think these gifts might have on the counter-transference?" I ask.

"The counter-transference?" she repeats. She stares down at her binder for inspiration.

All of a sudden, I feel frustrated by her impenetrability. Her refusal to be vulnerable enough to learn. Then I realize that it goes further than frustration. I feel the nudge of something cruel. I fight the urge to sit and wait it out while she looks for answers she won't find in her file, to watch her stumble through the humiliation of not knowing.

"It's the feelings that *we* are filled up with in the session," I explain. "Clues, if you like, as to what the patient might be feeling."

She nods.

"We all repeat things that are familiar to us," I say. "Patients do the same. The therapy room can be a place where they can act out all sorts of messy feelings about the past."

"Yes, of course. I remember now," she says breezily. "That's really helpful."

She takes a breath.

"So, what about all this baby stuff? How can I get it to her?" she says and she picks up her pen again. "The clothes are hardly worn. Boden, Monsoon, Baby Gap," she adds, as if this will prove the deciding factor.

I feel a heaviness as I sit back in my chair.

"OK. So, tell me about your wanting to give these things to Samira."

She stares back at me. "Well, she needs them. It's simple, isn't it? Something I can do to help. Something that will make a difference. Her family—the things that happened to her," and again, I can hear the emotion in her voice. "At least, she'll have some clothes, toys, a bed for the baby."

I hold up my hand.

"What's happening to you right now?" I ask.

"*Me?* What do you mean?" she says defensively, like it's a trick question.

"You're speaking very fast. Not taking a breath. How do *you* feel?"

She stops. "What's that got to do with anything?"

"Tell me. How do you feel?"

She blinks back at me. "Well, I just want to help—"

"And the feeling?"

It takes her a moment to answer.

"Overwhelmed," she says. "I feel overwhelmed—and helpless."

I nod. "So perhaps," I offer, "the chance to give her these things and make a difference will make you feel less overwhelmed? Less helpless?"

"Well, it's something, isn't it?"

"Let's assume the helplessness is coming from Samira. And you're picking it up. It's your job to use the feeling to help her with *her* feelings. Giving her the baby stuff might not help her feel any differently, but it might make *you* feel better."

Stephanie looks shocked. "So you're saying this is about me?"

"Not consciously." I shrug. "But in a way, yes. It's a response to the helplessness. A way of distracting yourself from the awfulness of what she's been through. Wouldn't it be wonderful," I say, "if a bag of toys and clothes would help a woman who's been raped and seen two members of her family murdered?"

I wait for a moment. "Do you see what I'm saying?"

Her eyes flash. "I'm not saying that a bag of clothes will make a difference."

"And if you *did* give the bag of clothes to Samira. What do you think you become to Samira?"

"Helpful? *Kind?*" she says with irritation.

"That's right. You will become her benefactor. And that will irrevocably alter the therapeutic relationship. It will stop you being able to deal with the difficult stuff. Transference isn't always about good feelings."

Stephanie sits tight in her chair.

"Bad things have happened to Samira. Her experience is dark and murky. Like a lake. You can walk around it, point to things in the middle distance, imagine what might be lurking at the bottom. At some point, you'll have to get into that dark water with her. To feel it as she does. And it will be awful."

She stares at me. Her hands are clenched in her lap.

I try a change of tack.

"One of the papers I recommended—the one by Bion?"

She scribbles the reference down.

"He worked with soldiers traumatized after the Second World War. I suggest you take another look at it," I say. "*Containment* in this context means bearing the feelings of traumatized patients. While part of the recovery is to get into the lake, it's not enough. You have to help her get out again. Incorporate the bad stuff back into her life."

Stephanie stares at me, a small ridge of tension across her forehead.

There's a moment of silence.

"This is all new to me," she says quietly, and as she lays her pen down, her hands collapse in a heap on her file. It's a small gesture of defeat and I feel a surge of warmth toward her for the first time.

"But I think I understand what you're saying," she says, "that to work in this way, using this model, I need to stop trying to be some kind of fairy godmother."

I smile.

I tell her about Freud. How he had a lot to say about the giving of gifts. "He wrote about the *storms of transference* that come from the simple exchange of an object."

Presents change things, I tell her.

Together, we come up with an alternative. She'll donate the items to Samira's local children's center, then alert the care coordinator, so Samira can buy them with her allowance. I tell her I understand her desire to save and rescue. "Giving her things would be helpful and kind," I say carefully, "but it's not your job."

In the last few minutes I ask her if there is anything else she has noticed about the work with Samira. I tell her how my supervisor always looks at how things start. "'It's all in the beginning,' is what he says."

Stephanie looks surprised to hear I have a supervisor.

"Everyone needs supervision," I explain. "The unconscious is not available to us. Things are hidden. We can't see what's right in front of us."

I press her. "Anything significant about the referral letter? How she started the work?"

Stephanie looks hesitant.

"She was late," she remembers. "She couldn't find the building. Then because she'd forgotten the referral letter, she didn't know where we were in the hospital. Front reception rang round. Eventually got hold of Paula."

There's a beat.

"So," I say quietly, holding my hands out, palms up, "she was lost."

As she's packing away her files, she asks about the blog.

"Who's Matt Johnson?"

I nod.

"He was a patient of mine. A few years back. He was nineteen years old, a student at Kent University on an exchange visit to Seattle."

I pause for a moment, remembering.

"There was a gunman on his campus."

Stephanie sits very still, holding her rucksack on her lap.

"Matt was with his best friend. They were hiding under a desk in one of the classrooms when the gunman came in. He knelt down and pointed a gun at Matt. Then, for no apparent reason, he swung the gun to the left and shot his best friend instead, then he calmly got up and moved on. Matt was physically unhurt, but left utterly traumatized. The usual PTSD symptoms, but he was crippled by appalling survivor guilt. He was in a catatonic state when he arrived back in the UK."

Stephanie shakes her head, stunned.

I think back to that first sight of him, the horror of seeing a six-foot young man, pale and mute, curled up like a fetus on a psychiatric ward.

"What happened?" Stephanie asks quietly.

"I saw him for a year. In hospital at first, then at home. Eventually, he was able to come to see me here."

I smile.

"That was some years ago. As I said, he's a junior doctor now. Works in emergency care."

"What did you do?"

I think for a moment as I recall those hours spent watching him slowly uncurl.

"The dark lake," I say simply. "We got in. We eventually got out. His catatonic state was a way of splitting it all off. All his feelings were gone. We had to retrieve them so he could come to life again. He remembered every detail—the weave of the wool on the man's balaclava, the smell of his breath, the small flecks of brown in his eyes. It was all there. Every single awful moment of it. The sessions offered him a *contained* place, so he could see that, in spite of such a devastating experience, the world was *in general* a good place. A place that was safe, ordered, and predictable. A place that he could choose to live in again."

"That's incredible," she says in awe, "to do that kind of work. I can't imagine."

"I had been working for twenty years by then. Here in this very unit," I say. "And anyway"—I shake my head—"if anyone was incredible, it was him. He was wise and courageous. An inspiration. His blog is about trauma. He writes about his experience of being a patient, about what we do here, our model of treatment, but he also writes about being a doctor in emergency care, linking back his life now to how things were before."

Stephanie looks pale. "All these stories—" She tails off. "They're so dreadful."

I nod. "It's a difficult placement. People come here with very painful life experiences. It can skew your view of the world—leave you feeling these things are normal, everyday occurrences."

I encourage her to look at Matt Johnson's blog. "It's very good. And helpful to remember our success stories—good outcomes, in among so many complex cases. People do leave us," I say. "They do get better."

I HAVE TIME to go out for some lunch. It's a relief to leave the hospital. The canteen is on the fourth floor and I already spend too many journeys in the lift squashed next to postoperative patients. Starched white sheets over bodies immobilized by anesthesia; eyes closed, heads lolling, and mouths agape. It's not always good for the appetite.

As I walk to the café across the road, I realize Matt Johnson then wasn't much older than Tom would be now. Then, almost immediately, my thoughts are drawn to Dan—his panic attack, the cuts, his sudden change of mood, and the way I ended up giving him exactly what he wanted. It's a struggle to order these thoughts, like having all the right ingredients in front of me, but not being able to turn them into a meal.

The café has a fridge of ready-made sandwiches to take away. Seeing them all in their neat packaged rows reminds me of Carolyn and her project in the last year of primary school. Each class had a week to raise funds for their designated charity, and all the children came up with different moneymaking ideas. Hers was a sandwich service that she and her best friend, Penny, took around to the offices behind the school at lunchtime. One of the teachers went with them, but it was Carolyn who made all the sandwiches in the morning before school. Great towers of egg and cress, tuna and cucumber, cheese and pickle. I can still remember her standing at the kitchen table, her small earnest face, her look of concentration as she sliced the tomatoes and cut through the bread. "In triangles," she said. "It looks better, I think."

Every morning, they worked for two hours, sold them at lunchtime, then came back after school to count their earnings. On Thursday, Carolyn came back alone.

"Where's Penny?" I asked.

There was a moment before she answered, and I could see she was trying to control the emotion on her face. "She didn't want to come today. Wanted to help on Suzanne's raffle instead," she said, her voice catching. "She said I was too bossy." Then it came, a small wobble of her chin, before her face collapsed in a big heaving sob. My heart ached. But by the time I got to her, it was over. Her sadness and disappointment had been folded neatly away, like one of her sandwich napkins. I pulled her to me. She yielded for a second. Then her shoulders became rigid, conditioned for self-sufficiency. As she resisted my hug, I let my arm drop away. She was ten years old. I should have held on tighter.

There's a voice behind me. A man trying to reach into the fridge. I select a feta and salad sandwich and take it to the register.

FIVE

Clingy" was how one of the nursery workers described Tom. She stood in the doorway, hair in pigtails, with a red-cheeked baby in her arms. "We've had this before," she said. "They always settle fine in the end. Don't worry," and she reached over to pat my arm. "Some children are just more clingy than others."

I recoiled at the sound of the word. Even more so, because of her pronunciation; "clin-gy," with a hard, metallic "g." I stared at the ribbons in her pigtails and her pink nail varnish. She looked about twelve. She went on to talk animatedly about "the module on attachment theory" at college. I stared at her incredulously as she told me all about Bowlby and transitional objects.

I smiled. "That sounds very interesting," I said tightly. "The thing is—while books can be really helpful, I'm his mother. And, well, you really don't know what it's like until you've had your own child."

I flashed her another smile. My tone was pointed and persecutory, but she was so pleased with herself, she failed to notice.

"We do see it," she said, "from time to time. And really, the best thing we've found is to simply 'drop and go.'"

"*Drop and go?*" I said.

"Give him a kiss and cuddle. Then go. Don't look back. Leave with minimum fuss. You know, the way you do with Carolyn."

"Carolyn is different," I said. "Tom is upset. You've seen him, screaming when I try to hand him over. Carolyn isn't."

She nodded. "Drop and go," she repeated breezily. "We find the children settle much quicker. If you draw it out, it makes it worse."

Her smile was knowing. Smug.

"Carolyn, she's a happy little thing," she said, "so independent spirited. Knows exactly what she wants. We were joking the other day that she'll be the next prime minister, the way she holds court over the sandwiches at teatime."

"I'm sure you're right about Tom," I said briskly, "but I'd like to arrange to speak to Gillian."

Gillian was the manager and I wanted to speak to someone who at least looked old enough to have had her own child.

"Sure," she said, obviously irritated. "You know," she continued, shifting the baby over to her other hip, "I was just thinking, when Dad brought him last week it was much easier. Perhaps Dad could bring him more regularly? See how that goes? Tom was so much less clingy with him. We all noticed the difference. Could Dad bring him?"

Dad. Dad. Dad. And that word again. *Clingy.* I wanted to reach across and slap the word out of her mouth.

You have no idea, is what I wanted to say. *You're just a kid. Clueless. What mother wouldn't be distressed by the sobs of her child?* At having to prize his small fingers from my hair, from my coat, from a curled position around my thumb? I dug my hands deeper in my pockets, my fists tight as buds.

"Do you know Jennifer?" she offered. "She used to have terrible trouble leaving Sam, then she followed our suggestions and he was fine. Settled just like that," and she clicked her fingers so loudly that the child in her arms startled with surprise. "Maybe you should have a chat with her. Might help?"

I had no desire to speak to Jennifer. I knew exactly who Jennifer was. She was one of the "Lycra Mums." The ones that had high-powered careers into their thirties, before they gave up work to have children. Jennifer's husband had a job "in the City"—and although she didn't need child care to go to work, she brought Sam to nursery to ensure he got time to socialize and spend time with other kids. "It's healthy for him," is what she said. What she didn't talk about so readily was her desire for "me time." I'd overheard her use that term at pickup, as she described her timetable of Pilates and yoga and training for her half marathon. Every aspect of Jennifer's life seemed project-managed; her social diary, her house, and her children were all on a meticulous schedule. I'd see her sometimes with a group in the mornings, striding along, pushing buggies with such determined efficiency, all ready to drop and go—like they were handing over a bag of shopping.

I did arrange a meeting with Gillian. But by the time we met, there had been several more mornings of distress—Tom's followed by mine. I'd felt the eyes on me as I cradled him on my lap. Pitying looks from some of the mothers, as they waved cheerily to their off-spring while I sat wiping away his tears, calming him down from near hysteria when I so much as tried to put him on the play mat. I'd heard the shushing that the nursery girls had taken to doing in response to the noise we were making. Even though we were tucked unobtrusively in the corner, they moved exaggeratedly around us, as if Tom and I were a tractor trailer restricting vehicular access.

So, when Gillian and I met to "discuss the situation," it was obvious that things had shifted. I'd already been cast into the role of the overinvolved mother. The tearful, emotional mother who was unable to separate, who couldn't let go. Gillian listened as I spoke, her head cocked to one side. "It *is* difficult, Ruth," she said, but I could see what was coming. More *drop and go.*

"Really, it's what we've seen to work."

"The thing is," I said, "I know my child. I don't think that would work with him. I just don't think he's ready."

She nodded kindly, then leaned forward and reached for my arm. "Perhaps the time *isn't* right," she murmured. "Perhaps it's you that's not quite ready. We say to all our mothers that they must do what's right for them. It's an individual thing. But obviously, we'll need a plan soon." Her hand was hot on my arm and I fought the urge to shake it off.

"We have thirty children here, and if we had all thirty parents doing different things? Wow," she said, shooting her fingers in the air like small fireworks. "It would be chaos. We need a routine."

"The difficulties," which was how she referred to my emotional outbursts and his screaming, "are becoming disruptive to the other children."

David suggested waiting until the end of term. "See if he settles? Or I can move work things around and take him more often?" I didn't even reply. I didn't want to acknowledge what I saw as an implicit criticism. My mind was made up. I began the nanny search that weekend, interviewed six potentials, and paid over the odds for one who could start in a week's time. In any event, a month later, David was offered a temporary teaching job in Oxford, so he was away from London three nights a week. It was a relief to have the nanny.

Tom was much happier in his own house, with all his things. And Carolyn—well, she seemed fine too. In retrospect, I'm ashamed to say that I didn't think much about her. Whether she would miss the nursery, the friends she'd made. It simply didn't occur to me. Besides, we couldn't afford to do both.

WHATEVER CAROLYN WOULD SAY NOW, and she's certainly had plenty to say on the matter, I didn't favor Tom over her. I simply saw that they had different needs and that he needed me more, and in a very different way.

Tom was always a worrier. When the twins were little and we read them bedtime stories, Tom was always overly concerned about the fate of the characters. *Tom Rabbit* was a story about a child's stuffed animal left out in the rain. He got to know and love the story, with its happy ending of reconciliation, but each time, the moment of abandonment in the rain on the hard stone wall left Tom's small face devastated. It was the same with all tales of missing things—the mislaid giraffe, the teddy left behind on the bus. The juxtaposition of loss and reconciliation both thrilled and terrified him in equal measure.

On the first day of school, Carolyn was up and dressed in her uniform, her hair brushed, all before breakfast. I was holding her hand as we stepped through the gate, but her fingers were desperate to wriggle out of mine. She searched for and found her class and then stood neatly in line. When it was time to file into the building, she was gone, without so much as a backward glance.

It was different for Tom. He clung tightly to my hand, and all the way up the hill he asked the same questions: When would school finish? Where would I be standing? How would he manage to see me over all the tall people? Would I *definitely* be there? What if I wasn't? What would he do?

After Carolyn had happily disappeared into the classroom and the last of the hesitant children were coaxed inside, Tom was still curled up like a monkey in my arms, hands tightly clasped around my own. Often, after he'd gone, I'd see the moon shapes of his fingernails in my palms, or the indentation of my ring where his hand had squeezed so hard. That first day, in the end, to prize him off me, I gave him my change purse. It was a long red one with a golden clasp that clicked open and shut. "You can have this," I said, handing it over, "so you know I'll be coming back."

His teacher, Mrs. Flynn, told me he could keep it with him in class, and all morning I pictured him sitting at the table, opening and closing that shiny golden clasp, clicking away the minutes until home time.

Now I wonder what I would think if a patient had told me this story. What conclusions might I draw? Would I wonder about this boy's separation anxiety? And what would I think about the mother giving her purse as a transitional object? Why would she think the boy would need to know she was coming back? Would I want to know more about the mother? About her own separation anxiety? Her own secure attachment figures?

I didn't ask myself any of these questions. I did what was required of me. If he needed me, I was there. If he was anxious and unsettled, I was there. I worked part time, so I could alter my schedule to accommodate pickups and drop-offs. Three out of five days I was there when they both came home from school. It was soon clear that the structure of term time was a struggle for Tom. Sports, lessons, the very act of attending school itself were all examples of large organized activities that he seemed to hate. Perhaps it was the herd mentality, but also the pressure to perform in a group. When I asked what he enjoyed the most, he always said, "Lunch break," when he spent his time helping the gardener dig over the flower beds. "Wet-play" days, the whole class cooped up indoors when it rained, were intolerable to him.

It was when the twins were at primary school that my mother embarked on her fourth, and what turned out to be final, alcohol detox program. This time, it was a twelve-week residential stint in Taos, New Mexico. She showed me pictures of a large red-clay adobe house, under the shade of cottonwood trees. The rehab program adhered to strict boundaries. "I'm sorry," she explained, "it's a silent retreat. So you won't be hearing from me for a bit. You can keep in touch, though—send letters or parcels. We're allowed to receive things, we just can't give anything ourselves. Silence is a way of encouraging self-reflection. Finding who we are and the root of our difficulties." It was hard to relax into this sudden silent exile. And for a while, I didn't trust the lack of drama, kept waiting for the phone to ring, with a teary or belligerent request to be picked up from the airport. But there was nothing. She rang the evening the twelve weeks were up. "Haven't I done well?" she said and told me she'd signed up to the advanced program. "Integrating the learning back into our lives," she said excitedly. "It's all about relapse prevention and sustainability." She told me that if she got through the next three months, she was going to stay on as a volunteer. "Run some groups, give something back. They picked me out. I was selected," she said proudly. I was in the kitchen making a cottage pie at the time. She sounded high and giddy. I smashed the potatoes against the saucepan as I listened to her incessant chatter. "You should see me," she gushed. "I look so healthy. Taken years off me." Her euphoria was exhausting. I'd heard it all before. I wished her luck.

"Luck?" she scoffed. "Luck has nothing to do with it." I put the phone down, grateful for the impending silence of the next twelve weeks.

It was around that time that Tom's night terrors started. He was eight. It was textbook stuff. Sudden and abrupt night waking, and I'd find him sitting bolt upright in bed, his body rigid, staring at something only he could see in the room, a look of dread stretched across his face. Sometimes he was crying, other times it was more of an animallike moan, and it could take up to an hour of lying next to him, stroking his back, to coax him out of his strange reverie. I read up about them: *Common at this age. Sensitive children were susceptible. Something they grow out of.* And sure enough, he did. But while the nights became more peaceful, he was left with a legacy of worry, a general state of free-floating anxiety that could land randomly on whatever was close at hand. He began to catastrophize about the world; an item in the news about a plane crash or a motorway pileup would cause him to ruminate about the event. Once, the local news reported a collapsed wall at a school that had injured a child. *What if that happens at our school? What if someone gets hurt?* It wasn't long before the worries escalated into feelings of unwarranted responsibility. One morning on the way to school he'd noticed roadwork on the street where someone in his class lived.

"I saw the trucks. They go so fast around the bend." His face was tense and earnest. "I must tell Charlie," he said.

"Why?"

"Because he might not be able to see around the truck. He might get knocked over crossing the road."

When I tried to make light of it, to point out that Charlie would see it for himself, he became agitated. "But *I* know about it," he said, "and if I don't tell him, and something bad happens, then it will be *my* fault."

I tried to reassure him, to help him see that the world, for the most part, was a safe place. But we turned off the news and stopped listening to the radio in the car. It helped, for a while.

As the twins got older, David was back teaching in London full time, and he got more involved in family life. "You're too enmeshed," he said, dramatically clasping his hands together, "you need to separate from Tom. Step back. Let him be his own person."

Let him be his own person. The words stung. He knew they would. And I felt a roar of hatred. It was what I'd wanted most for my children, because it was the very thing I'd struggled to achieve for myself. In my own childhood, any opaque rules of parenting would be further clouded by an open bottle of gin. I had to furrow my own path through the chaos. I was good. I was helpful. But I had no idea who I was. I was like a small limpet in a wide-open sea, desperate for a rock to cling to. I found those rocks outside the home. In teachers who took an interest in me—the PE teacher who made me captain of the netball team, the drama teacher who suggested I direct the school play, the English teacher who awarded me the annual poetry prize. I remember standing up in front of the whole school; the sense of feeling special, being singled out, was so achingly acute I thought my heart might break.

"Let him find himself. Toughen up a bit," David said. "He's just started in Year Six. Let him make mistakes. See if he can manage things. On his own. Without you."

I opened my mouth to speak but didn't know what to say.

"Ruth, in less than a year he'll be in secondary school," he continued. "Have you seen the size of those kids? You can't be hovering at the school gate handing over your change purse as a keepsake. He'll be ripped to shreds."

That was always the problem with David. He took something that had happened in one context and applied it to another. Once, after I'd confessed to being nervous in advance of a conference talk, he went on to assume I'd feel the same at all public speaking events.

"How are you feeling?" he'd ask earnestly, a hand on my shoulder.

"Fine," I'd say lightly, as I put on my earrings.

"It's just that I know you find these occasions difficult."

Initially, I'd read it as concern. His attempt to draw on a feeling of anxiety I'd previously experienced, a clunky and rather robotic way of nurturing and offering care and attention. And at first these links, these associations, didn't bother me. I'd laugh and say,

"No—really, I'm fine. I was nervous last year because Professor Bridgeman was there. This is different. I only have to say a few words of thanks. And anyway," I reminded him, "I'm collecting an award on behalf of the team. I'll be with all my colleagues. I'm looking forward to it."

As time went on and I became the director of the unit while David was passed over for successive promotions, I realized that there was something unhelpful, even undermining, about these comments. As if by mentioning a previous vulnerability, he was trying to drag me back to an earlier place of insecurity. Soon, I became adept at keeping things to myself, not telling him how I felt. In truth, that wasn't a new skill for me. It was a habit I'd already mastered, a survival technique I'd learned much earlier in my life. Perhaps it was something I'd always done—but it calcified the day my father left. I was ten years old when I came back to find he'd gone.

"I don't think that's relevant," I said, my voice tight. "I gave him the purse when he was in primary school. His first day," I said, "which was six years ago." I was angry. I hated the insinuation that I was babying him.

Of course, I wished Tom were more light and carefree. Especially when I could see there were times when he seemed happy and less burdened. It was usually on holiday, when absorbed in an activity—digging trenches in the sand, or making a dam across a stream. The task would consume him entirely. Everything else fell away and there was a purity about his immersion in something that gave him real joy. But his life couldn't just be constructed around these things, and I came to dread seeing his small frown when he came home from school. His worry made me tense, agitated. I can see it didn't help. And of course, the more he worried, the less he fitted in. Sometimes I could see his concerns loop around specific things, other times his anxiety simply multiplied like duckweed on a pond. I tried to tell myself he'd grow out of it.

"As parents, it's not our job to take it away, tell him everything is fine. We have to bear it," David said, "so he can learn how to bear it for himself."

He held his hands out in exasperation. "Ruth, you're the therapist," he said, "you know all this."

While I nodded in agreement, the next day I resumed my position, scooping up the duckweed into nets that I upended on the side, only to see the surface choked over the following day.

His worry became my worry.

You have to bear it.

Could I bear it? Maybe I simply couldn't. Maybe all I saw in him was my smaller, younger self, my stomach a tiny knot of anxiety. *It's fine.* And a rictus smile of tension stretched tight across my face.

SIX

Hayley's hair is scraped back into a punishing ponytail that pulls at her scalp. Several small greasy strands hang at either side of her face. She's wearing a shapeless gray tracksuit and dirty sneakers. Her eyes are set in a hard, mean stare.

"I dumped Tony," Hayley says, reaching into the side of her bag for a pack of chewing gum, "told him to fuck right off," and as she looks up at me, she slowly folds a stick of gum into her mouth.

Her eyes are small and watchful. I feel her waiting for me to slip up. To say something banal or stupid that she can pounce on and mock. Fleetingly, I find myself thinking of Carolyn, and the deterioration of our relationship.

I wait for her to say more.

"He was a deadweight," she says.

She holds my gaze. There it is again. That look, daring me, willing me to say something.

Her anger is exhausting. A great big wall of truculence that she wants me to run and hit myself against. I feel weary.

"I had to drop him," she says.

I think about the young man who accompanied her to the first session. His face pale with concern, offering to hold on to her coat in the waiting room as she and her father came down to my room.

"When I met him," I say, "he seemed very worried about you."

"Kept bringing me flowers," she scoffs. "Always there, following me round like a lovesick puppy. Fuck off, I said, and take your fucking roses with you. A deadweight," she says again, and she chews violently on her gum, her arms folded across her chest. "I'm better off on my own."

Of course she is. At the moment, she's the deadweight. The lump of uselessness. A blot on the landscape. Anything good that comes her way must be annihilated, such is the strength of her disgust for herself. It's so strong, I can almost smell it. Like something rotting at the back of a cupboard. I can see how hard she's working to get everyone to hate her as much as she hates herself. If you are repeatedly vile to other people, pretty soon they will move away. Leave you alone. Confirming the belief that you are truly despicable. I know how comforting it can be to have the way you feel about yourself reflected right back at you. I know that feeling very well. Head down, full of self-loathing, and batting back anything good that comes your way.

Once, years ago, when I was a trainee on an acute psychiatric ward, a patient got very angry. She was a giant of a woman, who was shouting and waving her arms about, kicking chairs and tables, hair wild around her face. People were afraid. Someone pressed the panic alarm. Staff edged away. I joined them, my heart pounding, my back against the wall, waiting for other staff to arrive. What happened next was extraordinary and unexpected. Mary, an Irish nurse, a tiny diminutive woman, stepped slowly forward. She walked toward the patient and gestured to a bench. "Can I sit down?" she asked quietly. Stunned, the patient dropped the chair that she was holding above her head. "You must be feeling really bad," Mary said. "Why don't you sit down with me?" And in that second, the anger seemed to fade from the woman's eyes. Mary reached for her hand and said, very gently, "I can't imagine how frightening all this must feel." And at this, this huge hulk of a woman slumped down next to her on the bench, head in hands.

I've thought of this incident many times over the course of my career—how much it's taught me about anger and aggression.

I spoke to the nurse about it afterward. "What were you thinking?" I said.

"I wasn't." She shook her head. "But I knew she was frightened. I could feel it. We could all feel it. Her anger was fear," she said matter-of-factly. "Fear that she was trying to get rid of and give to us. I wanted to give her something else. Something that showed I wasn't afraid. Something that told her I could bear it. That however badly she was behaving, I could bear *her*. I wanted to give her some warmth."

In my worst moments of guilt about Tom, I have almost willed judgmental comments from others. Sometimes, I've positively encouraged it. After his hospital admission, I felt undeserving of sympathy and kindness. I rejected all support and help. Some friends persevered, but for the most part, over time, people got the message and gave up. And pretty soon, I was left to glory in the comfort of the self-imposed exile that was my punishment. Yes, I think, looking at Hayley's thin, tight lips, her angry chewing jaw, I know just how comforting that place can be.

"It seems hard," I offer, "for you to bear anyone being nice to you."

"I told you," she says, her lip curling into a snarl, "he's useless. Going nowhere. And this," she says, jabbing a finger in the direction of my chair, "this isn't helping either. It's a waste of my time."

I nod and tell her that I imagine that at the moment, she feels so bad, nothing will help.

She stares back at me, almost writhing with fury in her seat. It's like the hatred she feels is poisonous, coursing through her veins, contorting her body into a shape that looks ugly and hateful. Her eyes are accusing, her jaw set out at an angle of defiance. A "say something useful" pout. She's trying so hard, I think, to be hateful and mean. It's so exaggerated, like a cartoon version of a moody teenager, I have to stop myself from smiling.

She lapses into silence. She looks down at the gray bag on her lap, picking at the zip, drawing my attention to it.

"S'pose you're wondering what's in here? You'd said to bring something—something that reminds me of Mum?" and then, in a deft move, she unzips it and turns it upside down, shaking out several hundred photographs that spiral out over the coffee table.

She curls her lip into a snarl. *What?* it seems to say. Again, that challenge. Willing me to reprimand her for the mess, or for the way some have spooled out over the floor.

With her face impassive, she leafs through a handful of photos in front of me. "Devon . . . Spain . . . first day of school . . . princess party for third birthday . . . Year Six party . . . sports day . . . ," and on she goes. Her voice is flat, like she's reading from a list. I catch a glimpse of some of the pictures. Sand dunes, an English seaside scene, the twinkle of Christmas tree lights, a villa balcony, a blue dress with a white ruff. She's taunting me with her flatness, her lack of engagement. Willing me to comment, or to reprimand. I do neither of these things. She continues to flick through them. A mound of family memories, moments between mother and daughter. It makes me think of our own family photographs, some of which have made it neatly into albums, while others still remain expectantly in packs, with dates scrawled on the outside, and then the most recent ones, now digitized, that may never make it off the computer. They pop up when I am at my desk, random pictures of Tom or Carolyn, holiday memories that nudge their way onto the screen while I am writing a report or shopping online.

"Thank you," I say eventually, "for bringing them to show me."

She shrugs.

I reach down for several that have fallen onto the floor and pick them up carefully.

"Tell me about this one," I suggest.

She peers at it. "Brighton," she says.

I continue to fan through the pictures, with a deliberate slowness. I think about the huge angry woman on the ward, and how the small nurse slowed everything down and sat with her, and did the opposite of what she was expecting. I pick up a photo from time to time and ask her about it. *Where was she? What were they doing?* And in that slow process of retrieval and reminiscing, of sifting gently through these memories, she, too, starts to slow down, to stop and look. She continues to answer my questions curtly. Just words, or monosyllables. "My brother. The beach. Christmas in Dorset. The Isle of Wight." But as I persevere, and she understands that I am not overwhelmed by the volume of pictures, and that I am interested, really interested in them, I feel she begins to soften. She leans in closer across the table. She stops fidgeting. Perhaps it's the care I am taking. The fact that I am really looking at the images. Really trying to see her—and see who she is. *I see you. I see the two of you. And because I see what you had, I see what you have lost.* And something shifts between us.

"What about this one?" I ask. It's taken outside, on a pavement. Hayley looks eight or nine, with an older woman with dark hair in a ponytail. She's standing by a red bike. Smiling a wide toothy grin.

Hayley reaches across for it, nods with recognition. There's the hint of a smile.

"My birthday," she recollects, "ninth, I think . . . my new bike—"

She hesitates. "Mum had wrapped it in brown paper. Put it in a box. Ribbons and tissue. I had no idea I was getting a bike. She wrapped it so well. Totally hid the shape. It must have taken her hours," and she twists her hands together in her lap.

She looks up at me.

"I am thinking," I say, working hard to hold her gaze, "that while it's hard for you to tell me how much you loved her, how much she loved you, and how dreadful you feel . . . you have brought these images, these memories, which tell me that story."

Hayley says nothing, but there's a softening of the silence.

She looks down at her hands.

"Lots of teenage girls argue with their parents. In fact, most teenage girls argue with their parents. Particularly with their mothers. It's normal. It's part of life as a teenager. And it's part of life as the parent of a teenager."

Again, I think of Carolyn. How her fierce self-reliance made my advice redundant.

"Lots of teenagers wish their parents would disappear. Simply go away. Parents—particularly mothers—with their questions, their concerns, their worries, they get in the way of freedom . . . getting what you want."

Hayley continues to stare. Lip out, jaw set hard and expectantly.

"But for many girls—and boys—it's a wish. A momentary wish. A fantasy."

There's a pause.

"If you're one of the many teenagers who's felt this," I say, "then I wonder how difficult it must feel, now that your mother really has gone away."

"It was the dress," she blurts out. "I'd just bought it, was showing it to her. Mum said it was awful. Tarty." She struggles to continue. "I saw it happen. It was like a film. Slow motion—and yet really fast at the same time. Like I knew exactly what was going to happen before it happened."

As she tells the story, I see the two of them on the pavement outside a crowded shopping center. The argument about the dress she'd just bought to go to the party. Too short. Too red. Too grown-up. Too cheap. On another day, it might have been about what time to come home. Or about drinking. Or not eating properly. The thinness of her arms and body. Or about not texting her the night before. Or not getting back in time to babysit her younger brother . . . or a million other things that might spark an argument between a parent and a teenager. Then she hears people shouting and she hears a woman scream. Then out of nowhere, behind her mother, a car comes careering off the road and onto the pavement.

"She was driving like a drunk," Hayley says.

There were no traces of alcohol found in the body of the driver. Mrs. Susan Hamilton was fifty-eight years old and suffered a massive and fatal stroke at the wheel of her car. Consequently, she lost control of the vehicle as it plowed onto the pavement on a busy Saturday afternoon in Wood Green. Hayley's mother died on impact, wedged up against the lamppost where she'd been leaning. There were other injuries, but she was the only fatality.

Hayley tells me how her mother had put down her shopping bags as they were arguing. "'I'm tired, Hayley,' she'd said, and I stopped in the street to shout at her, instead of walking on. She stopped, too. If I hadn't argued—or stopped—we would have been somewhere else entirely."

Hayley looks away.

"The last thing my mother said to me was something about how the dress made me look cheap. And guess what—," she says, looking back at me, as she picks the skin around her fingernails, "the last thing I was saying to her? Not out loud, but in my head. I was practically shouting it at her."

She drops her head down low.

"Why don't you just fuck off and die," she whispers. "That's what I was saying in my head. How shit am I? That just before it happens, I'm saying I hate her. The actual moment she dies, I'm wishing her dead."

She inspects her fingernails.

"So now you know. It was my fault," she says without emotion. "I did it. I made it happen."

She looks up at me defiantly. "You really don't want to mess with me. You don't even really want to be around me. Look what I can do," she says, "you never know what might happen," and there is real menace in her voice.

I do not feel threatened. I lean closer toward her.

"You were angry," I say simply. "You had an angry thought." I press my palms together. "Do you know what?"

I can feel her listening.

"You won't be the first or last teenage girl who's had a hateful thought about her mother. We can have a murderous thought without being murderous."

I have her full attention. "We can have bad thoughts without being bad," I say, very slowly and clearly. "I imagine the bad feelings you're carrying around must be really heavy. Awful to carry around with you. Maybe you can think of it like a rucksack, and put it down for a while. Give yourself a break. Pick up something else. Pick up some of these lovely memories," I say, gesturing down to the table.

She blinks back at me.

"Mostly what I feel listening to your story is great sadness. How awful for you to feel so bad. To feel so powerful. To feel like the bad girl who made the car swerve round the bend. I'm so sorry."

She sinks down lower as I'm speaking, as though the heaviness is threatening to crush her.

"What I also see here," I say, and I pick up a handful of pictures, "is that you are the girl who laughed and made sandcastles with her mother on the beach. The girl who appreciated how her mother wrapped her birthday present. These pictures show me that there was so much more than that single bad thought you had about your mother."

She says nothing in response, but I can tell she's still listening. I know that she can hear me.

I pick out one photo and hold it up. "Underneath all this fury, there is loss. Often, it can feel easier to stay angry. I know you feel it was your fault. It wasn't," and I shake my head. "But letting go of that feeling means you will have to let in a tide of other feelings. Grief and sadness. It will be very hard."

Hayley says nothing. Makes no sound. A solitary tear rolls down her cheek. Nothing follows and she doesn't move to brush it away. She ignores it. Simply pretends it hasn't happened. Then she looks up at the clock and starts to gather the photographs together and sweep them back into the rucksack. Her hands move more gently, reaching down to pick up the ones that have fallen on the floor. I help her pack them up. We do this together, in silence, until every last picture has been put away.

"Perhaps you can bring an album next time you come. We can start to put them in a book."

She gives a nod. Like a blink.

As always, at the end of the session, she sits poised on the edge of her chair, like a schoolgirl waiting for the bell. This time, the zipped-up bag is cradled on her lap. This time she doesn't ask if she has to come back, or "why she has to keep coming to this dump."

For the first time, she says good-bye. A gruff muttering, then, "See you next time," as she shuffles out the door.

It's a small triumph. Like a glimpse of green from the winter soil.

But I see it. I claim it for my own. It's what I am good at. Holding, bearing it all, waiting for the breakthrough that I know will always come.

It's in this state of triumph that I sit waiting for Dan. He's due at four o'clock—and at ten past I ring through to Paula. There is no sign of him. He has not called and left a message. By quarter past, I think perhaps he won't be coming, and I feel an acute sense of disappointment. Sessions when a patient doesn't come are marked as DNA on the system. Did not attend. They are hard to fill. The time that you would spend seeing your booked patient becomes a time that you spend thinking about them. Wondering about them, reflecting on the last session and their state of mind.

It reminds me of my previous supervision session with Stephanie.

"It's rude," she'd said, as she pondered over her three DNAs in the previous week. "If they could just pick up the phone and tell me they can't make it, then I could use the time to get on with something else. Instead," she said, "I spent the whole of the session waiting. Expecting them to come. Maybe they're running late. Or something's come up. Whatever. Common courtesy, don't you think? Just to call and let me know?"

Again, that impenetrability. That concrete thinking that was verging on obtuse.

"Perhaps," I offered, "that's the point?"

She screwed up her face, shaking her head. "What? I don't quite—"

"If a patient doesn't come, and doesn't let us know, we're left with all sorts of feelings. When they don't come, it's still their time.

Maybe they'll come. Maybe they won't. We are left with them, even if they aren't there. Let's think about rudeness," I say. "How else might you understand the feelings you're left with?"

"Out of sorts?"

Inwardly, I sighed.

"What does 'out of sorts' mean?" I prompted.

She shrugged. "Discombobulated?" she offered.

Perhaps it was her tone of voice—less obtuse, more like a child in class, hand in the air, desperate to give the right answer. I began to wonder whether her own feelings were somewhere underground, buried things she was trying hard to dig up.

"I understand what you're saying. What might be the *feeling* behind that?"

She stared back at me, "Well, it's irritating, isn't it?"

"Can you say, '*I feel irritated*'?"

She looked confused.

"Let's think about what the patient himself might be experiencing. Is it possible that the patient himself might be feeling angry and irritated? Angry about what's happened to him? Irritated by the fact he has to come here and talk about it? Angry that he is the victim, and in the hands of the 'expert' whose life might seem perfect? Do you think it's possible that he feels these things very strongly, and he might want you to experience a tiny bit of what that might be like?"

I paused for a moment. "Remind me—who was it that you had to cancel the week before?"

"When I was off sick?"

I nodded.

"Neil Dixon was one of them."

"Well, perhaps Neil Dixon felt angry at *his* sudden canceled session. Perhaps he was looking forward to coming . . . in need of help and support, given what has happened to him? Perhaps he wanted to retaliate. Perhaps he wanted you to feel what he felt. Let down? Rejected?"

She frowned. "I was ill. It wasn't my fault."

"I know that. And he *knows* that. He will have got the call from Paula. But what he knows and what he *feels* are two very different things. And all this is *unconscious*, of course," I went on. "It's not likely to be something he's aware of—at all."

"I can't help being ill—"

"No," I said, "you can't. That's not what I'm saying. It's about understanding the *impact* of your unavailability. In fact," I added, "our lack of availability is fundamental to the work. How a patient is able to internalize separation from the therapist says a lot about their early attachment figures. And vice versa." I reminded her about Winnicott. "His theory about the 'good enough mother' would be something to have a look at," I said, but she screwed up her face.

"I see it everywhere," she groaned, "almost every magazine article I pick up—*good enough* parent . . . *good enough* teacher . . . *good enough* partner." She rolled her eyes. "Sounds like a way of letting yourself off the hook if you mess up. An excuse for mediocrity," she says.

I shook my head. "It's become oversimplified. The original meaning's got lost. It's about the fact that maternal limitations play an essential role in separation and in the child's developmental process."

I glanced up at the clock, I could see we were running out of time, but I also wanted her to do the work and make the links. "Why don't you have a look at the paper again," I say, "then we can talk some more. I think the conference will really help. It'll cover attachment theory and you'll then be able to see how it relates so crucially to our approach to therapy with trauma patients."

She nodded. Then she told me she wasn't used to having DNAs as a trainee. "Up until now, my patients have mostly come. Perhaps it was the different model? The weekly homework tasks—"

"So this is important learning for you," I cut in, "something to really think about," I said, before she had the chance to tell me yet again about the structure of cognitive behavior therapy.

So it is, on that Friday afternoon, in the absence of Dan, I am thinking about him. After the initial disappointment, I then review our work together and I think about my confusion at the end of the last session. The pull to collude with his view of the world. His feeling of grievance, of being let down. I remember his sense of power at those closing minutes. The sudden shift, and how, as a result, he got what he wanted.

At my desk, I'm leafing through the notes and my thoughts turn to the brutal rape in the park. The subsequent panic attack in my office. How he might have been left feeling raw and exposed, and that it might have felt difficult for him to come back and see me again. His desperation. His hopelessness. The cuts on his arm. *The cuts on his arm.* The cuts that I failed to even ask about. Somewhere in the distance, there's the sound of a siren. An ambulance weaving its way to the hospital. I feel a sudden coldness. And then there was his comment about the dead plants. Was he trying to tell me something? Was it a warning? I think about Tom and the signs I might have missed. That dark night in the kitchen. The sight of him. Ashen. The black shadow that fell across his face.

Jittery, I ring Dan's mobile number. It goes straight to voice mail. Without thinking, I leave a message. *I was expecting you this afternoon. I hope everything is all right.* It's not something I would ordinarily do. But as I put the receiver down, I tell myself it's warranted. That it's an exceptional circumstance. And it's somehow a comfort to hear his voice.

I ring Paula. "Have we had Dan Griffin's medical notes forwarded from Hackney?"

When she tells me nothing's come through, I call the surgery. The woman on reception puts me on hold, then tells me there's been a problem getting them from his previous GP. She tells me Shirley, one of the administrators, is dealing with it. "She'll be in tomorrow. Can you call back then?"

I try to concentrate on admin but can't settle, so I go to the window, unlatch the catch, and push it open. The spring sunshine is warm on my arms as I reach for the pots from the window box. I lift them up, snapping off the dead leaves and twigs. Dan was right, some are dead. But others have strong roots, and when I fill a cup of water and pour it into the earth, they drink thirstily. I add more, until water drips down from the metal railings. It's as I'm placing them back that I look down to the car park and see the figure on the bench. Someone in a black jacket, or a hoodie. At six floors up, I'm too far away to be sure, but I think it's him, and I think he's looking up at me, watching me as I carefully tend to the plants. I feel exposed, to be caught acting on something he said. I step back to the desk to reach for my glasses, but when I return to the window, the person has gone. I look up and down the road. There is no sign of anyone. Perhaps I have imagined it. Perhaps there was no one there at all.

Seconds later, the phone rings. "Ruth, I have Dan Griffin here," Paula says, reveling in the misdemeanor. "Shall I tell him he's too late?"

"He has twenty minutes," I say. "You can send him down."

SEVEN

The relief I feel about his arrival soon morphs into a different kind of feeling when he's in the room. He strides in and sits down without a word. He's wearing a red long-sleeved T-shirt. There's no sign of a black hoodie. I find myself staring at the rucksack he's dropped on the floor.

When I tell him I was beginning to think he wasn't coming, he nods, offers no explanation for his lateness. "I wasn't going to," he says. He sits still in his chair, arms folded, staring at the floor.

"I'm sick of it."

When I comment on how frustrated he seems, he laughs.

"*Frustrated?* Is that it? Is that all you have to offer?"

His tone is more weary than aggressive. He wants the "tools"— the quick fix, and we're back to his "I want to get back to where I was before" conversation.

I tell him that therapy isn't some kind of magic. "I'm sorry. It doesn't work like that."

He talks about the effort it took him to come, how he had to walk, rather than take the bus. "Public transport still makes me feel panicky."

Then Dan speaks about the people he passes on the way. "All so happy and smiling, like they don't have a fucking care in the world."

I see how he uses the sense of grievance as a kind of armor. It stops him thinking about himself. How his victim status keeps him comfortably protected in his ironclad suit from any responsibility, from any need to think, reflect, or change.

"It feels unfair," I offer, "what's happened to you, and I imagine there's a part of you that's pretty angry at having to come here at all."

He says nothing.

"After our last session, I was left with some concerns about you. Then today, you arrive very late. Missing most of the session. It makes me wonder whether a part of you wanted me to worry about you?"

He rolls his eyes.

"One of the things I was left preoccupied with was something we didn't get a chance to speak about. The cuts I saw on your arm."

He shrugs. "What about them?"

"Can you tell me about the cutting?" I say. "When did you start?"

"Years ago." He is matter of fact. "I mean—it's just something I do."

His face softens. "Really—it's fine. Never deep. Always surface. I've never needed hospital treatment for them. I have it under control," he says. "It's not a problem."

He looks at me intently. "You must have seen loads of people who cut themselves. You know it's not indicative of any other risk factor."

He has all the right answers.

"It sounds like you've been asked about this before?"

"Not really. But I don't want to waste my time here on something that's been part of my life. Something that isn't a problem for me."

"OK," I nod. "So, let's think about you. The reason you have come to the unit."

When I ask for the questionnaire, he shakes his head. "It made me too anxious. I couldn't fill it in."

I feel a sense of frustration. That he's stopping me being able to do my job and thwarting any attempt at recovery. But I also feel there's something forced about his truculence, as if somehow he wants to pull me into reprimanding him.

"Let's go through some of the questions together," I suggest calmly.

We work through the practical information and the symptoms of his anxiety.

"There are a few other questions now," I say, "to help me understand a bit more about you."

He shifts in his seat.

"Can you tell me an early childhood memory?"

He laughs. "Aha. So this is the session when I talk about my abusive childhood. How scared I was of my violent stepfather. What a raw deal I had. How in the telling of my backstory, we'll understanding the link to my recent trauma. I'll cry. You'll hug me. We'll get down to the 'real work.' My *Ordinary People* moment."

My face is blank.

"Judd Hirsch? Timothy Hutton?"

He stretches out his arms toward me.

There's a moment of silence. I don't know what he's talking about.

"A violent stepfather? *Is* that what happened to you?"

He stares back at me. Holds my gaze.

"No," he shakes his head.

"I wish I did have a 'big story,'" he says. "Something filmic. A big moment I could tell you about. Something that you would instantly listen to and 'see.' Oh yes, I get it."

Again, that dispassionate gaze. "But there isn't."

I comment on his need to impress with a dramatic story. "You do have your own story," I say gently, "and I'd very much like to hear it."

He tells me about a family trip to West Wittering. "My parents and my baby cousin. Dad borrowed my uncle's car. We drove with the top down. Like something out of *Thelma and Louise*," he says. He tells me they had fish and chips and ice cream on the beach. "It was a happy day," he says.

It's an odd story. Disconnected. And it hangs in the air between us. I think about these film references and how they push me further away. Another sort of armor?

"What sort of child were you," I ask, "growing up?"

"Anxious," he says, "I was an anxious child. On my own a lot. I watched a lot of films." As he's talking he's absently twisting the handle of a plastic bag around his finger.

"What did you like about films?"

He thinks for a moment, twisting the handle tighter. "Other worlds. Places where anything could happen."

He pauses. "But mostly," he says, "they taught me to feel."

"*To feel?*" I repeat.

He looks up. A small moment of fragility. It's like I'm trying to reel him in, slowly, like a slippery fish that I imagine will quickly flip back into the water.

"And what about your parents?" I ask. "How were feelings expressed in the family?"

He's silent for a long time. I am distracted by the twist of plastic around his thumb. Tight, like a piece of string.

"When I think of my family," he says eventually, "there's nothing."

At first, I don't understand. I think he's being obstructive.

"Nothing?"

"A sense of nothingness. A void. Home was a hollow place. I always felt something was missing." He twists the bag tighter. His thumb is turning purple, like a plum.

"I tried to fill that space with films. With characters who were alive."

Alive. I think about this for a moment, about his choice of word. "So there was the opposite," I ask, "something *deathly* about your own family?"

He releases his grip on the bag. The blood rushes back to the rest of his hand.

"Like I said, I don't remember much."

I try to ask some more, but he shakes his head. "I'm sorry—I just don't remember very much about my childhood. There's nothing much to say."

That quicksilver flick of a tail, and he has gone, disappeared in a swirl of murky water.

I refer back to our previous session. How he had said what happened to him in the park felt like a punishment. "Karma, was what you said."

He stares back at me.

"Karma?" He shakes his head. "I don't know why I said that. I'm sorry. It was my Billy Bibbit moment. I wasn't making much sense at all. I don't remember what I said. I was in a bit of a state."

I ask some more questions. I get nowhere. The more he retreats, the more I probe, and the less able I am to comment on the process and what's going on in the room between us.

"Look," he says, "the park was brutal. I mean, *hello?* Perhaps I feel bad because of what happened? Does there have to be anything else to unearth? Some great big secret? I mean, who are you? Miss Marple?"

His gaze is unwavering.

"The attack *was* brutal and traumatic," I agree, "but from what you said in our previous session, I was left feeling that it had some kind of association for you. You said your flashbacks were of other things. Something from the past, perhaps?"

He's shaking his head, a mock "beats me" expression on his face.

"I can make something up," he jokes, "if that would help?"

I take a breath and sit forward in my chair. "Dan," I say, "something's happening here. Between us," I venture. "I feel pulled into the position of having to question you. All this asking, probing, and trying to find 'the truth.' It's stopping me doing my job."

He looks back at me. Says nothing.

"The sense of injustice and grievance that you carry," I say, "the parole officers . . . the police . . . the solicitors—it makes me wonder whether you've been let down before. Or had an experience of being unfairly treated in the past. Perhaps by parents, or by other people close to you."

There's a flash of something across his face. Recognition, I think. He sits still. He is watching me. He looks serious. Attentive.

"And I wonder, too, if that makes it difficult for you to show up and be truly present in the room. To really *be* here. To risk feeling vulnerable. Because there's always a danger—that I too might disappoint. That I too *won't do my job properly.*"

He looks like he's taking it all in. Like he is coming on board. I feel the session open out and expand, like a rush of air into the room. Like I am on the edge of a breakthrough. He sits back in his chair, interlocks his fingers, and stretches his arms, as if limbering up before a session in the gym.

"*People doing their jobs properly.* It's true—it does raise an interesting question," he says, and he moves his head side to side, stretching out his neck.

"I've been doing my own research about this place," and he waves a hand between us. "There's the Matt Johnsons of this world," he says. "But that's not the whole picture, is it?"

He leans forward.

"The thing is," he says slowly, "you haven't—have you?"

He's looking at me, waiting, in a way that makes me feel exposed. Like he's looking right through me.

"Haven't *what?*" I say, my throat suddenly dry.

"Haven't always done your job properly." His neck clicks as he moves it to the side. "You haven't been able to help everyone— have you?"

I feel everything slow right down. As he speaks, I see the pictures in my mind. The ones I try to keep away. David's shoulder against the bathroom door. Tom's boot on the floor. His blue lips. The smell of vomit. The bleached white of the ICU.

You haven't been able to help everyone—have you?

I know exactly what's coming. I feel caught in my seat. Trapped by his cool steely gaze. My palms suddenly sweaty. I look up. I am consumed by anxiety.

"Mark Webster," he says quietly. "It didn't turn out very well for him—did it?"

Mark Webster?

It's not what I expect. Not what I expect at all. I feel a momentary flood of relief. A feeling of escape. Then, it comes. A thud of confusion. I blink back at him, wide-eyed with surprise.

"Mark Webster?" I repeat slowly.

He nods. His face impassive.

There's a giddy moment when I can't focus. The shock of hearing his name after eight . . . or maybe nine years.

"Freedom of information," he shrugs, as if reading my mind. "I looked him up. An inquest is a public inquiry."

I stare back at him.

"If you're going to get your car fixed, you'd want to check out the credentials of the mechanic, wouldn't you."

This is when I should keep quiet. This is when I should explore what's going on between us. To find out what led him to carry out his research. To wonder with him what his motivation might have been. But in the moment, I am floored. I don't ask any of these things. I feel trapped, like a butterfly under a pin. I clear my throat.

"Mark Webster was very unwell," I say, and I can feel my cheeks are burning. "His suicide came in the aftermath of a terrible family tragedy. He was in a state of despair."

"I'll say," he nods, "letting a four-by-four roll over his own baby. Careless," he adds, looking straight at me. I'm not sure whether he means Mark or me.

"It was a horrible accident."

All of a sudden, I am back in that first session with Mark as he told me what had happened. It was the weekend his wife was out for a friend's birthday. Her first trip away since the baby was born. How proud he was that he'd taken the two kids out. How well he was managing. How his son, a toddler, was standing on the porch as he unclipped the baby car seat, how he placed his daughter on the driveway by the back of the car as he gathered the bag from the trunk. How he felt for his phone in his pockets. It was after he went back to collect his phone from the dashboard that the car rolled down the drive. I close my eyes briefly as I remember his tortured face. How he howled like an animal into his hands.

I struggle to find the right words. "There was an inquest," I say, "and much as the outcome was terrible and tragic, it wasn't seen to be preventable."

"I read that you'd seen him for his appointment that day."

"I did."

"Dead plants . . . dead patients," he says, swishing his hand around the room like a windscreen wiper, "it doesn't exactly inspire confidence."

"Mark Webster was clinically depressed after the accident. He was intent on killing himself," and then I stop myself. I have said too much. None of this is relevant.

"It was a difficult case."

"So, what you're saying is that you *can't*, in fact, help everyone."

He sits tall and strong in his seat. In contrast, I feel suddenly small, my hands holding on to the side of the chair.

It was the first year of my promotion to director of the unit, eight years ago. I was experienced. I'd been practicing for years. I didn't see it coming. Mark was getting better. We'd extended the contract. He was upbeat in the appointment that day. The flashbacks had been less frequent. He'd been sleeping better. He was airy. Light. Unencumbered. What I realized afterward was that this state of mind arose from euphoria—from the decision he'd already made to end his life. It was, he must have concluded, the only solution to what he saw was an insurmountable problem. We had our session. He thanked me, and he left. He stopped to have a coffee and a pastry in the park, called his wife, then took the Jubilee Line to Green Park, where he threw himself in front of a train.

John Grantham had only been chief executive for six weeks. He was brilliant. He supported me at the inquest. I was cross-examined, and my notes were pored over with a fine-tooth comb. As I explained my risk assessments and had them scrutinized by two separate independent mental health expert witnesses, my hands were shaking so violently I had to hook them on to the side of the witness box. My assessment concluded there had been a risk reduction based on the information he brought to the sessions. In the event, the care was seen to be "more than adequate." There were no grounds for negligence or a failure in our "duty of care." Sitting here in front of Dan feels like I'm back in the inquest all over again.

I'd been haunted by the small huddled shape of his wife, Jane. Her tight pale face of grief. Struggling to comprehend the loss of both a baby and a husband in the space of four months. She looked up when I spoke. I looked over at her. I didn't want to avoid her. What I wanted back from her was something—some hatred or admonishment. There was nothing. Her face was impassive. She was too distraught for blame.

Mark's brother was the one holding all the fury. He spoke eloquently and passionately about his need for some explanations. *A world-famous clinic. Renowned. The devastation to the family. A widow ... a son left without a father ...* At the end of his evidence, he looked across at me. *What went wrong?* What I remember most about Jane was her distracted, vacant expression. Her constant movements, pulling at her cardigan, checking her bag, her coat, her scarf, patting them feverishly to make sure they were still there. As if, having lost half the members of her family, she was now obsessively keeping tabs on all her things, keeping everything close to hand, making sure that nothing else went astray.

I saw a lot of my supervisor, Robert, over that time. "It's a myth," he said, "that we can always save people. Risk assessments can give an illusion of control. That we can somehow nail things down. That mental health is predictable. Black and white. If people didn't become mentally unstable, there would be no need for mental health services."

I nodded. I knew he was right. But I still felt fragile.

"You also know that if someone wants to kill themselves, has thought it through, has planned it in the way Mark Webster had— there is nothing we can do to stop them. Nothing," he repeated, shaking his head. "Even patients on a twenty-four-seven watch can find a way," he reminded me. "When a patient is angry with himself, the despair can be too great. There's nowhere to go. At the time, suicide can feel like the only response to such despair and fury. Mark Webster saw it as the only way out."

Robert, John, the doctors who were expert witnesses, everyone agreed. Neither I nor the Trust were found wanting. It was quite simply a tragedy that was unpreventable. I would have said the same to any member of my team. *Nothing you could have done.* I didn't believe it. I felt the guilt. I waded through it like treacle. Afterward, I was hypervigilant on risk assessments. I was overly cautious. For months, I'd wake in the night, seeing the dark tunnel and a tall, suited man stepping off a platform. I'd sit upright with sweat pouring off my face. Over time, things slowly got better. And then, six years later, there was Tom.

I breathe in and out. I sit up straighter in my chair. I release my hands from their grip on the armrests and move them to my lap. I begin to move back into my body. Take up my role.

"Dan," I say firmly, "we can spend what little remains of today's session on the tragic suicide of Mark Webster. We can talk about my professional capabilities, my possible failings, and my deficiencies as a therapist . . . but I don't think this is really about Mark Webster, I think this is about you and your reluctance to—"

Before I can finish, he stands up abruptly, looking at his watch.

"I need to go," he says, "my mate said he'd pick me up, so I wouldn't have to get the bus."

He's speaking quickly and moving fast. "Sorry to duck out early," he says, like I'm a friend in the pub. "I'll see you next week."

He is gone.

I ring Robert. I'm standing by my desk, looking out of my

window as I leave him a message. "I need to make an appointment," I say, "as soon as possible."

And that's when I see them coming out of the entrance to the clinic. Dan and Hayley in animated conversation as they walk together across the hospital car park.

I stare at them, a strange feeling in the pit of my stomach. But for all that I do notice, I don't see what's going on in front of me. I don't pick up what Dan is doing. That in directing my attention to what he wants me to see, he is stopping me focusing on the very place I need to look.

EIGHT

I feel it as soon as I get up. I'm like a cat that can't settle. Endlessly turning itself round, fidgeting this way and that until it can find a comfortable spot. But on days like today, I know there's no comfortable spot. How can there be?

I have no plan. I rarely make plans for the weekends anymore. Perhaps I should have made one. Today, the prospect of an empty weekend yawning ahead of me fills me with a kind of dread. The only event, the planned Skype call with Carolyn, was canceled yesterday. I'd switched my phone on after my session with Dan to see her text.

> Unexpectedly offered another shift on
> the boat. Celebrating my birthday out at
> sea. Will call on return Cxx

The morning starts badly with indecision over breakfast, whether to have a bath or shower, then what to wear. I can't concentrate on anything. When I pick up the notes for the paper I am presenting at a conference in June, my eyes skim over words that seem completely alien, ones I don't recognize as my own. I open the back door and pick up a trowel to weed the pots on the patio. But I feel heavy and lethargic under the grayness of the sky and have to fight the urge to retreat inside and lie back down on my bed.

David's text comes in when I'm making coffee. The small sound it makes into the silence of my morning is a relief, an external puncture in my solitary bubble. Most of the time it's fine. I'm good at driving the wheels and machinations of my life single-handed. Then there are days like today when I don't have the energy to push anymore. The relentless self-direction at the weekend is exhausting and often leaves me floundering. The working week, of course, is different. The unit fills my time, it's all-consuming. The needs of my patients are so visceral, so immediate, they drive me forward. At the moment, I am not sure who needs whom the most.

It's why I recoil when people are so full of admiration about the work. "Giving something back," they say. *Altruistic. Worthy.* They have no idea. They know nothing about the pull. The gratification that can soothe like a drug. The adrenaline rush of trauma work. For many of us, there's a comfort in the unpredictability. It tastes familiar. Sometimes I look at my team, their own chaotic lives, and their motivation for doing this work, and I wonder if we're all just high-functioning and better-informed versions of our patients. People who have learned sophisticated ways to manage the chaos. My own working day is carved out into fifty-minute patient-size chunks. Bite-size bits of grief and pain and trauma that serve to anesthetize my own.

In the bitter cleft that marked the end of our relationship, David said I lived for the distress of other people. He said being a therapist made me feel good about myself.

"You're a vampire," he said, "sucking on the pain and trauma of your patients to make yourself feel better. That way you can feel useful—like you're actually doing something *meaningful.*"

"More meaningful," I said, "than the study of long-dead poets?"

When we first got together, David used to leave notes for me to find. Quotes from poems that I'd find hidden in my bag, or on the bathroom mirror, or the one that made me laugh out loud: *Do I dare to eat a peach?*, which I found in my lunch box when I was studying at the library. I don't remember when the notes stopped. Probably somewhere amid the maelstrom of small children. But I thought about them back then, when we were simply trading insults, and wondered what poems he might have turned to if he needed inspiration. As it was, we both did fine all by ourselves, tossing words back and forth like a tedious ball game we felt compelled to keep playing. I mocked his own retreat into his books, his studies, his lectures. And of course, his students.

"You're a walking cliché of a midlife crisis. *College professor and his late-night tutorials with his PhD students.* Please—," I said, rolling my eyes.

"Well," he said, "I'm delighted you're so dedicated to your patients. At least you can have an intimate relationship, even if it is on the NHS. With people who are mad."

And so it went on. Before Tom's hospital admission, we used to row about him. *My overinvolvement. His underinvolvement. His retreat. My controlling nature. His bowing out of responsibilities.* After Tom came out of hospital, it was too raw. I remember the drive home as we crossed the Euston Road, sitting small and still in our seats. David driving carefully, like we were bringing home a newborn. After that, things shifted. We retreated. We skirted round it, like a couple of kids poking at a dead bird with a stick.

The texts from David have changed in the last year. Perhaps as Tom's disappearance became calcified and more of a reality in our life, he has softened toward me. We have softened toward each other. There's more warmth, less hostility. He's careful around me, like I might break. Ostensibly, he's texting about picking up his old printer. But at the end: Are you around? We could meet for lunch? It's thoughtful he's remembered. Even more thoughtful because he's not referred to it or asked how I am. He knows I would hate that. And because of this, I feel a sudden rush of goodwill toward him.

It also propels me out of my inert state and gives me a sense of purpose. A deadline.

Within fifteen minutes, I am dressed and out of the house. I text David on my way. My reply is friendly. That would have been nice. But I have plans. I'm out for the day. I tell him the printer's in the garage. Pick up anytime. See you soon. It's easier to be kind when we no longer see each other and now that the fighting is over. There's no energy for hostility, and somehow because of that we can enjoy the idea of each other. It may draw on the past, or it may be an entirely new construct altogether, but whatever it is, the fantasy is strengthened by seeing each other less. We've slept together only once since we separated. He came around to get some old papers from the loft. I made him dinner. We drank wine and went to bed. It was familiar, easy. A comfort at the time for both of us. But straight afterward, we were right back into familiar terrain. The edge of recrimination seemed sharpened by our union. After we'd put our clothes back on, we just had to look at each other. No words were necessary. Just the two of us together was a reminder of what was missing, and what was lost.

When I think of David now, it's hard to reconcile the life we shared for more than twenty-three years. As if our marriage was one of those houses that are close to a slowly eroding cliff edge. And when the marriage was finally over, the house fell away. The break so clean, you'd never know that anything else had been there before. Now I can barely even remember the rage I felt when he was seeing Kate. The repeated evening tutorials at the university. I can hardly relate to that version of myself back then. A person who was so angry, so aggrieved. It's like all the feelings have slid away into the foamy, crashing sea. It seems a lifetime ago.

Now that Tom has gone, his *disappearance*, his *departure* (I still don't know what to call it) has eclipsed everything else. There is no space for any other feelings. Carolyn, of course, would say there never was.

I walk briskly and purposefully up the hill, past Archway station. I walk with the pace and step of someone who has a destination. Over the months, walking is the only thing that helps shift the restlessness. On those days when I wake under a blanket of indecision and a low-grade unease, the simple act of walking, of putting one foot in front of the other, seems to help. Some days I walk miles and return exhausted. I know by now it's the simple act of moving, of keeping going, that uproots whatever has taken refuge inside me. Sometimes I imagine it's a slothlike creature, heavy and slow and dragging me into inertia. Going for a long walk seems to head it off at the pass. *Move. Wake up. Go. You're not welcome* is the message. And so, it shifts. It will come back. It always does.

I keep on walking. I move through the crowds on the high street, the groups gathering outside shops. The all-nighters grabbing breakfast before going to bed. The new parents pushing buggies who have been up since dawn, pacing the streets then sitting glassy-eyed in café windows. I keep on walking, and all the while I am looking, scanning the streets. The coffee shops, the restaurants, the staff that clean the pubs, the bodies sleeping in the doorways. I look, even though I know I won't find Tom here. If he's alive, he wouldn't be so close to home. So close to me. I think about Dan, the cuts on his arm. I think about this week's drama. Sweeping Mark Webster to center stage. Then I think of Dan and Hayley. Hayley and Dan huddled in a conversation. As I walk, my thoughts drift lightly, they dip and dive and fall away, like swallows in the sky.

I pass families, packs of friends. Things that were once part of my life. I keep my distance from people now. Relationships are tainted by the absence in my life. Conversations about other people's growing families, university, jobs, relationships, all feel strained because of Tom. I used to try to be interested. But I'd feel my face tense, the muscles tightening as I tried to find an expression that masked my fury. My envy and my jealousy. Sometimes I tried so hard, my cheeks were left stiff and aching. It became easier not to see people.

As I walk, I think about Carolyn. On the other side of the world, it will be dusk. I picture her on the boat with friends; happy, laughing, under a starlit sky. It's both a relief and disappointment that she has canceled. I feel sorry for her. Sorry that her birthday joy is now eclipsed by her brother's absence. I can't just separate out my grief and joy. It's not a surprise to get her text, but I can't pretend to feel something I don't. Neither of us was ever very good at pretending, and Skype emotions are tricky at the best of times. The juddering delay seems to exacerbate the nuances of our already faltering relationship. "I missed that? What did you say?" we stutter and fragment.

"—ip. Going on a tri—" She's shouting now. Her face in a twist of irritation. And then we are back to square one. *You never listen. I am invisible to you. You simply don't hear me.*

"A trip?"

"Yep."

"Where to?"

"To the Daintree Forest."

"Where?"

"The. Place. I. Took. Dad." She spells out "d-a-i-n-t-r-e-e."

And then her face distorts. Breaks up into small fragments that scatter then reemerge into a face. Her speech is often out of sync with her moving lips. I imagine she must find it weird to be talking back to a much older, graying version of herself.

We were at the kitchen table when Carolyn announced she'd decided to study law. I had no idea what was coming.

"So," she said, "Durham's offered me a place."

Her decision had already been a surprise and a source of tension, so I was careful to hold back, to read the mood on her face. I thought I saw pleasure.

"That's great," I said.

"But the best piece of news," she said and paused to take a breath, "is that I've managed to defer for a year."

She looked up at me. "I'm taking a year out. I'm going to Australia."

It was the first I'd heard of Australia. The first I'd heard of any desire for a year off. It was so like Carolyn to have everything signed and sealed before she mentioned anything. Nothing. Not even a whisper of a plan. I tried and failed to hide surprise.

"What?"

"Nothing," I said, "just surprised. I had no idea you were planning—"

"Well," she said briskly, "I didn't want to mention it. They might have said no. Then we'd have all been disappointed," she said with a strange, clipped laugh.

She looked at me. That look again—willing me, urging me to disagree, to find fault. To say something that she could pounce on. Several weeks later, she came right out with it.

"Why are you so angry with me?" Of course, I denied it. Looked surprised and feigned confusion, but I knew exactly what she was talking about. I could see how we had arrived at this place, as if we'd followed an endless trail of breadcrumbs through the wood. To a place, where, in different ways, I found myself estranged from both my children.

Australia? Really?

"That's great," I said. "If that's what you want, I'm so pleased for you." When really, I was thinking, *Could you have picked anywhere farther away from home? Why couldn't you have gone to Europe? Interrailing through the Italian cities. Rome? Florence? Island-hopping in Greece?* I could have managed a country where I could get back to London quickly, in three or four hours max, if there was any news about Tom. But a twenty-four-hour flight? It was inconceivable. We both knew it was. Why did she have to pick somewhere she knew I'd never be able to come? It seemed almost willful.

I swallowed. I was trying to be better. I had to struggle with myself to stay silent. To look pleased for her. I knew she could see through me. That she knew me too well.

"I want to learn to dive. Get a job on a boat . . ."

In an attempt not to be negative, not to say the wrong thing, I kept my face blank.

"The Barrier Reef? In Queensland?" she said, overarticulating, like I'm a small child that has failed to comprehend.

"Yes," I said, "that's great."

"The Coral Sea's supposed to be one of the most beautiful places to dive. One of my friends, her brother went last year," she added.

Which friend? What brother? But she'd moved on. She was saying something about visibility, "Forty meters or more." She was animated and excited. I wanted to feel happy for her, but had no idea what forty meters meant, or even looked like. All I could think about was how far away it was—and that I'd never be able to visit.

She left in September and David went out to see her at Christmas. It was our second Christmas without Tom. We wouldn't have gone at the same time, but the issue of whether or not I'd go never came up. It wasn't discussed. Once, I tried, but she interjected, "I know, Mum," she said, her hand up, like a stop sign. "It's fine. I knew you wouldn't be able to come."

David called around the day after he got back in January. I hid upstairs when he rang the bell. I heard him walk around, pictured him peering through the back door and the garden. Then soon after, there was the sound of the letter box shuddering and the slap of something landing on the mat. The pictures were bright and sunny. I fanned them out on the bed. Impossibly turquoise water. Flat millpond seas and sunshine. Their smiling faces, laughing into the camera. Arms slung around each other's shoulders. David was standing in between Carolyn and a young, blond, tanned man. David's face was tanned and healthy. They all looked tanned and healthy. Dark sunglasses. White teeth. Bright white sand. Bright sun. Bright blue water. It all looked too fucking bright and shiny.

He rang later that afternoon. "Rob," he said, "he's a really nice bloke," he said. "They seem happy."

"That's good."

"He adores her. He's a divemaster on the boat. She's having the time of her life."

The time of her life?

I wanted her to be happy. At least I think I wanted her to be— but I also wanted to ask, Did any of you think about him when you were cooking Christmas lunch on the beach?

"Sausages! Hog roast!" he said, and in the face of my flatness, he became more animated. "It's forty-two degrees and the shop windows in Cairns have these little snow scenes. Santa hats and reindeers and everything," he laughed.

I nodded. I said something—but all the while I'm wondering how his life could carry on as normal. How his life seemed untouched by the absence of his son. I wanted to put the phone down. It all seemed too loud. And that was always the thing. The issue I have always had with David is his ability to carry on—like he was in a parallel universe. One, where his son had disappeared off the face of the earth, and the other where he was drinking beer and cooking hog roast on the beach. They coexisted, but were separate and distinct. And just listening to him that day, to his frothy enthusiasm, made me feel so cold and angry that I had to get off the phone. It was stupid really, but without thinking, I picked up a book and threw it across the room. It hit the wall with a loud thump.

"David, sorry. I must go. Someone at the door. Call you back later," and before he had time to say anything else, I'd ended the call. I slumped back on the bed in the sea of bright blue photos.

WHEN I GET BACK FROM THE WALK, my body aches. I snack on crisps and an old carton of olives festering at the back of the fridge. After two large glasses of wine, I'm at the computer. The wine has done its work, has dulled my senses, and before I can stop myself, my fingers are on the keypad. It's a habit I'd weaned myself off. It's been weeks now, I justify to myself, it's good to check, to keep in touch.

In the early days, I pored over it. Fed off it. I signed up to all the chat rooms for parents of missing children. I only look at the site now. I don't participate. Not anymore. Not after what happened with Minty, the woman from Virginia.

When I first opened up the Missing Persons website, I'd been shocked. It reminded me of those adoption sites. Rows and rows of children, their small pleading faces, all looking for a home. This is different. They are not small children looking for a home. They are posted by families who want their relatives back. The sheer volume was extraordinary. I gasped as I scrolled down through the rows of faces—missing men and women, boys and girls, some just children really. Many of the faces are familiar to me now. The purple dress of the woman from Woking with a glass of white wine in her hand. Duncan, the accountant, smiling shyly into the sunshine. The cheeky-looking tattooed man in his twenties with a stripy scarf round his neck. I know them all. I have scrutinized their faces. Spent drunken late nights studying those missing faces, as if searching for some clue, some answer to my own missing person.

I like to think of Tom as missing. Missing things are a pair of glasses down the back of the sofa, misplaced keys. Lost by someone who is careless. Negligent. Missing things get found.

My cursor falls on Denis Watson. I know him well by now. He was twenty-two when he disappeared on holiday in Corfu more than ten years ago. The photo is of him standing in front of a marina, in the sunshine. He's wearing a Hawaiian shirt, laughing as he squints into the camera. He went missing from a place we'd once been to on holiday. There were posters up everywhere when we'd gone to the island eight years ago with the kids. I wouldn't have recalled his name, but as soon as I saw his story on the site, I remembered who he was. Now I know him so well, it's as if he's a member of my own extended family.

It was our first trip abroad. At my insistence, a nod to my student years, we'd flown to Athens, then taken a ferry to the island. It was a mistake. Languid hours of sunbathing on deck as a nineteen-year-old was a million miles away from keeping two kids entertained on a hot, sticky boat journey. We were staying in a small village called Messonghi, in an apartment on a rocky outcrop, overlooking the sea. The beach was sandy, shaded by tamarisk trees, and the twins spent the days in and out of the water with snorkels, tumbling on and off their brightly colored floats. Tom in particular spent hours floating in the shallows, head underwater watching the sandworms and the shoals of silvery fish.

It was on an early evening walk that we stumbled upon it, in the hills behind the apartment. Tom spotted it first. "What are those for?" he asked, pointing at a small, neat pile of stones. They were flat and smooth and some were initialed or had scribbled messages on the side. Nearby, there were posters of Denis Watson, laminated and fixed to the trunk of several trees. His smiling face, that colorful shirt of palm trees. "Missing" in bright red letters over the top.

"What's happened?" His voice was panicky. "Is that a grave? Is there a body?" Tom's face was stricken.

"No," I said. "A man's gone missing," I explained, pointing to the poster. "His family are trying to find him."

Tom read the poster, standing in front of it for a long time.

"He was here—and now he's not," he fretted. "So where is he? How can he just get lost?" He was on the verge of tears.

"I don't know," I said, taking his hand. "But all the stones are like good wishes. Left by other people. To help him come home."

He spent ages picking out a smooth flat stone. Then when he'd found the right one, he painstakingly wrote his message, COME BACK SAFE, in purple nail varnish I'd found at the bottom of my bag.

Denis's family now have a website. There's a link on the site. I often find myself idly trawling through. It's updated regularly, most weeks, in fact. Three times a year his brothers fly out to re-energize the search. They have reconstructed pictures of how he might look now. They are tireless in their efforts. They post photographs from family events, weddings, christenings, birthdays he has missed. There are messages from friends and family, new nieces and nephews that he won't ever have met. Then just a couple of weeks ago, a wedding picture: To my brother and best man. You are in my heart today. I miss you.

One time, I might have been judgmental. Perhaps it might have been something in the picture—a tattoo, a piercing, or a T-shirt that may have suggested a certain "type." The sort of person who decides to leave home and have no contact with his family. Now I have become part of this club, I view the rules of membership in an entirely different way. I know there's no "type." I am kinder. They are all lost. They all have people who love and miss them, who post pictures in the hope of fresh news. And then I scroll further down until I rest the cursor on Tom's face. I'd chosen a photo that was taken earlier in the year he disappeared. He was in the garden, digging at the unruly vegetable patch at the back. I called his name, and the spring sunshine caught his face as he looked up. There's a hint of a smile. He looks quizzical. Wearing the green sweatshirt that he always wore.

I click on the photo. No messages. No reported sightings. No nothing. I post a birthday message and stare at my son for a moment—then idly scroll down, to the new photos that have been added since I last went on the site. There's a blond-haired girl from Devon. Just sixteen. Recently been depressed. A man in his fifties who went to get cigarettes and never returned home. His wife and son write: Please get in touch. A young man in his thirties who took a trip to Southampton to see his team play, but then never got on the train home. What's happened to all these people? I scroll over the faces and the messages. It's addictive. All these lives.

Each person was a story opening in my mind. I became overwhelmed by the grief, the loss, but somehow I couldn't stop. In the end, it was Minty, in her burning Bible Belt of Virginia, who made me turn away. Minty was one of the regular contributors to the chat room site. In those early months, I was messaging all the time, as I topped up the glass of wine on my desk. I didn't know what to do with the ache in my chest. I poured it all out on screen and she was the first to respond. "Hi hon," she'd begin, before offering up words of comfort. She always seemed to be online. Her replies were almost instant, and she seemed to know the right thing to say. But some months in, something changed. Her support and sympathy took a more sinister turn, as she embarked on an attempt to save my "sinful soul." Things happen for a reason. It's an opportunity to find the Lord. To dedicate yourself to Jesus. Jesus listens to those who repent their sins. On and on it went. I had to get out before I said something I'd regret. No wonder your daughter ran away was what I'd typed one day. Luckily, I was sober enough to delete the message. I closed down the site and blocked her email address. Even Jesus couldn't find his way past my firewall.

It's just as I'm returning to Denis Watson's website that the email from Robert comes in. He can see me at eight o'clock on Monday morning. I reply to confirm, and quickly shut the computer down.

NINE

"One of my patients brought up Mark Webster."

Robert nods for me to sit down and pours me a glass of water. His movements are slow and methodical and solid. But I notice it. The small giveaway twitch of his eyebrow. For a demeanor that always presents unruffled acceptance, it's like throwing a rock into a pool.

I've seen Robert for supervision in the same consulting room for the last seventeen years. Nothing has changed—the pictures, the plant on the windowsill, the jade-green sofa, and the couch in the corner for his therapy clients. I could draw it all from memory. Once, I was unsettled by a change in the room, and it took me the whole of our time together to realize the old bamboo wastepaper basket had been replaced by a sleek black metal one.

Robert, I imagine, is in his late sixties, but he's strangely ageless. People who've known him longer than me say he's looked the same for decades. Sometimes I picture him in his twenties, with the same wisps of white hair, balding hairline, and those striking blue eyes.

There is something gently reassuring about him. He is intellectual, wise, and insightful. At times challenging. Always supportive. Usually just stepping into his room and sitting down can feel a source of comfort. My Atticus Finch. The father who doesn't leave. And in the seventeen years I've been coming, I've only seen him flustered once. It happened a couple of years ago, when he was unable to locate his mobile phone. It rang abruptly in the middle of our session. Disturbed by the sudden intrusion of noise, he checked his pockets to retrieve it. He searched his jacket, his briefcase, and yet, for some reason, he was unable to find the phone. His movements were still methodical and slow, but his increasingly flustered state was etched on his forehead. The ring became like a shriek. A wild animal he was unable to track down and silence. The more he searched, the more it seemed to evade him.

As he continued to look for it, he explained he'd just bought the phone. "I've resisted getting one of these for a very long time," he said with quiet exasperation, and when eventually he managed to retrieve it from one of the internal compartments of his briefcase, he was unable to switch it off, or turn it to silent mode. "And now I can see why," he said with a frown. When the room fell back into silence, neither of us seemed able to recover from the violent intrusion into the normally calm, quiet space. Robert was red and flushed and seemed distracted for the rest of the session, and while I pressed on with a description of my client case, I was conscious of his unease and of the echo of the phone ringing in my ears.

That was the last I saw or heard of the phone. I was never given the number. In my head, I imagined him ending our session, opening the back door, carefully lifting the lid of the dustbin, and calmly dropping the offending item inside. I then imagined him tying up the black bin bag tightly and securely, with several satisfied knots, as if to make sure that this wayward and disruptive intruder was properly dispensed with, and not able to find its way back into the house.

"Tell me about this patient," he says, his eyes fixed on mine.

And so, I talk about Dan. I tell Robert about the brutal rape. His symptoms of PTSD. I tell him how he seemed to come into the unit with a sense of complaint and grievance; against the clinic, the police, the parole officers, the whole system, all figures of authority.

"He said the clinic was scruffy—"

"He's right," nods Robert, the flash of a smile on his lips.

"He said he thought it would feel more 'special.'"

"And what about the beginning," he asks, "the very start of the work with you?"

I tell him that almost before I'd even started, he seemed to view us as a source of disappointment, "people who hadn't done their jobs properly."

I tell Robert how he drew attention to my dead plants, "how he said he hoped I do better with my patients." I tell him how he was reluctant to talk about the past and his family. I tell him about the cuts on his arms. The lateness to his third session. My pushback. His competitiveness with the patient who comes before him. I also tell Robert how all the film references confuse me, make me feel like I'm trying to solve a riddle.

"Then when he mentioned Mark Webster, I was completely thrown."

I tell Robert everything. Except for the most important part.

The fact that he bears a striking resemblance to my son. The fact that my heart aches when I look at him. That I have the sensation of falling when he comes into my office. That sometimes, I struggle even to formulate sentences because I am distracted by the very sight of him. By the urge to press my hands on his cheeks. To pull him to me and hug him. I don't tell him that when I dream about Tom, I sometimes see Dan's face. That their faces are becoming interchangeable. I don't say any of this.

Robert knows about what happened with Tom. He's the only person connected to my working life I've talked to. It was Robert who saw me through the worst times.

When I come on to talk about how he mentioned Mark Webster, how shocking it was, I feel the words clog up in my throat.

"It was eight years ago. I mean—an FOI request? Who bothers to do that?"

Robert listens very carefully. He nods. He asks a few questions, but otherwise he is still and calm.

After a while, he sits forward. Makes a few notes in his pad.

"We have a patient who has a sense of grievance before he begins. He's suffered a brutal attack. He wants a quick fix. He's evasive about his family and his past—and indications are that he probably has very complex attachment issues. He draws attention to the dead plants on the windowsill—"

I have a sudden and irrational urge to defend myself. To tell him that I've rescued some. That some are now thriving. *They're not all dead*, I want to say.

"—and so he wonders if maybe your patients (i.e., he himself) will suffer the same fate. Then," he says, leaning back in his chair, "he offers up his trump card, as it were. The suicide of one of your former patients."

As he's talking, I feel heavy in my chair.

"What did you feel when he mentioned Mark Webster?"

I tell him that I felt panicky. Guilty and exposed, "like I'd been *found out*. Like he'd uncovered my *dirty secret*."

I think for a moment. "But mostly I felt like a failure. Not good enough. That I made a mistake."

Why can't people do their jobs properly?

"So, he leaves you feeling criticized. At fault," he muses. "Perhaps he, too, has felt criticized or persecuted in the past. Perhaps he wants you to feel a little of what it's like to be him."

He pauses.

"What's the consequence of him exposing this 'big mistake'?"

"For him—or me?"

"Both."

"For me—a loss of confidence. It will roll into the work. Become a self-fulfilling prophecy. I don't do a good job. *I don't do my job properly.* He's right."

"And for him?"

I try to focus. But I feel filled with thoughts of Mark Webster. Of my own failings. I shake my head. "I can't think."

"So it's working," he says. "He's got inside you. Stopped you thinking."

I nod.

"For him, by deciding you are a 'failure' before you even begin—it stops him starting therapy. It's his way out. It keeps you at bay. He doesn't have to risk getting dependent on you. He can crush the work before it even starts. But without taking this risk—of entering into the therapeutic relationship—there can be no healing and reparation. He can thwart efforts that might be helpful. A form of self-sabotage."

I remember what Dan told me about friends. "He said they all let you down in the end."

Robert nods. "People who avoid dependency are people who feel it will always lead to profound disappointment. Possibly because it always has."

Afterward, I will think about that session. The things I said and didn't say. How it's Robert's job to work with the things I show him— and if I don't take him into a specific room, he can't shine his torch around and have a look. There were rooms into which I chose not to take him. And how, in many ways, it mirrored my work with Dan. There were rooms he didn't show me, but I also chose not to open those doors.

He nods. "So what's the common theme," he asks, "in all the things he's focusing on?"

I think for a moment.

"A lack of care."

"Exactly. Dead plants. Dead patients. He wants to know that you can take care of him," he says.

"Can he *really* trust you with his story? Or will you, too, behave how others have behaved before. Be negligent? Careless? Not do your job properly?"

"Will I be *good enough*?"

"Yes. He's testing you."

We sit in silence.

"I think he's frightened of his anger," I venture, after a while. "The violence of the attack—and his inability to retaliate . . ."

Robert nods. "What's his pattern of managing his anger in the past?"

"Avoidance, I think," and I refer back to the films. And as I'm speaking, I'm remembering I need to call the Hackney GP practice and follow up on the Bristol notes.

We talk some more about Dan's film watching. The references that pepper the sessions. How he said films taught him to feel.

"He's very split," Robert observes. "He cuts things off."

"He has an odd way of talking," I say. "When he mentions scenes from a film, or lines a character has said, I feel blindsided. One time it was *Dead Poets Society*, the other week, it was something else. I don't know what he's trying to say. I mean I've seen these films, years ago. I can't remember them all—but they get in the way of the work. All the time, I'm trying desperately to remember the scene he's talking about."

Robert's advice is to engage more fully with the films he brings up, "rather than simply seeing them as an obstacle to climb over. Ask him more. See if it offers a way to dig deeper, explore the feelings. Where's the anger?"

He's silent for a moment as he leafs back through his notes.

"Earlier you mentioned that he'd discovered your 'dirty secret.' Moving forward, we might wonder what *his* might be?"

I nod.

"Do you feel your boundaries pushed by him?"

"No," I lie.

"I get a sense that you might."

He pauses to glance up at the clock. "You're doing very well with him," he says. "He's not easy. Let's make another time soon."

As I reach into my bag for my diary, I feel calmer. Sometimes it's less what he actually says, and more the way he says things. His slow, accepting, and open stance. I stand up feeling lighter, unencumbered.

As he walks me to the door, he places a hand on my arm. It's a comforting gesture.

"Any news?" he asks.

I dip my head down low. I don't want to see his soft blue eyes. I can't bear to look at the kindness. I shake my head, then I push on the door out into the sunshine.

"Find the anger" I think, as I walk back up the hill to work.

It was waiting for me in the main office. A tray of six geraniums on the floor by the filing cabinet. The tight buds just beginning to unfurl in a flash of blood red.

"For you," Paula says, passing me a small white card with my name on it. Ruth Hartland, printed in neat blue ink.

"That's it? No note?"

She shakes her head.

"They were left on the front desk at reception this morning. The porter just brought them up."

Later that afternoon, I see Stephanie. She's ready with her case notes and binder, but she looks tired, a little distracted. She starts with a new referral, then talks about the PTSD group. It feels like she's avoiding Samira.

Toward the end of the session, I ask.

"It went well," she says flatly. "Jackie, the care coordinator, was great. Helped Samira buy a lot of the stuff. Most of the clothes, the bed. Lots of toys. Then she helped her set everything up. Made the bedroom look really nice."

There's a silence. She takes a breath. "When Samira came the following week, her daughter was still wearing that old undershirt and skirt." She fiddles with her pen. "All those new clothes in the bedroom—and she's dressed in the same dirty outfit."

I say nothing. We sit for a moment in silence.

Stephanie goes to speak, but her voice falters. She starts to cry.

I sit with her quietly, passing her the box of tissues. She's embarrassed by this unexpected show of emotion. I wait for her to collect herself.

"Doing this—day in, day out," she says, "all these dreadful lives. It's grim. How do you bear it? Don't you just want to *do* something," she says angrily, "something to take it all away?" She stops and reaches for another tissue.

When I ask her about the session, she says Samira told her about getting the new clothes and the baby things, "but she also told me more about what happened to her in Somalia. What those men did to her."

Stephanie closes her eyes briefly. "It was awful," she whispers. "But the way she told me—it was like a shopping list. Like it had happened to someone else. No emotion. No anger. No sadness.

Nothing." She shakes her head. "As I listened, I felt full up with it all. Helpless—and so sad. But I couldn't find any words."

I think for a moment.

"Have you ever seen a snake eat a rat?" I ask. "In a zoo? Or on television? They swallow the rat whole. It sits in their body. A perfect rat shape under the skin of the snake. It's like a cartoon."

She nods.

"Then gradually, it regurgitates bits at a time. Crushing the bones of the rat, reducing the body into smaller digestible pieces."

Stephanie blinks back at me.

"Sometimes the things that have happened to our patients are too awful. Too shocking to digest." I tell her about one of the first patients I ever saw as a trainee.

"Mr. Begum was a small, dignified Bengali man who ran a fruit and veg stall in Whitechapel Market. He'd been badly burned in a house fire. Had to have a leg amputated after the building collapsed on him. His two young daughters died in the blaze."

Stephanie is listening intently.

"We saw him in hospital. I was struck by how calm he was as he carefully detailed the events of that evening. While he remained detached, I felt engulfed by the horror of what he was describing. Then after a while, he reached for his watch on the bedside table, and looked up at us. 'I'm terribly sorry,' he said politely, 'but you must excuse me. I have to go and collect my daughters from school,' and with that, he began to shuffle his bandaged leg to the edge of the bed—"

Stephanie gasps.

"The nurses rushed forward, stopped him, just in time."

Stephanie is wide-eyed.

"The event for Mr. Begum was like the rat in the snake. Simply too big to digest. It was going to take him time to swallow the news, piece by piece. The emotions had been split off, projected on to us. They were simply too painful."

"Do you think that's what happened with Samira?"

"She's in shock," I say. "It's too overwhelming. She has to cut it off, disassociate from it all. It helps her survive, get up in the morning, take care of the baby."

She nods.

"The other thing to remember," I say, 'is that she's a refugee. She's holding a real sense of displacement. While she's safe here, physically, her safety comes at a price of alienation."

I tell her about an Iranian I once saw who had fled his country. Many of his extended family were tortured and didn't make it out alive, but his wife and children were safe. "He talked about the violence he'd witnessed, but he also talked about everyone telling him how lucky he was. He felt conflicted. Grateful, yet preoccupied with a feeling of wistfulness, a sense of longing he couldn't really put into words. 'The smell of my own country,' was the thing he missed the most."

"So you're saying the things I think Samira will like might actually make her feel more alienated from her country?"

"It's possible." I shrug. "But tell me what happened, after Samira told you her story?"

"I just felt really sad. I didn't know what to say. What you said about the rat? It's weird, because I felt like I couldn't swallow. That something was stuck in my throat. I said it was a very sad story and that it was brave of her to tell it to me. That I was very sorry that these things had happened to her."

"And then?"

"It was quiet." She hesitates. "I didn't really do anything. Didn't know what to do. My mind went blank. We just sat together. I really wanted to say something—something helpful."

"You did something very important," I say. "You were bearing it with her. You stayed with it. It's our job to connect people with their feelings. If we run away from them, they will too. You didn't run away. You did well."

I expect Stephanie to bloom under the compliment, but she simply shifts in her seat.

"But you know," she says slowly, "I'm not sure I really see the point—"

She bites her lip, blinking away the tears.

"The point of what?"

"Doing this. This type of therapy. I don't feel I'm making a difference."

"Making a difference?"

"Helping. Doing something. It's what I'm used to. What I'm good at." She looks away.

"All this emphasis on feelings—I mean," and then it comes, the question I've somehow been waiting for, "does any of it *actually help?*"

I listen as she tells me about her family. She's pragmatic with the details. The oldest of four. The only girl. A younger brother born with cerebral palsy. "Dylan," she says fondly, "he's such a character."

She tells me he was very sick when he was small, in and out of hospital for months at a time, "difficulty breathing," she says. As he got older, she explains, they had a family rota, for feeding, for physiotherapy, and for the exercises to prevent infections. "My other brothers were pretty hopeless," she laughs, "but I did what I could. Tried to fix things. I just got on with it," she says briskly. I think about the symmetrical bob. The color-coded binder. The first from Oxford. And I see that somewhere underneath all that perfection was a world of mess and chaos. And of loss.

"So, all this *staying with the feelings*," she says, "I'm just not sure I really see the point—or even want to—"

I nod.

I tell Stephanie that I don't know if this model of therapy is right for her. Or if trauma work is going to be the right fit either. "It's way too early to tell, and only you can make that decision."

Yet I can't stop thinking about a childhood where her own needs and feelings were lost under a rota of practical tasks. Being good. Being helpful. Trying to fix the unfixable. I want to remind her that something drew her to this unit.

"You fought hard to do this placement," I say. "I think there was something you wanted to learn."

AFTER SHE'S GONE, I think about those pretty Boden dresses. The toddler bed, the high chair. I think about all the items from our own baby years—the bath toys, the mobiles for the car seats, and the brightly colored play mats. My mother fed into all of this. By way of compensation for her erratic grandparenting, she showered the twins with expensive gifts and toys. "I know you'll say I shouldn't have—but I just couldn't resist them," she'd say as she staggered in laden with bags. One time, she brought two enormous stuffed animals, a tiger and zebra that she'd spotted in the window of Selfridges. "Too big to get on the Tube," she laughed. "I had to get a cab for the three of us." And on subsequent visits, her eyes would greedily seek the furry creatures out, as if successful sightings, or flickers of interest from the children, were a confirmation of their love for her.

We, too, bought into the consumer pressure to accrue the trappings of family life. The covert message being that if you buy the best, you'll be the best, as if somehow this would be a ticket through. A way of ensuring the smoothest and best possible childhood. We knew it was rubbish, but we were sucked right in. And so it continued for us, the bunk beds, the connected desks that sat side by side, the matching satchels when they went to school. The meaninglessness of all these things in the end. Gloss that covers the rotting wood underneath. There was a time, in his early teens, when Tom would only wear Adidas and Nike—eschewing these, and all labels, later on in life when he turned his attention to globalization and the destruction of the planet.

"All brands are feeding the devil," he said, "a step into the big wide jaws of consumerism." Shortly after, he got rid of these clothes. Exchanged everything for some old jeans, plain T-shirts, and that green Fruit of the Loom sweatshirt that he picked up in a charity shop.

It was in Year Six that Tom and Carolyn moved into separate rooms. They were ten years old, and I felt sad to sell the bunk beds.

To think they would never again giggle and chat together as they went to sleep. Perhaps they hadn't for a while. Perhaps that was a myth I wanted to keep going. Was it in Year Six that things began to change? At the time, I put it down to gender difference. Carolyn maturing faster than Tom, in the way that girls always did. I convinced myself it was a natural separation between them, and while I felt a sting of sadness, it was, I told myself, entirely normal. I realize, looking back, how frequently I used that phrase, as if it were a kind of mantra.

During the long summer holidays, I enrolled the kids in camps. Carolyn was happy with multisports, drama, almost anything I suggested. She made friends easily. Tom would only do the Forest Camps. Days out in the country, running wild. "Team games were a challenge," they would say at the end of the week, "but he's good with wood. Exceptional." The following summer, even these holiday activities became too structured and organized for him.

It was in the early years of secondary school that the bigger differences started to show. Carolyn grew tall and willowy, with long legs and fair wavy hair that cascaded down her back. Tom grew, but he seemed too big for his body. His hair, so gloriously wild as a boy, looked awkward around his adolescent face. He spent hours trying to smooth his hair down, then cutting it short, only to have it bubble up again above his ears. "I look ridiculous," he said, his hands slapping at the curls. As Carolyn grew older and became her own person, it left Tom exposed. Wide open. It was only years later I came to see this. She, in her wisdom, had seen it much earlier.

"Yes, I know he's having a hard time. It's not my fault. Why are you taking it out on *me*?" she'd ask during one of our many circular, nonsensical rows.

"I'm not," I said defensively.

Now I see it. I was angry with her for exposing something I didn't want to see. I was angry with her for stepping out of the way. For living her own healthy, independent life. What kind of a mother resents her daughter for that?

Why didn't I see it at the time? The truth was, I was good at looking the other way. It was a small muscle that I had worked on and strengthened since childhood. It was a good and hardworking muscle that made me sit neatly and eat my supper after school, as if everything were just fine, as if my mother didn't drink. Everything was fine and normal. I just never invited any friends round.

With Tom, not only did I look the other way, I went into overdrive to compensate. Gradually, the arranged playdates associated with his younger years all fell away. They were at an age to organize their own socializing. This became effortless for Carolyn, ringing friends, arranging trips to the cinema. For Tom, it was nonexistent. Looking back, my involvement was a form of denial. An obsessive need to look away from what was staring me in the face. It was at this point that the strain really began to show with David.

"Let him be," he'd say. "Let him find his own way" was his response to my persistent social organization.

"Don't you think you're overattached? Isn't it all a bit *Oedipal*?" he said, wobbling his head from side to side, in that irritating way he had of masking a serious point under a jokey facade.

And looking back, if Tom hadn't been a twin, I'm sure I would have found it easier. Maybe I would have been able to let it be. The fact was, Carolyn was a constant barometer to measure him against—academic success, sociability, friendship—and time after time, he fell short. It was around this time that Carolyn started playing hockey for the borough. She spent most Saturday mornings at matches. I think I only saw her play three times.

When Tom wanted a dog, we got Hester. When Tom showed a whiff of interest in a football, I got him onto a team. Tom played OK, although he had a slightly vacant presence in a group of other boys. Not unfriendly. Not rude. Just awkward. His absence was a space I quickly rushed to fill. I was like a builder with a fistful of putty, pressing and squeezing to fill the unsightly gaps. I was relentlessly chatty with the other mums. I brought oranges for halftime, baked cakes for the end of the match. "Is *he* enjoying it? Does *he* want to do it?" David would say. "Why are you driving this? This incessant need for control over his life?" But I couldn't stop myself. My response to feeling out of place has always been denial. Hide behind other people. Find a way to fit in. I didn't want to see a version of myself in him. Tall and tense. With a small knot of anxiety in my stomach.

Once at the station with Tom, waiting for the train, I spotted someone from the team on the platform. "Look!" I said. "There's Greg. From football."

Tom nodded, rooted to the spot. I felt his embarrassment, but still I pushed on. It was me who strode ahead. It was only as I'd walked forward, with Tom shuffling behind, that I saw Greg was with Finn.

"Hi!" I said too brightly. They looked startled by my intrusion.

The mumblings of teenage conversation were shattered by my sudden animation. I could feel their surprise. "You were robbed last week!" I plowed on. "That goal should never have been disallowed." Momentarily, they look confused. I could see they didn't quite know what I was talking about. In the life of a thirteen-year-old, last Sunday seemed a very long time ago. Eons of more important things have happened in their lives. Just not, I realized, in Tom's. And then I did a dreadful thing. I stepped back. So that Tom was left to finish the conversation, like I was a waiter lifting the lid, handing over my son as a tasty offering.

"Yeah," he muttered. "Well played," he said, to no one in particular.

He swung his arms back and forth, eyes darting nervously down the platform.

"Where you off to?"

"Cinema."

He nodded eagerly. A pause.

"What are you going to see?"

It was a beat too late. They'd moved on to something else. An exchange between themselves.

"What?" Finn said, turning back toward him.

I could see it—in excruciating clarity—that the harder he tried, the worse it was. The clunky, disjointed conversations. Slightly out of sync. The desperation to please, to be liked. It was painful. And as his back was turned, I saw the exchange of the sad and pitying glances. As they all got older, the looks were more ruthless, more mocking. Harder to ignore. And I'd look away, my face ablaze with a mixture of shame and hatred.

Naturally, the more anxious and uncertain Tom became, the more confident and self-assured Carolyn seemed. I came to expect the best from Carolyn, and understandably, it became a source of exasperation. "Tom only so much as has to make his way to school on time, and there's a bloody fanfare."

As she got older she had new interests and more friends; most weekends there was a huddle of girls in her bedroom, flicking through magazines and making clothes on the sewing machine she'd bought secondhand. All of this seemed to expose Tom's inadequacies in social situations. The more Carolyn's confidence grew, the more his eroded and ebbed away. I'm ashamed to say, it irked me. When Carolyn entered a competition, I found myself secretly hoping she wouldn't win, wouldn't be on the sports squad, or be picked for the main part in the school play when she went for her auditions. What kind of a mother thinks that? It wasn't a feeling I was proud of—and I thought I did my best to conceal it. Though, in the years to come, amid furious rows with Carolyn, it was clear I hadn't done as well as I'd imagined.

TEN

I have an unexpected free hour in my day. Hayley's father had rung on Monday to say they'd had the offer of a friend's camper in Hastings for three weeks.

"Is it OK to have a break?" he asked. "Can we book the other two sessions after she's back?" After we scheduled them in the diary, he told me things were a little better.

"She seems less angry. Been crying a lot, but that feels a big improvement on shouting and shutting herself away in her room. She even watched a film with us last night. Slowly, slowly," he said wearily, then thanked me as we ended the call.

The time I would be seeing Hayley I use to catch up on emails and letters to GPs. I'm at my desk by the window when there's a movement in the corridor. I look up to see Dan in the doorway. He's leaning against the frame, arms folded, head to one side.

"Hi," he says, then when he registers the surprise on my face, "am I too early?"

His voice is casual. There's a shy smile. It's an expression I haven't seen before. An expression so like my own son that it floors me.

Here you are, I think. *Here you are again.*

"I'm sorry," he explains. "I came a different way around. Up the back stairs. I saw the door open. Shall I wait?" And he gestures up the corridor.

He's still smiling, and I feel flustered, wrong-footed again.

"It's always better to make your way to the waiting room," I say. "Then you can let Paula know you're here." I should have left it there, but for some reason, I carry on, I overexplain. "I might be on the phone, or with a patient, or colleague," and then I make a vague gesture with my hand, "so it's better to let Paula know," I say again. I think about the session with Robert. The focus on boundaries. The need to be clear about the rules. To realign, without sounding judgmental, harsh, or persecutory.

His face gives nothing away.

"But you weren't," he says with another smile.

"Weren't what?"

"With another patient."

I open my mouth to speak.

"Is she away?" he cuts in. "The girl who comes before me?"

And before I have a chance to answer, he's darting his head back and forth to comic effect, *stay?—go?—stay?*

"I can go back and wait," he says. "Shall I do that?"

I glance up at the clock. It's five minutes before four o'clock.

I'd been doing my monthly figures. Various patient case notes are open across the table. A half-empty glass of water. I feel caught off guard. He has again shifted the power.

All patients are asked to report to the department reception, and then take a seat in the waiting room. The receptionist then rings through to us, and we come and collect our patients. The instructions are clear and consistent. It's the frame around the mess. For the most part, they are followed, but it's not uncommon for patients to try to challenge these rules. "The door was open," they might say, or "I was running late, so I came straight round," or "I didn't see anyone on reception." They may say all manner of things, present all manner of reasons for appearing unannounced, for choosing not to adhere to the instructions they've been given and have previously followed. Almost always, it's an attempt to push at the boundary that's been set. *Can the rules be broken? Is it really safe? Am I really contained?* It's a small display of rebelliousness to counter their own helplessness. Sometimes it's about control. About wanting to bypass reception, to have direct access to the therapists. It can be a desire to stand out from all the other patients. A desire to feel special.

Usually, when this happens, I look up politely and calmly and ask them to wait in the waiting room. It confirms the message they have already been given. There is safety in rules and boundaries. Usually, at some point, if not in that session then in the next, it will come up again. The patient may be angry. Feel rejected. The meaning gets explored in the session, becomes central to the therapeutic work.

That day, as I glance at the clock, I find myself reasoning that by the time Dan goes back down to the waiting room, I'll be back to collect him. I also know that I'm being pulled in. I know that he wants to feel special. I feel it that day, like a palpable ache in my chest.

"No," I say, "it's fine. It's nearly time. Come in. Sit down," and I gesture over to the chairs. "I'll be with you in a few minutes."

He wants to feel special, and I let him.

Hastily, I close the open files and find his own in the filing cabinet. I feel his stillness in the chair. I know I am flustered from his sudden arrival at the door. I am self-conscious as I return to my desk. As I sit there for those minutes until four o'clock, the small pocket of time expands like elastic. With the pen still gripped in my fingers, I pretend to continue with my notes. My face feels hot, and though my hand moves across the paper, I write nothing. Swirls and loops like a lovestruck teenager in class. As I sit there pretending to ignore him, the opposite seems to happen. The presence of him in the corner of my room burns in my chest. I feel it on my face, in the movement of my body. It's a strange sensation. Like when you're trying to ignore someone from afar, but out of the corner of your eye, every single pore of your body knows exactly where they are, and what they're doing. I can visualize the contours of Dan's body. The way he has crossed one knee over the other. The exact position of his head. And I know, without looking at him, that he is watching me.

At exactly four, I put my pen down, close the file, and cross the room to join him. I sit on the chair opposite him, the small coffee table between us.

"Plants look better today," he says, nodding over to the windowsill. "You've been taking care of them."

"I have some new ones," I say, and I scan his face for a sign that he had brought them.

"Nice," he says. His expression is neutral.

I ask him how he's been.

"A little better," he says. "I made it to college most days. We've been told to pick a film to analyze." He looks animated, excited.

"*Ordinary People*," he tells me when I ask.

"Why that one?"

He thinks for a moment. "I've watched thousands of movies," he says. "*Ordinary People* is a perfect film. A perfect piece of film-making."

"What is it that you like?" I ask, remembering the brittleness of the Mary Tyler Moore character. The husband played by Donald Sutherland. And a hazy memory of a scene with a camera and a family photograph.

"Family flaws. Parents. The limits of a mother's love." He sounds guarded. "I'll show you my essay when it's done. I like the way it ends," he adds, "the inevitability of the ending. There's no great Hollywood reconciliation. They separate. They have to. Some endings are inevitable—aren't they?"

"It makes me wonder about your own family" I say tentatively. "Were they fragmented?"

He feigns shock, shakes his head. "We were like the Partridge Family," he says.

I think about my time with Robert, the need to open more doors. I ask him more about how he became interested in films.

He shrugs. "There was a rental shop on the corner of my street, I watched everything. Films were exciting. Taught me to feel stuff—things I hadn't experienced before."

"Did you watch with your parents?"

There's a momentary look of surprise. "No. On my own."

"Did they work?" I ask.

"Dad was a teacher. Mum was a nurse, though she only worked part time." He looks vague. "She just wasn't around very much."

He tells me he liked films about misfits, kids who didn't fit in. "For years I thought I was adopted. There were no photos anywhere of me as a baby, or small child. For a long time, I thought that was why."

"How did your parents get on?"

"They were very compatible. A tight twosome. Never raised their voices." He gives an apologetic smile. "Sorry—I told you it wasn't very filmic."

The session feels achingly slow. I'm asking too many questions, going around in circles. Getting nowhere. As if at any moment, I might see that quicksilver flick of his tail.

I try again. I realize I'm leaning forward in my chair.

"What was the main thing that films taught you to feel?"

"Pain," he says without hesitation.

I feel a creeping sense of unease. A prickle at the back of my neck.

"I can't remember the film," he says. "I was very young, maybe five or six. I saw this scene where a family are in a hurry to go on holiday and the boy gets his hand caught in the car door. It was an accident. The parents were distraught." He tells me how they bandaged it up and took care of him.

"So I tried it," he says.

The prickle becomes a chill of fear. "Tried what?"

"Shut my hand in the door. Broke two fingers of my left hand. I felt so high. Like I was on drugs."

"You shut your hand in the door deliberately?"

He nods.

"Problem was, when I did it again, it wasn't as good. It's what a user says after the first hit of heroin." He pauses, meets my gaze. "I had to move on to other things."

"Other things?" I ask, and I can feel the moment slow down.

"Ninety percent of accidents take place within the home," he says. "It's amazing how much harm can be done with household appliances. A kettle. A toaster"—he pauses—"a cheese grater," and I wince as he looks down at his fingers.

I feel he wants to shock me, yet instead of saying so, I am pulled right in.

"What about your parents? Your mother?" My words come out too forcefully.

He blinks back at me, perhaps startled by the emotion in my voice.

"My parents cared for me—food, clothes, paid for books and my video membership, et cetera—but they didn't care *about* me," he says. His voice is calm, matter of fact. "They took me to the doctor, and to the hospital when it was necessary for X-rays or to fix any broken bones. My welfare didn't interest them."

The fear has turned into a different kind of feeling. My jaw clenches. He then tells me he went through a phase of watching films about missing children.

"It became a bit of an obsession," he says. "They were those 'every parent's nightmare' sort of films—when the child goes missing in a moment of carelessness. They're swept off by a stranger. Or they simply disappear."

They simply disappear. There's a pull in my stomach.

"These sound like films for grown-ups?" I say, alarm bells ringing as I try to understand.

"They were. I tried some of the things," he says jauntily. "I'd wander off when we were out somewhere. They were always so wrapped up in each other. It was easy."

My hands tighten into fists.

He tells me the first time was when they were all at a fairground. He was still in primary school. "I was about ten, I think. We were standing by the bumper cars and I wandered away. Away from the bright lights. I ran across a field and turned in to a road. It was dark. It wasn't long before a car pulled over. An old bloke, with a fat and sweaty face. I remember how the seat belt stretched across him, cutting his belly in half, like two big tires."

As I listen to the story, I can hardly breathe.

"As he reached for my seat belt, his fingers brushed across my face," and as he recalls the moment, he sounds excited, exhilarated. "I could smell the sourness of his breath."

He shrugs. "It didn't work out so well that time."

That time?

"He took me straight to the police station. My parents came to collect me."

I feel giddy. I'm struggling to find words. To make proper sentences.

"What about your injuries, the trips to the hospital? The police . . . the doctors . . . ? What did they do?"

Suddenly, it all falls into place. *People who haven't done their job properly.* The sense of injustice. Of grievance. His powerlessness. I feel rage and incomprehension; there's anger in my voice.

"My parents said I was accident prone, clumsy. Doctors diagnosed dyspraxia. Poor balance and coordination. I was referred to a specialist physiotherapist."

I look at him aghast. "But your parents?"

"By then my father was a headmaster. A magistrate. A pillar of the local community. My mother was a nurse. They were good people."

And then I ask the question that's been hanging there between us. The one I've been trying not to ask.

"Was there ever a suicide attempt?"

He looks taken aback.

"Kill myself? Never." He shakes his head. "I just wanted to hurt myself. It felt good to push myself as far as I could," he says, and again I feel a terrible shiver of fear, "and the closer I got to the edge, the more it became clear that my parents wouldn't be there to catch me."

What I remember most about listening to Dan was the absence of his emotion. A space where any feelings should be. And the emptier the space, the more I filled it with my own fury. I can feel my face radiate with heat. I am alarmed by the strength of my rage. By the rush of blood to my cheeks.

This is my moment to translate what's happening between us into words that will make sense to him. This is what I'm good at. Finding the right moment to comment on his detachment from his anger. To say how full of horror I feel at what he is telling me. *I am listening to you tell me a dreadful story. Something truly awful.* To comment on the fact that he seems to be normalizing his parents' behavior. How split off this experience feels. And that in the absence of any feelings in him, I am full of them. *Perhaps it feels too painful, or too frightening to connect with these feelings of rage?* Any feelings of anger have been cast to one side, they sit in the corner of the room like an unexploded bomb. It's my job to put my hands around his own and help him pick it up. To help him see that the bomb belongs to him. *His feelings. His emotions.* And by picking it up, he can control whether to let it explode or to work at understanding how it can be defused.

The problem is, I have picked up the bomb, and I don't seem to be able to put it down.

Perhaps he has noticed the flushed red of my cheeks or my fingers curled into a fist. He blinks back at me. "What's the matter?" he asks. "Are you all right?"

"I feel so angry," and it comes out like a spit of rage. "How dare they?"

"What?" He looks surprised.

"Why would your parents behave like this? Your mother? How could she?"

He bristles in his chair. "They didn't much care for me. I wasn't to their taste. It wasn't like I was *abused* or anything. Compared to what others go through. Neither of them laid a finger on me. Ever," he says emphatically. "In fact, I don't remember them touching me at all."

I open my mouth to speak, but I can't find the words.

"Indifference," he says, looking me squarely in the eye. "It's not a crime, is it?"

"*Indifference?*" I say. "You weren't *to their taste?* You make it sound like you were an item on a menu. Negligence and neglect *are* abuse."

"Perhaps they had a reason?" he says. "Perhaps I was someone that needed to be punished."

It's a struggle to concentrate on what he is saying. I feel a throbbing ache at the back of my head. I can't believe I'm arguing with him.

"Perhaps I did something to deserve it."

I think about the attack in the park. How he described it as a punishment. *Karma.*

"I believe there must have been a reason for my parents' dislike—and indifference—"

"You were just a child."

"I used to think that maybe it was connected to this odd nothingness feeling. Like there was a gaping wide hole. I used to fantasize there was a secret. Like my adoption theory. Something they kept from me. Perhaps I was the result of a rape? Or not my father's son? Or some other kind of secret."

A dirty secret.

"There was always something odd. Something just not there."

"The nothingness you described?"

He nods. "But like I say, it's not exactly a crime, is it?"

I talk about parental responsibility. The duty of care of a mother. The unwritten rules of parenthood. To protect. To look after. To love.

"She did the best she could," he says defensively. "Who are you to judge?" he adds with a flash of irritation.

It's like the bubble of tension has burst. I sit back in my chair.

"You're right. And I'm sorry."

I try to recover. To be his therapist. I tell him the things he has told me have been very difficult to hear. That they will be things we will need to return to at the next session.

"I do just want to say that there is no excuse, no possible excuse, for a parent to treat a child like this."

He brings his hands together, makes a steeple with his fingers. "Well—you say that," he says. "In fact there was something. Eight years later I found out what it was."

He glances down at his watch. I can see the clock behind him. We both know it's time to finish.

"Next time," he says, getting up from his chair.

When he has gone, I feel wounded. My body aches.

I know that whatever I have tried to do in those closing minutes of the session, I have failed him as a therapist. That regardless of the extent to which I tried to backpedal and recover myself, he has seen me. Furious. Outraged. Like an audience member of some puerile "true-life" chat show. I know I have not done my job. I have not helped him connect with his anger. And as he leaves the room that day, I am conscious of his rage, like white-hot fury, in freefall, somewhere high above our heads.

MINUTES AFTER HE'S LEFT, Paula rings through. She asks me to come down to the office.

"There's a delivery here for you." In the background, I can hear laughter. Animated conversation. It's a relief to get out of my room. To walk along the corridor.

"What's this?" I say, looking down at the large cardboard box with holes around the top and sides.

"A hamster."

"What?"

"It's for you. Just your name. No note."

I stare back at her.

"Delivered this afternoon. It came with a bag of food. And a book: *How to Care for Your Hamster.*"

Paula is laughing. She doesn't notice my blanched face. The hand that's on the side of the desk to steady myself.

"We looked it up," she giggles, "to see if 'live pets' were listed on Trust protocol for disallowed presents. A section on pets!" she roars. "Wouldn't that be funny?"

There's a small scratching sound from inside the box.

"New plants. And now a pet?" She leans in conspiratorially. "Secret admirer?"

News travels fast, and "Hamstergate" becomes the talk of the unit for the rest of the day. There's the curiosity about how it came to arrive and where it will go.

"I don't suppose you want it?"

"No," I say, "I don't."

After a series of phone calls, Paula finds a home for the hamster in the children's day unit, alongside a family of gerbils.

ELEVEN

It's on the Monday that I bump into Julie. A random encounter that changes everything.

I'm in South London to meet a team who have requested urgent support. When I'd briefly outlined the circumstances at our staff meeting, it was met with a horrified silence, then a flurry of questions that I answered to the best of my knowledge. I understood the need to visualize something, to make a picture from the details. Besides, it wasn't difficult to understand their shock in the face of the kind of tragedy I was describing.

The community drug rehabilitation team have their offices around the back of Balham High Road. Despite its proximity to the main road, it's surprisingly quiet. A no-through road, with a newsagent, some flats, and an industrial estate at the end. The entrance to the building is via a car park, with the team name and NHS logo on the wall by the video intercom. There's a strip of crime scene tape on the railing, flapping back and forth like a yellow ribbon in the breeze.

I close my eyes for a moment as I think about the sequence of events last Friday afternoon. CCTV from the flats opposite showed the man, a Harold Mason, weaving erratically along the pavement, rattling doors and shouting through letter boxes. He stopped in front of this same office, then peered down at the small logo. Three small navy-blue letters. NHS. Letters of hope and salvation, but also of disappointment. I wonder what he was thinking as his fingers pressed the intercom.

When I give my name, I'm buzzed through and I feel a sharp nick of fear as I step into the reception area. It's tidied up now, of course. The floor's been cleaned and everything's neatly back in place. The woman at the desk ushers me through to a windowless room with a bright fluorescent strip light. Orange plastic chairs are arranged haphazardly around a table. There's a coffee cup and a discarded *Metro* newspaper. The notice board by the door displays faded leaflets—a needle exchange, infection control, and one about joining the union.

I wait for a full ten minutes until I'm joined by a tall man with dreadlocks. He nods in my direction as he takes a seat. He's followed by a pale woman in a patterned floaty dress. Minutes later, two others come in, a man and a woman, eyes fixed firmly on the floor. I feel their heavy reluctance. I, too, am filled with a strong desire not to be there. Perhaps in response, the woman in the floaty dress reaches into her bag and brings out bumper-size packets of sweets. "Help yourself," she says to no one in particular, fanning them out across the table. They are children's sweets. The brightly colored sort I might have bought for the twins' birthday parties— Haribo Fizzy Colas, Starbursts. Treats, I think. An attempt to "sweeten" things for what's to come.

"Are we expecting anyone else?" I ask.

They all look round at one another.

"Some people are off today. Lots of sickness," the woman says with a vague apologetic smile. The others ignore her and seem irritated by her eagerness to please. There's a protracted conversation about someone called Toya. *Is she coming? Has anyone seen her?* The man with dreadlocks wonders if perhaps she's left a message, and this triggers an agonizing stretch of time as he laboriously scans his emails. He shakes his head. Nothing.

When I introduce myself and ask them to do the same, they shuffle in their seats.

"I'm Angela," says the woman who brought the sweets. Then the rest offer up their names—Tony, Farzal, and Wendy. I make eye contact with them all except Wendy, who doesn't look up from her phone, saying her name like a teenager at registration. I carefully write the names down as they are positioned around the table. I've facilitated many of these crisis staff meetings. Mostly for support in the aftermath of a patient suicide. Thankfully, what we are here to do today is extremely rare.

"What about Alia?" Wendy suddenly wants to know, her face hard, unforgiving. "Thought she was coming?"

Farzal explains that she rang after lunch from her home visit. "Got stuck in traffic," he says. There's another silence. This time, it's full of envy. Envy for those who have managed to find a reason to avoid coming today.

When I start to explain the purpose of the meeting, I'm interrupted by Farzal, who makes a point of reaching across the table for the *Metro* newspaper. "See this?" he says, jabbing at the picture. The others lean in. I know what he's pointing at. I saw it this morning on the train. The face of a Syrian refugee on the beach in Greece, clutching his dead two-year-old to his chest. He flings it back on to the table, and it lands on the bag of Haribos. "It's disgusting," he says. "Two ports wouldn't even let the boat dock. Made me think about my own kid," and he shakes his head, speechless. There are nods of agreement. Murmurs around the room about the lack of humanity. The lack of care.

"No one gives a shit," Wendy says, looking up at me coldly.

Resistance and unease have morphed into open hostility. I know I will have to tread carefully. To find a way to understand the anger. Not to alienate them any further. I think about the anguished face on the newspaper and I think about the reason we are here. Another man who was denied a safe haven. Another parent who tried to get refuge for their child.

"It makes me think about Harold Mason," I say. I know it's a risk to mention the man. To say his name out loud. There's a terrible silence in the room. They all stare back at me.

"From the little I know," I say, "he was also a desperate man. A man who needed something he wasn't given. And this, too, ended in tragedy."

I nod over at the newspaper, while looking at Farzal. "How near to drowning do you have to be before you're offered the safety of dry land?"

Angela and Farzal are both nodding now.

Tony and Wendy exchange a glance. It's a look of weary resignation. A look that's weathered the recent years of underresourced mental health services. I see it on their faces. The ward closures. The emphasis on "care in the community." They say nothing.

I start to tell them about the purpose of the meeting and how I have come to be here, but when I mention the three sessions I'd arranged with Karen Crosswell, Wendy snorts with derision. "Management trying to make themselves feel better by setting up a little support group for us," she says bitterly.

"They closed two mental health wards this year. That's why he couldn't get a bed," Angela explains, as if for my benefit.

"It's all about the money," spits Wendy, looking squarely at me, and the room bristles with a new kind of furious energy.

It's clear that my very association with Karen Crosswell, and my simply agreeing to the meeting, have somehow implicated me as well. I, too, am another "bad object" in an already rotten system.

I look back at them.

"You're right," I say, nodding, "and it feels unfair."

Wendy looks taken aback.

I comment on their feelings about the injustice. The faults in an already overstretched and underresourced service. I think about our own department's cutbacks; the long waiting lists, the staff under pressure to do more for less. "The anger you are all feeling is understandable. I feel it, too. I'm guessing that having me sent here feels like putting a Band-Aid on a broken leg."

I sense a shift in mood—as if the team is letting out a collective breath. Tony is nodding. Angela starts to cry silently.

"It's important for you to know that I don't work in your Trust. These sessions are confidential. I'm not part of the investigation and I'm not here to find a way to justify or explain what happened."

I lean toward them, dropping my voice down low. "I am here because a terrible thing has happened, and you have suffered a great loss." I pause for a moment. "And I believe that sometimes it can simply be helpful to come together and have a space to talk."

The silence feels different this time. Thoughtful. Contemplative. The hostility has moved away from me.

Tony lowers his head into his hands. "I just keep seeing her," he says. "On the floor. Her pale face. The blood." He presses his fingers at the side of his face. "I want to get it out of my head, but I can't—"

And like a faltering car, the story begins, stopping and starting, then juddering into life. They tell me they'd had a training session, and were going to the pub. "It was the end of the week," Farzal said, "we were in a good mood." They tell me Marion said she'd follow on. Wanted to try one last time to get hold of this GP for one of our service users, "a fifteen-year-old crack addict. She wanted to try to get something set up before the weekend."

His words trigger a flurry of conversation about Marion. How she was compassionate. Dedicated. Fought for her patients. Had relentless energy for the disadvantaged. The conversation is peppered with clichéd expressions—"a heart of gold," someone who always "went the extra mile" and was "first in and last to leave."

"Always fussing over us," Angela adds. "Making cakes. Buying us stuff from that health food shop. Telling us not to work so hard."

"Sounds like she really looked after you all," I comment.

Farzal nods. "Last week I'd hurt my back playing football. Next day, she's bringing me in this special cushion for my chair." He shrugs. "That's the kind of thing she did."

"She didn't have kids," offers Wendy, "said the team were her family."

"Not just the team. All the patients, too," Angela says tearfully. "They loved her. Couldn't bear it when she took a holiday."

"I can't remember the last time she took a holiday," Tony muses.

As I listen to them speak about their team manager, a picture of Marion grows in my mind. I know exactly who she is. My heart swells for a woman who has dedicated her life to her work. A woman who is drawn to disadvantaged groups. Relentless in her drive and commitment. People like Marion are the glue that keeps the crumbling public sector together. They are passionate. Committed. Relentless. But in the bottomless pit of referrals, they are also the people who find it difficult to say no.

"She sounds like someone who really cared," I venture. "Someone who was really devoted and dedicated to her work."

Farzal and Angela nod. Tony still has his head bowed.

"Nearly forty years in the Health Service, and this is how it ends," Wendy says.

"I just wish I'd waited with her," Tony says. "Five minutes. She told me to get a round in. *Mine's a pint of Guinness.* It was the last thing she said."

Angela picks up the story. And as they take turns, each slowly drawing out the different pieces of that fateful afternoon, it's like watching a horrific game of Jenga, waiting for the inevitable collapse.

"We rang her from the pub," she says. "It's only two minutes up the road. When there was no answer, Tony and I came back—"

They tell me how they found Marion McClusky slumped on the floor behind the reception desk, blood in a small pool at the side of her head. The reception area was in disarray, chairs and tables were upturned, two windowpanes were smashed, the desktop computer wrenched from its socket, and the office printer pushed over, spilling a path of white paper over the carpet. Marion could have been hit by any number of randomly hurled objects, but it was the fire extinguisher that dealt the fatal blow. Half an hour later, Harold Mason was found in the middle of Balham High Road, shouting at the oncoming cars, while slapping and punching at his own face. At the same time, three streets away, his elderly mother was at the local police station asking for help with her son's volatile behavior.

It would transpire that Harold was a fifty-seven-year-old man with a long-standing mental health problem. He had intermittent psychotic episodes, every three to four years, when he required hospitalization, usually because he'd stopped taking his medication.

"He had a part-time job," Tony says. "In the local greengrocer's."

They tell me how his mother had begged for him to be admitted that morning, but when there was no bed, the bed manager referred him to the Home Treatment Team.

"Care in the community," Angela adds with sarcasm.

"I knew Harry," Tony says. "He was obviously distressed. Out of control. He's a big bloke"—he shook his head—"but I know he wouldn't have meant to hurt Marion."

"Was he registered with your service?" I ask.

Wendy and Tony exchange a glance.

"No," says Tony. "But Marion knew Harry well. From when we both worked on the Community Mental Health Team. The team used to be based here, back in the day—before the service was restructured."

I look around at the group. There's an uncomfortable silence.

I know that no one wants to talk about the lone worker policy. The fact that service users aren't allowed in unless two or more staff are on site. The fact that patients not registered with the service should never be admitted. No one wants to say she should never have pressed the buzzer.

I wait.

"So what happened?"

"She let him in," Tony says quietly.

"But that was Marion all over," offers Angela quickly. "She'd have recognized him on the video intercom. Would have seen he looked distressed. Would have wanted to help. Always putting others before herself. She'd never have turned him away. Never have said no. That's what she always said: *We're the team that never says no.*"

"And anyway," says Wendy, "if he'd been given a bed in the first place, none of this would have happened. Robbing Peter to pay Paul. Now he'll probably spend the rest of his life in a secure unit."

"That'll cost a whole lot more than a bed on a psychiatric ward," nods Angela, brushing invisible dirt from the skirt of her dress.

Robbing Peter to pay Paul. Blurring the reality of cost savings. Organizational chaos. I have seen it all before. But it's a neat split that can feel comforting; "good" Marion pitted against the "bad" system. I listen as they talk about the flawed system, about being surrounded by other teams with such high referral thresholds that they refuse to take people on, "so the referrals all come our way." They talk more about Marion and her boundless commitment. *The team that never says no.*

I think back to the conversation with Stephanie. How she missed the point about the legacy of Winnicott. *An excuse for mediocrity.* How, of course, it's the opposite. That a "good enough" team manager would know the importance of limitations. The need to set boundaries. Would know that a perpetual readiness to say yes is unhelpful. Can be unsafe. Tiring. Destructive. And unsustainable in an already stretched and underresourced system. But while I know this is not the session to talk about this, it feels important to try to sow the seed.

I glance up at the clock. I have a few minutes left. I lean forward in my chair.

"I'm wondering what that was like," I venture, "to work in a team that never says no."

There's a still silence.

Tony's shoulders slump down. He locks me in a gaze. "Exhausting," he says.

And there it is. My small shoot of green.

Before people leave, we arrange the next session in four weeks. There's some uncertainty about the funeral date, and talk of wanting to involve the service users in some kind of memorial. "Perhaps this is something we can talk about next time," I say. As the team files out, they all make eye contact. There are murmurs of thanks. "See you next month," Wendy says, and Tony reaches across to shake my hand. Angela walks me to the door. She thanks me again, then lingers for a moment before asking me about my journey back. She seems to want to find reasons not to let me go. In truth, I can't wait to get out of the building and into the fresh air. My body feels rigid from holding all the emotion. All that sad anger and hostility in that tight, airless room. But also I'm thinking about Harold and

Marion, and I am consumed by thoughts of randomness. Small platelets that move and shift and are suddenly and inexplicably monumental in our lives. This is the thought in my head as I step into a seismic shift of my own.

The bright fluorescent lighting has left me with an ache at the back of my head. When I blink, I can still see the strip in a haze of white. As I walk to the Tube, it's this feeling, this hangover from the meeting, that makes me reluctant to go straight back down into the Underground. I spot the Holland & Barrett on my way to the station, and without thinking I make my way inside. It's an insignificant decision. A memory about Marion from the session perhaps. I've been run-down and tired, I'll get some vitamins, I decide on a whim, anticipating the almost childlike satisfaction in spending exorbitant amounts of money on small jars filled with multicolored sweets. I'm idly perusing the shelves, the Manuka honey, the bottles of zinc tablets. I can't say I was thinking about very much at all.

I'm aware of a woman and a buggy to my right-hand side, but only in a vague and unfocused sort of a way. It's only when the child kicks his legs out and knocks off several jars of magnesium tablets that I really notice they are there. I reach down for the jars as they roll across the floor. I am at eye level with the baby. "Thank you," I hear the woman say. By then, I am transfixed by the sight of the boy.

It's a blond-haired baby wearing a blue-and-white hat and denim overalls. I'm staring into the baby face of Tom. I reach out for the frame of the buggy and push myself up to a standing position. It's then that I see the young woman with a pink fringe gaping at me, openmouthed.

"*Julie?*" I say in a whisper.

TWELVE

Over coffee in the café opposite, Julie tells me everything. My hands are shaking as I lift the cup to my mouth. In the end, not trusting myself, I set the cup down on the saucer and place my hands in my lap and leave the coffee to go cold.

She looks the same, but motherhood has changed her face. She's still wearing funky clothes. A tie-dyed T-shirt. There's still a streak of pink in the fringe of her hair and a stud in her nose, but she looks older. I am listening intently to her, even as my eyes are drawn to the small boy. "Nicholas," she'd said, when I was unraveling in the aisle of Holland & Barrett, a tub of high-dose magnesium in my hand.

I watch every movement he makes. Every pat on the table. Every facial expression. The way his face breaks out into a sudden smile.

"He's beautiful."

"Thank you," she says. Her voice is soft. Kindly. It is nothing like the tone of our last meeting.

There are so many questions I have. So many things I want to say, but I feel the fragility of our chance encounter. It could so easily not have happened. I could have passed the front of the shop and slipped away down into the train, and our paths might never have crossed. The small, papery butterfly wings of an encounter that might never have taken flight. The very thought makes me want to weep. I try to find a tone that's casual, nonchalant. I don't know how to ask.

In the end, she helps me out.

"It was just the once," she says. "What are the chances? I was sixteen weeks pregnant when I found out."

"Oh," I say quietly. I don't trust myself to say anything else.

"Tom and I were friends. I really liked him. That day—after the accident, he was really upset. When he came over—he looked so lost." She shrugs. "I just wanted to look after him. I made him some food and we hung out. . . ."

She looks away. "We slept together. Just that once."

Tom slept with Julie?

When she looks back at me, she tells me she knew it was a mistake. "As in," she adds quickly, "we were good friends. Anything more—I didn't think it was a good idea. Besides, I was going away to college."

"And Tom?"

"He agreed." She pauses. "But I had a feeling—well, that he might have liked it to have been something more."

I feel a dull thud. A pain in my chest.

"When he asked to stay—" She looks away. "I—well, I didn't know—"

"It's OK," I say, "it's not your fault."

She looks startled. "I know."

I feel my face flush.

"You weren't much older," I say. "How did you manage?"

She nods. "It was tough, at first," she carries on, "being on my own. But look at him," and she speaks with such warmth and pride. "I wouldn't change a thing. And my sister really helped."

"What about your parents?"

"My dad has Parkinson's. He's quite frail. And my mum, well, she died when I was young. So, no grandparents on hand, but I have some really good friends. We do OK."

No grandparents. And I feel the rush of something, a wave pooling into a sand hole on a beach.

I have to battle with myself to stay silent. Not to reach across the table for those thin shoulders and shake them. I want to blurt out, *Why didn't you tell me? Why didn't you let me help? Why didn't you let me see my grandson?*

I don't say any of these things. We both remember the last time we spoke. That day when she came over with Tom's things. I was desperate. The bitter recriminations. I said awful things in my fury. I blamed her for Tom's departure. I blamed everyone for Tom's departure. Why on earth would she have called me? Why would she have wanted me in her life?

"I am assuming—" and of course, I don't finish my sentence, my eyes feasting on this sandy-haired boy.

"What is it they say?" She smiles. "A baby is designed to be the spitting image of its biological father. Ensures the survival of the species—nature's way to make men stick around—and be monogamous. Not that that applied to Tom and me." She laughs, then looks embarrassed. "I'm so sorry."

She doesn't need to say it, but she does. "It's his. There was no one else."

It's mesmerizing. Magical. Like I have a small video camera in my hand, and I have the chance to watch and play back Tom's early years. I'm utterly transported. And yet, at the same time, it's another feeling. This is not my son. This is my grandson. And I feel awash with love for this delightful, small, innocent boy, while simultaneously feeling full of sadness for Tom, that he, too, isn't sitting here with me.

"And what about Tom?" I ask. Again, I try to sound casual. "Any news since then?"

She shakes her head. "Nothing. When I heard he'd gone, well, I needed to move anyway. I had a friend around here. She managed to get me a housing association flat. It wasn't an easy time for me," she says carefully.

I nod. I understand.

I look down at Nicholas. "How old is he?"

"He'll be one in a few weeks. A May baby."

Suddenly, she glances at her watch. "I'm sorry, Ruth," she says, "I have to go."

I feel a sudden lurch of panic.

"So soon?"

"I have to pick up Jess from nursery."

"Jess?"

"Frank's—my boyfriend's daughter," she says. "We met at one of those baby music groups. He's a single dad. We hung out. Kindred spirits, I guess. And then—well, we got together," she says simply.

Frank. I can see she loves him, but I have the feeling that she's trying to downplay it all. Perhaps she's thinking about Tom. Trying to protect me. I'm not really thinking about any of this, I am just panicking that this person is about to exit my life, just as quickly and unexpectedly as she has come into it.

My words sound clunky and clumsy. "I would really like"—I look down at my hands locked in my lap—"I'd really like to see you and Nicholas again." There's a pause. I feel desperate and exposed and acutely aware of the circumstances of our last encounter. I wince. She'll remember it as well as I do.

"That last time," I say, "I'm really sorry I—"

I am fortunate. Motherhood has softened Julie. She shakes her head as she picks up his plastic beaker. "It's a long time ago." She hesitates. She looks at me across the table, a knot of fingers in my lap. "Let me take your number," she says.

She doesn't offer hers, and in the days that follow, I will admonish myself for not asking. How stupid of me, I'll think. She doesn't put it on her phone. Instead, she scribbles my number and email on the back of a leaflet she'd found in her bag.

I feel a lurch of anxiety watching her stuff it back into her bag. This small scrap of paper that could flutter away in the wind, or be accidentally thrown out with the recycling when she gets home. I say nothing. What can I say? By then, she's distracted by Nicholas, who is pulling on the straps of his buggy, arms stretched out for the door.

"Please," I say, "do get in touch." And then we hover awkwardly, not knowing whether to embrace; in the end, I reach forward and give her a small, jerky hug. I brush my hand over the soft hair of my grandson. "Bye-bye, Nicholas," and I wave. *My grandson.*

THE TRAIN AS IT HURTLES along the tunnel feels loud and dirty. The platform is full of people. I look at them all, reading papers, looking at their phones; I want to go up to each and every one of them and shake them, rouse them from the stupor of their own introspection. *I am a grandmother. I have a grandson. Nicholas is my grandson*, is what I want to say. Not say, but shout into their faces. Sing. Laugh. Run along the platform waving my hands above my head.

The train is crammed and I hear the child as soon as I step onto the carriage. It's full, people are clinging to the handles, bobbing and jerking with the movement of the train, faces set into expressions of stoic resignation. The boy is small, no more than two, in jeans and a red anorak. If it wasn't for the fact that he was pulling on the bottom of her jacket, it would have been impossible to tell whom he was with.

"I. Want. Water. At. Home," he wails. He's repeating the words in between great hiccupping sobs. His tearstained face is red with the crying.

I can remember traveling on the Tube with the twins, caught out suddenly in those early years, mistiming food or drink, and how quickly the situation could spiral into something intense and catastrophic. One of them starting to whine. Trying to comfort them, the other one starting to cry, me feeling embarrassed in front of my fellow passengers as they exchange looks of discomfort.

This woman doesn't look around at us. Her straight, dark hair is tied back. Her face is pale. The boy is on the seat next to her as she stares straight ahead, her face impassive. The Tube rattles through the station. The doors open and close, people get off, more get on, we all shuffle up. The boy repeats the phrase over and over, his lips making a small circular shape as he lingers over the *o* in *home*. Still nothing from the woman. Only her stony-faced expression, staring out of the window opposite. His crying ratchets up a gear. More hysterical, more plaintive. Still nothing. *I. Want. Water. At. Home.* Some of us are exchanging glances. One man looks over, irritated by the noise, but it's the mothers among us who feel a sense of unity and camaraderie. I feel we're joined in our incomprehension of the woman. Her poor mothering. Her negligence. Her ignoring the needs of her small child.

The anger settles in my chest. It creeps up to my throat. Without thinking, I scrabble through my bag. I find a bottle of water. Unopened. I hold it out to him.

"Here," I say, "water." The little boy is stunned by the sudden movement. He stops crying. He holds his hand out and grabs for the bottle. His eyelashes are heavy with the next downfall of tears, and when he blinks at me, they tumble down his cheeks. "Water," he says, a look of glee on his face. I look over at the mother. I'm expecting a smile. Gratitude. A hand on my arm. A mouthed *thank you*, as the relief smooths across her stressed face.

But none of these things happen. Instead, she leans forward and snatches the bottle. By now the boy has his small fingers clamped round it. He's holding on tightly. Shaking it up and down, delighted by the bubbles. With a quick deft movement, she prizes his fingers off and holds it out to me. She says nothing. The boy is now stamping his feet. Waving his arms above his head, as if trying to bring the bottle back down toward him. "Water," he wails, "water."

He turns his face desperately up toward me. His big brown eyes are pleading. The mother's face is hard. Bitter. *Mind your own business. How dare you?*

Perhaps it's my surprise, or the sight of the small boy waving his arms, but I am slow to take it back from her. So slow, in fact, that she gives up waiting—and simply releases it from her fingers. It drops onto the floor. It rolls back and forth as the train shudders into the station. We all follow its erratic journey as it hits a man's shoe, a suitcase, then rolls into the corner. The boy moves to run for it. The woman pulls him back sharply. More shrieking and sobbing. "Ow," he cries. Now everyone in the carriage is staring at me. The attention has moved away from the mother and her boy. Like I am the source of the disturbance. Another jolt of the train, and the bottle slams against the door. A man tuts. A sigh from someone behind me. The bottle seems to have a life of its own. Each lurch reminds the boy what he was given and has now lost, and reignites a crescendo of sobbing. I make a quick grab for the plastic bottle and stuff it back into my bag.

By the time I get home, the earlier euphoria of my chance, life-changing encounter in Balham has dissipated. Having felt so full, I now feel utterly bereft. I begin to feel panicky at the thought that Julie may not contact me. Short of hanging around the Holland & Barrett on the High Road, I may not see her, or Nicholas, again, and the realization sits like a lumpen weight in the pit of my stomach. In the days that follow, I wonder if I imagined it all. That I have conjured him up out of nowhere, because that's what my mind does. Over and over, I admonish myself for not having asked how to reach her. The need to tread carefully overtook my need for certainty, to have a telephone number on a piece of paper in my hand. I feel stunned by the poor choice I have made.

The email appears a few days later. It's short, noncommittal, but friendly. I've attached some photos. A few milestones for you to see. I click on them, elated. I look at each one in turn. Amazed all over again by his small face, the likeness to my son. There's one of Nicholas at a barbecue, with ketchup around his mouth. One of him in a park, a yellow bucket balancing on his head. There's another of him laughing as he sits in a blue pedal car. The one I like the most is of him on a beach. It reminds me of an almost identical photo I have of Tom and Carolyn on the Isle of Wight when they were the same age. Nicholas is wearing swimming trunks with fish on them. He has on the blue-and-white gingham hat and he's looking up, grinning and pointing at the camera with his small sandy hand.

I print them all out. I pore over them, my eyes scanning every inch of his face and body. I print out smaller versions. I scrabble about for magnets to display them on my fridge. I move them about, this way and that, to make a collage. I stand back and admire them. I do this because I am full of pride, but also because I want to feel like an ordinary grandmother who puts pictures of her grandson on her fridge. All day, my eyes are drawn to these new smiley colorful additions. Whenever I come into the kitchen, I see them straight away, and when I do, I feel a new sense of warmth, of satisfaction, for their newfound place in my kitchen and in my life. I email Julie back and thank her.

In the morning, I pick the beach picture from the fridge and put it in my purse. I tuck it behind that plastic see-through part of the wallet. It's what I see other people do. And because I want to feel like everyone else, I do it, too.

THIRTEEN

That week my sleep is erratic. The pattern is the same. I fall asleep quickly, then get pushed awake by vivid dreams. That night, I'm out at sea. I'm on a small boat with a group of people wearing life jackets. We are there for a reason. There's the air of purpose, but I have no idea what it is. It's after dusk, and the sea is choppy, rocking us back and forth in dark, navy water. I'm following the others, scanning the surface, but I don't know what I'm looking for. All of a sudden, there are shouts, people point, and we swerve in that direction. As the boat dips and falls in the waves, I see the face of a child. It's a baby. Nicholas. I reach out to heave him up onto the boat, but he slips through my arms. I call to him, then I feel a surge of horror as I see all the waves have small bobbing faces. There's Tom, Dan, and others I don't know. There is panic. Mouths open. Arms reaching up out of the water. Their faces are pleading. Desperate. The people on the boat aren't helping—they are talking, looking in the other direction. Each time I lean down, the waves roll over and the faces disappear. I wake with a start, I sit bolt upright, my eyes pinned and alert. It's 5:25 A.M.

As the week edges toward my session with Dan, I feel an

increasing sense of dread. Just as he made references to being on a cliff edge, I, too, feel like I have been left hanging, as I await the next installment in his dreadful narrative. Given his uncharacteristic level of self-disclosure at the last session, I have a strong feeling that he might not come, and I already know I'd feel both relieved and worried by his absence.

In the event, Dan arrives on time, and while I am prepared for a withdrawal, a retreat from me and the process we have started, he starts with an attentive eagerness.

"I was looking forward to coming today," he says, striding into the room. Then as he sits down, he makes a point of looking me in the eye. "I wanted to thank you," he says. "Last time I came, it's the first time I've ever talked about that stuff—I've never been able to talk about any of it before. There's something that happens—here with you," he says, "that makes it OK to talk."

His gaze is still, intense, and I feel a rush of something. A kind of satisfaction. But in the next breath, he mentions something about college, then the name of a film that I don't catch and immediately I feel him pull away from me. He sits forward in his chair, drapes his hand over his forehead for dramatic effect, and in an Eastern European accent, he says, "*Ich kann nicht wählen. Ich kann nicht wählen.*"

He waits for a moment, then looks up at me expectantly.

"Any ideas?"

I feel a stab of irritation, and before I can find a way to turn this into words, I feel the nudge of a memory. Being a student, sprawled out on the floor of the common room watching a film late at night, eating spaghetti with garlic butter. The memory pushes back and forth, like a wave on the beach. Nothing comes. I stare back at him. My face is blank.

"*Sophie's Choice*," he says eventually. "She says she can't choose—" and he flutters his hand winglike in the air between us. "But then," and he folds his hand into a fist that he bangs into the side of his leg, "she does. Her son lives. Her daughter is sent to the gas chamber."

There's an odd expression on his face. Totally unreadable. I feel a heavy weariness.

I make a comment about the split between reality and fantasy. I talk about how perhaps it feels safer for him to be back in the world of films, the world of "make-believe," rather than in his real life— which sounded so painful.

"The film references feel distancing," I say, "like you want to push me away."

He reels back a little. "They're important," he says. "Perhaps if you paid more attention to them, you wouldn't find them distancing—but quite the opposite."

I feel stung.

He sits forward again.

"Sophie is in Auschwitz. She's forced to make a choice. If she didn't, both her children would die." His tone is educational, informative, like I'm a student in a class. "Most mothers don't have this dilemma on a daily basis, but it illustrates an important point. A taboo."

"A taboo?"

"Mothers have favorites," he says simply. "We have preferences for everything else in life, yet it's such a taboo to think that applies to children. The party line is that parents love their children equally. Every parent will say they don't have a favorite. It's a lie."

He pauses, looks at me pointedly, and again I have the sensation that he can see right inside me. That he's talking about me. I feel uncomfortable. Exposed. As if he's referring to Carolyn and Tom.

"I don't understand," I say, shaking my head slowly. "I thought you were an only child?"

"I was," he says, "or thought I was," he corrects himself. "Turns out I had a brother. Michael."

He speaks quietly as he tells me what happened. Tells me he always had a sense of something hidden. A secret. And how one day, he climbed up to his mother's wardrobe, where he knew there was a box. An old-fashioned hatbox with candy stripes.

"Hidden," he said, "but colorful, like a present waiting to be unwrapped."

Inside, there was a small wooden box, where he found a pile of photos of a baby and a birth certificate for Michael, who was a year and a half younger. There were lots of Michael with their parents. But only a few photos of the two boys together. He tells me that in every single photograph, this baby was ridiculously happy. "Michael was joyous," he says, "like a ray of sunshine."

There was also a small hospital wristband. Dated two years after the birth certificate. He tells me there were no more photos after that.

"It was as if time stopped."

"What happened?"

"I don't know." He sighs. "I guess he got sick. Went into hospital. Never came out."

"You have no memories of him at all?"

He shakes his head.

There's a pause. He looks preoccupied. Then after a few moments of contemplation, it's as if he makes a decision. He reaches into his pocket with a careful, slow movement.

"I've never shown this to anyone else," he says.

He pulls out a photograph that he places on the table. He nudges it toward me and looks up at me. A face that's expectant. I feel the weight of anticipation.

It's a picture of a woman with a baby, taken side on.

"May I?" I say, reaching for it.

He nods.

The woman has long dark hair and she's lifting the baby into the air. The baby's in a blue romper. His face is stretched into a big gurgle of a smile. The two of them are locked in a gaze. There are people in the background, but it's as if no one else were there. Her arms are lifting him up, and the baby is reaching his hands in to pat her cheeks. They are both laughing and smiling at each other. A picture of joy. Their faces transfixed. Like a bright white beam of love was flowing between them.

"My mum and Michael," he says. "You can almost feel it, can't you? Their love. Their happiness," he says. "How could I compete with that? How could anyone compete with that?"

There's a palpable heaviness in the room.

He tells me about finding the picture. "Suddenly, it all made sense. Everything fell into place."

He said at first he felt like he couldn't breathe. "I was dizzy and giddy, like I was going to fall." Then he said he felt relief. Realized that all his efforts were pointless. That anything he did or didn't do was never going to make a difference.

He leans forward. "It was my third act epiphany," he says theatrically. "I stole it that day, slipped it into the pocket of my shorts. She must have known it was missing, but she never mentioned it. Michael's name was never mentioned in our house. And yet after that, I could feel him in it. The emptiness. The void. The gap. It was him."

I stare down at the picture, still pinched between my fingers. I think about Nicholas. Tom as a baby. Michael and his mother. It's an undeniably happy picture. But while she is looking at Michael, she is not looking at Dan. I feel a wave of unbearable sadness. For the mother. For the tragedy that felled this family. And for Dan. The small boy left behind. Uncertain, anxious, bewildered, and desperate for his mother's love. Trying constantly to find ways to get the spotlight of her love, her interest, and then her care, to be turned back on him. Yet whatever he did, the light didn't shine his way. I feel the well of tears. The heaviness of his loss and how his desperation calcified into self-loathing that became willful acts of self-harm.

"I'm so sorry," I say.

His head is down. He rubs at his eyes.

"And when you saw this picture, did you remember anything?"

A small shake of his head.

"It explained everything, though. The feeling I had growing up. That there was always something missing."

We sit for a moment in silence.

"The death of a child is traumatic," I say, "but what you describe are parents who seemed unable to recover from their trauma. Seemed unable to fulfill the basic job of parenting. To love and care for and protect their child. It was negligence that was a form of abuse."

I'm conscious of saying the word again. Gently this time. To nudge it back into the room.

"It sounds like they were traumatized by their grief. Do you think it's possible that your mother was depressed? And unable to care for you as a result?"

He pauses. "I've thought about that. And I'd like to say that was true, but I have memories of my parents together. Happy. Just the two of them. Sometimes, I imagine the death of a child can make the surviving child more precious. It was the opposite with me. I think it would have been easier if they'd been left with no children."

There's a long silence.

He tells me that in the days after he'd seen the picture, after the initial relief, he had other sorts of feelings. "An ache," he says, and he puts a hand on his belly, "and it spread all the way up, until I could hardly eat or speak. I kept looking at the picture of Michael. I felt so jealous."

He shrugs. "That's when I decided to let it go."

"Let it go?"

"I started to cut myself. It was a release. The bad feeling calmed right down."

"And what were you feeling?"

"Rage," he says.

"So, the bad feeling, the rage—was turned on yourself?"

He nods. "The joy of family life," and as he sits back in his chair, he makes a gentle hissing sound.

He sees my frown.

"Sophie's choice? There's always one kid that gets sent to the gas chamber," he says.

"Is that what it felt like?" I ask. "A death sentence, not to be chosen?"

He looks down at his fingers, picks at the skin around his nails. He pulls sharply and blood rushes to the surface in a small crescent of red.

When he asks the question, it comes out of nowhere and lands with a thud in my chest.

"Do you have kids?" he asks casually, all eyes on me.

In that moment, I see a small boy getting himself lost at the fairground while his parents looked the other way. I think of the photograph. A mother and baby son shining with happiness. The glow of love that never came his way. I look at his face. It looks pleading, desperate.

Do you have kids?

"No," I say, shaking my head, "I don't."

He raises his finger to his lips and sucks the blood away.

As I walk to Robert's after the session, the lie sits heavy on my chest. I turn the moment over and over in my head. I think of all the ways I could have answered the question. I think of all the ways I have answered the question in the past.

Sometimes it's been buried in a series of questions that sound casual and nonchalant. "Are you married? Where are you going on holiday? Do you cycle to work, or get the bus? Do you live locally?" The seemingly innocuous questions are all about power. One of my patients, Ellen Taylor, whose daughter was critically ill in hospital, was able to put it into words. "You know the terrible thoughts I have. The things I want to do to myself. The despair I feel. You know things my closest friends don't know. You know everything about me—and I know nothing about you. I don't even know if you have children."

Sometimes, the question can feel more accusatory, as it once did in a Mother and Baby Unit with sleep-deprived mothers. I was helping them develop sleep routines for their babies, a task that was challenging, given their own complex issues around attachment and abandonment. Trish, the mother who sat in front of me, had dark rings under her eyes. Her eyes swam in front of the charts I'd asked her to fill in the preceding week. "Do you even have a baby?" she snapped.

Usually, questions that probe the personal life of a therapist are not searching for concrete answers. They hint at something more elusive. An unconscious search for certainty, safety, and trust. The flesh and bones of real children aren't the issue. It's about being an imagined child. It's about their own experience of being parented. The issue is more about their concern, their terror. *Will you be there for me? Can you help? Can I trust you? Can you be a good enough mother to me through this experience? Will you let me down as others have done in the past?* The rule of thumb is to understand the meaning behind the question. To use it in the work. To think beyond the pull to answer the concrete question. The rule of thumb is not to lie.

WHEN I'M SITTING WITH ROBERT, I tell him all about the last two sessions with Dan. I tell him about the sad loneliness of his childhood. I talk about his parents. The curious way he described their abusive and neglectful behavior, "indifferent," and "not to their taste." We talk about the revelation of a dead brother. His parents' grief. How they were unable to think of his needs. "They seemed not to care. They were negligent," I say, more fiercely than I'd intended.

I describe Dan's self-harm, and as I do, the image that haunts me returns. A small boy alone in the kitchen, rooting through the cupboards for sharp utensils. I tell the fairground story, and as I talk, I notice how Robert sits forward on his chair. He stops writing notes. He places his hands carefully in his lap, as if he wants to give me his full attention.

"I'm sure there are other worse things," I say. "I feel a kind of dread of what might come next."

I pause to clear my throat. There's a stillness in the room as Robert waits.

"I'm not sure I want to hear about them."

Robert nods thoughtfully. He makes no comment, but I see him squirreling it away.

Robert talks about self-harm as a defense against emotions that can feel overwhelming.

"Like the rage?"

He nods. "He'll have a fantasy that his rage will be out of control. Unmanageable. Annihilating. Easier to simply block it off, through pain."

He thinks for a moment. "He was six, you say, when he first hurt himself?"

I nod.

"Young," he says. "It's unusual. And worrying." He takes off his glasses and cleans them as he thinks.

"Putting himself at risk in the ways you've described, it's like a death wish," he says.

We talk about his compartmentalization.

"Splitting off his rage seemed to work well for him—until the rape. Then everything caved in. It opened the lid," I say. "No wonder it was traumatic."

"Sometimes there's a predominant feeling. Was there one for him around the rape? Did you get a sense of that?"

I think back to the session.

"He talked about feeling small . . . and powerless . . ."

I stop for a moment, remembering. "There was a thing with a lighter. A fear that he was going to be burned. He wasn't—but he talked about a strong sense of shame."

"Shame?"

"It's been a theme," I nod, "that he's to blame. Is responsible in some way."

"For the rape?"

"Yes, but also for the way his mother behaved. In one session, he talked about karma. Then denied it the next."

Robert makes a note, then he's quiet as he flicks back over the pages, rereading notes from our previous sessions.

"And what do you feel?"

"Lots of things—but at the moment, pulled in to help him. To look after him."

He nods. "To be the mother he didn't have. He was young when he shut down."

To be the mother he didn't have.

I tell him about the gifts. "Anonymous," I say, "but I'm pretty sure they're from him. Plants, first. Then a hamster."

"A hamster?" he repeats, his eyebrows rising in surprise.

I nod.

He thinks for a moment.

"He gives you living things to look after. To keep alive. *Can you take care of him?* he wants to know."

I'm careful with the next bit, when I tell him how the story about his childhood left me full of his anger. "I felt a sense of outrage. It was the way he was telling the story. Excusing their behavior. Protecting his mother." I fiddle with the edge of my jumper. "It was powerful. I got very caught up in something. Like I was left holding all the bad angry feelings. Like a bomb in my lap."

"That will be your focus," he agrees, "handing him back the bomb. Helping him understand that it doesn't have to go off. Doesn't have to annihilate him."

There seems to be something that's troubling Robert, something he can't quite work out.

"Any relationships?"

"He mentioned someone. A woman, but he didn't elaborate," I

shake my head. "He seems ambivalent about friendships. He's been let down."

"And his attachment issues—how do they manifest in the room with you?"

"The usual," I shrug. "He retreats and withdraws. He came late one day. Early another."

I tell him how it's taken time for him to trust the process, that it's only now I feel like he's present in the room, willing to engage and work. But that it feels fragile, could turn at any moment.

"Nothing else?"

I tell him he wanted to be offered more than the standard six sessions.

"What did you say?"

"I offered him more. I think it was about trust. I wanted him to commit to the process."

I feel myself overexplaining, but if Robert notices, or thinks it odd, he makes no comment. Another nut to store away.

"Any other attempts to push boundaries in the session?"

I shake my head. "Not so far," I say, and my stomach feels heavy and leaden.

Do you have kids?

It's as if the lie I told Dan sits between us in the room. It grows bigger, taking on a shape of its own, calling for attention, like a demanding child. I feel uncomfortable in my seat. My cheeks flush. My throat feels dry. I reach for the glass of water.

"Are you all right?" Robert inquires gently, and he asks with such kindness and concern that I have the sudden urge to tell him what's happened. Instead, I flap a hand in front of my face. "It's hot," I say.

And perhaps it's his disinclination to further probe into what might be the uncharted territory of a menopausal woman, but he doesn't press me further, and simply reaches behind him to open the window.

The guilt burns my cheeks. In an attempt to hide my face, I reach down for a pen from my bag.

I've never lied to a patient before. I lied because he was desperate.

I lied because I wanted him to feel special.

I lied because I wanted to feel special to him.

"Any recent self-harm?"

"He still cuts regularly. But it's controlled. I'd categorize him 'low risk.'"

Robert thinks for a moment.

"Seems highly unlikely this man has got to adulthood without his defenses breaking down. What about his previous contact with mental health services? Any hospitalization in the past?"

And that's when it happens. That stricken, hollow feeling.

"I haven't seen his notes yet," I say.

There's a beat. Robert looks up, surprised.

"I keep missing the GP," I say. "There seems to be a problem with getting the notes from the previous practice. The one in Bristol. There was an admin person off sick." I hear the excuses. The edge of defensiveness in my voice.

"It sounds like an administrative error. The place in Bristol's a small single-handed practice," I add, "probably still operating with paper notes. In the process of updating to an electronic system. Welcome to the twenty-first century."

Robert nods. It feels cursory. "Well, as you know, it would be useful to get hold of them," he says, looking directly at me, "as soon as possible."

I feel admonished. Unprepared.

Perhaps it's my guilt, my keenness to shift away from the thing I have not done well, but I find myself moving on to the film references. And as I do, it strikes me that I am using them in the session with Robert in much the same way that Dan does in his sessions with me. A barrier. A block to feeling exposed.

"I'm still struggling with all these film references," I say, flipping open my file. "I feel pulled in. I'm still finding them confusing. I said I felt they were a distraction."

"How did he respond?"

"He was angry. Said if I paid more attention to the films, I might find them a revelation."

"A *revelation?*"

"Yes."

Robert asks me to list the ones I remember.

"They seem so random," I say, "mostly old films. Classics. Not much that's recent—last session he talked about *Sophie's Choice*," I say, "then there was *Dead Poets Society*. *Ordinary People* he's mentioned a few times. He's writing up an essay on it. *Thelma and Louise*," I add, remembering his trip to West Wittering, which I'm now not sure he ever took.

"There are others—I don't really remember. Early on, there was *One Flew Over the Cuckoo's Nest*," I say. "He mentioned Billy something or other, he likened himself to this character, after he'd had the severe panic attack in our session. Each time, I'm busy trying to remember the film and he's whoosh—he's on to something else—and yet, I keep being drawn back to them as if—"

"Billy Bibbit," Robert interrupts, "the character in *Cuckoo's Nest.*"

I nod. "That's him."

"I don't know all the films," he says, "but I know this one very well. He's a patient. And along with others, he's given a new lease on life when the McMurphy character, Jack Nicholson, comes into the ward. At the end, Billy sleeps with one of the girls McMurphy has smuggled in. He's made to feel dreadful shame by Nurse Ratched. She tells Billy she'll have to tell his mother. For Billy, it's the very worst thing. The shame, the notion of both disappointing her and being rejected by his mother, is too much. He kills himself."

I'm startled by his words. "Kills himself?"

I'm in the conversation, making all the rights sounds and noises, but my desire to leave the room is so intense, I'm not really concentrating at all. The information that he gives me does not land. Instead, it floats off, as my mind stays firmly focused on the clock behind his head.

"See if you can get a push on those medical notes," he says as we both stand up. "I can't help feel there's a piece missing."

I move toward the door.

"Let's make another time," he says.

When I open my bag, I see I've forgotten my diary. "I'll call you with a date."

"Take care," he says, as I step outside.

FOURTEEN

I'm at home when I see the email from Julie. She's taking Nicholas to a music event at the South Bank the next day—in the afternoon. Short notice—but would you like to meet us for coffee afterward? My heart leaps. I feel a surge of joy. A rush of excitement. I have to stop myself from replying straightaway, in case my eagerness scares her off. I type back a reply. Then delete it. I write a more measured version. Thank you. That would be lovely. I look forward to seeing you both. Let me know when and where. Ruth.

It's a beautiful spring day. We've agreed to meet by the "beach," a long trough of sand by the Thames, but I wake with a nervous kind of anxiety. I get dressed, then get changed again. In the end, I change my outfit three times. I want to take a gift for Nicholas, and in the toyshop that morning, I peruse the shelves, agonizing over what to choose. I feel nervous about being too ostentatious, and equally so about getting something he might not like. Eventually, I settle on a bright yellow plastic digger. My indecision continues as I wrestle over whether to wrap it or not. In the end, I buy tissue paper and a gift bag patterned with brightly colored cats. My hand is clasped tight around the handle as I walk down the steps toward the river.

The sunny afternoon has brought everyone out, and in the throngs of people my panic shifts away from the choice of gift to the fact that we might simply not find each other and meet up at all. I feel a rising concern that I'll have forgotten what Julie looks like. When I try to picture her sitting in the café that day, I can't remember her face. I scan the crowds, nothing. Then, from my elevated position on the steps, I see her.

She's some way off, by the stalls of food, pushing the buggy. She's wearing a patterned dress and flip-flops. There's a man next to her. Frank, I think, as she stops to hug him. I feel a pang. A pull in my chest for Tom. They have a brief conversation. Then he leans down to kiss Nicholas before moving off in the other direction.

We sit on a bench on the edge of the big sandpit. It's awkward at first. Nicholas hides his face in her lap. But as Julie unpacks an assortment of plastic toys to play with in the sand, his shyness is eclipsed by curiosity. There's a green trowel, a blue rake, and a series of multicolored cups that fit inside one another. To my great relief, no digger appears. There's a water tap close to the bench, and Nicholas crawls over to fill the cups, waves at me from the safety of the tap. I wave back and offer to get us coffee and cake from the kiosk.

The sun is dancing on the water and the usually sludge brown of the Thames looks silvery and bright. The place is packed with faces that are uplifted by this unexpected warmth so early in the season. Coats have been discarded, shirtsleeves rolled up, and the tables are crowded with ice cream wrappers and cans of cold drink. The fountains are on and a trail of squealing children run in and out in underpants and T-shirts. As I carry the tray back, I suddenly see myself carrying cake on paper plates, meeting my grandson in the sunshine.

I feel it like a gently rippling wave. This is what it feels like to be normal.

When I hand over the gift bag to Nicholas, his face is a picture of wonder. For a long time, he simply grins and points at the pictures on the bag and makes car noises.

"Nuts about cars." Julie laughs. "Well, vehicles of any kind," she says, as my excitement grows. I reach in for the gift and hand it over. Julie helps him unwrap the tissue paper. Instantly, his face lights up. He looks at his mum, then me, back and forth, like he can't quite believe his luck, his good fortune.

"For you. For Nicholas," I say, patting his hand.

"Brrrr," he says loudly, as he wheels it along the ground. He squeals when he realizes the digger bucket moves up and down and he quickly pushes it into the sand. He scoops and empties, over and over again, making an accompanying creaking noise. Each time he extends it to its full height, he laughs and claps his hands, as if astonished by his expertise. When he smiles, it's like watching the opening of a flower. His face is wide open, aflame with joy.

"Thank you," Julie says. "What do you say, Nicholas? Thank you. Ta," and she presses her hand to her lips. He looks at me, and copies his mum. A small pudgy hand planted clumsily on his mouth. He throws it forward, showering me with kisses.

My cheeks glow, and my heart swells, and the sudden rush of joy makes me giddy.

For the next hour, he crawls around in the sand, and I kneel down to join him.

"Why don't you have a break? Sit back on the bench. I'll play with him." I nod toward the paperback poking out of the top of her bag. "You could read for a bit?" She looks uncertain, then coaxed by my insistence, and my own recollection about how hard it was to have a break, she nods gratefully and picks up the book.

She's only a few feet away, and every now and then he crawls over to her and passes her something, to check on her, to feel safe, and to reorient himself. Though, for the most part, it's me and him, playing in the sand on a sunny afternoon. He comes back and forth with a green cup, fills up the blue, and comes back again, empties both in the well of sand he has made with the digger. He watches solemnly as the water drains away, then repeats the sequence all over again. I remember my own children doing the same. That safety, that certainty of repetition. Perhaps she sees it on my face. "*Peppa Pig*," she laughs. "We broke our record last night. The same story, eight times in a row."

I think of *Tom Rabbit*. How for weeks, it was the only story Tom wanted to read.

"What?" she says, as she sees the memory flicker across my face.

I smile and shake my head, turning back to Nicholas.

On it goes, until he directs me to a new patch of sand, a bit farther away, where we begin all over again.

"You've got a fan," she laughs, as he pats me on the knee. "He's not always so friendly with strangers," and then she stops short, looks embarrassed at her choice of word.

I pretend not to notice.

"The digger seems to have gone down well," I say. "Tom used to love his cars and diggers. Was never happier than when he was making a traffic jam out in the garden."

That's when it happens. Perhaps it's the combination of my

memories mingling with the physicality of this small, beautiful boy in front of me. The collision of the past and present. My own nostalgia laced with the feel of him; his sandy hands on my knees, his fingers on mine, and the slosh of water as it spills over my hands. Still, it takes me by surprise. The tears fall like rain. They drop soundlessly down my cheeks. I feel raw, like I have been suddenly unzipped, and opened out onto the sand.

"Ooh," Nicholas says, pointing at the small pockmarks in the sand, "ooh," he says again.

He looks up at me, trying to find the source of the water. His look of curiosity becomes one of concern as he comes over and pats my cheek. Then he begins to find it funny, watching these small raindrops of water landing in his construction site. He laughs. A gurgle that rises up from his throat and explodes across his face in a rush of laughter. Soon, I am laughing, too, as the tears still fall.

Nicholas leans in and scoops up the patches of wet sand with the digger scoop, giggling as he pours them into a separate pile, introducing a new dynamic to his game.

I pat my bag and pockets for a tissue. Julie produces one instantly. "Always have tissues at the ready," she says. I take it gratefully.

"I'm sorry," I say, "I—" but she's waving away my words.

"Tom. He seemed a lovely person," she says quietly. "Gentle. Thoughtful. Something special about him. I wish I'd got the chance to get to know him better."

I nod, dabbing at my face.

Perhaps it's an attempt to reduce my own embarrassment, but she talks about the loss of her mother. Her recent unexpected sadness. "It was so long ago," she says, "but I've been struck by it, sometimes out of the blue. That missing of her. Like an ache. It floors me sometimes."

I nod. I don't need to tell her I know exactly what she means.

"It's a funny mix. It's missing her, but it's also a sadness about her missing this," and she nods toward Nicholas. "She would have loved him, and then I feel sad for him, missing out on her, as his grandmother."

She looks away. I can see she feels she's said too much.

There is more digging and scooping, then at four o'clock, she looks at her watch and tells me she's meeting Frank and Jess in twenty minutes by the steps of the station. I feel apprehensive about saying good-bye. Julie gathers up the toys and then reaches down to put Nicholas into the buggy, maneuvering the straps carefully around hands that are tightly clenched around his yellow digger. We walk slowly together, past the theater, then along the main road.

"I'm glad we met," she suddenly says.

And perhaps it's this comment, this small opening, that gives me the confidence to ask.

"I was wondering," I say, my voice tentative, "you said his birthday was coming up. I wondered if I might send him something. For his birthday? Something in the post?"

There's a beat. Suddenly, I feel embarrassed, intrusive. "Or perhaps I can give you something—next—another time." I feel clumsy. Like the words are too big in my mouth. Like I've been too eager. As I look down, I feel her hand on my arm.

"That's really kind of you. Of course," she says. "Let me give you my address."

I don't know why I do it. Instead of entering it on my phone, I flip open my wallet and take out the photo. "I'll put it on the back of this," I say.

Perhaps it's what she said about her own mother, and my own need to step into her shadow and show how much Nicholas means to me. Perhaps it's also something about the accidental nature of our meeting; the fragile nature of our burgeoning relationship that means it feels too formal to simply type the address into my phone. Perhaps I want to imbue everything about our contact with a sense of ceremony and of secrecy. But perhaps, too, it's an affectation, born out of my own need to assume a false sense of connectedness to a child I have met only twice. It may be any, or all, of these things. Either way, it is something I will come to regret. A small act that will come to haunt me.

"Ah," she says, smiling over at the picture. "I'm glad you like that one, one of my favorites."

I write the address down and pop the photo back in my wallet.

She stops some way from the station steps. "Thanks for this afternoon," Julie says, "and for the digger!" and she reaches in to give me a warm hug.

As I kneel in front of Nicholas, he lurches forward into my arms, and I feel his soft peachy cheek against mine. As they walk away, I look up and see Frank by the steps, staring at me.

A few days later, the text comes through.

> It was lovely to see you on
> Saturday. Thought you might like to
> know that the digger is like a new
> member of the family.

She's attached some pictures. There's one with the digger perched next to Nicholas's bowl on the high chair. One with it clasped in his hand, mouth wide open as he's asleep in a car and the last one—tucked up in his cot, the digger on his pillow. His sweet peachy round face. Hair plastered across his face, fast asleep.

The second text comes in the next day.

> We're having a lunch for Nicholas's
> birthday on Friday 16th May 1—4 at the
> cafe on Balham Common. There's a little
> garden at the back. Just a small
> gathering. A few friends . . .

She mentions other babies from her antenatal class. That she'll totally understand if I have other plans. I don't think I even read the rest. My eyes glaze over as I stare down at the text, charged with a kind of energy and happiness I haven't felt since Tom disappeared. I'd like to say that I gave it more thought. But I didn't. I texted back straightaway.

> Thank you. I'd love to come.

Afterward, I would wonder about my decision not to tell David. I can put it down to the tenuous nature of the new relationship with Julie and our grandson. That there was something dreamlike about it, like a mirage, and that if I spoke the words out loud, it would be like getting too close, and the beautiful oasis might suddenly and inexplicably disappear. I wonder also if it was something selfish, too.

Something tight and withholding. Like a child refusing to share, and wanting to keep a present all to himself for as long as possible. This delicious gift that I want to keep unwrapping all by myself. The joy of having something that belongs to me. I flip open my purse and peer at the smiley boy in the picture. His fish-patterned shorts. Waving a sandy hand to the camera.

It's only after I have replied that it occurs to me it's a Friday. That given it's on the other side of London, I'll have to reschedule most of my patients that day. While I'm not sure what other appointments I have, I know I'll have to cancel Dan's regular slot at four o'clock, and prior to that, Hayley's first session back after her holiday.

I feel an instant stab of guilt. Apart from when I took extended leave, I can probably count on one hand the number of times I've canceled patients. A funeral . . . ill health . . . a tribunal. All sudden and unavoidable reasons. Emergencies. Did this constitute an emergency?

My actions and emotions that day have something of the furtive excitedness of a teenage crush. My focus is one-dimensional. All I am concerned about is clearing my path to my destination. My reasoning is measured and pragmatic. I conclude that there is enough time to reschedule. That I can offer him something sooner. That the inconvenience will be minimal. All this is true. But even Stephanie would now be able to tell me that such rational thinking has no place in our therapeutic realm. Any doubts are lost and buried under my pressing thoughts about first birthdays. My memory of the twins' first birthday at home. The relief when my mother was admitted into hospital and couldn't come; the first of her many rehab programs. My mind drifts onto the fervent question about what to buy for Nicholas's present. It takes a huge act of will not to send another text to press Julie for ideas.

Later that evening, I'm at my desk and I'm on the Missing Persons website. I check on Tom's profile. Nothing. I scan the others. Then I come to rest on Denis Watson. I click on his website. Perhaps it's the energy the family put into updating the website that pulls me in, their rigorous posting of pictures and updates. A life unfolding. There's a new picture. Denis's best friend—the one, I remember, who got married last year. His wife, Sarah, has had a baby. There's a picture of a man with a baby curled up on his chest, tiny, like a brooch. My eyes fill with tears.

When I'm back in the office, I write to Hayley and draft a letter to Dan, but then I decide to call him as well. On the second ring of his mobile, he picks up. I explain the need to alter one of his forthcoming sessions. "An unexpected appointment out of the office."

There's a pause.

"No problem," he says.

He sounds good. Jaunty even. When I offer up several alternative sessions, he opts for the soonest. I'm pleased. Coming sooner than he was due to come assuages my guilt. He's getting more, not less, is what I think. I confirm the date in the drafted letter and put it in the post tray. I'm ashamed to say, I think no more about it.

FIFTEEN

Tom's adolescence marked the moment when things broke down entirely in his relationship with David. Looking back, I can see it was on the cards, and while I was unable to recognize it at the time, I played my own part in the downward spiral. The more I smothered any hint of Tom's anxiety, the more irritated David became, and the more Tom withdrew. Equally, while Tom still had a tendency to fret unnecessarily about things, he was expressing a new exasperation in David, and in us as parents. The frustration about his life had a different energy about it. In a way, I saw it as a good sign, something that was appropriate to his age and perhaps simply linked to the stress of impending exams.

There was one row I remember particularly well. It was during one of my mother's visits from Taos. It was the trip when she told us that she'd got married. *"Married?"*

"To Ted." She nodded. "An arrangement," she added matter-of-factly. "My visa. Now I can stay and carry on with my work." *My calling,* was what she had said. She was now working at the rehab center. She also chaired a couple of AA groups in town, "twice a day," she said. "Sometimes more. We meet in cafés. Sometimes we sit in the desert. Under that big, wide Taos sky," she gushed. "We offer what people need. Whatever helps. Sometimes it's just about being there for people." She was excited, breathless with her evangelical desire to convert others to her abstinent ways. I had to look away.

The row between Tom and David was sparked by an item in the news about two young men climbing El Capitan, the famous rock in Yosemite in California. The men, both in their twenties, were planning to scale Dawn Wall, the sheerest side of the rock face. Their plan prompted news coverage about previous attempts to climb the rock and the twenty-one or more casualties it had produced over the years. David had no time for such risk taking. Citing the worry for friends and family, "Ultimately, it's selfish," he concluded. "One of them will probably die. I mean, what's the point?"

Tom was incensed. His face hardened. "If you think it's selfish . . . you just don't get it. Don't understand it at all."

My mother rarely listened in on conversations that didn't focus on her, but that day, she glanced up at the sharpness in Tom's voice. David looked back at his son in surprise. We were all in the kitchen, and I held back, stopping myself from getting involved. Carolyn was chopping vegetables for a stir-fry.

"I've read up about them," Tom said. "They've been climbing for years. They've planned for this particular climb for four years. *Four years,*" he repeated. "Can you imagine that level of commitment? Of planning. Of dedication—" His voice tailed off. That's when I saw it on his face. Envy. Aspiration. The desire to have that passion. Something similarly all-consuming in his own life, and with it, the simple admiration for those who do.

"And what about everyone else? The rescue services that will inevitably be called? The waste of money . . . the waste of life?"

Tom glared back at him. There were several moments of silence. Father contemplating son, and son contemplating father. At first Tom's look was one of disdain. It soon became something more akin to pity. "It's about being free," he said, "being out in the elements. At one with nature."

"Just like in Taos," my mother interjected. "Like living alongside nature. As if you've been invited in. It's all about the freedom," she said, stretching her arms out wide. You and me," she said, nodding at Tom, "we're so similar. Free spirits."

I closed my eyes briefly.

David ignored her. "What if one of them died? How do you think their parents would feel?"

Tom paused for a moment. Carolyn stopped chopping.

"It's possible—just possible," he said, "that as well as feeling sad—they might feel proud. Proud that their son had managed to find something that fulfilled him. That he died doing something he loved. Maybe they got how important it was to him?" Then, more pointedly, "Maybe they understood their son."

"They're twenty-six and twenty-seven. They're adults. They should know better," David muttered.

"And do what instead?" Tom shot back. "Work in a bank? Become an accountant? A lawyer? Teach *at a university*," he sneered, "enjoying all the trappings and privileges. The wine? The college dinners? Yep—all sounds a totally unselfish existence."

David snapped. "Well, until you've managed to find a way of

supporting yourself in dreamland, then I suggest you keep quiet about my career choice."

There was a stinging silence. Carolyn swung round. Tom looked appalled and I could tell David regretted it as soon as he'd said it. It grew not out of malice, but out of exasperation, a divide with his son that he didn't know how to repair. Tom just shrugged and left the room. By way of avoiding my recriminations, David followed him.

"Teenagers," my mother laughed. "He's stretching his wings. It's the same for a lot of the young people I see."

I was standing by the kitchen table, my hands on the back of a chair.

"I always encouraged you to do the same," she said. "And looking back, you probably should have taken a few more risks when you were his age."

I felt my hands grip the frame of the wood.

"Always such a homebody," she continued. "A worrier. Skulking round the house with that small frown on your forehead." She sighed. "I was always trying to get you out more—"

As she was shaking her head, I saw myself. A child, early teens perhaps, I don't remember. We were shopping for an outfit for a party. I had my heart set on a blue silky dress. "This is the one I like," I said, my fingers reaching for the shimmer of turquoise. She glanced over, her face a portrait of displeasure.

"Don't you like the green?" she said, holding up a dull, pond-colored shift.

"Not so much," I said carefully. "I prefer the blue."

Her head was shaking ever so slightly. "I think the green is *lovely,*" she said tightly. "It's my favorite color," and she held it up against me, triumphant, before taking it to the till.

"*Furrow your own field*, is what I used to say," my mother continued. "Do you remember?"

My hands ached. I could barely speak.

My mother was heading back to Taos the next day.

"Yes," I said. "I remember it well."

When I thought about Tom, of course, I understood that sixteen was a tricky time. It wasn't helped by the fact that David and Carolyn were forever in cahoots over her studies, their heads constantly huddled together at the kitchen table over books for her exams. And in many ways, the umbrella of adolescence became a relief, an excuse to hide behind to explain away his disaffected behavior. "Teenagers," people would nod sympathetically. "He'll grow out of it."

David withdrew. He was stressed, and over time, his anxiety became lodged in his body. As the cracks and fissures in his family continued to show, so he felt the failings of his body as he entered middle age. And with it came a localized worry about his own mortality and related physical signs and symptoms. Moles he was convinced were melanomas. A headache, a brain tumor. A sore throat, the early signs of throat cancer. There was never any way of talking about it. His concern was only assuaged by regular and anxiety-inducing hospital appointments that eventually gave him the all-clear. Once, after a CT scan had not detected a tumor, his jubilation was marred by a Google search that indicated there was a particular type of tumor undetectable by the traditional scanning equipment. It was only available privately, he discovered. This led to a lengthy debate about the merits or otherwise of private health insurance, which, after a career in the NHS, was an anathema to me. Knowing there would be nothing I could do to push against him, that it would be a decision he would make, I said nothing.

I could see what was happening. Everything, including his recent unsuccessful application for head of department, was being focused on his health. After what he'd thought was a good interview, the post was offered to someone younger and more dynamic, whom David described as "knowing jack shit about literature, but good with a spreadsheet." Sometimes at night, I'd see him in the dark, prodding and poking at a gland in his neck, his hand turning it into a cancerous lump as he worried it under his fingers. In his pocket, I found a receipt for a trip to the Mole Clinic for five hundred pounds. A GP friend had advised against it. "It's a business," he shrugged, "not a charity. It'll always be in their interest to find something they can hack out—at your expense. These places have their doors kept open by anxious patients with money to spend."

In the run-up to GCSEs, the house was tense. Carolyn was studious, conscientious, and organized regular study-group meetings with her wide circle of friends. She was sociable and led a full life, albeit curtailed for those months. I simply couldn't bear the gaping cavern that had widened between my children.

I spent hours helping Tom plan a study timetable and testing him on his subjects. I could see he was low, but rather than look at it, engage with it, contemplate it at all, I pushed on, with an intricate schedule of work, exercise, and healthy food.

"Let's just get through the exams," I said to David when he tried to intervene. Generally Tom allowed himself to be led by me, less out of enthusiasm than because it felt the path of least resistance.

Other times, he gave in to the heavy weight that he seemed to carry around with him and decided to "study in his room," and I let him be.

The exams came and went. Carolyn, I'd overhear giving a detailed analysis of each exam to her friends on the phone—she said little to us about any of it—but she seemed to sail through it. Tom was pretty much unreadable. Mostly he came home and disappeared up into his room. "That's what they all do," said one of the mums I bumped into. I pictured her son, Ben. A tall gangly boy with a mass of curly black hair, who was good at music. I imagined him downloading new tracks, strumming his guitar, and hanging out with his other lanky friends in his room. Once, when Tom left the door of his room slightly ajar, I saw him, lying on his bed, pale and still, just staring up at the ceiling in silence. I hurried along the landing, mostly wishing I hadn't seen him.

After the exams, Carolyn picked up her social life, which had been simmering away on the back burner. It was like turning the flame up on the gas. She was out all the time, fixing events with friends, playing hockey and football, going to parties and gatherings at other people's houses. Never our own.

One evening, she was on her way out, and I'd overheard what was a protracted and elaborate plan to choose a place to meet her friends. At the cinema, at the café, at the station. On it went. All the while, I was in the kitchen and Tom was next door in the living room, aimlessly surfing the channels on the television. Some minutes later, I heard him in the hall. "Just popping out." he said. "For a walk."

After the door closed behind him, I went to find her. I couldn't help myself.

"I just think if Tom had some good friends," I started, "like the ones you have. If he just had some people to hang out with—"

She stared back at me, her face unreadable.

"Then I think maybe things would be different for him."

Carolyn was putting on her coat, standing in front of the hallway mirror. After wrapping a silky scarf around her neck, she lifted the curtain of trapped hair and it fell about her shoulders like a fan.

She said nothing.

"You know—good friends. Some focus in life—"

Still nothing.

"Anyway, where are you off to?"

"A band," she said, "in Chalk Farm."

"Oh. I'm sure Tom would love that," I said.

She froze.

"He hasn't been out," I said, "for weeks. It just can't be good for him lolling around in his bedroom all day. I really think he should get out more."

Somewhere there was a question that Carolyn chose not to answer.

"Is it something you could take Tom along to?"

A cool moment of silence.

"No," she said. "He wouldn't like it." Then she turned slowly to face me. "But more importantly, nor would I."

"Sometimes it's good to think of someone other than yourself."

Her face was ablaze, but when she spoke, she kept her voice low and controlled.

"You've got to stop doing this," she said carefully.

"What?"

"Trying to compensate. Trying to do things he doesn't seem able to make happen for himself. Blaming me. He's not my responsibility. This isn't primary school. It's not like sorting out playdates that we had in Year Three. This is different. He's grown up. He's sixteen. It's so naive, and I'm sick and tired of being made to feel responsible for him. For his happiness, for his unhappiness. For making his life good. It's not my job."

She stopped and took a deep breath. "My counselor—" and there's a pause as she waits for the grenade to explode.

"Your *what?*"

"My counselor," she repeated with delight, "at school. She thinks you're guilty. Can't bear it that he's floundering and that's why you put it all on me. Can't bear the fact that I have friends. Have a life. It kills you. Sometimes I wonder if it would be easier if we were both a mess."

I was horrified. "A counselor? Why on earth do *you* need to see a counselor?"

As soon as the words came out of my mouth, I wanted to take them back.

There was a beat of silence. Carolyn opened her palms in an "I rest my case" gesture. Then she turned away and I heard the gentle click of the front door as she left.

It happened a few days later. It was a Thursday. June 24. From the outside, there was no trigger, no specific incident. I had been aware of Tom's low mood, of course, but hadn't seen, or was in denial over, the extent of it. Perhaps the yawning summer weeks after the exams were a factor. Who knows? It certainly wasn't just his sister having fun; the whole world seemed to be out in the sun, laughing, drinking, enjoying the summer. I suggested things for us to do together. He declined politely. In the absence of your own social life, it's doubly torturous to have one that revolves around your parents. We were eating dinner. I was talking about a film David and I were going to see. "You could come if you like. It's had good reviews," I said, nudging the paper toward him. He picked at his food, turning over the pasta as if he might find some answers underneath.

"Thanks," he said, shaking his head. "Think I'll stay in tonight," making it sound like it was an unusual occurrence. A night in, after so much social activity. Afterward, I turned that brief exchange over and over in my mind. Did he look any different? Was there a clue on his face? Was there anything I missed? Something in his voice I failed to notice?

We were home by eleven. The house was quiet. In itself, that wasn't so unusual. But generally, when we went out Tom watched TV in the kitchen, sprawled on the sofa with the dog. He wasn't there, and Hester was behaving oddly, disoriented somehow.

"Tom," I called out.

No answer.

"Perhaps he's gone out?" David said, but we both knew that was unlikely.

It was as I walked upstairs that I felt a deep sense of unease. A shift of something in my bones. When he wasn't in his room, I called again. No answer. The bathroom door was locked. I shouted and rattled at the door. Silence.

"Tom," I called.

Then I shouted for David.

I hammered on the door, calling his name. No sound. The dog was at my feet, anxiously moving from the door, then back to me, barking at my raised voice.

"It's locked," I said uselessly as David appeared on the landing. Perhaps it was the look on his face, but I felt something drop in my stomach, white and cold, like a stone.

It took David three shoulder rams to the door to break the lock. We found Tom lying on the floor on the bath mat, his face in a pool of vomit. He was unconscious, but still breathing. David called an ambulance. He relayed the instructions that were given to him by the switchboard. His hands shook as he gripped his phone. He spoke them out clearly and carefully and I repeated them and followed them with the diligence of a frightened child. We did everything they said—we kept him warm, we cleared his airways, we moved him into a recovery position. We were methodical in our silent terror. The two of us said nothing as we nodded and repeated the instructions out loud. Everything slowed right down. An aching cavern of time in which we were barely even breathing. As we waited for the ambulance, I sat small and still, my son's head cradled in my lap.

These are the things that wake me, even now. The hot thump of my heart. The sight of his blue lips. The anguish on David's face. Hester twirling round our ankles, yapping in panic.

The first hour was crucial, they said. It's what they say about missing children. But in our case, we had no parameters for our golden hour. When did it start and finish? After several hours at the hospital, we were told the vital signs were good. Carolyn came straight to the hospital. It was the first time we'd hugged for a long time. We said nothing, just held each other and cried. Tom was in ICU for three days, and on the third day he was well enough to be moved to a rehab ward. He was under the care of a psychiatrist, a Dr. Hanley, whom I'd met once through work. He was kind and conscientious, and most importantly, Tom seemed to like him.

The shock was like a hard shell. A suit of armor that moved me through the daily tasks of life in a metallic, robotic fashion. I got up. I drank coffee. I washed my body. I pushed food into my mouth. It was a week later, when Tom had been on the ward for a few days, that whatever it was that was holding me upright fell away. I was folding laundry at home in the bedroom, flapping out each item before sorting them into neat piles. A towel, a pillow case, David's shorts. Then, as I reached for Tom's green Fruit of the Loom sweatshirt and felt the familiar worn fabric under my fingers, my legs gave way. It was sudden and brutal, like I'd been kicked from behind. I fell to my knees. There were no tears. Just dry heaves that came from somewhere empty and hollow. They shuddered through my body, part sobbing, part retching, like the noise of an animal.

I took two weeks' leave of absence, giving the excuse of my mother's ill health "after a sudden fall." Of course, I didn't tell my mother the news. I could already hear her sighs of blame, and then even worse, her likely suggestions for his rehab. "We have programs here. Just get him on a plane."

Tom recovered physically, with no lasting damage, but he was quiet, subdued, and made no attempt to explain how he felt and what had happened. On the advice of Dr. Hanley, we didn't ask. Visiting hours were spent in an anxious haze; I jumped about like a rabbit, avoiding the shape of the thing neither of us could mention.

When I wasn't with him, I read books, I consulted specialists and sought out their advice. I learned everything there was to know about teenage suicide, but ended up learning next to nothing about my own son's attempt to take his life.

"It's not like a hat that's fallen from the sky and landed on his head," said David. I ignored him. I told him what I was doing. What I thought would help. "Ruth," he said wearily, "this isn't about you. You need to move out of the way."

All the tension became located between myself and David. How do other parents survive such things? How do people pick up their lives and carry on? The worst was what was left unsaid. The undertow of recriminations and blame built up into a corrosive and hard seal of resentment. We crashed against each other. Hard-edged, bitter, and hateful.

Carolyn was intermittently concerned for Tom, and silently furious with us. Or furious with me. The only thing that seemed to shift for the better was Carolyn's relationship with Tom. Almost overnight, they slotted back together, huddled in whispered conversations like they were kids again.

When Tom was discharged from hospital, he was referred to Child and Adolescent Mental Health Services and attended a day program at the local unit.

"You're lucky," the director said, "we've got a pilot program targeted specifically at people like Tom."

"People like Tom?"

"Teenagers who've tried to kill themselves."

We didn't tell many people. Those we did were kind, supportive. Each time, after saying the words out loud, there was always a small

204   • *Bev Thomas*

pause. Sometimes, there were questions to fill this pause. Sometimes, there were no questions. Just the flash of a look, like a small
dark shadow across a face.

Why? What happened? Why didn't you see it coming?

Without a logical explanation, we somehow became pariahs
overnight. As if, by association, their own families, their own flesh
and blood might also suddenly and imperceptibly fall between the
cracks. Mostly, I understood. People want answers when bad things
happen. I understood that fervent desire to understand something
completely. It was reassuring to find differences from their own situations, to convince themselves it could never happen to them. We
were all selfish, really. It was a natural instinct, a primitive desire to
protect your own. When they came looking for reassurances from
me, I refused to give them. I simply wouldn't do it. I had no explanation. I didn't know. I shook my head.

It could happen to any one of you was what I wanted to say, but I
knew that wasn't true.

Why? What happened? How has this happened?

It was like turning an alien object around in my fingers, trying to
make sense of it. What would be an easy explanation? *He was struggling with his peer group. He was anxious. He was depressed. It was the
pressure of exams.*

But lots of teenagers struggle with all these things.

Not many try to kill themselves.

The trauma did recede. It was, as I knew from the nature of my
work, physically impossible to stay in that heightened state of nervousness and shock. It gets replaced by something else. Sometimes
it's a sharp anxiety that takes your breath away. Sometimes it's more

grating, like the scratching of an animal at the door. I came to find a way to live and manage the constant worry. The *what-if? Is he all right? What's he doing? What's he feeling?* Given that, in my mind, Tom's mood that evening, that day, that week, and that month hadn't been any different from his mood on any other occasion, there was something deeply unsettling about this unknowability.

He went to rehab every day. It was a four-week program; it gave some structure to his summer, which was a relief, while Carolyn was busy Interrailing with friends around Europe. She sent him post-cards of different cities, Venice, Rome, Prague, and Budapest, and she made a point of ringing twice a week, on days she had prear-ranged with Tom. She rang on the landline, and we'd hear him dis-appear upstairs to his room to talk. He didn't say much about the rehab unit, and we were advised not to probe too much. A state of "detached interest" was what Dr. Hanley recommended, and I re-frained from asking how well he'd manage that if his own son had tried to kill himself. After a few days, Tom did mention Oliver, a boy he'd met in the unit. It was Oliver who introduced him to the book about Christopher McCandless.

At the time, I felt I had much to thank Oliver for. To my knowl-edge, *Into the Wild* was the first book Tom had read in two years. Not only had he managed to finish it, but it had sparked real inter-est and enthusiasm. There was something wistful about the way he talked about the book—and about McCandless. Tom was clearly gripped by the story, and he went on to read all the books that were quoted by Christopher—*The Call of the Wild* by Jack London, and books by Henry Thoreau. He talked animatedly about Christo-pher's brave decision to turn against commercialism. Giving away his trust fund to charity. Abandoning his car. Turning his back on convention. The pointlessness of possessions, of consumerism. The way Christopher embraced nature and a life out in the elements. His affinity with the outdoors. His bravery in living the life he wanted. "Alaska became the place that symbolized freedom for him." At first, I was pleased. He hadn't shown an interest in anything for a long time, so it was a struggle to maintain detached interest and not become overeager. It wasn't long, however, before the book, and this young man's life, became something of an obsession.

His care coordinator, a lanky, tall man called Declan with a soft Irish accent, said it wasn't anything to worry about. Often, he explained, there was a need to focus on something else very quickly after such a period of despair. *Despair?* In the past, as a child, Tom had fixations with things. Full-blown immersions in new hobbies or interests that were passionate, fervent, and utterly consuming. Then, like the flick of a switch, the interest would stop, and the piano, or the rock collection, or the telescope would remain untouched. It was almost as if, in his attachment to these external things, he was trying to find the answer to something much more profound in himself. To that extent, I wasn't particularly concerned by the introduction of Christopher McCandless into our lives. At first, I took it as another passing fad.

"It's all he talks about," I said as the weeks went on, during one of the key-worker sessions with Declan.

"Chris McCandless this, Chris McCandless that. Then he talked about someone called Alexander Supertramp. *Who's that?* I asked him. Turns out it's the same person. His *alter ego.* I mean, doesn't Tom need to be building himself up—not constantly quoting someone else? Someone who sounds like he's got a few problems of his own? How is that going to help develop his self-esteem?"

At home, Tom began to quote chunks of *Into the Wild* when debating issues with David. In answer to some of the arguments around consumerism between him and his father, he began to come out with some sentences he simply wouldn't ordinarily have said. I came to see afterward, when I read the book, that he was lifting passages straight from the text.

Declan shrugged. He was a man in his early forties, I supposed, yet he looked much older, ravaged by a lifestyle I didn't want to know about. But I was relieved, too, that whatever he did and said seemed to be helping my son. One day, when I was there for a family meeting, I spotted them out in the garden, talking cross-legged under the trees. Tom looked animated, deep in conversation. When I came over, he was quiet, sullen, and noncommunicative.

"It's normal," Declan reassured me. "He's working some things out."

And in any event, I was grateful. He seemed to be looking well. Coming out of himself at last, talking to someone outside of the family. I was crushed by my exclusion. And yet at the same time, I saw the benefits.

"There are worse aspirations," Declan said, when I spoke of my worries about the book at Tom's midprogram review.

"But the boy dies," I said.

"Yes," he nodded slowly, "although I'm not sure that's the point. Have you read it?"

I shook my head.

"Well, bits," I said.

"Do you perhaps see what Tom aspires to in Chris? Do you see what draws him to a young man like that? A man not afraid to tread his own path? To be happy with his aloneness? To be independent?"

"He leaves his family," I said. "They don't hear from him. He dies alone. He starves to death in an abandoned bus in Alaska. What part of that is good?" My voice trembled.

He is silent for a moment. "I suggest," he said, "that you read it all, putting yourself in Chris's shoes. What might it feel like to be Chris? Look for something else in the pages of that book. Look for what might have ignited something in your son."

I nodded. But of course, I didn't do what he suggested. Was I too worried, as I claimed to David? Or too inflexible? Too self-absorbed? Too attached to my view of the world? Or maybe I was simply too angry to be told what to do by a man I barely knew.

"I'm not sure about him," I voiced to David one night.

He was silent as I ranted about my concerns and worries.

"You hate the fact that someone else has got close to Tom."

I said nothing. Tom's copy of the book stayed unopened on my bedside table.

SIXTEEN

The time away was my idea. "It's a cabin," I said, "by a lake." Neither of these two facts inspired any great enthusiasm from the family, apart from Tom, who seemed mildly interested in getting out of London. "How remote is it?" he asked. "Does it have electricity?" and was disappointed to discover it did. I booked it anyway. Carolyn was just back from Interrailing and wasn't keen to be going away again. "I had plans to see friends," she protested. But Tom had finished his four-week rehab program and had a gap before starting twice weekly therapy in September—and we had ten days before the GCSE results. I felt it would be good to get away. A break, I called it. Not a holiday.

As we set off late afternoon, Tom started telling us how he'd seen the film of *Into the Wild*. "We watched it at the unit," he said. "We were all allowed to suggest a movie. Mine got picked." I can feel David's frustration as Tom talked in detail about the pros and cons of the book and the film. "The film's directed by Sean Penn. Really gave you a sense of the space. The sheer beauty of Alaska." Again, that wistful tone. "He'd been wanting to adapt the book for film for years, but the family had resisted." And on he went. His fixation showed no sign of abating. David said nothing, but fiddled with the radio, constantly switching channels to catch the traffic updates. I made the odd comment, trying to navigate the tricky path between showing I was listening to Tom while not "indulging" him in this single-minded obsession, but my words were vacuous and placatory. I saw this on Tom's face as he reached into his bag. For the rest of the way, we drove in silence. The kids were encased in headphones, Carolyn listening to music, Tom engrossed in a film.

The cabin was in a part of Devon we'd never visited. As David drove, I followed the owners' directions, through smaller and smaller villages, until we took a right turn by one of those old red postboxes buried in the wall. After a narrow twisting road through dense woodland, we reached the cabin. It was high up, nestled in the trees, and the only houses in sight were way across the valley, or down in the village. It was a simple wooden construction, and had once been the engine house for the slate quarry up the hill, winching the containers up and down. There was a deck out to the side that overlooked the deep rolling hill. A simple kitchen, a double room, and a small room with bunk beds. The kids hadn't shared a room since primary school. Perhaps they were tired from the journey, but I was struck that they didn't complain. Any disdain was directed toward the lack of wi-fi. We ate the fish and chips we'd bought on the way and went to bed. I lay awake wondering if this was a huge mistake.

In the morning, I rose early to see the rich green in the distance. I sat on the deck with a mug of tea, the sun warm on my face, and I watched the light on the trees and the hazy mist of heat as it moved across the sloping hills. Great golden lines of sunshine fanned out over the velvety valley. The only sound was the birdsong and the hum of bees. I laid out melon, bread, and jam on the deck and one by one the chairs were filled. I could see straightaway that Tom liked the place. He was eager to walk up and find the lake, the now disused slate quarry. He ate quickly and set off.

"Can we swim up there?" Carolyn asked.

I had no idea. "I can bring our swim stuff," I offered.

"I'll catch Tom up," she said, getting up and draining the rest of her coffee.

While the simple kitchen was fully equipped, there was a sink and draining board outside in the sunshine, and without any discussion, David washed and dried up outside, like he'd done on camping holidays we'd had when the kids were small.

The way up to the lake was a steep incline, and the old iron tracks that carried the slate trucks were still there, embedded in the wild undergrowth where the pulley had once winched the slate up and down the hillside. And as man had retreated, nature had taken over, to the extent that it seemed unimaginable that the place had once been a busy, thriving work site. The pathway was almost prehistoric in its color and the density of its foliage. Giant fans of ferns were uncurling like great beckoning fingers. Thick gnarled trunks were encircled with twisting ivy and the ground was carpeted with a soft and springy layer of moss.

"It looks like nobody's ever been here," Tom said later that morning, "like the land that time forgot."

Both David and I were breathless when we reached the top of the incline. The path that twisted through the trees was flat, and as we emerged from the woodland, we caught the first glimpse of the lake, spreading out before us, a deep jeweled green.

Tom was in the water, lying on his back.

"There's fish," he said excitedly, "carp and pike. We can catch some and cook food up here later."

There was a small wooden hut by the side of the lake where Carolyn changed, then myself and David. The sun was bright. Whorls of dust swirled in the shafts of sunlight that cascaded on the floor. Outside, there was the whoop of a bird and the gentle lapping sound of Tom swimming across the water. A shriek as Carolyn jumped in. Other than that, a still quietness. As I wriggled into my swimsuit, I caught David smiling at me, and at the door, he reached for my hand, pulled me to him, and kissed me. A different sort of kiss from the perfunctory pecks we'd exchanged in recent months.

The water felt crisp and clean on my skin as I pulled my arms back and forth. I twisted onto my back, squinted up at the clear blue sky. I felt surrounded by great bands of bright primary colors—the blue sky, the deep green lake. It seemed unreal, like we were encased in a child's drawing of a woodland scene. "It's the depth of the water," Tom explained, when I marveled at the color, "together with the angle of the sun at this time of year."

"We saw deer," Carolyn said as we dried off by the lakeside.

"A mother and fawn," Tom added, "just in the clearing before we got to the lake."

Carolyn sounded unsentimental. Perhaps too full of city cynicism to understand that such things were not run of the mill. It was only at the end of the week, when their sighting proved the only glimpse of these two beautiful creatures, that their faces seemed to glow when they mentioned it again, full of pride and wonderment for this moment they had shared.

No one wanted to leave the lake. It was creeping toward lunch-time and we were all getting hungry. In the end, David offered to go to the shops and get food.

"We'll do what Tom suggested," he said, "we'll eat up here today."

"Can you get bacon?" Tom said. "For fish bait?"

David laughed. "Will do. Might also get some sausages in re-serve. Just in case."

But there was a lightness in his voice. Devoid of the judgmental and cynical tone of recent months.

"Trust me," Tom said, "we won't go hungry," and together they made a list of things that would cook easily on a fire.

While David had gone, Carolyn and I spread towels on the rocks and read, outstretched in the sun.

Tom set himself the task of making us all fishing rods. He went off into the forest to collect wood. In a sealed tin in the hut, he found old penknives, a length of rope twine, and a couple of firelighters. While I was reading, I stole looks at him as he worked. I marveled at the time he took. The care, the way his fingers smoothed over the wood. The patience as he whittled the sticks. He made holes care-fully in the other ends of the rods. He unraveled the twine to pro-duce small lines that he threaded through the holes. It wasn't long before Carolyn joined him, and they sat hunched over together, their heads almost touching. I smiled as I recalled school holiday weeks spent at Forest Camps. "He's good with wood," they'd said.

"They're so beautiful," Carolyn said, her fingers stroking hers. "Thank you."

The handles were thicker and on each he'd carved our initials.

"So smooth and clean," I said, "just lovely."

Tom was beaming under the sun hat he had fashioned out of fern leaves. "Ash," he said, "always comes up so smooth. But—we'll see," and he nodded over to the lake. "The proof of the pudding..."

As instructed, David returned with potatoes to bake, bacon for bait, bananas, mangoes, chocolate, and tinfoil. I unpacked the crisps and wine and beer, but kept the two packs of sausages hidden in the bottom of the bag.

We all collected wood. Tom made a tripod. Built a fire without using either of the firelighters. He caught four fish, David two—but one got away—and Carolyn and I one each. Tom found wild thyme in the woods and we cooked the fish skewered on sticks that Tom had whittled to a fine point. We ate them with our fingers on shiny plates of enormous dock leaves, followed by baked banana and chocolate and slices of mango that ran down our chins.

Those first few mornings, I still woke with panic, momentarily gripped by the pressing worry about how the four of us would fill the yawning hours ahead. How would we rumble along until bedtime? What would we do? What would we talk about? We so rarely spent time together—and when we did, it was always fraught with tension and unspoken recriminations.

Yet somehow, over the course of the next few days, we sank deeper into the place. There was a slow, languid quality to time, a dreamy reflective state, like our lives had been dabbed with watery brushstrokes. There were no endless debates about schedules or about when and what we were going to do. We did the same thing every day, without discussion. The weather was relentlessly warm and sunny. We breakfasted outside, then made our way up to the lake, staying there until just before dusk. While we had identified the nearest pub, there was a general reluctance to go, one of us always finding a reason not to, until eventually we abandoned the idea altogether. Trips to the local store were made only out of necessity, and the planned trip to Exeter that had been suggested in the car on the way down was never mentioned again. Even David, who loved his fix of daily news, became less and less inclined to make the morning trip to the village shop for the paper. By Wednesday he concluded, "It's always going to be bleak. I don't think I'll bother."

In the cabin, the television reception was poor, so on our return from the lake, we sometimes played cards, or we watched a film from the old stack of DVDs in the cabin. They were old family movies—*Mrs. Doubtfire, Parenthood,* and *Indiana Jones*—ones that would have been disregarded if we'd been at home. Carolyn had her sketch pad and she did pencil drawings of us all. I displayed them on the windowsill in the cabin. I still have them pinned to the board above my desk at home; one of Tom whittling his sticks, David asleep in the sun, me reading lying on a rock. "These are really good," I said after she gingerly handed over the sketch pad. She said something about not being able to draw hands, but her face under her sun hat was so aglow with pride, it made me want to weep.

We took a couple of photos, but for the most part, the camera and iPhones lay discarded on the table. It was as if all of us had signed some unspoken treaty to avoid any intrusion of the modern world that might break the spell we had created. We moved gently through the simple domestic chores. Laying the table, sweeping the floor, washing the dishes outside in the sun, all these tasks became ritualistically slow and enjoyable. One day, chopping up fruit to make a fruit salad, I noticed the feel of the fruit under my fingers; the sleek shine of the apples, the thickness of a mango and the hard callousness of the pears, the dimpled skin of an orange. My fingers lingered over these different textures as I chopped methodically, looking out over the sunny hillside. Tom was on the grass reading, his long hair flopping down over his face. Something happened to me that week. Something happened to all of us that week.

We became the best of ourselves.

I have never found relaxation easy. The need to be useful pumps through me like blood through my veins. Relaxation wasn't a feature of my life growing up, and I had simply never learned the habit. In pockets of empty time, I was always moving on to the next thing before I had finished what I was doing. The simplicity of the cabin soothed me. A small functional kitchen. A table outside to wipe down. A wooden floor to sweep. We wore the same clothes every day. We lived on little, needed little, and somehow it made us gravitate toward, rather than away from each other. All our rough edges rubbed away. We were four smooth pebbles tumbling along the shoreline.

I stopped wearing earrings and makeup. I pulled my hair back into a ponytail. I caught the sun on my face. My freckles appeared. Carolyn's, too. And in two days, Tom turned a deep shade of brown, his hair bleached blond in the sun.

"You're so lucky," Carolyn said, flicking his back with her sun hat, "look at the color of you—I'm like a mottled tomato."

Tom laughed. "Come on, tomato face, let's take the boat out," and I watched as the two of them pushed the small wooden boat away from the sandy bank into the lake. Tom rowed, while Carolyn languished at the bow, her fingers trailing in the flat green water. Pretty soon, he dropped the oars and let the boat drift along the bank. I listened as he read from his book, quoting passages out loud. "*Nature was here something savage and awful, though beautiful,*" he said. "*Think of our life in nature—daily to be shown matter, to come in contact with it—rocks, trees, wind on our cheeks! The solid earth. Contact. Contact,*" he shouted, dramatically, laughing as he beat his fist against his chest. "*Who are we? Where are we?*" and he suddenly stood up in the boat, so Carolyn shrieked. "Henry Thoreau," he said, flipping the book closed. "One of Chris's favorites. Amazing stuff, eh?" And for once, I think we all agreed.

Away from home, the twins were able to avoid their usual points of difference and allowed themselves to be who they once were. Carolyn, who I imagined would quickly tire of life in the woods, seemed, in fact, to revel in it. As the days wore on, she allowed Tom to take center stage, like an actor stepping aside for the understudy, who, nervous at first, then shone brightly in the spotlight. He showed her how to whittle wood into a point. How to carve a design with the knife. "No," he said, moving her fingers gently around the knife, "more like this movement." He taught her how to build a fire and to light one without matches. On Thursday, when he said he was going to spend the night in the small wooden shack by the lake, I was surprised when Carolyn asked if she could join him.

We all saw a new confidence in Tom. In the hustle and bustle of our everyday life, he constantly found himself in situations that demanded things from him that he could not give. Even David and Tom developed an unprecedented ease between them. Away from the points of usual contention, they were stripped back, like the pale, carved pieces of his wood, to father and son. David, away from the pomp and status of college life, wore shorts and an old T-shirt. They gathered kindling together and chopped logs for the fire. David, for his part, was able to see Tom in his element, to marvel at the skills none of us had really seen before.

It seemed hard to believe what had happened just six weeks earlier. That bleak place he'd been. And perhaps what was also suspended in that week was my sense of reality. The cabin by the lake enabled me to pretend that things were fine. Those awful moments that I revisited in the dark hours of the night—the rush up the stairs, my thumping heart, David's shoulder hammering against the bathroom door; I could pretend for those seven days that none of it had happened. I could look at that green jewel of a lake and blink it all away.

On the day when David had to make a trip into civilization to send a work email, the three of us took a walk. It was Tom's idea to follow the stream that was below our cabin, "Check out how close we can get to the source," he suggested. We found a path alongside the gushing, bubbling water. We crossed rolling green hills dotted with sheep and scampering lambs, tracking the stream until it came out into the open field. Ahead was a large farmhouse and an odd movement in the distance, up and down between the trees.

"Look," I said, pointing, as we got closer. "It's a boy—on a trampoline."

The garden was large. The boy wore jeans, his chest was bare. Next to me, I felt Tom tense up at the sight of another human being. His torso was thick, muscular. He was not a boy. He was a teenager, and when he caught sight of us, he waved. "Do you want a go?" I felt Carolyn's enthusiasm, a surge forward, just as Tom flinched back.

"Let's head to the lake," he said. "We can go for a swim." We all agreed. For Carolyn and me, there was something mesmeric about the sight of the boy twisting and turning and flipping like a bird through the air. For Tom, the boy seemed a threat, a source of anxiety. A reminder of all the things he was not.

What perhaps we all realized, but did not want to acknowledge, was that Tom excelled in situations away from people. He shone when he was alone. It was something I found unbearable. Perhaps for someone who has spent her life inextricably entwined with the lives of others, it was incomprehensible. I needed others, relied on them, and so his isolation seemed a failing, not a source of strength.

It was a concept I found so alien it scared me.

The morning we were due to leave, I woke with a profound sense of dread. The thought of leaving was like an ache, a sharp pain in my chest. I felt tearful as I folded the clothes and wiped down the wooden breakfast table. While David and I cleared up, the twins went up to the lake for the last time. Perhaps it was my wanting to parcel up what had happened, perhaps it was my wanting to defend against what would come with our inevitable return to London, but in trying to celebrate what had happened with Tom, I was turning it into something else.

"Wasn't it great," I said, "to see Tom whittling the wood? Catching fish at the lake? Did you see," I continued, "how he lit a fire without matches? And that raft from the logs . . . the tripod for the fire . . . It was like one of those reality shows in the jungle. He'd have done well in one of those," I laughed. It was stupid. Of course, he wouldn't actually have coped well with all those people. I was describing it all to David as if he hadn't been there at all. It was clear from his silence what he felt.

David nodded, but he said nothing, and I should have left things well alone. Instead, I rambled on, as if by talking about Tom I could capture the essence of him, preserving him as one might a small, rare plant in resin. "Amazing," I said, "how he managed to make a raft. A raft!"

It was then he snapped. "Jesus, Ruth. What the fuck's wrong with you? Six weeks ago, he was facedown in a pool of his own vomit. Excuse me for not being excited over a Bear Grylls Adventure," he spat. "Shall we crack open the champagne because he can take a crap in the woods and whittle a few sticks?" His eyes were blazing. "Nothing's changed," he said. Then he looked squarely at me. "Nothing's ever going to change—is it?"

We packed silently. The twins returned, and as we'd asked, Tom had brought back the hand-carved fishing rods and laid them outside the cabin to take home. When David reversed the car to load up the boot, there was the unmistakable sound of splintering wood.

"What the bloody hell was that?" shouted David, as he leaped from the car.

"Dad—," Carolyn shrieked, as she ran to the back of the car and picked up the broken pieces of fishing rod. "Look what you've done!"

"What on earth did you put them there for?" and he swung around to Tom.

Tom glared back at him and shrugged. "Not going to be much use in London anyway." He picked up the pieces and hurled them into the woods; they made a clattering noise as they tumbled down the valley.

"I wanted to keep mine," Carolyn said, turning a piece of splintered wood over in her fingers, and it wasn't clear whether her sadness and anger were directed at her father or Tom.

"Stupid place to put them," David muttered under his breath.

That was when I began to think Tom had left them there deliberately. As if he knew that, just like him, they had no place in London.

On the way back in the car, I talked about the week, how perfect it had been. "We should come back." While everyone was quick to agree, I knew it wasn't something that we could ever replicate. What I didn't know then was that it would be the last time we would be away together as a family.

Before we got to the motorway, I suggested stopping at a country pub on the way home. "We could get some lunch. Enjoy the last of the sunshine." I heard my voice as they did. Too jaunty. Too jolly. Needy and irritating. There was little enthusiasm for the idea.

"I have some stuff to do," Carolyn said eventually, and David concurred, said he'd rather get back. "I need to check in on emails before the onslaught of Monday."

Tom said nothing.

We drove back mostly in silence.

As we turned off the motorway and began the drive across London, I felt an ache for the family we had been.

SEVENTEEN

Dan is late for his appointment. While I'm waiting, I place a call to the Bristol surgery. When I ask the receptionist about the notes, she tells me she's just sent something across to the Hackney practice. "Can you forward it to me?" I ask. But of course, I know she can't. She's only authorized to pass the information to his new GP—so she refers me back to Dr. Davies. I then leave a message for her to send it on to me.

It's half an hour into the session when he arrives. He looks pale and agitated and sits small and hunched in his chair. There are dark shadows under his eyes and a fresh bandage on his wrist.

"Talking about it all," he says, "lifting the lid on it . . . the feelings were really hard." His words are clipped. "I tried to resist." His eyes fall to the bandaged hand in his lap. "But the voice got louder."

"The voice?"

"Haven't I told you about the voice?"

"No," and I feel a sudden chill. "What voice?" I ask.

He shrugs. "Hers, I guess. Mary Tyler Moore," then seeing the look on my face, "my mother," he says quietly. "*The wrong one died* is what it always says. I felt anger for the first time. I felt furious. I felt glad she lost the thing she loved. Glad she lost Michael. Glad that she was punished by his death." His words come out in a rush. "But feeling those things wasn't enough. I didn't know what to do with them. I cut myself. Just a bit. It didn't work. Didn't make me feel better like it usually does. I needed something else. I thought about what you said," and as he looks up at me, I feel suddenly alert. Wary. "About not keeping it all in here," and he presses his bandaged hand to his belly. "I called her."

"Your mother?" I feel a creeping sense of unease. Free floating. Nonspecific. Like a dusting of something.

He nods. "I knew she wouldn't have moved. I rang the same number. It was strange hearing her voice after all these years."

"What happened?"

"When she picked up, I didn't answer. She said *hello?* a few times. Then I put the phone down. I think it would be better to see her face-to-face. It's not a conversation I can have on the phone. I need to go to Bristol."

I can see that we only have ten minutes left in the session. His plan worries me. We don't have much time. I need to find a way to share my unease, without lecturing him.

"I can discuss things with her," he continues. "You know—an eye for an eye," he says tightly.

"An eye for an eye?"

He nods.

"If people have been negligent, they deserve to be punished. Don't you think?"

"You're talking about revenge? A sense of retribution for what happened to you?"

"All this stuff," he says, nodding around the room, "it was better when it was packed away."

He sounds breathless. Panicky.

I acknowledge how the coping mechanism had worked for him before. Now things have been opened, they feel out of control.

"Being attacked in the park has opened the floodgates," I say. "Flashbacks from that incident—but perhaps more significantly, from your childhood. These are very complex feelings. Things have become muddled and confused, and can feel very difficult."

His hands are twisting in his lap.

I tell him to imagine a chest of drawers. Drawers opening randomly, the contents of clothes spewing out all over the floor.

"As fast as you try to clear them up," I say, "another drawer flies open and there is more mess. More chaos."

I tell him that the idea is not to get rid of the mess. Not to change the life he has had. It's the cards he's been dealt. Instead, the aim is to have some control and order over it.

"The purpose is to open a drawer yourself, when you want to. Look inside. Rummage around with the contents. Place them neatly back, or mess them up, whatever you want."

He's looking at me intently.

"But the point is—you will be able to close the drawer when *you* want to."

He seems to settle, to like this concept. The image of the chest of drawers.

I see his hands relax in his lap. Something has shifted. In a short space of time, I have turned things around. I feel relief. A small flash of pride.

"At the moment, it feels as messy as fuck," he says and shrugs. "And like I can't clear it up on my own."

I nod. "I understand," I say, "and I'm not saying this will be easy. Or that it will be something that happens overnight. It's the very process of looking back, getting the contents of the drawer out, examining it carefully, understanding the messy feelings that have been locked away, that is the focus of our work *together*. I will be here to help you."

He is staring at me with a fierceness I haven't seen before.

There's a silence.

"So," he says, "not a good idea to turn up on her doorstep?" His tone is lighter. He smiles.

I smile back.

"It's not my job to advise," I say. "What I do say to people is that when you are full of a strong feeling—when you have perhaps connected to a feeling that you have shut away—such as rage or anger—it can feel very uncomfortable and unfamiliar. The desire is to quickly get rid of it. I would urge caution."

I talk with him about how cutting and hurting himself has served this purpose in the past, that these overwhelming feelings have been kept at bay, but now something has changed. "The wound will not close up," I say, "the trauma is wide open. What worked before won't necessarily work anymore. You need a new way."

"A new way," he repeats, as if trying to understand the concept.

We talk about his desire for revenge. How it shows he is in touch with his anger. I tell him I can't say whether it's right or wrong to see his mother further on down the line. What I do know is that it is helpful to wait. To hold on to the feeling—and the desire to act.

"I suggest suspending any action until you've had a chance to open the drawers. Put the things back in the way you want to."

He's nodding.

"I'd like to suggest that you work through the feelings here. *With me*. Bring them here. Direct them here."

The mother he didn't have, was what Robert said.

And as he nods, he fixes me with such a stare that I have to blink, then look away.

It's a moment I will come to look back on. To turn over and over in my head. *Direct them here*. The intense look on his face. *An eye for an eye*.

When I tell him it's time, that we need to finish, he looks calm. His breathing is measured. His face relaxed.

"Thank you," he says. "That was good. Really helpful." He stands up.

"See you next week," he says. "And good luck."

I frown. I don't know what he's talking about. My face is blank.

"Your appointment? Next Friday. Out of the office?" he says as he reaches for his rucksack.

I don't know, for a moment, what he means.

"But I'll be seeing you on Thursday?" I say.

"Yep, of course," he says, tapping a hand to the side of his head.

As he leaves, I feel a pull of something. A small snag. Like the thread of a jumper caught on a nail, gently unraveling as I walk away.

THAT EVENING, I'm looking for a film to watch and I come across *Ordinary People*. I feel uneasy as the movie begins. A boy, not unlike

Tom, trying to settle back into his home life after a suicide attempt. I am transfixed. How can I have forgotten this film? Mary Tyler Moore and Donald Sutherland. Her brittle departure at the end. It reminds me of what Dan said he liked, *the inevitability of the ending.* I sit for a moment watching the credits. Her grief is like a boulder. Tears are streaming down my cheeks. I find myself thinking of Dan and his mother—and the similarities between Mary Tyler Moore's preference for the son who died. Lovely, handsome, talented Bucky. Her love, her joy for her older son. It's so obvious why Dan chose the film as his project. How it spoke to him and his experience. *A revelation.* It's only then that my mind drifts to the other films he's talked about. I can't remember them all, but the ones he's mentioned recently come to mind. *Cuckoo's Nest . . . Sophie's Choice.* And it's only when I think of *Thelma and Louise,* and that final freeze frame of the Thunderbird, that I gasp and make the link. I quickly look at my watch. It's too late to call Robert, so I email him instead.

"The films," I type, "they are all linked. Linked by suicide."

ROBERT'S CALL COMES in first thing Monday morning.

"I'd been thinking about your case," he says, "even before I got your email. Do you have some time to talk now?"

I have fifteen minutes before my first patient.

"I was left with something," he says, "after our last session. A sense of shame. It was in the room with us. Between the *two of us.*" He's speaking slowly and carefully.

I feel myself redden.

"It was focused on the notes, but it was palpable. Something very powerful in the counter-transference. Something about shame. It got me thinking about *his* shame."

I can't tell him that the shame was real. That it *was* in the room. But that it was *my* shame. My shame about the notes. The lie. I don't know what to say.

"The notion that his mother despised him," he says, "is this his perception? Or real? I feel this might be linked to his shame. The missing piece? The something else you felt he hadn't told you?"

"But what about the films," I ask suddenly, "the suicide link?"

"I don't know," Robert says quietly. "I think we should keep an open mind."

I feel a sudden stab of irritation that he's not taking it as seriously as I imagined.

"Tell me about your last session with him."

"He got in touch with his mother. He just rang her."

There's a silence on the end of the phone.

"They didn't speak. He hung up. He was very distressed. Angry. Let down. Confused about his feelings for her. He cut himself," I say. "But he said it didn't help."

Robert is quiet for a moment.

"His defenses are breaking down," he muses.

"I advised waiting," I say, "before making further contact with his mother. To talk things through in the sessions with me."

"Well done," he says.

There's a pause.

"Any news on those notes?"

"Chased them up last week," I say, relieved to have made the calls.

"Good. Let's arrange a session. To talk further. He's going to need a lot of containment. He's a complex chap," he says.

I hear the sound of pages flicking in his paper diary.

"I have a slot this Friday. Any good?"

"I'm actually on leave," I say. "How about early next week?"

When we've agreed on a time, he asks if I'm away for the weekend.

"No," I say, "just the day off. A family birthday."

"Enjoy," he says. And then, "Take care of yourself."

FOR THE REST OF THE WEEK my attention is on getting to Friday, and Nicholas's birthday party. After deliberating long and hard about a present, I go up into the loft and find Tom's old cars. There's a complete set of metal Dinky cars—all still in their cardboard boxes. I feel a pang as I remember Tom's fastidiousness, the care he took over his toys and belongings. As the day draws closer, I frequently find myself opening my purse and looking at the picture of the small boy, sitting on a beach in his gingham hat, patting his hands on the sand. So often, I've felt the burn of envy when I see other people casually open their wallets or purses. In my grimmest days, it has felt willful, punishing. Salt in the wounds of my own broken family. One afternoon, in the café across the road from the unit, I am standing in the queue, and I find myself opening the wallet flap of my purse unnecessarily. I hold it open as I pass over my coins. Not closing it even after I have reached across for my coffee. Look at me. Look at my life. Look how normal I am. As if by saying it loud enough to those who might listen, I might start to believe it myself.

OUR FAMILY HARMONY was short lived. I knew it would be, but not that it would end so abruptly. Back at home, Tom's mood darkened. The GCSE results were predictable. Carolyn couldn't have done any better, and if anything, Tom exceeded expectations, but still needed to retake three exams. It was agreed he'd do these, and defer A-levels for a year. It wasn't long before our trip to Devon seemed surreal, a holiday that had happened to another family that we once knew. It was as if the isolation at the cabin had heightened Tom's sense of his inadequacies in "the real world." A reminder that the stiff, uncomfortable coat of his real life increasingly didn't seem to fit. I wonder if, looking back, he simply decided he wasn't going to force his arms into the sleeves of the coat anymore.

It was a few weeks after the half-term break when I came back from work to find him in the kitchen. He didn't look up as I came in, and spoke quickly.

"I haven't been to college," he said, "not since half term. I just can't."

He was hunched forward over the table, digging his thumbnail into the grain of the wood.

He looked pale, thin, and very tired.

I clicked on the kettle and braced myself against the worktop. For the past two weeks, he'd been leaving for college in the mornings. Then after supper, retreating to his room to do his coursework.

"It's difficult," I said gently, "to get back into work mode after a break."

Absentmindedly, I reached for the slab of leftover lasagna and a fork, and ate a mouthful. It was cold, like a boulder in my mouth. I swallowed it down.

"I bumped into Finn's mum the other day. On the Tube."

Tom sat very still. I picked up the fork again.

"Finn's joined the football team at college. She said the new coach was very welcoming—you know," I nodded, "to new players—"

"I can't go back to college," he said flatly.

I put down the fork.

"Perhaps I could come in? Speak to your tutor?" Already I was turning around, glancing at the calendar on the wall, thinking how I could schedule a meeting into the week.

"Mum," he said quietly, "I just can't." He paused, twisting his hair around his fingers. "There are just so many things—so many things to worry about. I just can't deal with them all."

It was then that I allowed myself to look at him. To really look at him. To see the terror on his face. My heart lurched. A brief glimpse into the darkness that was his world. The sudden horror, the realization of what the bleak alternatives might entail. In that frightened face of my son, I saw the white of the ICU. The blue of his lips. I felt the pain of it all thudding on my chest. The robustness, yet flimsiness, of life. The frailty. Life. Death. Sometimes unfathomable. I saw small decisions and moments that can be utterly irretrievable, like dropping a stone into a deep, dark lake.

"Of course," I said, smoothing the cling film over the lasagna and putting it back into the fridge.

In that moment, I had caught a glimpse of something dark, and I wanted to look away. I didn't wait for him to elaborate. I didn't want to hear what he might have wanted to say. It scared me and I wanted to shut it down.

"Then you must leave," was all I said, reaching for his hand across the table. "You must leave. And I will help you."

It's then I had a memory. Christmas as a child. My mother in her smart purple dress, the slide of makeup on her face, the stain of red wine at the edge of her lips. The twinkle of Christmas lights. A table with gold and red decorations and the empty place set for my father. When she slumped at the table, the cooking fell to me. I piled the plates high—turkey, roast potatoes, and bowls of steaming, shiny vegetables. "Two different types of stuffing!" I said. Somehow, behind my back, her glass was refilled, with the deftness of a magician. My mother lurched forward, glassy-eyed, knocking over her wine; it seeped across the table like an open wound. "Let's eat," I said, jauntily, "before it gets cold," and I picked up the serving spoon.

Very quickly, my thoughts were racing forward, running through the alternatives. A different course . . . an apprenticeship . . . work experience with one of our friends. Something else we could offer up to him—so we could smooth over the unpleasant, painful feelings in the middle. There I was again, decorating the table with shiny Christmas baubles and piling plate after plate on the table, trying to make everything look normal. I made many suggestions to Tom that evening. Some were wild and fanciful. I was scrabbling around in the dark. "What about carpentry?" I said suddenly, and his eyes lit up.

Of course, it was a mistake not to have discussed things with David. There was the opportunity and occasion, but I chose not to.

My logic was that David wouldn't be able to handle the problem well, and I wanted to wait so I could serve it up with a solution. Something more palatable.

At earlier points in our marriage, David would pace up and down in front of me. "Why on earth didn't you tell me?" he'd say, dragging his hands through his hair in exasperation. "I could have helped, if you'd talked to me."

I didn't lie, just hid the truth, until I'd managed to sort everything out. Besides David's reaction, there was also my own sense of independence. The need to do it alone. Now I see the selfishness of this decision, but at the time, the need to find a quick solution was a priority. Yet I was trained to do the opposite at work. My job was to stay in the mess, to bear the pain, for as long as it took. At home with Tom, it was different. Like a hot potato I couldn't hold between my fingers.

By January, I had Tom enrolled in a carpentry course. In the following months, he took up kayaking, and by the spring he'd made his own canoe and was volunteering for weekend shifts at the club. Life seemed good. Two weeks later, my mother came home.

The call came out of the blue. "Ruth?" the voice drawled. "This is Ted."

Ted?

"Your mother is unwell."

Unwell. I knew that word. I'd used it many times over the years. The great euphemism for an alcoholic relapse.

"No," he said, as if reading my mind. "She's had a seizure of some kind. It's left her"—he paused—"rather confused."

He explained that she'd had a few days in hospital. "She'll be out on Tuesday. I'll need to bring her home. As you probably know," he said, "we had *an arrangement*." He stopped. "I can't—well, she obviously can't stay here."

Three days later, I met them at Heathrow. I didn't see them at first. They passed right by me. I noticed the elderly woman waving and smiling at the placards that were held by waiting people. It was the wheelchair; I wasn't expecting it at all. Ted was all big jaw and silver hair, and wore a large Stetson and cowboy boots. "I'm from Houston. Originally," he boomed. "Found my way to New Mexico, like the many waifs and strays. I've yet to meet anyone who was actually born in Taos." His laugh was loud and hearty. Below us sat the birdlike body of my mother. She had white, wispy hair and was smiling benignly, like she'd been wheeled onto a game show. He handed me her bag. And a small suitcase. "Cheerio," he said, and he swiveled on his Cuban heels.

I was grateful for the simple life she'd led in the desert. Her savings had been left untouched. She still had money. I did my research. I found a good care home in Finchley. They looked after her well. Her moods were erratic. Sometimes she recognized me, sometimes not. Sometimes she was benign, sometimes not. I felt nothing. I was ashamed of my lack of pity. My lack of empathy. But there was nothing there. I visited once a month. It was as much as I could bear. As it was, I steeled myself for those visits. I'd mark them on the calendar, willing some untoward event, some act of God, to prevent my passage.

When I went, she was greedy for attention. Her narcissism had morphed into a cloying state of neediness. While she sat, small in her chair, frail and watery-eyed, underneath all that fragile vulnerability was the familiar roar of desperation. With her eyes wild and hungry, and her hand on my arm, my stomach heaved. All feeling in the rest of my body receded. It's all I felt; those clawlike fingers pressing into my flesh. I bore it for as long as I could. Sometimes it was only seconds until I had to lift my arm. I'd fish for a pen in my bag, or a tissue to blow my nose—anything to move my hand away.

The staff looked at me in silent judgment. I felt their whispers when I arrived. *Living so locally, visiting so infrequently.* Claire, one of the nurses, was very fond of my mother. "Such a sweet lady," she'd say, and made a point of striking up a conversation when I came. "She'll be *sooo* happy to see you," she gushed and then proceeded to tell me what activities she had "taken part" in over the preceding weeks. I nodded and smiled. "And you work in the NHS? A therapist?" she said, her voice laced with accusation.

One visit I was later than usual. Claire told me they served a light supper at eight o'clock. "In ten minutes," she said, glancing at her watch. "Perhaps you'd like to wait. You could feed her?"

"Next time," I said, hurrying along the corridor.

Some days when I was leaving and felt their eyes on me, I was tempted to sit with them and reminisce about the past life of their "sweet lady." Perhaps I'd tell them how heavy she was for a ten-year-old to lift when she fell. How when I'd try to remove her sodden underwear, her mouth was thick with alcohol and abuse. Perhaps I'd tell them how I'd often wake up to find she had crawled into my bed, weepy and drunk and full of self-loathing, clinging to me like a baby. I could tell them that when my father left, her rages got worse, her anger uncontrollable. I could tell them about her hunger to control. That when I was a child, there was nowhere to hide. Nothing was sacred. Nothing private. That whenever I tried to move away from her, to find some respite, I was something to be clawed back. Diaries were read and mocked. Phone calls listened in on. She saw me as an extension of herself. I had no shape of my own. I was invisible.

Who are you to judge? I wanted to roar.

EIGHTEEN

Hayley curves her mouth into the briefest of smiles as she enters the room and sits down. She seems shy in her seat. She's wearing jeans and a T-shirt with a dog on the front. Her wavy hair is loose around her shoulders. She looks young.

She talks freely and easily about things at home. How she went with her dad to watch her brother's football tournament at the weekend. "Zak's team came second," she says proudly. She tells me they stopped for pizza on the way back to celebrate. She talks about how she's been reading local news stories, watching the national news, and noticing how the world is full of these small, random events. "It's everywhere," she says, "a train accident. A faulty wall that falls on a passerby. That coach crash in the Alps—those schoolkids . . ." She trails off and looks out of the window. "All these random decisions people make every day of their lives. Sometimes things go well." She shrugs. "Sometimes they don't."

As I listen to her speak, I notice her voice sounds different. Less harsh. Less accusatory. She turns back toward me. "I understand it wasn't my fault. That someone having a stroke at the wheel of a car is beyond my control. Beyond anyone's control. I just wish we weren't arguing when it happened," she says. "I wish we'd been having a laugh and a joke—that her last moments were full of fun."

I nod. "And how would you feel now if that were the case?" I ask.

"Terrible. We'd all feel terrible," and she looks down at her lap for a moment. "But you know, it would be a terrible thing out there," and she twirls a hand in the air. "Something unconnected to me. The thing I can't get away from is that she never would have gone to Wood Green that day if it wasn't for me. She didn't want to go. I made her. I wanted to get the dress. It was all about me."

She pauses, then looks up at me. "Everything aches," she says suddenly, pressing her hand to her chest. "It all hurts. I miss her," she says simply, tears filling her eyes. "Poor Zak. He's only nine."

There's kindness in her voice. She sounds less blaming. There is none of the bitter fury of the earlier sessions. What I hear most is a sense of resignation. A real feeling of sadness. And with this, I have the sense that she might be ready to begin the long process of grieving.

"You agreed to come for the six sessions, but I have been thinking that it would be good if you had some further work—some bereavement counseling—to just think about your mum. It can be helpful," I say, "to have someone to talk to. Someone outside the family. Someone—just for you," and I can see her eyes are misting over as I speak.

She blinks back and nods. "I'd like that," she says slowly, clearly pleased at the suggestion. "That would be good. So we'll just carry on with that after next week?"

There's a beat. She has assumed it will be me.

I shake my head gently. "In terms of our work here, we have one more session left. This new work will be with someone else—"

As I am speaking, I can feel her body stiffen. Her face drains of color.

"It won't be you?" she says, her brow drawn into a knot of confusion.

"No," I say, "one of my colleagues. As I said in the beginning— our contract was for six sessions, specifically around the trauma. It's the same for all the people we see. And then sometimes we refer on to other people."

"Why?"

"It's the way we work here at the unit," I explain. My voice is calm, even, in spite of her change of mood.

I could tell her about the budget cuts. That we used to have more resources. That we've lost staff. That even a few years ago, there was more flexibility to carry on seeing the person you've started with, and for a longer time span. But I don't say any of this because it's not relevant. What's relevant here is that Hayley Rappley needs therapy for her bereavement, not her trauma.

"So, are you saying you never see people here for more than six sessions?"

I hesitate for a moment and can feel the tension in the room.

"No," I say carefully, "that's not what I'm saying. Sometimes that's enough, sometimes people need more. And I think you would benefit hugely from some more sessions, some bereavement work."

"These sessions, they'll be with someone else? In a completely different place?"

"Yes," I say, "that's right."

She looks back at me incredulously.

"And how many sessions will that be for? Until I say I want to stop?" I can see there are tears forming at the corners of her eyes. She blinks them away. "Or will that be someone else's decision?" she asks, twisting the silver charm bracelet on her wrist.

"That will be something to work out with the new therapist," I say. I pause and fold my hands together in my lap. "I think we have done some very important work here together, Hayley. You have been courageous in coming here and talking about what has been a most incredibly traumatic and stressful—"

"You're lying," she cuts in. "This 'we just offer six sessions' crap. It's simply not true. A while ago, you told another patient he could have 'as many sessions as he needs.' Why can't I?" Her eyes are ablaze.

I feel a flush spread quickly up my neck.

"I'm not sure I understand—"

"That bloke who comes after me. Dan. How come you told Dan he could have as many as he needed? Did he score more points than me? Is that how it gets worked out? Three of his family died and only one of mine . . . is that how it goes? Points for people? Or does arson trump a car crash?"

I keep my voice even and calm. "I'm not at liberty to discuss other patients' treatment plans," I say. "We make decisions on a case-by-case basis. Our initial offering is six sessions. Some people need more. Some less. That's it."

As I'm speaking, repeating the same instructions, my thoughts are scattered, trying to get a handle on what she's talking about. *Dan? Losing three members of his family? Arson?* Most of all, I'm trying to regain some control. Her rage is quietly simmering, heating up to a boiling point. I know I need to move beyond this focus on sessions, to an understanding of what all this really means for Hayley. The pain and distress of endings, in the midst of so much loss. The loss of her mother. The loss of me. But as I go to speak, she bats away my words.

"So that's what you do here, is it? Make us talk about the worst thing that's ever happened to us, then say *fuck off*. Go and talk to someone else."

I try to speak, but she's gathering momentum. Her body upright in her chair. Her hands clasped, white knuckled in her lap. Her voice has hardened, her face has twisted into that old defiant stare.

"*Bring your photos, Hayley. It's not your fault, Hayley,*" she says, mocking my voice, "*I really want to be there for you, Hayley.*"

Small bubbles of spittle are gathering in the corner of her mouth.

"How do you live with yourself?" she demands. "People like you make me sick. All smug and above us all with your perfect life. Your poncey consulting room—" and as she speaks, saliva sprays over the case file in front of us.

"Hayley—"

"Your perfect leafy life," she says again, spitting out the words. "Bet you live in one of these big fuck-off houses around here. People like you make me sick. Literally. In fact, I want to puke. Right now," and she mimes poking her fingers in her throat and retching. "I want to puke my guts up over your carpet." She takes a breath. "Look at all this," and she jabs a finger around the room. "These silly chairs. The box of tissues at the ready. That stupid picture," and she turns toward my desk. "I mean, what *is* that?" she says. "Looks like it's been drawn by a five-year-old." I follow her gaze. It's one of the sketches that Carolyn had drawn at the cabin in Devon.

"Cherry-picking," she continues. "That's what you're doing. Choosing who you want to be with—and you've decided not to choose me. Are you worried that something bad might happen to you? Are you scared of me?" she says, and she wiggles her fingers in the air, "*Woo-hoo,*" like a ghost. "Is that why you're palming me off to someone else?" she continues, without taking a breath.

"Hayley," I say, quietly, "I can see you are angry and—"

She cuts in again. With her clasped fists and a mean face, she sits rigid in front of me.

"I'm glad I won't be seeing you," she snaps. "You're evil. It's you who has the problem. My mother's dead. But at least she was kind. At least she wasn't selfish, like you. Thank God I had a mother who was kind. Thank God I didn't have you."

Thank God I didn't have you.

The priority is to bear her fury. I know how to do this. The four walls of my consulting room have been splattered with rage over the years. Most of the time it's been raw, but not such a personal attack. The important thing is to contain it. Then try to understand it together. As she continues to berate me—a relentless assault on my room, my clothes, my very existence—I realize there's no space to intervene. For a few moments, I simply watch her mouth move. Her arms and hands flicking back and forth. Her jaw set. When she takes a breath, I say her name.

"Hayley," I say calmly, "when you are shouting, it's impossible for us to talk. And it's hard for me to listen."

"You're useless," she snaps, "useless, stupid, and unhelpful. In fact, you make me feel worse. I feel worse coming here. Is that what you want?" she says, looking at me.

I let her words go over my head. I know she feels abandoned, alone, and rejected. And I know that all her rage is being funneled into this small moment with me. All I can see is her taut angry face leering in at me. All I can hear is her hatred.

"Hayley," I try again.

Perhaps it's the calmness in my voice that ignites her further, because she lurches forward. Her eyes are a bright, flared blue, and I'm close enough to smell the cigarette smoke on her breath.

"I hope to God you don't have kids," she says, pushing her face close to mine. "What kind of a useless cunt of a mother would you be?"

These are the words that don't drift over my head. Instead they land hard, like sharp slaps across my cheeks.

It's at this point she stands up. I'm aware of a strong desire to get her to stay, and I stand up, too. It's all I can think about. Finding some way to get her to sit down, and a way to contain her anger before she leaves.

She hisses with venom, "If I was a child of yours, I'd get as far away from you as possible."

It's like a body blow.

As she turns away, I move toward her. I reach my hands out. Palms down, a sort of fanning motion. A soothing gesture. A way of trying to calm things down. And as she moves away, the hands that are fanning and placatory reach out. I want to try to get her to sit back down with me.

"*As far away as possible,*" she repeats very slowly.

I hear her words thundering in my ears. I see my hand reach for her. My fingers touching her skinny white arm.

She startles.

"What the fuck are you doing? Don't touch me," she shrieks, spit landing on my cheek. The exact sequence of events is a little hazy. I remember how the emotion on her face seems to course right through me. It's like a sudden and unexpected flaring of my own blind rage. Then, seconds later, we're both staring down at the tangle of our arms. She says something. I let go, quickly. She jerks her arm away, shock on her face.

"Bitch," she says, leaning into my face, "you're a fucking disgrace," then she grabs her bag, slams the door behind her, and is gone.

I slump down into the chair. My hands are trembling. Her rage. My rage. I wash my face at the sink and open the window. I gulp in fresh air. I feel jittery and panicky, but I make myself sit at my desk and take some slow, deep breaths and then I realize I have twenty minutes until Dan is due to come.

It's four o'clock. No phone call. At ten past four, I ring through to Paula. There's no sign of Dan. It's a relief. I sit with my hands clasped together almost willing him not to come.

At 4:45, it's clear he's not coming, and I start to gather up my things to go home. The phone rings.

"It's Dr. Jane Davies. Dan Griffin's GP?"

She tells me she had a call from an A & E department to say Dan was waiting for treatment, "but then he up and left. He'd given the doctor your name."

"What happened?"

"Not sure," she says. "Wasn't local," and I can hear the sound of the shuffling of papers.

"Bristol," she says.

"When was this?"

"Couple of hours ago. That's all I've got. Seems it was a physical injury."

I walk home quickly. Already the episode with Hayley has taken on a surreal quality. It plays and replays in a loop in my head, spooling back and forth. I feel ashamed by my feelings of anger. Ashamed that I let her words get to me, and I realize my mistake. My focus was on getting her to stay, but it was wrong. She was too angry. I should have simply let her go. Sometimes the most containing thing to do is to let someone leave. Let them calm down. My thoughts flit back and forth between Hayley and Dan. I feel jumpy. When I shift away from the image of Hayley and the enraged look on her face, my thoughts turn to Dan. To his trip to Bristol. And then my feelings of panic are free floating, exploding like fireworks, way above my head.

NINETEEN

When I get back home, I call Robert straightaway. I send a follow-up email. His email sends back an "out of office" until Friday lunchtime. I email back, asking for an urgent appointment on his return. That night, the house feels empty. I sit on the sofa. When I close my eyes, I see Hayley's face. That twist of fury. Her hot angry breath on my face. *Bitch*. I pour out some red wine and watch it splash around the huge bowl of a glass. Wine in a glass. The sound of a bottle opening. It used to be celebratory. . . . Now it's often the opposite.

My body is tense. I realize I'm perched on the edge of my seat, as if ready for the dramatic moment of a production. I have my monthly visit to see my mother on Saturday. I already know I won't be able to go. I sit very still. I am staring at nothing, just listening to the sound of the rain on the windows in the kitchen. I think about how the skylights were part of the kitchen extension, the side return to give us a wide-open family space. When the twins went to secondary school, I'd imagined they'd sit at the long table and do their homework side by side. I often had images of how I imagined our life would be. I still do.

The rain is lashing harder now, like handfuls of grit being hurled against the glass. I always think of Tom when it rains. I close my eyes and try to picture where he is. I wonder if he's out there, walking the streets, head down, and bent forward, without a coat on his back. Sometimes I can catch myself, and picture him inside, somewhere warm and sheltered. That evening, my mind drifts to darker places. A shop doorway? The bottom of a lake? I remembered the conversations in those early days, when it was quickly established he took no bank cards or cash. "He can't have gone far," they said, "without funds or resources." Then, as an afterthought, "Don't forget it's easier to disappear when you're alive than when you're dead. Bodies always turn up sooner or later." At the time, I felt the words like a punch. The cold blunt words of a middle-aged policeman. Now that all this time has passed, when I repeat them in my head, they have become the reverse. A strange sort of comfort. Perhaps a misguided source of hope—but hope nonetheless.

I'm at the computer after the second glass of wine. I can't help myself; it's a weird sort of solace these days, watching the mouse track the faces that are now so familiar. After checking in on my son, I move to Denis Watson and click on the website. It all looks different. The black ribbons. The statement posted over the top of the montage of pictures. As my eyes scan the words, I feel drained.

———

As you may have seen in the press reports, human remains were discovered in a cave close to the beach where Denis was last seen in Corfu. Officers from the UK have been working in conjunction with the Greek authorities and it is with great sadness that we report that forensics have confirmed that it is the body of our Denis. Denis Watson—much loved by many. RIP. We will be bringing his body home to rest.

After such a long period of uncertainty, grief, and hope, we now have to deal with a huge loss as our tireless search has now ended. We hope for rest and peace for both Denis and ourselves, as we focus on the precious memories we have of Denis and of his wonderful life.

We would like to take this opportunity to thank both the public and the media for their support over the years, but we now ask for privacy as we come to terms with our loss.

———

The words swim in front of me as the tears well up. I Google his name and Corfu, and sure enough there are many reports of a body unearthed at a rocky outcrop of caves. I click on the press reports, reading each one greedily for new information. By the time I click back to the website, moving the mouse over the pictures I know so well, I am sobbing. There's the birth of his best friend's baby. His brother's wedding. The death of his granddad. Twelve years of all these lives moving forward. His own stopped all of a sudden, like the hands of a clock. There's no detail on when he died, but the implication is that it was on that night, on holiday, all those years ago. All that time, all those posted blogs and pictures. All those visits by his brothers. All in vain. He was long dead. I lean in close. That cheeky smile. That casual pose against the backdrop of the bright blue sea. I refill my glass. I gulp at the wine. My hands are feverish on the pictures. Entering into the life that ended so abruptly. The family that lives on. I'm crying as I gaze into the void of their lives. The space they have filled with him, with their hope, their search; their expectations have come to nothing. It's not much later that I notice my glass is empty and I'm weeping in a strange and uncontrollable way. My body lurches back and forth in great dry heaves, and the tears continue to flow, like I am punctured and leaky.

When the doorbell rings, it's close to midnight. Maybe even later. There's barely an inch of wine left in the bottle. And the sound of the shrill bell in the silence is jolting. I stand up too quickly, light-headed from the alcohol. I feel dizzy, and in my flurry to move, my foot kicks into the coffee table. The bottle rocks and teeters, then falls to the side. The wine tips, a red gash across the carpet. The bell rings again.

Perhaps it's because I'm thinking of Tom. Perhaps it's because my thoughts are curled around him at that very moment. Perhaps because I can think of no one else who could possibly call so late, I move with a surge of hope and expectation. And in my mind's eye, I see him. Standing on the porch. No coat. The water running down his face.

"Hey, Mum," he'll say, stepping past me into the warmth of the house. The bell rings again, more urgently. I turn into the hallway and I see his figure in the porch. I open the door. A stooped head in the darkness.

"Help me," the voice says, "please?"

Dan is standing on my porch. His lip is swollen. It's pouring. His face is pinched and white. His hands are trembling.

Without hesitation, I open the door wide, and he steps inside.

There are many moments I will come to look back on, turn over, and scrutinize. The decision not to refer Dan on to another therapist, the first blurring of my boundaries that led to the bigger lie. And one of those moments will be how quick I was to open the door and let him in. Let him into my hallway. My house. My world.

Water pools onto the wood of the floor, "Sorry, I'm very sorry," he mutters, looking around helplessly as though parts of himself were dripping to the floor in a puddle.

In the light of the hallway, I can see his bloodied nose and a bruise emerging on his cheek above the bleeding lip. His teeth are chattering and it becomes obvious that he needs dry clothes. Without thinking, I go upstairs and gather a jumper, trousers, underwear, and socks from Tom's room. Do I think this through? I simply don't remember. What I do remember is how I stumbled drunkenly on the stairs as I came back down.

"Here," I say, opening the utility room door off the kitchen, "you can change in here." He steps in, but doesn't close the door. Quickly, he peels off his wet hoodie; I see the flash of his torso. Tight, muscular, but patterned with old scars. I look away.

I should call the police. I can see he's very frightened. I can see from the way he's walking, gingerly and with caution, that he's been hurt. I should take him to a doctor. I don't know why I don't do either of these things. I don't ask him how he knows where I live. I don't tell him that he can't be here. That I'll have to call him a cab. All of these things are the things I should say, but I don't. Instead, I make him hot chocolate in my kitchen.

"I went to Bristol," he says, mumbling into his fingers. "I didn't know where else to go," and he looks up at me. It's his face. Open. Pleading. "I'm sorry."

I don't know whether the apology is for coming to my house or for going to Bristol after we'd discussed it at the last session.

"I didn't know who else to turn to—" He's gulping in air. His body is twitching, his hands flying up to his face, then wringing his fingers together. "I knew you would help," he says.

Bitch. You're a fucking disgrace.

"How did you know where I live?" I ask. And I can hear the slight slur in my voice.

His face falls into his hands. "I'm sorry. I followed you home once. It was ages ago. I'm really sorry. I know it was wrong," he says simply. "It was the day I left early. I waited and followed you home. I'd been rude. I wanted to say sorry. But then I changed my mind. Thought you might think it was creepy."

It's odd, looking back, how many things I chose to ignore. How many things shoot up in the air. Some like small damp squibs of fireworks, others are bright and clear, like red flares. There are things I see, but make a conscious choice to look away from. To choose denial. If my childhood taught me anything, it was that denial was a place of comfort, a place that was easy to hide in. If I was in my consulting room, if I hadn't drunk nearly a bottle of red wine, I might have said something else. Instead, I say nothing. I make him a sandwich. As I turn my back to him and pick things out of the fridge, I drop a packet of ham over the floor. The pink flesh tumbles out, glistening on the black slate of the tiles. I scoop it up into the bin. My head is throbbing from bending down. I feel myself holding on to the side of the worktop to stop myself from swaying.

As I'm reaching into the fridge, seeing him in my mind's eye in the clothes I have brought down from upstairs, I imagine, just for a moment, that it's Tom in my kitchen. That we are sitting at the table late at night and I'm making him his favorite sandwich. Perhaps it's because of this fantasy, I don't ask what Dan wants to eat. I simply make him what I know Tom would have liked. He eats greedily, hungrily. I make him another. I cut up an apple in small neat slices, like I did for the children when they were little. When I go to the cupboard for a plate, I am standing behind him. I move closer. I'm too close to him. I'm close enough to press my hand against his cheek. To sling an arm around his shoulder and pull him toward me. I put the apple on the plate, set it on the table, and make myself a strong black coffee.

"I felt—" He falters. "I don't know. I just had this urge to see her. Face-to-face. I didn't think about it. Just went to Paddington—got the next train."

I nod.

"On the way, I felt a rush of something. A sense of anticipation." He shrugs. "Some kind of an ending."

"What happened?" The words are thick and heavy in my mouth. It's not just the wine, I can feel my throat is dry. There's a tension I can see in his face. Fear in his eyes as they dart back and forth.

He tells me he went to the house but it looked different from the outside. When he summoned up the courage to ring the bell, the door was opened by a young woman with a baby at her hip.

"They'd lived there for three years . . ." He pauses. "My mother had moved. Must have kept her telephone number—so still in the area, I guess—" His voice drifts.

I don't trust myself to speak. If Dan has noticed my blotchy red face from crying, or the slight slur in my words, or the clumsiness in my movements, he doesn't say. He's too caught up in his own story.

"I asked for a forwarding address, but the woman didn't have it. She'd been given it when they moved in, but that was ages ago—and then she sort of looked around her, at the baby in her arms, like it was a lifetime ago."

He tells me he stumbled away, into the nearest pub. "I was all pumped up. Ready," he says, "and I felt so angry that she wasn't there. That she'd gone. Moved away. That I just didn't fucking matter." His hands are clenched into fists.

"I sank three pints. Way too quickly. Played pool. Pints of beer and tequila shots. I was humming," he says.

All of a sudden when he looks at me, he does a double take. "Oh," he says, "are you all right? You look—"

"I'm fine," I say. "I'd fallen asleep. It was late when you rang the bell."

"I'm so sorry," he says again.

His green eyes are dazzling. Intense. I look away.

"I got into an argument. I can barely remember what happened. I was trashed by then. I hardly ever drink. Not like that. I was steaming. Totally out of order. A complete wanker," he says. "Ended up insulting some meathead on his turf, surrounded by all his mates." He laughs. "Talk about a death wish."

I have the nudge of a memory. The conversation with Robert. *Almost like a death wish.*

"I must have passed out. Woke up in hospital. Had a load of stitches." He turns to show me a neat crisscross row at the back of his head. "Couple of broken ribs." He shakes his head. "What a wanker, eh?" he says again.

"All this grief . . . for a mother who really doesn't give a shit. All I can say is," he laughs bitterly, "you've had a lucky escape. Kids . . . families—what a minefield."

It's then I feel a stab of something. The flash of something dark that I catch a glimpse of underwater. Something I know I should be paying attention to. Something that is fighting to get to the surface. But keeps bobbing away. Out of reach.

He tells me he saw one of the blokes from the pub. "I'm sure it was him, hovering about in A and E. I was scared. I left. Before the result of my X-ray."

His head drops down. "You were right. It was stupid to have gone to Bristol. I just wanted some answers. I just don't understand," he says. "What did I do to make her hate me so much?"

Then, out of nowhere, he starts to cry. I realize that I have never seen him cry before. He leans forward. Tears slide down his cheeks. Then he starts to sob. Loud heaving sobs that send his body jerking back and forth. For a while, I say nothing. I get a box of tissues.

"I felt so panicky. Just going back to the city. Scared, like I'd done something bad," he says, and his hands and legs start to shake.

When I look at the clock, it's gone 1:00 A.M.

"Is there a friend you can stay with?"

He shakes his head. "Please?" he says. Again, that plaintive voice. Those trembling hands.

The police will ask me why I didn't call them, or take him down to A & E. There is no rational response. The sight of his frightened, lost face in front of me will be no kind of answer. Nor is the fact that

I am incapable of driving him anywhere in my car. Fleetingly, I think of calling a cab, but it never becomes a coherent plan. Just something that passes like a shadow across my face.

I'd like to say it was a decision I reached by weighing up the pros and cons. The reality is that it feels more like a drift, like a leaf that floats down from a tree. An indefinable feeling propels me up to Tom's room. "It's late," I say. "I will take you to hospital in the morning. You can stay here tonight."

His face crumples with the weight of exhaustion and gratitude. I go into the bedroom, switch on the bedside light, find some clean pajamas and a fresh toothbrush from the bathroom. By the time I have returned, his mood has shifted. At the time, I put it down to a sense of relief, a sense of safety—but he looks and seems different.

"Can I take up some water?" he asks. I pull out a bottle from the fridge.

As I close the fridge door, he's nodding over at the photos, "Cute kid," he says. Gone is the wounded hesitancy. The terror. The fear. He is moving around my kitchen with a confidence I haven't seen before. He's standing up straight. He looks tall. Older somehow.

As we walk back to the hallway, he's looking around. "Nice house," he says as he follows me up the stairs. It's then that I sense him slow right down as we pass the walls of photographs. I feel his eyes feasting on the montage of family pictures—seaside holidays, Carolyn and Tom canoeing on the river, camping holidays in Devon, birthdays and cakes with candles, the four of us on snowmobiles, camels in the sand dunes. "Morocco?" he asks, pointing at the desert. He looks at them all. All the endless pictures of the children. Pictures of the children I said I didn't have.

I show him to the bedroom, the bathroom next door. He hands me back the pajama top. "I won't need this," he says, fixing me with his bright green eyes.

I take it back. "I'll get a towel," I say, by way of an answer.

"And what about your husband? Will he be OK with this?"

The sensation is like a sudden darkening, as if the light is dimming in a tunnel. There's a twist of discomfort that leaves a heavy weight of tension. I feel my cheeks color. What would David say if he were here? I can't even imagine a situation when I would have conceived of the idea had he been here.

"Of course," I say. I try to look nonchalant. Dismissive. But something about the way he's looking at me makes it obvious to both of us that this is a lie. Gone is the sorrowful, wounded expression. He looks alert. Watchful.

"He's at a conference," I say. "He might be back late tonight, or first thing tomorrow. Depending on the trains."

He nods. He knows I'm lying. How does he know? Am I such a bad liar? I know I am. Can he see this? Again, it feels like he can see right through me.

"Dan—," I say, then stop and start again. "Giving you a bed for the night. A place to stay, it's not usual practice. It's an emergency. It's not something—" Again, the words feel big and unformed in my mouth. "It's exceptional."

"I understand," he says, nodding gravely. "It's not something you usually do. Exceptional," he repeats, rolling it round his mouth, like he's enjoying the taste of a new food. Again, there's something that nudges at me.

"We can talk about this at our appointment next week."

"I understand. I do. And I appreciate it," he says, resting a hand on his chest, a gesture of sincerity.

As I hand him the towel, it falls to the floor. Did I drop it? Or did he fail to take it? Either way, we both lurch to pick it up. We clash shoulders on the way down awkwardly. We each pull back. "Sorry, here we go," I mumble, opening the bedroom door.

He looks at me. A strange indecipherable look, and I have that feeling again. That we are having two different conversations. Speaking two different languages. As I move to go past, he steps toward me.

"Thank you," he breathes to the side of my face. Then he reaches out his arm and leans in toward me. I pull back, but he moves forwards. The flash of his green eyes. His face moving toward mine. As I turn away, I feel his lips brush against my cheek.

"Dan," I gasp, pulling back sharply. "What are you doing? What—?"

I'm struggling to speak.

"It's fine," he says. "Exceptional circumstances. I understand." He leans back in toward me conspiratorially. "Really, I get it. And anyway," he says quietly, "it's not like I'm going to tell anyone, is it?"

I stare back at him, feeling like I'm about to fall from a great height.

"Good night," he says. Once again, he's reverted back to how he was before. Shy almost in his gratitude and appreciation. But I have seen something else. Something dark and menacing. It leaves me with a feeling that he has stolen something from me and I'm not sure what it is.

I don't know it at the time, but this turns out to be the last conversation that I ever have with Dan.

I mutter a good night. He turns. I walk away and push my bedroom door shut. My face is hot and my cheek smarts from the brush of his lips. The sight of his fiery green eyes. His relaxed stance. His moving round my kitchen, light, like a dancer.

Nice house.

In my room, the error of judgment is like a burn. I sit on the bed, then stare at the back of the bedroom door. I get up, wedge the chair under the door handle, then get into bed. The house is quiet. What was I thinking? I am gripped by pure white thumping fear. I take deep breaths. Strangely, I think of calling David. Asking him to come around. I know he'd come. But I can't bear the conversation. The look of horror on his face when I tell him what I've done. "A patient? In your house? You just can't help yourself, can you?" he'd say. I sit blinking at the chair wedged under the door handle and get up again. I move the chair away and move the chest of drawers across the doorway. It's heavy and in my drunken clumsiness, a mug falls off and crashes to the floor. I don't think about this, or care what Dan might think. I am beyond that now. I push it across the doorway. Only when it's firmly in place do I begin to breathe.

I get into bed fully clothed. My phone under the pillow. The house is so quiet. I can't sleep.

I lie there, blinking my eyes in the darkness. Rabbitlike and fearful. I am aware of him down the corridor in Tom's room; the image looms in my mind. My face, my whole body burns with the wrongness of what I have done. At one point, I close my eyes, then I think I hear a noise in the house. I sit up with a start. I am rigid as I listen. All is quiet. Just the rain and wind against the window.

At 3:00 A.M., I am still wide awake. Wired, thinking about the impact of this on the work, on the therapeutic relationship. To say nothing of my lie. The impossibility of being able to work with him again. My head throbs with last night's red wine, a tight band of pain across my forehead. I take some ibuprofen and watch the clock. The last time I register the time, it's 4:40.

When I next look, it's 6:30. I get up. The chair in the middle of the room and the chest of drawers against the door both look ridiculous. Morning brings relief, and sobriety; now everything feels more manageable. I push the furniture away from the door and as I walk along the landing, I know instantly the house is empty. When I walk past Tom's room, I see the bed is neatly made, the towel folded in a square on the duvet. Dan has gone.

There's a note in the kitchen. It's pinned to the fridge.

Thank you for your hospitality. I'm very sorry for the inconvenience. I am feeling better. I will see you at our appointment next week. Best, Dan

At first, I am filled with relief that he has left. It washes over me like a wave. I feel light and airy. I read the note again. It sounds normal. Appropriate and boundaried—back in the realm of patient and therapist. I almost want to laugh at the ridiculousness of my fear. Just hours ago, I was barricading the door with a heavy chest of drawers. What was I thinking? It was like a scene from one of Dan's films. I stand in the shower and let the water run over my body. I close my eyes. I tilt my head back and feel the water on my face. I think about Hayley. How I tried to stop her leaving. *Bitch.* I need to get in touch. A letter? Or maybe a call? I need to remind her of the date of her next appointment. I need her to know that I am here for her. That she can come back. I keep my eyes closed tight and I turn the tap up higher. I feel the needles of water jab on my cheeks. And I think about Denis Watson. The ring on the doorbell. Dan in my house. *In my house.* My relief about Dan has become something else. I see the two of us outside Tom's bedroom and I feel a burn of shame. I don't want to think about any of it. I flick the shower off, then sit on my bed wrapped in my towel.

I look over at the outfit I'd planned to wear to the birthday party. Blue cords, sandals, and a white shirt. It crosses my mind not to go. To simply climb under the duvet and stay in bed. The state I'm in. The lack of sleep. My face is so drawn and pale, I look ill. Then I think of the carefully wrapped box of cars. And I think of Nicholas. His small peachy face. That smile. His cheek against my own. And I heave myself up and off the bed. I get dressed and sit in front of the mirror. I'm at the age when makeup doesn't seem to do much anymore, but I work on my face. I do what I can.

It's odd not to be at work on a Friday. I can't remember the last time I've had a day off. The party is in a room at the café in their local park. I feel gripped by nervousness as I walk through the gates and make my way over to the small redbrick building. As I step inside, there's a hub of noise. There are plates of sandwiches and biscuits and drinks laid out on tables. Several babies are crawling across the floor among boxes of plastic toys and musical instruments. The parents clutch paper plates of food, having half-finished conversations as they watch over their scampering children. One little girl is walking, taking big drunken steps as she staggers across the floor, flapping her arms, her face shot with surprise. I can't see Nicholas or Julie. It's loud and noisy, but perhaps it's the wine and lack of sleep. I have a dull ache across my temple and my eyes are gritty. I feel exposed, standing alone among huddles of young parents who all know one another. For something to do, I move toward the drinks. The smell of the sausage rolls makes me nauseated and when I pour out orange juice, the cup shakes in my hand. I set it down and close my eyes briefly. I want to be at home.

Then suddenly, I hear my name. I turn. Julie is behind me. Her embrace is warm and welcoming. She's dyed her hair a bright peroxide blond and it's twisted into bunches. I gesture to the box I've put down on the table of presents.

"More cars, I'm afraid. I wasn't sure what to get," I explain. "It's something of Tom's. Something that he used to love when he was a boy. I hope that's OK?"

She smiles. "Thank you." She reaches for my hand. "It'll be nice to think of him playing with something that belonged to his father," she says, dropping her voice down low.

I smile, too.

"I'm so glad you could come. Nicholas will be happy to see you—"

She's interrupted by the sudden appearance of another woman. They hug. Then she turns to introduce us. "Bella from my antenatal class," she says, "and this is Ruth," she says. *Ruth. Not Nicholas's grandmother.*

"He's outside," she says, when she sees me scan the room, "with Frank."

I nod, and edge toward the door.

I see him from the doorway. There are blankets and toys on the grass near the baby slide. He's wearing a red-and-blue T-shirt and is peering intently at a balloon tied to the side of the chair. He's prodding it with his fingers, then shrieking with laughter as it bounces back and forth, bopping him on the nose. I sit on a chair by the door, content simply to watch him, even though my hands are twitching to reach for him, to feel his small body in my arms. Back and forth he goes, up to the balloon and back again. More shrieks of laughter.

"Ruth?" I look up. It's the man I saw with Julie at the South Bank.

"I'm Frank, Julie's boyfriend," he says pointedly. We shake hands politely.

"Nice to meet you," I say. He looks older than Julie, by more than ten years. He has a kind face.

We nod. It's awkward. I feel his reticence. His caution.

Julie comes out. Perhaps it is then that Nicholas looks up and sees his mother and shuffles over to us. Halfway across, he stops midcrawl, staring at me. It's as if he makes a connection, reaches for his digger on the blanket, and looks at me. His face breaks into a smile and he speeds across the grass.

"Here comes the little man," Julie says. And then he scoots past Frank toward me. It would be a lie to say I'm not delighted. My heart swells with joy that he comes to me. He stops by my legs and pulls himself up to my knees. He comes to *me*.

He lifts his hands up. "Up . . . up," he says. I reach down and lift him high into the air.

"Happy birthday, lovely boy!" I say, pressing my cheeks to his, then I stretch my arms out. He laughs as I fly him through the air. Perhaps I am showing off. Perhaps, under the watchful eye of Frank,

I am glorying in my moment. Marking my territory. Look at me, I'm saying. *He knows me. I matter.*

He waves his hands in the air when I go to put him down. So I do it all over again. And again. And again. And there we are, locked together as I hold him up above my head. His face chuckling with joy.

When the party games start, my head is throbbing. It's time to go home.

"I'll leave you all to it," I say.

Julie protests at first, then reaches in to hug me. Frank nods. He doesn't try to dissuade me. As I walk out of the park toward the Tube, I check my phone. Three missed calls from John Grantham. I never get calls on my mobile from the chief executive of the Trust. And on my day off? My heart lurches. Then his text comes in. Please call me asap. On my way, I also see there are two missed calls from Paula. I feel a growing sense of unease as I push through the ticket barrier down to the Northern Line.

On train, I text John back. I'll call in twenty minutes.

I ring through to his office as I step out of the station. He picks up straightaway.

"Can you come in now?" he says, and in the beat before I answer, I realize it's not a question.

TWENTY

The accident wasn't Tom's fault. No one suggested it was. Not even the boy's mother, who, as it transpired, had clearly overestimated her son Jack's swimming ability on the waiver form. It was one of the weekend activity camps for the Scouts and Tom had done everything by the book, checking each child off against the life jackets as they came off the water. Once the area was cleared, he washed down the deck, put all the jackets in the troughs, turned on the hose, and went to get changed. If anyone was to blame, it was the Scoutmaster who was supervising the changing rooms. No one saw Jack run out through the café. No one saw him searching for something, then slip on the wet decking into the water. It was only when Tom stepped out to turn off the tap that he heard the cries for help. He found him, clinging to the leg of the jetty, and pulled him out.

Tom was more shaken up than the boy. After the call, I drove out to meet him, and as soon as I got there I could see his hunched body. That dark hooded look. He was sitting on the bench, staring out over the water. "The kids are my responsibility," he said heavily. "I let him down," and no matter what I said, he was convinced of his negligence. Of not doing his job properly. He shook his head in defeat. "He could have died." Before we left, I spoke to Geoff, the center manager, and he was impressed by Tom's quick thinking. "We have someone out on the jetty with the younger kids," he explained, "but we've never needed to for the over-twelves. The Scoutmaster should have spotted him leaving. We'll have a review of the policy." He told us there'd be an incident report, but Tom had nothing to worry about. "Jack's fine," he said, "still more bothered about the Scout badge he's lost."

I drove us home, heavy with dread. I knew the blame wouldn't need to come from outside. That Tom would be serving it up all by himself. In spite of all the reassurances, I knew that none of my words would stick, that nothing anyone could say would make the slightest difference. "It was me," he despaired. "I left him outside." It reminded me of his small anxious face, poring over the *Tom Rabbit* book. The stuffed animal left out in the rain. I reasoned with him. I repeated what Geoff had said. I couldn't bear it.

"Just stop it," I said eventually.

That evening he was jittery. Then Julie rang, and he went out for the rest of the evening, returning later that night. In the morning he seemed worse. He had a panic attack after breakfast and was anxious for the rest of the day. Then he had a call from Geoff, which he asked me to take. I explained to him that Tom might not be in for a while. When I talked to Tom later, I mentioned Julie. He was evasive and irritable. "What about Julie?" he said. "She's just a friend from work."

The next morning he was up early, and when I came down to the kitchen, there was a faint smell of wood smoke, like a bonfire. I was immediately distracted by the sight of him. He'd hacked off his hair.

His raw, shaved head looked brutal and punishing and I collected up the spirals of curls he'd left in the bathroom sink. In the ensuing days, he was unable to go to his course. There was something child-like about his terror. As if he was once again the five-year-old who needed to hold on to my change purse in order to leave the house. I worried it would set him back after his improvements over the summer, so with his permission, I set up a session with Dr. Hanley. Perhaps I was overly reassured by his agreement, his readiness to go. Perhaps, again, I only saw what I wanted to see.

Two days later, on the day of his appointment, the house was eerily quiet when I returned from work. Given the almost involuntary thud in my chest in the face of a silent empty house, it was a sheer act of will not to rush upstairs too quickly. I had to focus all my attention on keeping the urgency out of my voice as I called out to him. Similarly, to keep calm, I made myself walk slowly up the stairs to check his bedroom and the bathroom, saying his name with a nonchalance I didn't feel. "Tom?" I said. He wasn't home.

I made coffee, and I looked out the back, expecting perhaps to see him in the garden. I called his phone, which went straight to voice mail. I rang off without leaving a message. Then I tried again, a little later, leaving a message to see whether he'd be home for supper. My voice was calm, even. "I'm making roast chicken," I said. Supper came and went, and I rang again. This time when I called, I was walking on the landing, and heard the distant hum of his phone. In his room, I found it on silent, on the floor by the bed, vibrating as I rang. It was then I felt a cold and creeping sense of dread.

Afterward, I would scan back over our conversations in those days after the accident. Wondering if my lightness, my reassuring comments that were intended to minimize Tom's worries, had the opposite effect. "It could have happened to anyone," I said. "And anyway, the Scoutmaster was responsible for the boys after they left the front deck." Perhaps all this simply meant that he felt unheard. Not listened to. That I'd underestimated the strength of his feelings of responsibility.

I rang David. He was in Los Angeles. I didn't factor in the jet lag, and when he picked up, he sounded groggy.

"Have you heard from Tom?" My voice was breathless.

There was the briefest of pauses. And then a mocking voice. *"Hello, David. How are you? How was your flight? Good luck at the conference tomorrow. Sorry for waking you. You were probably trying to catch up on some sleep before the big day."*

"I'm sorry," I said, "but I'm worried about Tom."

David didn't need to tell me what he was thinking.

"I know," I said, "but this time, it feels different. He hasn't come back for supper. He's not home," and as I was speaking, I heard my voice speeding up, "and he left his phone. Then I found it. Here, by his bed." By now my voice was shrill.

I can't remember how we ended the call. Short and curt, I expect. A great cavernous divide widening between us. Whether there were any words of comfort. Of connection. Of endearment. Probably not. Later, I remember I walked from room to room, listening to the silence of the house. I remember how I picked up the paper, a magazine, then flicked through the TV channels, but all the while, I couldn't concentrate. There was something, just on the edge of my vision, like the thread of a dream, that fades before it can be properly realized. I rang Dr. Hanley, but of course, it was after hours and the call went straight to voice mail. On instinct, I picked up Tom's phone and scrolled through. I played the solitary voice mail on his phone. It was from Dr. Hanley's secretary. Tom hadn't gone for his appointment. She asked him to ring for another. I thought about Mark Webster and his last jaunty session with me. I saw the dark tunnel. The whoosh of the train. His shiny black shoes as he stepped off the platform. Anxiety swelled in my chest. I was having difficulty formulating my thoughts and staying calm. It was then I called the police.

I don't remember much about the call. It was by now 10:30 P.M. I must have been panicky and agitated on the phone. "My son is missing," I remember saying with urgency. And it must have been this that led to the confusion.

Within ten minutes of my call, there were two officers on my doorstep, a female officer and a man in his late fifties, tall, solid, with a bristly beard and salt-and-pepper hair.

"*Seventeen?*" he repeated, frowning with confusion.

I nodded, launching in with my story. The words tumbled out. The accident at work . . . his mood . . . not in a good space," I said.

He stared back at me, then as he consulted his phone, he said the message they'd received was of a missing seven-year-old. He sat forward. He had a wide, buff face. His jaw hardened.

"You said your son was seven. Now you're telling us he's seventeen. Practically an adult?"

There was an edge to his voice. The other officer, the female one, took over.

"There must be some confusion," she explained in a soothing voice. "I'm sorry. It may well be that the confusion was at our end.

On the switchboard. I can see you're very distressed. Why don't we come in and you can tell us what's happened?"

We sat at the kitchen table, and as I spoke, she listened intently. I wondered if she had children. I fought the urge to ask.

"So, when were you expecting to see him?"

"Around six or seven o'clock," I said.

As I was speaking, the man suppressed a yawn and glanced at his watch.

"So perhaps he's stayed out a bit later?" she asked. "Have you called his friends?"

I blinked back at her.

"I think he's in trouble," I said.

"What sort of trouble?" she said, opening her notepad.

"There was an accident, at the canoe club where he works," and I gave them the details.

As I spoke, I pictured Tom at the end of the day. Hardworking. Diligent. Rinsing and hanging up the life jackets. "It was a small metal badge," I said. I told them the boy had taken it on the boat, in his pocket, but couldn't find it afterward. "He slipped on the jetty. It was Tom who fished him out."

I knew I was telling them too many details. As if I were trying to get it straight in my head, looking for something I might have missed. "The center manager's name is Geoff," I said. "He told me Tom was a great asset. A good worker. Good with the kids. Geoff told him it would all be fine. But Tom just shook his head. 'It was my fault,' was what he said." Fleetingly, I thought back to the times I'd worried in the past. Things I'd been able to bandage up and repair, and mend. How much easier it was when he was seven.

"So the kid that fell," asked the policeman, "he was fine?"

I nodded.

"No charges? Nothing?"

"No."

"So your son is not in any trouble?"

"No. But he felt the weight of responsibility," I said. "He *felt* it was his fault, even though it wasn't."

There was a silence.

"And he left his phone here," I said triumphantly, as though playing my trump card.

The policeman looked back at me, his face impassive. He was still smarting over the misunderstanding. There was an accusatory tone in his voice. A hint of blame. As if it were somehow my fault that my son was missing.

"Do you work, Mrs. Hartland?"

"Dr. Hartland," I corrected him unnecessarily. "Yes. I'm a therapist, the director of a trauma unit."

"Ah," he said, as if this provided the answer to all his questions.

I felt the pull of exasperation.

"This thing at the canoe club," I said, "he won't be able to bear it." I twisted my hands in my lap, I could hardly bring myself to say the words. "He—he tried to kill himself. Over a year ago. He was in hospital," and the tears came, sliding down my cheeks.

The man made some notes on his pad, then gently and wordlessly the policewoman took over. She sat forward. I felt ashamed of my tears. The tears that have made the woman sit forward, and the man sit back. The woman had short, dark hair, neatly cropped, with flecks of gray. She looked efficient, organized. She spoke calmly.

Immediately, I felt in safe hands. Her voice was quiet, low. I felt reassured.

She asked about the preceding year. His mental health. Whether he was still having any treatment. "We need to assess the level of risk," she said. There were forms to fill in. They wanted a description and recent photos.

She asked more questions and I duly offered up the information she requested. I decided to wait for her to finish, to hear her out, before I posed the question I most wanted to ask.

There was a brief pause. Finally, it was my turn.

"So, when do you think you will find him?"

There was a slight twitch in her face, and again, the policeman took a less than surreptitious glance at his watch.

"According to his assessed level of risk, a number of things will immediately be set in motion."

"Like what?"

"You will be assigned an investigating officer. Notifications will be sent to the Missing Persons Bureau and Children's Services."

"What does that all mean?" I cut in. Everything seemed suddenly blurry around the edges.

"Because he's under eighteen. And because of his previous suicide attempt. His risk will be categorized as high—"

"High?"

"Yes. There will be an immediate deployment of resources. He'll be on a nationwide police alert. We'll circulate his description and photos."

There was a pause.

"Is that it?"

"If there's a sighting, we'll notify you immediately. You'll also be offered family support."

"I don't want family support," I said.

There was another pause.

"There are other categories, but I don't think he—"

"What categories?"

"A learning disability?"

I shook my head.

"Detained under the Mental Health Act?"

"No."

"Likely to cause serious harm to another person?"

I shook my head. I stared back at the two of them. "He's my son. I'm worried about him," I whispered into my hands as I slumped forward in my chair.

"Has he taken anything with him?"

I must have looked confused.

"Money? Clothes? Passport?"

"What? I—I don't know—"

"Can you please have a look?" and her voice was soft.

I went upstairs. Opened the wardrobe. As far as I could tell, nothing was missing.

When I went to look for the passport in the desk drawer in the study, I remembered it wasn't there. He'd needed it for the job.

"He took it in to the center," I said, "for the canoe job. He needed it for ID. And his background check."

They exchanged a look between them.

"It must still be at the center," I said, sounding confused.

A beat.

"He keeps money in a tin in his room. It's still there. Fifty-five pounds and some change."

The policeman shifted in his seat, glanced up at his partner. He felt it was time to go. She didn't look back at him. She sat still.

I had a sudden urge to keep them there. To lock them in my house, to stop them leaving. I felt that all hope would disappear the moment they left. His radio blasted. He lowered the volume, then stood up and walked toward the patio door, stood facing the garden as he spoke into the radio. He turned. She looked up and nodded. A glance exchanged between them. She rose to her feet.

"The assigned investigating officer will be in touch tomorrow," she said. Then she opened up a folder and handed me a leaflet. "These are the organizations we recommend."

As we walked out of the living room and into the hallway, I slowed down. I had the urge to point them up the stairwell. To show them the walls of photographs. Or to pull the pictures from their neat wooden frames and push them into her hands. Photographs from holidays. Birthdays. Tom on the beach. Inside, I was screaming.

Please. Please look at us. Please see us. Please help us.

"Thank you for coming," I said at the door.

The man was gone quickly down the path, speaking into his radio. The woman lingered on the porch. "I'm very sorry," she said. "I hope you hear from your son." She tells me that a third of all the cases reported missing are young people between sixteen and eighteen. "Most of these are home in forty-eight hours," she said. "Some just want some space. It scares the parents. But it shakes kids up a bit to realize how hard it is out there. They're more than grateful to head home. Back to the comfort of their nice warm beds." She was trying to find a tone. Hopeful? Jokey? Reassuring? It didn't feel any one of those things.

Back upstairs, I scanned his room for clues. It was neat. The bed was made. Clothes hung up. His bookshelf and desk were tidy. Bedside table. A clock. A pile of books. I skimmed over the titles. Then I looked again. Under the bed and along all the bookshelves. Nothing.

"A book is gone," I said, when I rang the police station.

"*A book?*" There was a silence.

"You asked me to call if I discovered if anything was missing. His favorite book. That's the only thing I can see so far."

There was no news that night. David called later and said he'd booked an early flight home. Carolyn was on a school hockey tour, and we both agreed not to interrupt her trip. "She's back on Saturday. He'll be home by then," David reasoned. The investigating officer came the next morning. There were more forms. Photos and information gathering. He carefully explained what would happen next.

"What's the usual timetable," I asked, "for finding boys like Tom?"

There was a moment of silence. "We'll keep you posted," he said, and again, I am referred to the websites and the organizations. There was no news the next day. Or the day after that. It seemed incomprehensible that nothing else could be done, that no one could find him and bring him home.

The investigating officer reassured me he'd pass on any new information immediately. But when I pressed him, he gently reminded me of Tom's age.

"Dr. Hartland." His tone was kindly, but with an edge of insistence. "We're doing everything we can—but London is full of missing children. Young boys and girls of thirteen and fourteen, younger sometimes. Perhaps there are problems at home. Drugs. Family breakdown, mental health problems. But they are missing. Look at any local paper. Tom's still technically a child, but he's not far off adulthood in the eyes of the law. At eighteen he'll be deemed equipped to make his own decisions. If we find him, we'll encourage him to make contact, but it will be his choice. We'll do what we can."

For those hours and days afterward, I barely slept, and if I did doze off, I woke in a hot sweat, with a shutter stock of awful images. The most recurrent one was of him falling into a lake. Sinking downward, stones bulging in his pockets, his arms outstretched like giant wings.

I rang Geoff the following day to ask about the passport. He told me he'd given it back to Tom a few weeks ago.

"But we've got his sweatshirt," he said. "He left it here that last day. It was in his locker. With a book. I'll drop it round."

In fact, it was Julie who came over with his things. She refused to come in, but stood on the step, twisting her pink braids between her fingers. She was evasive about the evening he'd gone around to see her. Shrugging off my questions, like it wasn't any of my business. But perhaps it was how tired I looked, or the worry etched on my face, that finally prompted her to offer up some details. She told me when he'd come around to her flat he was all panicky and worried, "blaming himself," she said, "but then we talked. And he seemed to chill a bit. We hung out for the evening." Then she hesitated, picking at her nails. "He asked if he could stay for a few days. On my sofa. Said he wanted some space—"

"Some *space?*" I shot back. "From what?"

She was shaking her head. "I said it wasn't a good idea. It was a friend's flat. She was already doing me a favor."

"You said no?" My voice was stony.

"Well, I—it wasn't my flat."

"But he was asking for help."

I'm not proud of my behavior. I was tired and anxious and looking for someone to blame.

"What were you thinking?" I said with venom. I said her timing was appalling. I think I called her selfish. "He's only seventeen," I shouted hysterically. "This is your fault." The last thing I remember is her slamming Tom's things on the porch and the swirl of her tie-dye dress as she marched away.

It's hard to describe how devastated I was to see Tom's copy of *Into the Wild*. I turned it over in my fingers then flicked it open. It was well thumbed, with bits of the text underlined in pencil. He never went anywhere without it, and so I realized how much I'd been linking the absence of the book with a premeditated departure on his part. Much as the idea he'd made a willing choice to leave was painful, it would have showed intent, a decision, and to my mind was a better alternative to the other, darker images of him. Lying in a ditch. Or at the foot of a cliff. Or at the bottom of a lake. I realized how much I'd dreaded the book turning up, under a pile of papers, or tucked behind bills on the mantelpiece. So when Julie brought it back, I didn't so much want to shoot the messenger—I wanted to annihilate her.

It was later that day that I found the remains of the bonfire in the garden. The metal firepit we used to take camping was tucked by the side of the shed. I knelt down. On the grass, tossed to one side, was Tom's wallet. It was empty. I sifted through the pile of white ash. My fingers found the hard edge of something. I lifted it up. A small triangle of blue plastic, melted on one side, but the unmistakable edge of an Oyster card. On the ground, to the side, was a scrap of paper. I peered at it. I could see exactly what it was. It was the corner of Tom's filled-in, but not yet sent off, application for his provisional driving license. I sat on the grass, tried to imagine him coming out here the morning he cut his hair, or maybe it was late the night before. I tried to picture him building the fire and setting light to the kindling, then systematically feeding all his documents into the flames. His college ID card. His passport. His bank cards. I thought about him watching them curl and burn and melt in the heat. Setting light to the things that defined who he was. Destroying all traces, all evidence of his identity, one by one. What was he thinking? I wondered. Then I stood up abruptly. I didn't want to think about what he might have been thinking.

David came back early from Los Angeles and by Saturday Carolyn was home. It was obvious she knew something had happened when she saw the two of us had come to collect her. Together, we sat around the table and made a plan. David channeled his energy into a massive outward search. He left the house first thing and spent hours driving round London, going to all the hostels, with photographs of Tom that Carolyn had printed out. He pinned a map up on the living-room wall and marked out areas he thought that Tom might go. He tracked places where Tom had been happy; on childhood holidays, camping trips—he even went to Devon, to the cabin by the lake. Carolyn set up a targeted search on social media, with accounts on Twitter and Instagram that she updated regularly, casting the net wide. At home, I coordinated the links with the police and Missing Persons Bureau. Every evening we came together to eat and update each other on our progress. There was no word, no sightings. Nothing.

TWENTY-ONE

In the immediate aftermath I was in shock. Freefall. I obsessively checked all our bank accounts and each time I went online, I hoped to see some sort of unusual activity, the removal of a lump sum that might have given us some sort of clue to his whereabouts. There was none. I was empty and aching as I moved through my life. For a while, things looked normal on the surface. I saw patients. I supervised my staff. I chaired the team meetings. No one knew. I held myself together, until the day I bumped into Sally Adams. I realized afterward, it was only a matter of time. A small tap of a spoon on the eggshell that was my life.

Sally was Finn's mother. The last time I'd properly seen Finn was that time at the station, after the football match. She was chatting in a huddle by the bus stop. I judged if I carried on walking at speed, looking straight ahead, I'd get past without her noticing. Just as I thought I was home free, I heard her shrill voice.

"Ruth?"

I froze, then turned.

"Ruth! I thought it was you."

And then it started. "I'm on my way to the uniform shop," she said. "Finn's got that football tour in Holland." She sighed. "You should see the amount of stuff they need . . . Holland? *Holland?* What happened to tournaments inside the M25?"

She rolled her eyes dramatically.

"They're staying in Eindhoven. An international tournament. Bloody hell. Seventeen years old? Where do you go from there, eh? Finn's so happy. It's all he wants to do—football . . . football . . . football . . . ," she said in mock exasperation.

Suddenly she pulled out her phone. "Look at this," she said, scrolling through her photos. "Remember how fed up Finn was about being so short. Look at him now," and her pearly pink nail tapped onto a picture of a lanky boy in football kit. He looks unrecognizable. For a second, I saw the two of them at nursery. Finn and Tom, sitting together in the sandpit. Their small intent faces as they poured sand from one bucket to another.

"Bill was moaning last night, *When are they going to ship out and bloody leave us alone?*" she laughed. "He loves it, really. In fact, Adam's back now from university. The boomerang years! Last year at medical school and he's moving back home for a while. It's impossible—with London rents—"

On and on she went, feigning annoyance while reveling in her delight about her family. I stood immobilized, as if impaled by the glittering sword of her shiny, prizewinning children. When she took a breath, I was so anxious to ward against any questions coming my way that I found myself saying, "Is it four or five you have? I can never remember."

"Four," she said proudly. "I would have been happy to carry on, though. I wanted six, but Bill put his foot down. Or rather, zipped up his trousers," she shrieked, leaning in conspiratorially.

"It does always feel like more than four. They all seem to hang out at ours—friends, girlfriends, boyfriends. Often, it's like feeding a football team. I never know how many I'm cooking for; I can't remember the last time it was just the six of us. I always end up doubling up stuff—don't you find that?" she said, not really waiting for an answer, as I pictured our long, empty kitchen table.

I remember once going around to pick up Tom from Finn's house when they were in Year One. She had four children under the age of seven; the youngest, a baby, was in a sling strapped to her chest. Her hair had a silky shine to it. She was perfectly dressed in Lycra and a matching sweatshirt. She was pureeing a fish pie, "for Molly," she explained, jiggling the baby and scooping the potato mixture into small ice cube trays, while wiping down the surfaces at the same time. I felt tired just watching her.

"'*Liberty Hall*,' Bill always mutters under his breath. But you know—" and she suddenly stopped. "God knows what we'll do when they're gone. It's the graveyard time for relationships, isn't it, the big fat *empty nest*? I'll have to take up basket weaving—or hope that a couple of them will be poorly paid creatives who can never afford to leave home," and she roared with laughter.

"Yes," I said, "thank goodness for work," and she was chortling so hard at her own joke, she didn't seem to notice my dry tone.

She shook her head. "God knows how I'd have fitted in gainful employment. And especially your job—all that good work that you do."

I was feeling hot and clammy. There was a smell of damp wool. I loosened the scarf from round my neck. Her face went blurry. And for a moment, everything went quiet. Her relentless incessant chatter continued. I could see her mouth moving. Her hands weaving and gesticulating in front of me. I didn't hear any of it.

It took a great effort of will to glance at my watch.

"Listen to me rabbiting on. How are *you?* The twins? David?"

"Good," I managed to say, "but I have to get a train," I said, backing away, a hand up, like a shield.

"Catch up soon," she called out after me, as I stumbled away toward the station.

I TOOK THREE MONTHS OFF WORK. I told them I had to have emergency surgery on my back, after slipping on an icy pavement. Maggie stood in for me in my absence. The only person who knew the truth was Robert.

"I don't want to tell anyone at work," I said. "I want to keep it separate. Work helps. It's part of who I am—and someday soon, whatever happens, I will want to go back. I don't want them looking at me in a different way. All sympathy and pity and kid gloves. I won't be able to stand it. It won't work," I said fiercely.

Robert listened, and if he didn't agree, he didn't say so. Still, I could tell it didn't sit well with him. That it wasn't what he'd have recommended.

"Whatever you think will work for you," he said. "That's the important thing. But if you don't open this out to John, to the wider team, then when you go back to work, you will need to be your own barometer of what you can manage and what you can't. What cases you take on. What to say no to. These are things we must discuss here. And I'd like your assurance that you will do that. Here, with me."

I gave him my word—and he seemed satisfied with the spine surgery story. In many ways, it wasn't so far from the truth. I could barely hold myself upright. Keep two feet on the floor.

And the day I called in sick after "my fall," I literally collapsed, at such an alarming rate that I wondered if it had been a bad idea to have a break from work. I spent Christmas in bed.

I developed flu symptoms and then a postviral illness that meant I was confined to my bed for three weeks. I was floored, literally. David took a week off and fielded calls and emails from well-wishers from the unit. Then the second week, when I was no better, he worked from home. He was considerate and helpful. Unusually available and attentive. Perhaps we both saw that this sudden collapse was my body's way of coping with the stress and shock and, while we'd been unable to speak of the events without recrimination, he could now focus on finding ways to nurture and heal my body.

Many of those days passed in a haze. I'd wake to find a cool washcloth on my forehead, a freshly filled glass of water or lemon barley by my bed. Once, when I went to have a bath, I returned to find he had removed the sweat-drenched sheets and exchanged them for new crisp linen. It was so unlike him, and such an act of kindness, it made me want to weep. Afterward, I discovered he'd even gone to visit my mother for me.

Carolyn was a quiet presence in the background, doing the

washing and ironing and making a constant menu of delicious food; healthy soups, casseroles, and salads, which she left on the hob, or in the fridge, with small Post-it notes. The weeks passed. The twins' eighteenth birthday came and went. Carolyn had an English paper the next day, and wanted to revise. David had offered up various suggestions that I waved away. In the end, he took himself off to the cinema and I spent the evening in Tom's room, just sitting on his bed.

Carolyn expressed doubts about her forthcoming trip to Australia, was in a mind to cancel, but David and I were uncharacteristically united. She had to go. There was no point staying in London. A waste of her year, "and anyway," I reasoned, "you can carry on the social media updates wherever you are," and it was this that seemed to sway her.

In the months that followed, up until our inevitable separation and David's departure from the house, I was grateful to have his acts of kindness to remember. We waited until Carolyn had gone to Australia. If she was surprised at the news of our separation, she didn't say.

In those weeks after I recovered, while I was still off work, I threw myself into a continued search for Tom. I joined the Missing Persons support group that was linked to the website the policewoman had given me. I went on chat rooms for parents. I gained support from others, mainly mothers from all over the world who were struggling with the very same torment. I was horrified at the numbers of "children" who were sixteen, seventeen, and all those over the age of eighteen, who were beyond the reach of the law. Still babies, really. Whatever their age, they would always be our babies. We emailed. We supported each other through difficult times.

There were many lovely, helpful people. Then there was Minty. After that, I closed down my account.

Weeks became months, which eventually became a year. A year of no news. It seemed inconceivable. I came to accept that the police could do nothing. I came to accept that my world was on the constant sharp edge of anxiety. A tension that heightened around birthdays and anniversaries, but also around many other entirely unpredictable and unexpected moments. I came to accept that I would see him everywhere. I came to accept living in a state of heightened anticipation, of anxious limbo. Of grief and loss. A missing person was an ambiguous loss, and with nothing to hook on to, it was like trying to hang a coat up in the dark. I came to expect that memories of him would nudge themselves unexpectedly into my daily life.

I didn't expect Dan Griffin.

TWENTY-TWO

John doesn't smile. He's not unfriendly, but his face is pinched with worry. He looks tired, is what I think when I come in. He's lean and fit for a man in his early sixties. Today he looks gray, and weary. When I hover in the door, he stands up from his desk and gestures me toward the chairs by the table. He picks up a large brown A4 envelope from his desk, then joins me, sinking heavily into his chair.

"Some photographs arrived at the porter's lodge at lunchtime," he says. I feel a creeping unease as I recall my errors of last night. I look up at him. This is it, is what I'm thinking. I am going to have to explain to my boss, the chief executive of the Trust that I've worked for, for twenty-five years, that I allowed a patient to stay overnight in my house. I have no idea what I'm going to say. It seems impossible— no, inconceivable—that there are photos of Dan leaving my house. How can that have happened? Who could have taken the pictures? He shakes open the envelope and fans out six or seven pictures across the table. I force myself to look down at them.

The pictures are blurry and flesh colored. For a moment, it looks like bodies, the side of a face perhaps, and I have the sinking memory of his lips on the side of my cheek. There's a tense moment of silence as I peer at them. John is quiet. Too quiet. I am confused. I lean forward. At first, it's hard to work out what the images are.

I pick one up and it appears to be skin. I select another, there's a red mark. And then I see it. The bracelet with small silver charms. A wheelbarrow. A star. A small heart. I look up. I feel the color drain from my face.

"Hayley Rappley," he nods gravely. "Photos of her arm. She left this set at the porter's lodge after posting them all on Instagram at two o'clock this morning, followed shortly by Twitter. The tag line, #Killorcure with Ruth Hartland at the Trauma Unit."

I hold my breath.

I select another. It's less blurry. It's possible to see the imprint of my fingers on her arm. The images seem to zoom in and out. I feel a dull ache at the back of my head. I think back to that moment in my room. My ears ringing with the sound of her fury. My desperation to stop her from leaving. My hand on her arm. I briefly close my eyes.

"Well?" he says, and his voice is kind, gentle. There's the briefest of pauses. "Please tell me it isn't what it looks like."

John's face is a picture of grim determination, his body still braced for imminent disaster. The last thing he needs is another scandal. He's waiting for me to tell him it's a mistake. That I've been the victim of a patient fabrication. A hoax. That this will be no more than a headache, an irritant. That we can get the Comms Team to release a statement and smooth things over quickly.

I open my mouth. My face flushes with shame as I look back down at those marks. A squeeze of fury branded on her arm. *Bitch.*

It's an arm held up in defiance. I can see the time recorded on the picture and I imagine she went straight to the toilets on the ground floor and took them right then and there, in the bright strip lighting by the sinks. I shake my head. He breathes out heavily, defeated.

"I—I don't know what to say—," I stammer. "Something happened. There was a scene. She was very angry—she said some things. I tried to stop her from leaving. I reached for her. I don't remember it very clearly," and I press my fingers to my temples. Her sour face. The words that stung my cheeks. "I did touch her arm. I do remember that. But I don't remember squeezing it." I shake my head. "I just remember being very angry," and then I cover my face with my hands.

A long breath out. "Jesus, Ruth." For a moment he sits very still. Then he slowly wipes a hand over his face like a washcloth.

It has not been an easy year in the Trust for John. Financial cuts across the hospital had seen widespread job losses, and the resultant fury led to a line of hefty HR grievances. On top of this, a member of staff had been implicated in a suicide on the adolescent unit. There had been court cases, endless press releases, and just when things were improving, his wife had been taken ill. She had surgery for breast cancer and was now in recovery. All in all, it's been a bleak and stressful year.

THERE'S SOME DISCUSSION. Not much. John says Hayley's spoken to the police. That they'll be getting in touch with me for a statement. Criminal charges, I hear him say. He says he'll do what he can. "Minimize the damage," he says. Then he tells me I'm suspended with immediate effect.

"What about my patients?" I say helplessly. In my head, I run through my timetable for next week. The team meeting. Supervision with Stephanie. My second session with the Balham team. All my patients who depend on me. All of them who I see once a week or once a fortnight. And what about Dan? I feel a sharp pain in my chest.

"I have about twenty-two open cases," I say. "There's this one patient—"

John is pragmatic. I need to write a list of current patients to hand over. "Paula will be in touch with them all today. By phone and by letter." He says he'll draft something for her to send out. "They'll be offered an alternative therapist."

"Who?" I say. "We're all stretched. There's no one—"

"Ruth," he cuts in, "they will need to be offered an alternative. Work out from the list who is most at risk, who needs to be prioritized," he barks. "We will be nonspecific about time frames. Someone else will need to pick them up."

I watch him speak. I see him open and close his mouth.

"Time frames?" I ask weakly.

"The investigation," he says. "It'll be three months, minimum."

I work my lips. I can no longer find any words. I nod. All at once I remember the patient investigation in the adult department last year. In the end, it was more like six months before the therapist was back at work.

"We may need a substitute," he says, "or someone junior to step up until this is sorted."

"A *substitute?*" I say. We never get substitutes approved. You never agree to extra staff, is what I want to say. "Why now?"

It's then that he looks irritated. Like I'm a child that isn't following clear instructions.

"Ruth. You're the director. You hold a position of seniority. Someone will need to lead the team."

"But it shouldn't take long. It'll blow over? Won't it?"

His expression changes. He looks at me. A hard, intense look.

"*Blow over?*" he says, in exasperation. "Ruth, do you understand how serious this is? Hayley Rappley may bring *criminal charges.* I sincerely hope not. I am due to meet her father later this afternoon. But if she does, well—" He holds his hands palm up. "She could. Sounds like she'd be entitled to," and there's more than a hint of accusation in his voice.

He stops, scratches at the side of his face. Something he does, I've noticed, when he's worried.

"What happened, Ruth? How on earth did this happen?" He has respect for me. For my status and professionalism. For my years of service in the Trust. He wants to understand. He searches my face for an explanation.

This is the time to tell him about Tom. To tell him my son is missing. That I don't know where he is. That I haven't seen him for over a year and a half. This is the time to offer him something. Some small crumb. Something he can use and understand. But I know this would be no kind of excuse. There is no excuse.

I shake my head.

"I'm so sorry. Really. I'm sorry."

I tell him I'll sort the admin stuff out now. That I'll go to my office.

"Yes. Good," he says briskly. "I've given Paula the heads-up. She'll be expecting you."

I'm taken aback by the urgency. The swiftness. I stand up to go.

"And I'll need your ID," he says.

It's only then, in that moment, that I come close to crying. As I feel my eyes mist over, I put my head down and make a prolonged search for the badge in my bag, then place it on the table. *How quickly things can change*, I think.

PAULA LOOKS TENSE. "You've seen John?" she asks, her face pale.

I nod. It's her sudden hug that releases my tears. She pats at the chair next to her.

"Let's get this done," she says gently. "Let me help."

"My patients for Monday—can you try to get hold of them? Let them know in advance. And Dan Griffin," I say, "can you please call him?"

As I step out into the car park, I feel bruised and dazed. But somewhere, there's relief. Some recognition that the last forty-eight hours have spun hopelessly out of control and now I'm being rescued. That I'm limping away from a car crash that could have been so much worse. Squeezing a patient's arm? Letting a patient stay at my house? What next? So there's a small voice that's telling me I'm lucky. That this enforced exile will be helpful. That I've been saved from myself. In less than twenty-four hours, it's a thought that will seem grotesque, given the reality that is to come.

TWENTY-THREE

When it happens, I am one of the last to know. It's a Friday afternoon, a week since my suspension. So I am at home, and still reeling from the sudden shift in my working week. I'm struggling to adjust to empty afternoons that were once too full, too crammed with helping and listening and being useful. Time now yawns ahead of me as I search about for things to fill my days. I feel stunted. Lost. At sea.

Sometime during that week, Paula forwards a card from Stephanie. It's a coastal picture of a windswept beach with sand dunes and multicolored beach huts. I imagine her sitting at her desk to write her message, wrestling with her feelings at being let down midway through her placement and her desire to do the right thing. "Thinking of you" is what she settles on in her neat and careful handwriting.

In the days that follow, I will wonder exactly where I was when it happened. Perhaps I was at the sink? Washing up a cup? Sorting through old work files? Or perhaps I was weeding the flower beds and planting yellow primulas in the pots on the patio. Were those soft velvety petals smooth under my fingers at that very moment? It will take some time for me to realize the significance of the timing. And of course, much will be made of this in court, the fact that it took place at the exact time of our booked appointment at the unit. It's later I find out that in spite of Paula's message, he turned up for his session in what was described as a "highly agitated state." And then he was told I wasn't there. Perhaps he came remembering our last session, the image of the chest of drawers. *I will be here to help you.* Perhaps he came with hope. An opportunity to create order out of chaos. Perhaps not. Who knows?

I can only imagine the sequence of events that afternoon. It would have been Paula who took the call. They would have asked for me. Given the high profile and criminal aspects of many of our cases, calls from the police were not unusual. At first Paula would have explained that I was not at work. She would have relayed the brief response that had been agreed by John, "She's out of the office for the next few weeks. Let me take a message and get someone else to call you." *Foreseeable future* is of course the term that was agreed, the phrase that John recommended my colleagues use. Perhaps they're not ready for this yet. They, too, were easing themselves into the news, gingerly and slowly, like a swimmer sinking into a too-cold pool. It's funny how none of this matters now. Now there is no secrecy. No place to hide.

When the urgency of the police request became apparent, Paula, in her efficiency, would have offered up one of the more senior therapists; Maggie or Jamie, both of whom stand in for me when I am away. In turn, I imagine each of them, in their offices, going about the business of work, sending emails, seeing patients, reviewing case notes. A regular Friday afternoon. Down the corridor, the PTSD group will have started. Stephanie will be seeing Samira. It will be a normal afternoon, unpunctured by the news that is to come.

At some point, very soon after, John would have been called. Perhaps it's after this initial call, or perhaps it's a little later, when the police come to seize my files. I have a pang of sympathy for John. For what is coming. Poor John. A week earlier, his biggest worry was managing the fallout from a fifteen-year-old's Instagram account.

There is a flurry of activity, all this news and tragedy bleeding its way through the office. The overfull bath is reaching the top. A curl of silvery water creases over. One finger, then another. Until a giant hand of water slowly rolls over. It hits the floor, then gently creeps across, soaking into the fabric of other people's lives. And all the while I am at home. Washing up a cup or feeling soft petals under my fingers. In my exile. In a bubble of ignorance.

The first I know about any of it is when my mobile phone rings at 6:35 P.M. I reach for it, I see it's John, and as I tap to answer the call, the doorbell rings. I'm walking into the hallway. There's a small shaft of sun coming through the patterned glass in the door; it creates a swirl of light on the wooden floor. I step across it as I press the phone to my ear.

"Ruth," he says. His voice is low. "Something's happened—"

I'm opening the door now. A middle-aged man and a woman in her thirties are on the step, police IDs in hand.

"Ruth Hartland?" says the woman. "May we come in?"

For a brief moment, I think these two events are unconnected. That John and the detectives at my door are two random events that have collided on my Friday afternoon. When I see the police, I instantly think of Tom. I feel a plummeting sensation, an intense and desperate urge to get off the phone. In that moment, his call seems secondary, a distraction from the important issue in hand.

"I have to go," I say to John, a lurch in my belly.

There are some other words he says, but his voice is more distant. It's receding, as I let my hand drop away from my ear. "I'm on my way around," he says. I think I hear him say something about a lawyer. The papers. If there's any association at all, I think he's ringing about Hayley. Perhaps she's decided to press charges. It's a vague and fleeting thought, and I park it away somewhere else. This is not a priority, is what I'm thinking as I sweep it away. Making room for the other important news of my son. Perhaps John does give me more details. Perhaps he sketches out some events. Perhaps he doesn't. I simply don't remember. All I do know is that I am bracing myself for news. I am preoccupied with my own panic. My terror about Tom. Whatever John has said falls away when I usher the detectives inside.

We move into the living room. I sit down, perched on the edge of my chair. Then I am baffled when the female detective gets out a transparent folder. It contains a small picture that she doesn't remove, but places down on the coffee table in front of us. I stare at her blankly. I don't look down.

"Is this about Tom?" I ask. "Has something happened to Tom? Please?" I say urgently, "I need to know."

"Tom?"

"My son . . ."

The woman glances up at me. Her face is blank. There's a small, almost imperceptible shake of her head. At this point, their knowledge is patchy. They are still piecing things together. At this stage, her demeanor is kind, but of course, this will change.

"Can I please ask you to take a look at this photograph? Do you recognize it?"

I peer at the small snap taken on the beach. The little gingham hat. The hands that are patting at the sand. The joyful smile on his baby face.

"It's Nicholas," I say, "my grandson." I'm confused. "Where did you get this? It's my photograph."

I flip it over. On the back is the address. Julie's home address written in my excited handwriting.

She nods and moves it gently to the side.

"It was in my wallet—in my bag. Where did you get it?"

"And what about this one?" she asks, and all of a sudden there is another photo on the coffee table. This one is grainy and out of focus. The camera has zoomed in on the faces. I pick up the plastic envelope and peer at it. It's me. With Nicholas in my arms. Lifting him up above my head, like a bird in the sky. His face is creased into a chuckle and the picture has been taken as I am pulling him back toward me—our faces touching.

I don't understand. "It's me," I say, "it's a picture of me and Nicholas."

She writes in her notebook and there's something about their strange, still silence that makes the moment shift. A darkening of mood. A creeping sense of dread.

"Can you tell me where it was taken?" she asks.

I can see the red brick of the café. I take in his red-and-blue striped top. My own white shirt.

"At his birthday party," I say, "last Friday."

"And Julie and Nicholas McKenzie? Can you state your relationship to these two individuals?"

"Julie was a friend, a sort of ex-girlfriend of my son. Nicholas is my grandson." My words are impatient, brisk, like I'm trying to clear through the fog to get to the other side. It's as though, at this stage, I still somehow see all this as irrelevant, the warm-up to the main act that will feature Tom.

Their faces are unreadable. There's an eerie silence. It's the moment before, and I will remember its purity. I will remember the woman's hair pulled back into a shiny brown clasp. The small wisp of hair on her forehead. The small loose strand of cotton on her gray jacket. I will remember the slowing down. The small details. A sense of lumbering heaviness that takes shape before the moment when I learn what has happened.

"Where did you get this?" I ask, but of course, before she tells me, I already know. I know who has taken the picture. I don't know it in my head. It's not yet formed into a word, but I know it in my body. It's a sudden thrust of fear. Like a full intake of breath. The sensation and realization of fear is a rush of ice-cold air. Inhaled sharply, with a shocking chill to my lungs.

"Dan Griffin," she says. "Can you confirm he was your patient?" and she then produces a mug-shot-type picture that she places on the table between us. I peer at it. It's Dan wearing his black hoodie. His hair is unkempt. A blank expression. When I look at it later, it's not blank at all. It's something else much more terrible. It's a look I haven't seen on him before. It's relaxed. If I had to identify the expression on his face, it would be serenity.

Dan Griffin and Julie McKenzie. This is the first time I hear these two names in the same sentence; it's incongruous, jarring, like two discordant notes of music. Dan Griffin and Julie McKenzie. Mismatched names linked together in the same sentence, though in the months to come, given the press reporting of the trial, it will feel commonplace. Something we will all come to expect and associate together. Bacon and eggs. Fish and chips. It will feel normal to line them up together in one single sentence.

"A young man presented himself at a local police station, and we have arrested him in connection with the murder of a twenty-three-year-old woman whom we believe to be Julie McKenzie. The man in custody you will know by the name of Dan Griffin, but his birth name is Stephen Connolly."

I have the sensation of falling. Plummeting a long way down.

"Do you have any idea how the photo from your wallet came to be in the possession of the accused? Was there any occasion when he might have had access to your handbag?"

I try to speak. No words come out.

"I don't— What are you saying?"

"Stephen—or Dan—broke into the property of Julie McKenzie and Frank Martin at approximately four forty-five this afternoon. He was there when Julie and Nicholas returned to the flat."

"Nicholas?" and my voice comes out like a whisper.

I feel dizzy and sick. There is a sharp pain in my temple, and for some moments, I see her lips move, but I am unable to hear what she is saying. I hold on tightly to the side of the chair.

"We'll need a witness statement," she says. "You'll need to come to the station."

I close my eyes.

"Mrs. Hartland?" she asks gently. "Are you all right? Can we get you some water? Can we perhaps call someone?"

There's a pause when she goes to the kitchen. She hands me a glass of water and a cup of sweet tea. I put them on the table. My hands are shaking.

I sit paralyzed as I listen to what I now know she's going to say. The man takes over. Perhaps it's because she hesitates or perhaps they have planned it that way. But it is he who tells me the horrific details. The facts are unembellished, pared down. It is up to me to fill in all the emotions. The fear. The pain. The terror. The feeling that dominates is the feeling that belongs to me alone. It sits heavy as lead, the weight of my own guilt.

IN THE WEEKS AND MONTHS TO COME, I will learn the full and horrifying details. That Dan (or Stephen) was in the flat when they came home. That he had neatly and deftly cut his way through the glass panel in the back door. While I have never been to their flat, over the months of the trial I will come to know it like my own. The position of the lamp, the dining table in the middle of the living room. The exact distance between the sofa and the windows overlooking the garden, and the number of paces that it will take to get there. I will be shown photographic evidence. And as I look away from the things I don't want to see, I will see other things that I might one day have come to know about—the pattern of the curtains, the slate-colored coasters, the pink roses in the garden.

Their flat was arranged over two floors, on the basement and raised ground floor. It was part of a large, rambling Victorian terrace with shared communal gardens. It was the back door in the basement that was his entry point. He walked through the kitchen, took the knife from the drawer, and climbed the stairs. He was waiting for them in the living room when they came back, armed with the four-inch blade.

I will learn that Julie had taken Nicholas to Monkey Music, a local singing and music group she'd once told me about. A weekly class where he spent the session grinning and laughing away as he bashed at a cymbal. "Totally out of time," she'd laughed, "but he does seem to love it." I can imagine her pushing the buggy into the hall, unclipping Nicholas's straps, lifting him out, and him crawling to his toy box. The exact sequence of events is not entirely clear, but between the crime scene report, forensics, and the statement from the neighbor, police were able to piece together the story.

There was an initial scuffle by the sofa in the living room, which then veered over to the window. The evidence suggested that Julie had engineered this movement to the window in order to save her son. There was an unequivocal belief among investigators that Dan had come for the boy. That his primary intention was to harm Nicholas. Little Nicholas. The boy he saw me swing up into the air. The boy who pressed his cheek against mine. The boy who brought me joy. The boy who took his place, just like his brother had so many years before. The baby boy who sucked up all the love.

A neighbor in the adjacent basement flat, working at his desk, gave an account of what happened next.

There was the sound of screaming, then breaking glass, and I saw an object fly down onto the grass. I thought it was a large ball or something. It was only when I stood up from my chair that I saw to my horror it was a baby. My neighbor's little boy. Nicholas. It was then that I rushed outside to him.

The police report concluded that it would have been obvious to Julie at this stage what her assailant's intentions were. She managed to keep Dan talking long enough to find a way to get over to the window, smash the glass, and hurl her son down onto the lawn. The postmortem revealed that the injuries Julie sustained in the attack were instantly fatal.

While the drop from the window was high enough to cause injury, Nicholas's age and size worked in his favor. He rolled himself up like a ball. He suffered a few minor scratches from the glass, and a bang to the knee from a stone on the lawn, but was otherwise unharmed. The press reports of the incident made much of his miraculous escape—and of Julie's bravery.

One can only imagine the horrifying ordeal for this young woman. In her final moments, her thoughts were for her son, as she made efforts to save him from their frenzied attacker. Sacrificing her own life, for the sake of her child, embodies the greatest and most unselfish act of motherhood. It's a tragic loss of life, but her bravery will, one hopes, be some comfort to her partner, Frank, and her young son, Nicholas, in the years to come.

TWENTY-FOUR

The desire to hurt myself is visceral. And for the first few weeks, it's overwhelming. It's not something that creeps over me, it arrives straightaway, like a visitor at the door, presenting itself as an answer to my responsibility and guilt. An answer to the pain of this terrible ending.

Once the visitor has arrived, it steps forward at different times, giving me alternatives, showing me the things on offer. The things I could do. I allow myself to look. I stand by the roadside of a four-lane highway, watching the trucks as they thunder past, and I wonder what it would be like to step out and feel that hard metal against the softness of my flesh. Or when I cross the footbridge over the main road near our house, I wonder what it would feel like to simply drop down, my arms outstretched, and have my limbs break, or my face smash against that hard, black tarmac.

These aren't suicidal thoughts. I don't want to die. I just want to hurt myself. To make the pain go away. In the early days, I am wired and jittery and unable to sleep. Robert comes around most days. Sometimes he just sits as I pace up and down the kitchen, and on other days, when I feel lifeless and heavy, he reads to me, as I stare vacantly out into the garden.

Guilt has left a metallic taste in my mouth, and my stomach feels lined with acid. One afternoon, in the early days, before David comes to stay with me, I'm in the kitchen, making a cup of tea. The sky is a watery gray and the last of the white flutes from the magnolia have fallen, littering the grass with brown, faded petals. As I stand in front of the kettle, the steam rises in great majestic swirls, and there's a gentle rattle as the water comes to the boil. I reach across and press my hand flat against the side. The steam billows, the kettle roars, and the blue light clicks off. The pain is searing.

I watch the skin on my palm turn red. It's not enough. Not nearly enough. It doesn't touch me. Two large, soft blisters that I press and poke with my other hand. It's nothing.

If people have been negligent, they deserve to be punished was what Dan said.

The decision about what I need to do floats up, out of nowhere. And of course, once it's there, it's the most obvious thing to do.

If the nurses at the care home are surprised by my change in visiting hours, they say nothing. It's only Claire who wants to know. "Are you on holiday?" she asks, when she sees me for three days in a row. I tell her I'm on extended leave from work.

"I'm so pleased to be able to spend it with my mother."

I visit every day at two o'clock and stay until six. Sometimes my mother says nothing the whole time I'm there. Sometimes she is lucid and the conversation is benign and noncontroversial—the weather, the décor, the woman in the room next door. Other times it's like being battered by a raging sea, great hurling waves of fury and resentment that lash across my face.

In the afternoons, all the residents are wheeled into the day-room. It's an oddly opulent setting, with a grand antique table and red velvet curtains. The wheelchairs are lined up to look out over the gardens, a great sweeping lawn, with red roses in the flower beds.

Mostly the people stare out misty-eyed and vacant, hands constantly fidgeting in laps, as if searching for lost things. When I have settled my mother down, a blanket over her knees, she leans toward me, her hand pressing into my arm.

I usually arrive after lunch, but today I am there for "tea" at five o'clock. Over the last few months her mobility and dexterity have deteriorated. She can no longer feed herself, and a more recent problem with her stomach lining means she can't keep solid food down. Her food is mostly pureed. Depending on her mood, it can be a painstaking process. I prefer it when she's irritated, resentful, and full of spite. The other days are worse. The days when she sits small and birdlike in her chair, her face set in an ache of need. Her thin hair adrift, like cotton wool, so I can see the flaky skin of her scalp. Her pleading, watery gray eyes are locked on mine, as I spoon the food into her mouth like a baby.

The first time it happens, the nurses are surprised.

"It never happens at other mealtimes," Claire says, shaking her head. "She's usually really regular. And good with the commode, never has accidents." She fusses about. She's embarrassed, as if her own child has let her down.

They try to usher me away, back into the dayroom. "It's fine," I say, "I can manage. Just show me where everything is."

I wash my mother down. I clear away the mess. Help her into clean underwear. Still the eyes are fixed on mine. Her "accidents" at teatime become a regular feature of my visits.

I wheel her to bingo in the dayroom twice a week. She stares vacantly at the numbers as I move them on the board. Sometimes, she finds enough movement in her arm to swipe it across the table, and the small plastic squares are scattered over the floor. She is quiet and still as she watches me on my hands and knees, picking them up from the carpet.

I bear the foul, putrid smells. The disinfectant. The stale, stagnant air. The heavy anesthetizing air freshener that covers up the smell of body fluids. The sight of those shrinking bodies, papery thin and leaking. I swallow down my nausea. I let my mother rest her clawlike hand on my arm. I bear the forced jollity from the nurses. The fact that time seems frozen, punctuated only by the menial tasks of a mealtime, a trip to the toilet, or a visit to the dayroom. In between these activities, there's a vast, slow expanse of nothingness, when minutes seem like hours and I have to ration the compulsion to look at my watch. I bear it all because people who have been negligent deserve to be punished.

Negligence. It can mean so many things—doing too little, looking the other way, staying in a state of denial. At other times it can mean doing too much, and taking on a God-like responsibility over others. Over the years, I have been guilty of both, a kind of willful myopia when it suited me, and an overzealous desire to control when

I felt that was called for. Somewhere in the midst of all this were other people's lives.

JULIE'S FUNERAL WAS A SMALL, private event for family and close friends. I was not told about it. I didn't ask to come. I did write to Frank to express my condolences. No doubt I was looking for forgiveness. Some nod, some recognition of my own sorry situation. He didn't want to see me. I sent him books and links to organizations for support. Help for him, but mostly information on early childhood trauma for Nicholas. He didn't return my calls, and after the third parcel I sent, he returned it with a short note.

> Please do not contact me again. We are leaving London. We are moving to Scotland. I have family there. I want to build a new life for Jess and Nicholas.

He didn't say he blamed me. He didn't need to. *I have family there.* I thought back to our one meeting at Nicholas's birthday. He was polite and civil and made conversation, but there was a guardedness, a wariness about him. No great warmth. He couldn't have been delighted about my appearance out of the blue. And who could blame him? A connection to his girlfriend's missing one-night stand? His mother she met by accident, who ended up getting an invite to her son's first birthday party? How did Frank feel? I wonder. I don't think I gave much thought to him at all, so preoccupied as I was with my own joy, my own sense of entitlement. My own need for gratification. If he'd had his way, I'm sure he'd have preferred to have nothing to do with me. Been happier if Julie and I had never met that day in Balham High Road. And of course, given how things turned out, he'd have been right.

When David discovered what had happened, he was incredulous. "*Julie?*" It was so painful to see his sadness. It would have been easier if he'd shouted, had admonished me for what I'd done. When he discovered the news about Nicholas that had been hidden from him, he merely paced up and down the kitchen with a look of total incomprehension on his face.

"Grandparents have rights," he insisted, much later on.

Poor David, he never even knew he had a grandson before he was quickly whisked away.

I looked back at him. "I know they do," I said, "and if that's something you'd like to pursue for yourself, then you must. But for me, this is the end." I shook my head. "I have no rights." David was silent, his face slack. He didn't disagree.

Carolyn wanted to come back from Australia. I told her not to. "It'll all take ages. You'll be back by the time his trial starts." And she was. While she was away, she sent me letters and pictures; sketches that she'd drawn on the boat, giant sea turtles and latticed sea fans in purple and red. The legal process involved months of preparation. Delayed court dates, witness statements, psychiatric reports, meetings between solicitors and barristers, an endless back-and-forth. When the trial began, the press coverage was extensive. There was interest in the trauma service, both as an NHS organization and as a prestigious unit with a distinctive therapeutic approach, and this added another dimension to the normal salaciousness of a murder trial. There was also the nature of the case itself.

When people do terrible things, we want to understand. After unspeakable acts, we want answers. A gunman shooting innocent students on a campus, two young boys killing a toddler, a young man with a knife, lying in wait for a woman and a baby he has never met before. We want to know why. Of course we do. These acts are abhorrent and shocking. They make no sense at all. And in the search to understand them, there's an intense wish to move away from the dreadful act itself, so it has no connection to us anymore. A diagnosis or a label can offer us some refuge. It sets the person and their actions apart. Makes them abnormal. Alien. It offers some relief. I understand all this. I have felt this pull many times. But while I know these acts are not normal, I know, too, that things are more complex than the black-and-white categories of "mad" and "bad." Most things are a murky wash of gray. Over the course of my career, I have seen ordinary people do extraordinary things, both good and bad. I have come to understand that life is complicated. That chance encounters and fierce emotions can come together. In Dan's case—there was me, of course. My actions and inactions. But there were others—his mother, Michael, Tom, Julie and Nicholas, small unconnected shards of a kaleidoscope that twisted together into a final tragic shape.

In the numbness of those months, whenever my name was in the press, I sometimes allowed myself to imagine that somewhere out there in the world, Tom was in a café, casually reaching for a newspaper. That he'd read the story and feel propelled to pick up a phone and call us. But the call never came. Even as the thought sparked a tiny glow of light, it quickly blew itself out. I knew it was the stuff of fantasy.

It took Carolyn coming back from Australia for me to see the house through her eyes. The empty space where David's desk had been. His missing coats and shoes. The books that had been removed. Perhaps it was the state of the place, and the combination of my aimlessness and her restlessness that led to the suggestion. "The kitchen's looking tired," she announced. "I think we should redecorate."

The very idea exhausted me. But with no legitimate reason to refuse, I let myself be swept along with her proposal.

When she asked about colors, my mind went blank.

"Greens? Something neutral?" I shrugged. "Or maybe gray?"

"Not gray." She shook her head.

In the days that followed, the kitchen table was awash with strips of paint cards and swatches of material, small and neat like dollhouse tablecloths. I had no interest in any of it. It took an enormous act of will not to hand it over completely, so I could slump back and watch from the sidelines. But I made myself sit at the table, poring over the different colors as we whittled them down to ten. The next day, she brought home sample pots that she painted onto the wall, a mosaic that morphed from dark to light green, then into shades of stonewashed colors. I touched the chalky paint under my fingers as she read the colors out loud. We laughed at the names: *Elephant's Breath, Sager Than Green, Skimming Stone*. She left out piles of home styling magazines for me to look at, pages earmarked with orange Post-it notes and scribbled messages. *This lamp by the bookshelves?* or *What about these?* with an arrow pointing to a pair of oatmeal-colored cushions. Her plans made no mention of the old navy-blue sofa under the window. It was the place Tom liked to sit and I was grateful she didn't suggest replacing it or getting new covers for the well-worn cushions.

The whole project could have been completed swiftly, but there was an unspoken decision to linger on it. It was good to have something to occupy our minds. Something to focus on during those endless months of waiting. A distraction from conversations we didn't know how to have.

Before we started painting, we cleared out the big wooden cupboard by the window. It was like opening a museum from the twins' childhood. Together, we sifted through pictures and drawings and misshapen clay pots. Carolyn studied school photographs, trying to remember the names of long-forgotten classmates. We found boxes of toys and games, a half-grown crystal from a kit, a semiconstructed cardboard castle, dried-up paints, and an unopened box of science experiments. I lingered over these unfinished things, incomplete childhood projects that had littered the journey of motherhood.

Carolyn was oblivious, caught up in reading little scraps of paper she unearthed from the drawers. At one point, she sat cross-legged on the sofa, totally absorbed in some written pages. She laughed out loud as she reached the end.

"What's that?" I asked, looking up.

"A story Tom and I once wrote," she said. "Can I keep it?" she asked.

"Of course," I said quietly, and stopped myself from asking to see it as she folded away the words.

As we began to prep the walls, Carolyn suggested the audiobooks. "The classics," she said. "Women authors only." We listened as we started at different ends of the room, working our way along with masking tape and cleanser, until we met somewhere in the middle.

On the surface, they were days of quiet and soporific repetition; the movement of the brush, the metronome of spoken words in the background, but in my own internal world, there was turmoil. I was a little battered tent in a storm. Sometimes I'd blink, startled to find myself in the kitchen, feet on tiles, brush in hand, and it often felt like my daughter was the one small guyline that was tethering me to the ground. I have never been more grateful to have her by my side.

We painted through *Jane Eyre, Wuthering Heights, Pride and Prejudice,* but when I suggested *To Kill a Mockingbird,* she hesitated. "A courtroom drama? Really?"

I chose Mary Shelley's *Frankenstein* instead.

After the painting was done, she busied herself with finishing touches, fixing two new lamps over the table. Big frosted globes that she picked up at a market.

"Come and see," she called out to me.

I gazed in awe at the finished room.

I thought about her homemade cards. Her pencil sketches. The clothes she used to make. How she always took such care and attention over the details. How she would make small choices over the preparation and serving of food that transformed a simple meal into a thing of beauty.

"You always make things look so lovely," I said.

She flushed under the compliment and I felt a stab of guilt that this light had shone down on her so infrequently. That she wasn't more accustomed to such praise. Or able to glory in her talents and achievements. The fact that they came to her so easily should have made them more, not less, of note. I found myself questioning her decision to read law. I worried that this flair and creativity would get lost under the weight of Contracts and Tort. Still, I knew better than to voice this out loud.

Less than a week later, she told me she'd been sent her reading list.

"I thought I'd feel more excited," she said flatly.

I willed myself to listen. Not to jump straight in with advice.

"I worry that I might have been swept along with something," she continued. "That it was the right thing to do. In the midst of"— she stopped—"everything else."

I nodded.

We were both silent for a moment.

I sat down next to her, held her hands in mine.

"I'm sorry," I said.

A few days later, she was reading on Tom's sofa. She looked up and told me she was going to take up the place.

"If it's not for me, I can always change my mind and come home." She shrugged. "Would that be such a disaster?"

"No," I said, "it wouldn't be a disaster at all."

TWENTY-FIVE

When I stepped into the court to give evidence, I looked over at Dan. He was unrecognizable. His hair was cut short. He wore a plain white shirt, gray trousers, and a navy tie. Whether he was Stephen Connolly or Dan Griffin, he looked nothing like my son. I stared at him, but he never once glanced in my direction. He kept his head still, his eyes fixed forward, gazing into the middle distance.

Frank had come to London for the trial; sitting next to him was a small gray-haired man. Julie's father. He looked thin and papery in his grief. At times, during the most painful parts of the evidence, I saw him wince. More than once, I thought his frail body might crumble under the weight of those graphic witness statements.

A defense of diminished capacity placed considerable emphasis on Dan's previous contact with mental health services. As the Trauma Unit had been his current place of treatment, my work as both the director of the unit and his therapist came under particular scrutiny. Understandably, much was made of my professional failings and the domino effect they had on the outcome of events.

When I stood in the witness box, the defense barrister began her cross-examination with my training, the history of my career, and the rise to director of the unit. She asked about the model of work. She wanted the psychodynamic approach explained for the court.

"Can you explain the importance of 'the transference' to the court?"

After a lengthy explanation, she clarified it for the jury.

"So, it's the relationship between the patient and therapist that's particularly significant in this type of therapy?"

"Yes. That's correct."

"This very relationship is the place where the patient can bring his or her issues from childhood, feelings about their own parental figures, and reenact them, as it were, in the sessions?"

"'Reenact' sounds a little contrived," I say. "But yes, the relationship is the place where unresolved and difficult feelings around parental figures can be surfaced."

"And for the court, can you tell us therefore, about the importance of boundaries and containment within this model of therapeutic practice?"

Afterward, she moved on to my family. To the breakdown of my marriage. Then to Tom and his difficulties. His suicide attempt. She asked why I didn't tell people that he had gone missing. The court was referred to my email requesting leave for my "back surgery."

"You lied to your employers?"

"Yes. That's correct."

"Can you tell the court why?"

For a moment, I didn't know what to say.

"I was—" and I searched for the right word, "struggling." I take a few moments. "Grief is not linear," I explained. "Nor is it rational. I made the decision at the time to keep it hidden. Not to let my personal life contaminate my professional life." I paused for a moment. "I felt it would be better for my work. Better for my patients, to keep it away."

"*Better for your patients?*" she repeated and couldn't resist a smirk.

And that's when I see it very clearly—by hiding it from work, I was hiding it from myself. My denial. My own undigested rat. Splitting it off was a way to keep going.

I didn't say this. It wouldn't interest her. Why would it?

When we moved to the likeness between Dan and my son, the jury were referred to a selection of photographs in their evidence packs. The woman on the end, with the cropped gray hair, studied the photos carefully. She looked up at Dan, shook her head ever so slightly, before shooting me a cold, hard stare.

"If a colleague presented you with a similar conundrum—a likeness between a patient and a member of their own family, a likeness that they thought could have a detrimental impact on the work, what would you do?"

"I'd advise them to refer the patient on to someone else. It would be in the patient's best interest," I said without hesitation.

The court was still.

The barrister looked around at her audience. "*In the patient's best interest,*" she nodded, as she flicked over a page of notes. "Can you explain why you didn't properly chase up the notes from the surgery in Hackney? Records show that you left messages, but failed to follow it up successfully. Can you explain why you didn't speak to the Bristol GP yourself?"

I told her I had spoken to the Bristol receptionist, who had referred me back to Dr. Davies. I talked about the fact that Bristol was a single-handed practice. I listed my various phone calls, explained that my attempts had been thwarted by an administrator off sick. I said all the things I had been reminded to say.

She was nodding as I spoke, as if to hurry me along.

"Ordinarily, are a new patient's notes transferred to their new GP?"

"Yes."

"And when a patient is referred to your unit, is it normal practice to request the notes?"

"Mostly. Particularly if the patient is not known to the referrer."

"And ordinarily, when the notes don't arrive, what would you do?"

"I would follow it up. Ring the surgery. Look into what the holdup might be."

"Did you do all of these things?"

"Yes."

"Would you agree there was a significant delay in you obtaining the notes?"

"Yes."

"If you had seen the notes, you would have known all about the defendant's previous hospital admission." A deliberate pause, for dramatic effect. "A three-month stay in a psychiatric unit in the north of England," she said looking up, "two years prior to the defendant's arrest. Might this knowledge have altered your work? The focus of your therapy?"

"I don't know the details. But yes, quite possibly."

Obtaining the notes from his previous surgery would have alerted us to his different birth name. And this, more than likely, would have alerted us to his complex past and his previous psychiatric admission. I did make a number of calls, but I didn't follow them through with the rigor I ordinarily would have. I could say that following up the notes slipped to the bottom of a list of priorities. But that wasn't the whole story, of course. Freud would say there's no such thing as forgetting, and that, by then, I was too tangled up in my own web, my own version of the truth. The narrative I wanted to see. Somewhere, I think, deep down, I knew he was very disturbed. And somewhere, wrapped inside all of that, was my own omnipotence. However damaged he was, I felt that I could save him. I accepted the unknowability of him because I didn't want to discover a reason to stop seeing him. In the void where once stood the trophy of my son, he was the small consolation prize I'd wanted to cling to.

After the recess, she moved on to the other dominoes that I had set in motion.

"Is it your usual clinical practice to lie to your patients?"

"No."

"Is it common practice to cancel sessions with your patients?"

"No. But the session wasn't canceled. It was rescheduled."

She raised an eyebrow. "Have you *rescheduled* sessions in the past?"

"Yes."

"What for?"

"A tribunal . . . a funeral, are two reasons that come to mind."

"Can you tell the court the reason you canceled, sorry, *rescheduled*, the session with the defendant on the sixteenth of May?"

"To attend my grandson's birthday party."

The court was silent.

"Thank you. And for the record, please note this was the day after Stephen Connolly, the man you knew as Dan Griffin, was invited *to spend the night* in your house." She paused.

The judge looked up. "Is there a question for the witness?"

"It was on the sixteenth of May that the defendant followed you to South London, and saw you with your grandson, and took a series of photographs of you holding the baby."

Members of the jury were referred to the relevant pictures in the file.

"Can you confirm that this took place *after* the therapy session when the defendant told you about his dead baby brother, and had shown you a photograph of his own mother cradling her son?"

"That's correct."

I felt hot and dizzy. I reached for the water.

"Is it common practice to let patients stay overnight at your house? Are you operating some kind of *therapeutic B & B?*" she said, with another smirk.

"No."

"Can you confirm that it was during this overnight stay when the photographs of your children on the walls would have made it obvious to the defendant that you lied to him?"

"That's correct."

"We put it to you, that it was your own trauma, the physical likeness of this patient to your missing son, Tom, that altered your professional judgment."

There was a collective intake of breath.

The barrister was all puffed up when she said this. As if ready for some sort of combat. A war of words. These were the sort of moments they thrived on.

"Yes," I said, nodding, "that's correct."

She looked momentarily deflated.

"So are you saying it was your own selfish need that swayed your judgment, and it was this that led to the tragic event on the twenty-third of May?"

It was shocking to hear it out loud. It was like a sharp slap against my face, but it also came as some relief not to try to duck away.

"That's correct," I said too quietly.

"I'm sorry, can you repeat your response?"

"Yes. That is correct."

"Would you say it constitutes a serious clinical misjudgment?"

"Yes."

The defense pursued this line, snaking her way to the impact of my own blurred boundaries on the therapy work . . . the lie . . . the overnight stay.

"You stepped out of role. Would you agree?"

"Yes."

"I suggest that you became more of a mother figure to your patient, and it was this very confusion that became a trigger for his subsequent anger and jealousy. *Anger and jealousy* that you had already surfaced in therapy—that it was *your job* to contain."

She was stepping from side to side now, her hands gesticulating in front of the jury.

"Is it possible," she asked, "that the sight of you holding another baby, so soon after he had described the torment of his own childhood rejection, was difficult for him?"

"Yes."

"Is it possible that this, coupled with the altered appointment time, left him feeling rejected all over again?"

"Yes. It's possible."

"Then once you are suspended from work, he has *yet another* canceled appointment. It was reported that he arrived in an agitated state. Perhaps desperate to see you. And you were not there. He then went to South London, and it was precisely during your booked appointment time that the murder took place."

I nodded.

"Perhaps," she mused, looking around at the jury, "none of this would have happened if you'd done your job properly."

I thought then of Robert. His quiet, wise voice. "It's all in the beginning" is what he always said. And so it was. *People who don't do their jobs properly.*

After the break, there was a long session that focused on my "fixation" about Dan's suicide risk, and my belief he was likely to harm himself. When it was proposed that I may have been misled by the films he talked about, his barrister was prepared.

"But what about *When Harry Met Sally? The Deer Hunter? The Godfather?* Stephen claims he mentioned many films in the course of your sessions." Then she peered dramatically down at her papers. "*The Sound of Music?*" she said triumphantly. "Where's the suicide there?"

There was a murmur of laughter around the court.

It was suggested to the court that I was caught up in my own unprocessed drama, my own hypothesis of suicide and self-harm, to the detriment of everything else. Links were made to the Mark Webster case, and then to "the very shocking suicide attempt" by my own son.

Hayley was, of course, called as a witness. She looked small and terrified in the dock and I felt sorry for her. She kept her eyes from mine. Answered as quickly as possible.

"Did the accused tell you that he could see Dr. Hartland for *as long as he needed?*"

"Yes."

"Did Dr. Hartland lose her temper?"

"Yes," she said quietly.

"Can you please describe what happened during your fifth session with Dr. Hartland on the fifteenth of May?"

Hayley's words were hesitant, her hands holding tightly on to the stand.

The photographs were produced as evidence.

"Can you confirm that these are the photos you took? That these are the marks on your arms?"

And so it rolled on. The court felt airless. Tight. Things moved incredibly slowly, sifting over small, grainy details. It was an atmosphere very far from the image presented in the media or on a fast-paced entertainment drama. Mostly, it was tiny movements. Back and forth over the minutiae. It reminded me of the fairground slot machines I loved as a child, where a bar pushes back and forth, gently nudging a pile of money forward, until one or two coins eventually fall over the edge. On a daily basis, the biggest challenge was trying to find enough air to keep breathing.

There were many inconsistencies. Things I didn't pick up. I was thrown many breadcrumbs by Dan. Some, I gobbled up eagerly. Others, ones that might have led me on a different path, I chose to ignore. What wasn't in question was the fact that he was a deeply disturbed and troubled man.

There was a brother, Michael. He was eighteen months old when he died. Dan was three and a half. According to the records, Michael was in the living room, playing by an open fire in a polyester dressing gown that caught alight. The flames roared up his small body in seconds. He had 90 percent burns and died five days later in intensive care. Dan's mother had left the two of them alone when she went upstairs. She was convinced the fireguard was in place when she left the room. How it fell away from the fire was unexplained. Did it fall? Was it kicked away? It didn't really matter. Dan was only three. Such a little boy to be burdened with such a traumatic experience. It was reported that he had no recollection of the event. It was highly likely that the event had been "forgotten," and was buried somewhere deep inside, leaving him with a scar of blame and shame.

As I listened, I recalled the session he told me about the rape. His fixation with the lighter. The flame next to his cheek. *That smell. Burning. I felt like I couldn't breathe*. It was soon after that Dan had wondered if the attack had happened for a reason. *Karma*, he'd said. *Because I'm bad*. Perhaps there was an unexpected association. Perhaps the sense of smell had triggered a fleeting, but unidentifiable memory, some connection he couldn't make.

There were lots of things that weren't clear. The two dif-

ferent names. Two different NHS numbers. A false National Insurance number. Layers of truths and untruths. Some of what he
told me was true. Some was expanded so far away from the truth so
as to be unrecognizable. Whatever was true or untrue, it didn't really
matter. What I knew, beyond all doubt, was that the session when
he talked about his childhood was real. The drive away from the
fairground in the car, his memory of searching the kitchen cupboards for sharp utensils, whether they actually happened or not
(and I suspect they did), they were real in his mind, and an accurate
reflection of how he felt. The feelings of isolation. Of not being
loved. Of finding ways to hurt himself to take away the terrible pain
and emptiness. That was real.

A number of weeks into the trial, the faces of the jury had become as familiar as my own family. I knew the members of the public gallery who came in every day. The court reporters, the unruly
quiff of hair on the usher's forehead. I knew them all. It was amid all
this familiarity that a new face came into the public gallery one
morning. It was a woman about my age. She walked with purpose
and precision, looking straight ahead. She had short, dark hair. The
woman in the photograph. Her face was blank, cold, impassive. Dan
sensed her presence as soon as he stepped into the dock. Like an
animal, his eyes sought her out. There was a brief moment when
they stared at each other. By lunchtime, she was gone.

Over the course of the trial, the barristers picked over the details
of the case. In their long black cloaks and white shirts, they were like
magpies swooping down on the glittering prize of murder over manslaughter. There were reports from clinical professionals who had

treated Dan in the past. Expert witnesses with a litany of diagnostic terms that were leveled at him: psychopath, sociopath, and pathological narcissist. Different forensic psychiatrists, witnesses for the defense and prosecution batted the terminology back and forth. Most frequently mentioned was "borderline personality disorder," the blanket categorization for those individuals who were undeniably disturbed, but seemed to evade any other specific diagnosis. One forensic psychiatrist referred to his "early attachment disorder," and another's theory was of an "acute psychotic episode" triggered by the "delusional transference" in therapy.

The experts were in unanimous agreement about childhood trauma, and his emotional deprivation. Loneliness. Neglect. Severe and long-standing attachment issues. Unresolved anger issues toward his mother, in a family that was broken by the death of a baby. It was accepted that the work at the Trauma Unit unearthed some of these very difficult feelings and failed to contain them. Instead, he was inadvertently given a platform to vent his anger.

Perhaps he was looking for someone like me. Perhaps I was looking to be found.

In her summing-up, the judge highlighted many contributory factors for the jury to consider, but the ones I remembered were the "errors in clinical judgment" and the "failure in due care and attention" by the Mental Health Trust responsible. It was acknowledged these issues were beyond the jurisdiction of the courts, but were a matter for ongoing investigations by the Trust and external professional bodies.

In the end, the verdict from the jury was unequivocal. The photographs Dan took, the planned break-in at the flat, the seizing of the knife from the kitchen. All were clear signs of intent, and indicated the premeditated nature of the crime. It wasn't clear whether Dan was coming to the flat for Nicholas, or whether, because of my absence at the clinic, he somehow believed I, too, might be there, and he was coming for me. Or perhaps, in his deranged and distressed state, the three of us; his mother, me, Julie, had somehow all become one. We'll never know. There was insufficient evidence to charge him for the attempted murder of Nicholas. Given the defense of diminished capacity, he was found guilty of the manslaughter of Julie, and was sentenced to life, with a minimum of twenty-two years. He was transferred to Rampton Hospital straight from the court.

Subsequent internal hearings for professional misconduct found me negligent in my duty of care. Incidents cited included the session with Hayley, the deviation from my normal therapeutic standards with Dan, and the decision to let him stay overnight in my house. The "complications in my own personal life" were seen to have contributed to my failure to make clear and informed judgments about the care of this seriously unwell patient. The adjudicator concluded, "It wasn't so much what you did, but what you failed to do. On realizing the difficult feelings evoked by the similarities with your son, you should have stopped seeing this man. You should have referred him to one of your colleagues. You had the experience and knowledge to do so."

All the character witnesses were kind, almost reverential in their respect for my career, my status and experience. Robert was especially helpful in his careful assessment of my expertise, outlining my skills in the clinical field. But all had to conclude that given my unresolved grief, and the complications arising from the likeness to my son, it was impossible to perform a high standard of therapeutic work.

My license to practice was suspended. My solicitor, with support from Robert, and Maggie from the unit, urged me to appeal. Almost before they had finished speaking, I was waving away the suggestion. I was aghast. They didn't understand how wrong it felt. How utterly misjudged the idea was.

"No," I said, "I won't be working again." And until I said the words out loud, I hadn't quite realized the extent and clarity of my decision. The relief was palpable. Like letting go of a heavy weight I'd been clutching to my chest.

Maggie was frantic. "But all your work?" she said. "The unit?" She was tearful.

I tried to speak. "I—"

I glanced up at Robert. He nodded.

"—I can't do it anymore," I said, faltering.

Robert stepped forward. A small movement. A hand pressed lightly on my shoulder.

"I . . . It's like other people's pain," I said carefully, "is a shield against my own." I shook my head. "I have to let it go."

"How will we manage," Maggie wanted to know, "without you?"

"Exactly as you have been," I said. "You will carry on."

So, after more than twenty-five years of clinical service with hundreds of patients, I was stepping away. Like an addict going cold turkey. A life without the rush of helping. The itch to save and rescue and make myself feel worthwhile.

I was lucky enough to have an NHS pension that I could draw down in seven years. I had some savings. For the most part, I intended to scale back. Live a simpler life. The obvious solution was to sell the house. Neither David nor I needed a family house to rattle round in. But while I didn't want to live in it, selling the house was inconceivable, at least for now. It was our only connection to Tom, and it was an anchor I wasn't ready to pull up, if I ever would be. I told David that in a year or so, I'd look at getting tenants, maybe people we knew. Then I'd rent somewhere smaller. A flat perhaps, near the coast.

Carolyn did go to university, but she left after the first term, deciding to apply for an art foundation course instead. She spent hours working on a portfolio for her application and got a part-time job in an art shop in Bloomsbury. It was a beautiful place, old and wood paneled and stashed from floor to ceiling with specialist equipment and materials—leather-bound sketchbooks, paper, chalky crayons, and glass jars of powdered paint pigment in bright blues, reds, and oranges. We'd sometimes meet for lunch nearby, and then I'd go on to the British Museum, where I'd simply sit quietly in the courtyard, under the great white dome of a roof.

The weeks immediately after the trial, I slept a lot. In fact, I found it hard to stay awake. My body went into a sort of shutdown, almost like a self-induced coma. When I emerged, I spent my days in the garden, weeding and potting and turning over the flower beds. A friend of Maggie's was taking a job abroad for eight months and asked me if I'd like to look after her allotment while she was away. I took it on readily. I grew vegetables—cabbages, leeks, and broccoli. I liked the feel of the soil under my fingers. The physical exertion of digging. Standing out in the sun, the rain and the wind felt somehow therapeutic.

Then, I saw an advert for volunteers for a charitable gardening project in the backstreets of Haringey. It was a beautiful walled garden that was owned by a charity, a small green jewel in the midst of an urban sprawl, called St. Margaret's Secret Garden. It ran sessions for people with mental health problems, recovering addicts, the lonely and the isolated, kids from the local residential home. I began to volunteer three mornings a week. I worked the vegetable patches and one of my daily tasks was to keep the vase in the office filled with fresh flowers. I did it first thing, before the others arrived. I didn't like to see people. I didn't want their morning greetings, their nods of hello, or gestures of kindness. I wanted to keep all that away.

One day, Joyce, who organized the volunteers, asked me if I'd like to do more. "Perhaps be a group helper—help supervise one of the afternoon therapeutic groups?"

If she was surprised by my involuntary flinch she didn't say anything. She must have been used to all sorts there.

"No, thank you," I said. "Looking after the vegetables and plants is all I want to do.

"Besides," I added, "I visit my mother in the afternoons."

In the evening, I wrote letters to Tom about Nicholas. I wrote to him about his son—what he liked to eat, how strawberries were his favorite fruit, how he liked apple juice from a grown-up glass. I wrote about his favorite song at bedtime. How he liked to sit on the small window seat in the sun, his small hand pressing the book into my lap. I wrote about how I'd made the spare room into his special place, kitted it out with a digger duvet cover and a string of car lights over his bed. I wrote about how Nicholas loved to help me in the garden, on the morning after a sleepover.

His favorite food? His stuffed animals? The song he liked to sing at nighttime? Of course, I had no idea about any of these things. None of these details were available to me. But at night, or when I was weeding the garden, I allowed myself to dream, to imagine, and to make a picture that he and I were in.

I also wrote letters to Nicholas to tell him all about his dad. How sensitive and thoughtful he was. How he cared deeply for other people. Sometimes too much. How he worked hard. I wrote how he could carve beautiful things out of wood. And that one day, he would carve him his very own fishing rod with his initials on the handle. I wrote to him how his dad loved trees, the woods, the sea, and nature. How he loved to be free, out in the wild.

TWENTY-SIX

That spring, Carolyn went on holiday to Australia to see Rob, and David was away in France with his new partner, Simone, whom he'd met at a conference. When he first told me about her, he was quick to say she was a divorcée, with a daughter at university. I told him I approved. It was such a relief to hear he'd found someone born in the same decade. Once they were all away, I booked a trip to Corfu.

Messonghi was the small village we stayed in when the kids were little. It has bled out in all directions. It's now more like a small town. I chose to stay in a place outside the main hub, up in the mountains. It's a simple whitewashed pension, with blue shutters that open out to views of the sea. The old woman who looks after the place is short and stocky. Walnut lined skin, and a simple black shift dress. She serves breakfast on the small terrace at the back. It's a sheltered courtyard overhung with grapevines. I watch her from my room as she lays out my table with such care and patience—the cutlery, the folded napkin, the fresh yogurt, and a plate of sliced melon. She nods and smiles as I take my seat. I smile back. I use the few Greek words I know to express my appreciation. Sometimes I catch her watching me with curiosity. Perhaps she senses my need for solitude. She leaves me well alone.

The weekend after I arrive is Greek Easter weekend. In the preceding days the village is busy with preparations. I have only ever come to Greece in the height of the tourist season, and it's a different place in the spring. I like the bright, crisp sunshine, and the sudden chill of the evening when the sun sets. I watch from the sidelines as the village cleans. Doors of the houses are flung wide open, carpets beaten outside in the street, pots and pans are polished until they gleam. Outside the two tavernas at the top of the village, the tables and chairs are stacked up to be repainted for the summer season.

On Easter Saturday at midnight, the street is full of people. There are families, small children, teenagers in groups, babies in arms, they hug and embrace. The priest comes to the door of the church with a lit candle. He lights the candle of the person next to him, who reaches across to the next, and so on. Lights pour out like fireflies and soon there's a sea of flickering candles as the trail of lights snakes down the mountainside. I press my back into the wall as they pass.

Christos anesti.

Alithos anesti.

The lights glow in the distance, there are firecrackers, the sound of laughter and music. The tavernas are soon full. Families are together, holding hands, faces pressed together. There's an air of expectation. I feel awash with the glow of the lights and as I stand by, I feel anointed with a rush of hope and renewal that marks the season.

On Easter Sunday, after the service has finished, I walk up to the small mountainside church. It's decked with garlands of herbs, olive branches, and eucalyptus leaves. On a tree outside, there are little posies of flowers hanging in the branches, and in between, there are glints of silver. I watch as a group of people come closer; they help a man forward. He is young, but limping with a crutch. He reaches up to hang something on the tree. When they move away, I edge closer to look. They are small rectangles made of tin, hanging from the branches like Christmas decorations. They shine as they twist in the sunlight. I pick one out. It's an indented picture of an eye that is closed tight. I select another. The knee joint of a leg. I trace the imprint under my fingers, examining the details, and I look up. A man is watching me. I tap it with my finger. "What are these?" My face in a frown of confusion. He says something in Greek. Turns to his companion. They exchange some words. "For make better," he says, "for God. When you ill," and he clutches his head and pulls a face, "for make better health," he says, and then he presses his hand onto his forehead. Then his arms. His eyes. I look back at the tree. I see that all of the small tin shapes show parts of the body. An arm. A leg. A kidney. Another one of the lungs. I nod. "*Efharisto*," I say, and we nod. They smile, happy with themselves.

Later that evening, I make my way down into the town, to the place we stayed as a family all those years ago. I can't remember our exact apartment, but it doesn't take long to find the stones. The small pile that was once knee-high is now taller than me, and stretches over an area of more than fifteen feet. Many of the stones and pebbles have writing scribbled on them with felt-tip, paint, or pen. Some have initials, some have names, some have longer messages. My eyes linger over the ones I can see. *We miss you. Stay safe.*

We love you. Pete RIP. And on the back of a large flat pebble, *CT—sorry I couldn't save you, the way you once saved me.* There are letters and notes fluttering in the breeze. Paper letters, where the ink has run in the rain, and photographs that have been carefully laminated against the elements. Missing children. Missing people. Missing daughters. Missing wives, husbands, and sons. It is a shrine to lost people. People who may be alive and may return. Some who are already gone.

To the left, in the shade of a lemon tree, is a wooden bench with a small plaque.

In memory of Denis Watson. There's a picture of him, the one from the website, fixed onto the back of the bench. *Denis. At peace. Forever in our hearts* is carved at the side. The place where his remains were found is less than ten minutes away.

The place is deserted. It's too early in the season for tourists and the whole village is quiet after the celebrations of the night before. I sit down on Denis Watson's bench to retrieve the envelope from my bag. All my letters to Tom about Nicholas. The ones to Nicholas about Tom. I fold them in half and tuck them carefully in between a pile of stones. I place photos of Nicholas and Tom, side by side, in an envelope together. I select three stones from the olive groves and place them gently on the top. Julie, Tom, and Nicholas.

I walk farther up along a small mountain track, to the tiny chapel on the hill that the children found when we'd visited. It looks unchanged since we stepped inside all those years ago. White walls, small simple makeshift wooden benches, and then amid such rustic simplicity, an ornate golden altar at the front. Behind is a large fresco of Jesus on the cross. A clutch of angels in the corner. I sit down, instinctively clasping my hands together. The air is cool. Quiet. The time drifts. I light candles. For Julie. For Tom. For Nicholas. And one for Denis. As I stand up to go, there are footsteps behind me. A woman comes in. Her face is covered with a dark head scarf. She looks at me, a nod of recognition. It's the woman who looks after the pension I'm staying in. *"Yassas."* As I pass, she reaches for my arm, presses something hard and metallic into my palm, and says something in Greek that I don't understand. Outside, I blink in the bright sunshine and open my hand. It's one of the small tin decorations that I'd seen hanging outside the church. I turn it over in my fingers. It's an indented shape of a heart.

That moment is like a cool drink after a long and self-imposed drought. A simple act of kindness that makes me want to weep. After months of punishing myself, instilling a self-imposed exile from all that was colorful, good, or joyful. I'd seen myself as undeserving, as if on hunger strike, starving myself of the good in life. I sit down, my eyes closed, face tilted up to the sun, my fingers clasped tightly round the small tin heart.

When I stand up, the light dazzles my eyes. I feel the warmth of the sun on my face as if for the very first time. I take a different path back, one that meanders through the olive groves, and as I turn back toward the village, I breathe in the smell of wild thyme as it rolls down the mountain. The sun is shining and the sea spreads out before me in a deep cobalt blue.

I spend the rest of the week walking the rocky paths by the coast. I take a day trip to follow a trail through a gorge inland. It's a steep climb for seven miles, through blankets of spring flowers, rolling hills of blue and purple and white. The oleander bushes are just beginning to flower in bursts of pink and red. I cross stone bridges where streams gush underfoot, pass cascading waterfalls where the spray cools my face. The walk takes me six hours. By the end my ankles are swollen, and when the path comes out into a small cove of white pebbles I take off my shoes and socks and feel the cold salty waves on my toes. Along the way, people say hello. They make moves to chat. I am polite, friendly, but I keep to myself. That evening, at the little taverna on the beach, something has shifted. While still I keep my distance and eat alone, I find myself lifting my head up, enjoying the roar of laughter and camaraderie as it drifts from the surrounding tables.

It's two days after my return from Greece that the card arrives. I see it on the mat from the top of the stairs. It's a bright colorful picture of a mountain and some trees. From a distance, it looks like junk mail. A promotional advert for a car, or an insurance policy. It's only when I'm closer, reaching down to pick it up, that I see it is a postcard.

The moment slows right down as the picture comes into view. It's a view of a dense, rugged pine forest. There's a river cut between the trees, racing through the woods in a cascade of crashing water. A big sky with snowy mountains in the distance. The sun is coming up. A glint of gold on the water. High above the trees, there's a bird with wings outstretched. A bird of prey. A black hawk perhaps. It shoots like an arrow across the big, wide, cloudless sky.

There's a thud in my chest. I can barely breathe.

Alaska.

I flip it over. The card is blank. No message. Unsigned. Just Mum, Dad, and Carolyn, and our address written in his familiar neat slanting handwriting. A postmark dated nine days ago. The tears come instantly, sliding down my cheeks as I drop to my knees. I don't know how long I sit there on the mat by the door. The card pressed against my body. After nearly three years, I hug the news to my chest as if it was his very head cradled in my arms.

When I phone David, then Carolyn, we cry across three countries. *He's alive*, is all I manage to say.

Later on, I'm at the computer, Googling a map of the area. I'm poring over the terrain, astonished by the vastness of Alaska. Somewhere, I think, in that huge wildness is my son. *My son.* Of course, I have the urge to track him down. To go and find him. To wrap my arms around him. The computer mouse moves over the screen, slowly and carefully around the vast and uninhabited landscape. My fingers walk the paths, as if to trace his steps. Into the wild. A thought filters up. I could take a plane. A trip up from Seattle. But as quickly as it's formed, I fold it away. I look again at the card. At what he is trying to tell me. Going to find him is not what he would want. Instead, I go to the bookshelf and find his copy of the book he fell in love with. The book that touched his soul. The book I didn't read properly before. There are lots of passages that he has underlined in pencil, extracts from the diaries of travelers over the course of history, but there is one that catches my eye. I write it out and pin it to the fridge.

As to when I shall visit civilization, it will not be soon, I think. I have not tired of the wilderness; rather I enjoy

its beauty and the vagrant life I lead, more keenly all
the time. I prefer the saddle to the streetcar and star-
sprinkled life to a roof, the obscure and difficult trail,
leading into the unknown, to any paved highway, and
the deep peace of the wild to the discontent bred by cities.
Do you blame me then for staying here, where I feel that
I belong and am one with the world around me?

He's now a twenty-year-old man. I think of him in the splendid isolation that he so often craved. When I picture him out in the wilderness, in that immense wild landscape, I think of that week we all spent in the cabin in Devon, and it makes me smile. I think of his joy as he whittled sticks, built a fire, and carved our fishing rods. That week when he showed the best of himself. That week when we all showed the best of ourselves. I think of his determined resourcefulness. His sense of self-sufficiency. His love of wild places.

The postcard has a home in my bag; I carry it with me always. It sits with the small sketches that Carolyn drew of us in the cabin in Devon, and the small tin rectangle with the beating heart.

I think of Tom all the time, but it now feels different. It's a less frantic and desperate kind of thinking. Before, my thoughts were formless and anxious, a search for an image that might give me some kind of answer. Now I have the luxury of a picture, of some certainty, and I can make a frame around his life.

There are bad days, when I'm gripped by how far away he is. When I get frightened by his smallness, out alone in the wilderness. There are days when missing him feels like a hole in my chest. When I have days like this, I simply try to breathe.

On a good day, I think of him happy and fulfilled. And I wish him love. I see him in my mind's eye: tall and lean, his skin weathered by the wind and sun. I imagine him moving with a confidence. Hacking his way through the undergrowth. A scarf pulling back his hair from his face. His hair is long now, uncut for weeks, hanging in golden spirals to his shoulders. He has made himself a dwelling, somewhere in the woods. He has blended into his environment. He has built a shelter. I know he will have visited the abandoned bus, the place where Christopher McCandless died, but I don't imagine him lingering there. It has become a mecca for tourists, a symbolic place for travelers. He would have left at dawn. Surveyed the empty shell of the bus, read the messages from fellow travelers, and would have gone on his way, silently and alone. I see him seeking out paths that have not been trod before. Making his footsteps on new, unmarked soil. He stops to watch a bird overhead. It swoops and soars, high in a sky that is a deep, dark blue. I watch him as he looks up and smiles, his face turned to the sun.

This is how I like to picture him. And imagining him like this is my way of trying to let him go. In the hope that if I do, he might one day find his way back home to me.

A PENGUIN READERS GUIDE TO

A GOOD

ENOUGH MOTHER

Bev Thomas

An Introduction to
A Good Enough Mother

Ruth Hartland is an experienced therapist at the top of her game. The director of a renowned therapy unit for trauma victims, she is wise, intelligent, successful, and respected by her peers. But her calm professional demeanor belies a personal life full of secrets and sadness. The mother of grown twins, she is haunted by the fact that her son Tom, a beautiful but fragile boy who could never seem to fit in, disappeared eighteen months ago. So when Dan— a volatile new patient bearing an eerie resemblance to Tom— wanders into her waiting room, it's not long before her judgment becomes clouded, boundaries are crossed, and disaster ensues. A fascinating family drama with a ticking time bomb at its core, Bev Thomas's debut novel, *A Good Enough Mother*, is a powerful page-turner about motherhood, grief, obsession, and the importance of letting go.

A clinical psychologist herself, author Bev Thomas has in-depth knowledge of therapy and mental health, and takes readers inside Ruth's head with rich detail and realism. Who among us hasn't wondered what goes on in the private thoughts and life of a therapist? What is it like to be a sounding board for someone else's troubles—and how do you deal with your own demons in the meantime? A deeply compelling narrator, Ruth is poised on the outside but troubled within, incapable of moving on, fixated on how she failed her son and whether he can be found. With her family in pieces and her marriage crumbling, Ruth finds her new patient Dan is both a balm and a landmine—he is clearly unstable and manipulative, but he is also the shadow son she might actually be able to save. As Ruth twists herself into knots about her duties as a mother and a therapist, she becomes frantic and reckless, events spiral out of control, and her once calm and orderly life is violently disrupted.

A Good Enough Mother will have readers on the edge of their seats, but it is also a brilliant, beautiful story of parenting, of how love consumes us, and how difficult it is to heal from tragedy, even when we must.

A Conversation with
Bev Thomas

The protagonist of A Good Enough Mother *is Ruth Hartland, an experienced therapist who specializes in helping trauma victims. You were also a clinical psychologist for many years, and have an in-depth understanding of this world. What made you want to explore the patient-therapist relationship in fiction and how did your real-life experiences inform the novel?*

In my work, I had always been very interested in grief and loss—powerful emotions that not only underpin the human condition, but frequently find their way into the therapy room. But I was initially reluctant to explore the therapeutic world in fiction, as I didn't want the focus to be on a patient. It was only when I flipped the concept and made the protagonist a flawed therapist instead that the story began to emerge. What if a brilliant therapist is blindsided by feelings of grief about her own missing son? What if one of her new patients reminds her of him? And so the story began.

All the detail around the case work is fictionalized, but the world is real. The workings of a National Health Service [NHS] department, the therapy work, and the understanding and treatment of psychological difficulties are very much drawn from my experience of working as a clinical psychologist in the public sector.

How do you feel about the way therapy is typically depicted in popular culture, including books, movies, and television shows? And why do you think people are so consistently fascinated with this subject?

Popular culture often uses therapy as a plot device rather than something to be explored in its own right. Given my background, I was interested in exploring the psychoanalytic model of therapy in fiction. It places emphasis on transference, the relationship between therapist and patient, and the importance of boundaries, and these are the elements that get played out in Ruth's story.

Therapy is about enabling a person to make sense of his own life story. I think the general fascination with therapy in the media is partly because it's such a private world: just two people talking in a room. There's both an intimacy and secrecy to that relationship. In my book, people come to therapy feeling desperate, and hope their lives will change for the better. By opening a window into this world, the reader becomes a fly on the wall, and by seeing it all through Ruth's point of view, the reader is simultaneously party to, and full of, her anxieties and struggles. People are endlessly fascinated and intrigued about other people's lives, but I believe it's more than just curiosity. I think people want to "listen in" to learn about what makes people tick, in order perhaps to apply that learning and wisdom to their own lives.

A Good Enough Mother *is also, as the title suggests, about the responsibilities and challenges of motherhood. Why did you choose to ground the novel in Ruth's role as a mother and in her relationships with her children—and were there particular themes or issues you hoped to explore?*

In my clinical work, I became particularly interested in attachment theory and the title is taken from the writings of Donald Winnicott, a British pediatrician and psychoanalyst. It refers to the necessary progressive maternal detachment, so that the child is able to develop appropriate independence. The aim is for something less than perfect, not all encompassing, enabling a child to learn to thrive. In the book, the irony for Ruth is that, despite her best intentions, it is her own difficulties in separating from her son that contribute to his problems.

Attachment and mothering are key themes in the book, reflected in the relationship between Ruth and her mother, Ruth and her son Tom, and also what we come to learn about the relationship between Dan and his mother. We also see how patterns can unintentionally be repeated through the generations. And in making Ruth the mother of twins, I wanted to help the reader to see differences in the way she parents her two children.

The book highlights a general tendency toward "over parenting" and taps into the maternal anxiety of our generation. We are bombarded with messages that encourage perfection and while we of course need to offer love and support to our kids, we also need to know when to stand back and let them find their own way, however painful that might be.

Because of your background, you already had firsthand knowledge of psychological therapy and psychoanalytic theory before beginning this book. But you did do some additional research while writing. Can you talk a little bit about what that process looked like, and what you learned more about?

I did further research into the psychology of trauma. It was something I had encountered in my clinical work, but I was able to deepen my understanding of the psychoanalytic understanding and treatment of trauma. I came to appreciate the difficult and enormously valuable work done by therapists who treat the survivors of awful tragedies. We might read those stories on the front page of the paper, or see them on the evening news, but we don't always think about how those people go on to live their lives after experiencing such terrible events.

In addition, research into missing persons left me appalled by the statistics of young people and adults who go missing every year. My research focused on the lives of families and loved ones who are left in limbo, a state that has been described as an "ambiguous loss"—a particularly painful psychological experience that is punctuated by hope, uncertainty, and a lack of closure.

From the first introduction of Dan—Ruth's new patient who bears a striking resemblance to her missing son—it is clear that he is damaged and manipulative. Yet Ruth is drawn to him all the same, and the reader must wait with bated breath to see just how bad things get. How did you go about building suspense, and were you inspired by any other novels or films?

The opening chapter needed to set up the book, revealing simultaneously both the risk and the inevitability of Ruth's choice to continue seeing this patient. The reader needs to know it's unwise, but also to understand the pull. In the book, the two parallel stories of Dan and Tom are interwoven, and in each strand, there are questions to which the reader wants answers. It is the slow and steady revelations that build suspense, continuing until the narratives collide and come to a climax at the same time.

Unsurprisingly, I'm drawn to books and film that explore psychological and emotional complexities. One film that gets a mention in the book is *Ordinary People*, which is an extraordinary film about the aftermath of grief and loss in a family.

In many ways, Ruth represents the archetype of the "wounded healer." Can you expand on that idea a little further, and what it means in the world of this book?

The "wounded healer" was a term originally created by Carl Jung. It refers to the idea that analysts are compelled to treat patients because they themselves are "wounded." Many people in the caring professions come to the work because they are interested in it, but also perhaps because they have also had difficult personal experiences. Therapists, just like all people, deal with the complexities of emotional and family life, and this can often add, rather than detract, from their ability to do a good job.

A problem arises if work becomes a way of trying to heal a personal problem. For Ruth, helping and fixing was something that was rooted in her complicated childhood. She was the child of an alcoholic, and after her father left her family, she was the sole caretaker of a mother who was volatile and inconsistent. Undoubtedly, this life experience played a part in her decision to train as a therapist—and probably contributed to her being an extremely good one. Yet it is her more recent, current grief for her missing son that is her undoing. She is "wounded" by this trauma, so at the very time she needs to be pulling back, she sinks in deeper, and Dan becomes a focus of her feelings of grief and despair.

Without giving too much away, A Good Enough Mother *culminates in a terrible act of violence. But the book doesn't end there, and instead shows the characters working through the aftermath— confusion, grief, penance, acceptance. Why was it important to you to examine the effects of trauma and to grapple with the toll that this violence takes on the characters?*

There is a multilayered aspect to the book, as I wanted to create mirroring between the emotional experiences of the characters. We see how Ruth's childhood feeling of suffocation and lack of individuation at the hands of her mother is mirrored in her relationship with her son. We also see how her unresolved trauma regarding the disappearance of Tom draws her inexorably to Dan, as she's compelled to try to find a way to "fix" him, in a way she has failed to do with Tom. Dan was looking for a mother; she was looking for a son. It was a perfect storm. Interweaving these stories was fundamental to the plot, but I also wanted to make sure the emotional fallout following the tragedy was similarly multilayered. It couldn't be a clear-cut line of blame and responsibility that would fall at the door of one person—life very rarely works that way. It felt important to show the subsequent emotional unravelling in all its complexity.

What do you hope readers take away from A Good Enough Mother?

First and foremost, it's a book of fiction, and so I hope they enjoy it and find the narrative thought-provoking. But I also hope readers learn something about the model of therapy, and see the value in acknowledging and experiencing feelings. While Ruth thinks she is in control of her world, she is in denial about the strength of her grief and these suppressed feelings seep out. It's this that has devastating consequences for her and others.

I've worked in the NHS for many years, and currently work with staff teams in mental health services. The system is stretched and under-resourced and referrals are increasing. I wanted to highlight this pressure in the book. In one chapter, when Ruth works with a traumatized staff team, we see firsthand the tragic impact of the unavailability of in-patient beds for a desperately unwell patient. Mental health services are underfunded and the patients are often disenfranchised and without voice and power to demand better treatment. One in four people will be affected by a mental health problem in their lives, regardless of culture and social class, so this is an issue for us all. In particular, the focus on adolescent mental health issues draws attention to our responsibility for the youngest and most vulnerable in our society.

QUESTIONS AND TOPICS
FOR DISCUSSION

1. Though we often put health professionals on a pedestal, Ruth battles her own demons from her childhood and is certainly not perfect; she's a flawed individual and makes mistakes both as a parent and then, because of her grief, as a therapist. Do you think the author's portrayal of Ruth—a person torn between her two selves—was believable? What do you think Ruth could have done differently?

2. The book deals with various themes—mental health, trauma, grief, motherhood, heartbreak, and emotional attachment to name just a few—did you connect with a specific topic or topics? Why or why not?

3. *A Good Enough Mother* delves into the complicated intersection of ethics and emotion. Working with, yet still remaining objective to, a patient who closely resembles your son is an impossibly difficult task. Was Ruth's decision to work with Dan inappropriate from the get-go, or is she justified in taking him on? When did you think she began to behave inappropriately, if ever?

4. People are often curious about what goes on during the private, intimate conversations between therapists and their clients. At times in the novel, the reader is privy to interactions between staff and patients at the trauma clinic. Did you enjoy being a fly on the wall during these sections or did that make you uncomfortable— or both? Were you surprised by anything you "overheard" or noticed in these sections?

5. *A Good Enough Mother* is about complex relationships: between therapist and patient, between mothers and children, between husband and wife, between the private and the public. Do you think the author has done a good job exposing the layers inherent in these dynamics? Did it make you consider your own relationships differently?

6. Ruth is haunted throughout the book by her son's disappearance; the hopes and terrors of motherhood that she experiences are laid bare for the reader to witness. Do you think she handled Tom's childhood and subsequent loss as best she could? What would you have done in her place?

7. What did you think about the resolution of Tom's story? Were you satisfied with how his story was resolved at the end?